ESCAPE
from
COMMUNIST
HEAVEN

ESCAPE
from
COMMUNIST
HEAVEN

ESCAPE
from
COMMUNIST
HEAVEN

Based on the true story of Viet Nguyen

DENNIS W. DUNIVAN

First Sentient Publications edition 2013
Copyright © 2013 by Dennis W. Dunivan

Cover and book design by Kim Johansen, Black Dog Design, www.blackdogdesign.com
Map by Cher Leedom and Garth Heckel

Library of Congress Cataloging-in-Publication Data

      Dunivan, Dennis W., 1964-
       Escape from communist heaven / Dennis W. Dunivan. — First Sentient Publications edition.
       pages cm
       Summary: The communist takeover of South Vietnam in 1975 is very hard for Viet Nguyen, fourteen, and his family but when Viet foolishly tries to speed up their plans to escape he is arrested and sentenced to the harsh life of a labor camp in the jungle.
       ISBN 978-1-59181-229-6
       1. Vietnam—History—1975—-Juvenile fiction. [1. Vietnam—History—1975—-Fiction. 2. Communism—Fiction. 3. Family life—Vietnam—Fiction. 4. Labor camps—Fiction. 5. Survival—Fiction.] I. Title.
       PZ7.D9209Esc 2013
       [Fic]—dc23
                      2012048708

Printed in the United States of America

10 9 8 7 6 5 4 3 2 1

SENTIENTPUBLICATIONS
A Limited Liability Company
1113 Spruce Street
Boulder, CO 80302
www.sentientpublications.com

To the children still searching for freedom

6

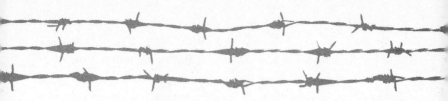

American Evacuation

On the evening of April 28th, 1975, two days before communist tanks rolled through our neighborhood on their way into central Saigon, Dad burst through the kitchen doorway as my brother Vinh was scraping the last bit of rice from his plate. Mom was in the bedroom, tucking Tu into bed, and my sisters were already asleep. "Go to your room!" Dad shouted to Vinh and me, even though I was fourteen and could usually stay up with the adults. I wanted to ask Dad what was happening, but when I saw the angry glare of his eyes, I hurried to my room. Vinh climbed into bed, but I squatted against the wall, beside the doorway, so I could hear what my parents were saying.

"The Americans are evacuating," Dad said. "The communists are closing in on the city. We must leave the country in the morning." I couldn't believe what I heard. I had never thought my father would run from the communists.

"We can't leave," Mom pleaded. "This is our home, our country."

"The communists will overthrow Saigon in less than a week," Dad said. "It will be their country then." There was a long silence. I waited for Mom to say something, but she didn't. In Vietnam, the father is the head of the family and his decisions are final. I crawled under my mosquito net, blew out the lantern and fell asleep, wondering where we would go.

I woke the next morning to the banging of Mom's spoon against the wok. The smell of fried eggs and pork drifted through the darkness. Vinh was still curled in his covers, so I bounced my pillow off his head to wake him. When I walked into the kitchen, Mom was packing clothes and food into our backpacks. Dad sat silently in his chair. "We're taking a trip," Mom said, but she didn't say where we were going.

By the time I had finished breakfast, Mom was pushing my brothers and sisters out the door. I wanted to take one last look around the house, but Dad rose from his chair and told me to hurry. With Mom and my two sisters on one moped, Dad and my little brother on the other, and Vinh and me on our bikes, we rode single file out our drive, through our neighborhood, and onto Highway 1.

At first, it seemed like a normal Saigon morning, except for a few more people on the streets. White flares lit the sky, and produce trucks bounced along the highway, delivering their goods to the city. As we rode, I watched fishermen load their boats on the banks of the Saigon River. We circled north of the city for a half hour before turning onto the airport road. There the scene changed. Abandoned cars and pushcarts blocked the road, and people on bicycles and mopeds weaved between them. People with anxious faces were all around us, pushing forward. A chain-link fence ran along the right side of the road, and buildings lined the left. As we moved forward, the road narrowed and the people poured into the funnel. The roar of jet engines blended with the roar of voices. I could see planes taking off above us, but I couldn't see the airport gates.

Dad weaved through the people, beeping his horn, and we followed in single file. The street became too crowded and we had to stop. Dad yelled for people to get out of his way, then he jumped off the moped and pushed it through the crowd. My little brother Tu hung on his shoulder crying, and Mom was right behind him shouting, "We'll never make it! We'll never make it!"

When Dad finally stopped, he told us to leave our bikes and follow as close to him as possible. But Mom kept saying that we couldn't make it, and I thought she was right. Sweating bodies rubbed against me as Dad tried to convince her we had to escape. We were pushed tighter and tighter until my bike was held up on both sides by the crowd.

"We'll never make it," Mom kept saying. "We should get the children out of this mob and go to Grandfather's house." It was unusual for Mom to argue with my father, and I was surprised when he finally agreed with her. We pushed our way out of the crowd, then rode south to Red Cross Street.

Grandfather lived with Mom's brother and his family only a few miles from the airport. I loved spending the night there because I could stay up late reading Grandfather's kung fu books to my cousins, but this night Mom made us go to bed at eight. The steady rhythm of machine gun fire and occasional rocket blasts echoed through the house, but I didn't feel scared. I thought my father could solve any problem. But not knowing what would happen next or where

I was going gave me an empty feeling. I still had that feeling when Grandfather shook my shoulder early the next morning to wake me. I got dressed and went to the table for breakfast. Before I sat down, Dad motioned for me to follow him outside. We stood face to face on Grandfather's porch. The yellow street lights reflected in Dad's tired eyes.

"Viet," he said and then paused for a moment. "We'll try to escape as a family. But if we can't get to the airport together, I'll tell an official I found you and your brothers and sisters on the street with no parents. If we can convince them you're orphans, they may let you into the airport and put you on a plane." What was Dad saying? We couldn't leave my parents. Where would we go? Who would take care of us? But before I could resist, he went on.

"I'm depending on you because you're my oldest son. You'll have to act like you don't know me, and you'll have to pull your brothers and sisters away before the officials realize it's a plan to get you on a plane." I tried to speak, but he wouldn't give me a chance. "I know you don't understand what's happening, but you must do what I say. It may be your only chance to live a free life." I told him I would do what he said, but I thought nothing could be worse than splitting up our family. Dad walked back into the house, and I followed.

It was just before five when we said goodbye to Grandfather and my cousins and started walking to the airport. Abandoned cars still blocked the streets, and luggage, bikes and trash were scattered on the sidewalks. Dad said he thought we were early enough to make it, but as we walked onto the airport road, I saw the crowd was as thick as the day before. Everyone was fighting for position. As we followed Dad through the crowd, I watched people trying to climb over the airport gate and soldiers knocking them back with the butts of their rifles. We moved forward, and the crowd packed tighter until I could feel the hot breath of those around me. We were packed so tight that when the soldiers opened the gate to let a few people in, I was carried forward by the crowd. Then the soldiers beat us back as they closed the gate. Bloody faces pushed by me. I knew my whole family couldn't make it through the gate, and I was glad we couldn't get close enough for Dad to give us to the officials.

By noon, we were back at Grandfather's house. We had just finished dinner, and I was wrestling with my cousin on the living room floor, when Dad turned the radio up and told us to be quiet. I rolled to my feet as President Minh made the announcement. "Soldiers of the Republic of Vietnam. Cease firing. Stay where you are. We are waiting to meet with the Provisional Revolutionary Government to discuss the turnover of our civilian and military administrations."

I knew the Provisional Revolutionary Government was the same thing as the communists and watched Dad to see what he would do next. He was silent for a moment, then he rose from his chair and raced toward the door. Mom ran after him, grabbed his arm and pleaded for him to stop. "If we can't escape," he said, "we must fight until the end."

Grandfather followed them to the front porch and told Dad to listen to the rest of the report. Dad argued at first, then came back in. After we sat listening for a few minutes, Nguyen Huu Hanh, the man in charge of the South Vietnamese military, came on the radio. He ordered our troops to lay down their weapons and surrender to the communists. Dad's eyes were on fire. He glanced at Mom, stood up slowly, and walked out the door.

Grandfather said to let him go, but Mom motioned for

us to follow and ran out behind him. Without saying a word, she sat Tu on the back of Dad's moped, then climbed on hers with my two little sisters. Shouts of "Peace! Peace!" echoed along the street. A young woman in a red wedding dress shuffled up the sidewalk, singing, "The war is over! I will see my husband again!"

Dad looked at the woman and said, "The war is not over. This is only the beginning of our suffering." Then he started the moped and zoomed out of Grandfather's yard.

We were home less than a minute before Dad had his police uniform on and his gun in his hand. Mom pleaded with him as he ran out of the house, but I knew he wouldn't stop. He returned a half hour later with eight of his men in full combat gear. He said they were going to the church tower to fight until the end. His eyes were wide and his face determined, but I could see fear in the other men's faces as Mom cried out, "The French couldn't beat the communists! The Americans couldn't beat them! Our whole army surrenders to the communists, and now you think you can beat them with one squad. You will accomplish nothing! You will die and leave your families with no fathers!"

Dad told the men in his squad to step out if they wanted to surrender, and one by one, they all did. I was seeing my father as a new man—a man out of control. "Go home!" he shouted to the men. "Go home and be cowards. I'm going to our station."

As soon as he left, Mom started hiding our valuables. Then she carried things to the back yard—she took furniture, books, toys, my father's uniforms, photo albums. She stacked them in a pile, and I watched silently from the porch as she lit everything on fire. I was terrified. "Why are you burning our things?" I asked. "Why are you acting so crazy?" She kept running in and out of the house, bringing out more to burn. "You have to tell me what's happening," I said. "I have to know."

Mom sat beside me on the porch. Her wavy black hair hung over her eyes and tears rolled off her soft, round cheeks. "These things are no good to us anymore," she said. "The communists will take our things anyway, just like they did in the North. We need to get rid of everything that links us to the Americans. If the communists find out that your father was an intelligence officer for the Americans, they will torture him."

I knew Dad was an officer in the Army and that after getting wounded he became a police officer, but I didn't know he was an intelligence officer too. I became more frightened when Mom told me this, but I still didn't understand what was happening. Most of our neighbors were going about their business. Some of the people on the streets were cheering because the war was over. "How do you know they will torture him?" I asked. "Why isn't everyone scared?"

She stood up, poking the fire with a bamboo stick. A pale blue flame blazed up, igniting one of my father's uniforms. "People don't realize what life under the communists is like. Your father and I know because we lived in North Vietnam when the communists took control there."

"I want to know what happened to you in the North," I said. "I want to know the whole story."

She poked the fire a few more times, then sat next to me. "The communists took over our village," she said. "They were disguised as peasants, and they asked the farmers in our village if they could work in the rice fields in exchange for food and a place to sleep. They didn't want money. They wanted the trust of the farmers who rented land from people

13

like my father. When the communists earned the trust of the farmers, they told them to rise up against the landlords. They organized groups and preached that all men should be equal. They convinced the people that the landlords were cheating them."

Beads of sweat covered Mom's face as she stared deep into the flames. Anger flashed in her eyes as she remembered. "The communists broke into our house. They took your Grandfather away! Then two of them moved in with our family. They ate our food. They slept in our beds. Every evening after chores, we had to sit in the living room and listen to them ridicule what my father had done. And when they brought him back, they made him get on his knees in front of our family and the people who worked for us. I had to stand in front of him and say he was an evil man, that he should be punished for cheating his countrymen. I had to say these things or the communists would have tortured us."

She stood up and walked over to poke at the fire. She wiped her hair from her face, then she turned to me and shouted, "They made one of our servants spit on my father!" She walked slowly back to the porch and sat next to me again, grasping my arm. The air must have been ninety degrees, but her hands were cold and shaking.

"But we're not rich," I said. "We haven't cheated any-one...have we?" I told her I thought everything would be fine, but she didn't reply. Her black eyes were set straight ahead, gazing into the flames. When she let go of my arm, I stood up and walked to our front yard. The neighborhood was silent, but in the distance I could see South Vietnamese airplanes flying and hear explosions as they bombed villages outside Saigon. I thought the pilots must have been diehards like my father and were refusing to give up. Later I heard

14

they were trying to keep the communists away from the airport so the officials could evacuate.

Dad didn't speak when he came home. We hadn't eaten, but no one was hungry, except my little brother Tu. He had been crying all day and was starting to irritate me. Mom and Dad whispered to each other most of the evening, and I could tell Mom was trying not to cry, but every few minutes she would shake, and tears would roll down her cheeks.

They didn't seem to notice we were there, so I walked to the river and sat on the bank. It was evening, and the orange sky reflected across the water. Fish splashed and birds raced around the trees. I sat on the bank for a while, listened to the current, and wondered how nature could be so peaceful when my life was so confused. I skipped rocks until it was too dark to see them, then I walked home. Mom and Dad were still sitting in their chairs, staring at the floor. I went to my room and collapsed on my bed. The problem was too big. I knew the adults would have to work it out.

The morning sun was over the trees and glaring through my window when I woke. I didn't want to get out of bed, but the sun was so hot that I rolled into the shade on the floor. The only sound was a strange voice on the radio. "This is the Vietnamese Liberation Front," it said. "Everyone remain calm. We have won our independence. Vietnam is one nation. We are free from the imperialist...."

The Liberation Front was another name for the communists—they had taken over the radio station. I didn't know it at the time, but they had seized most of the city, including the Presidential Palace. Dad came into my room right after the announcement and said we were going to the airport again. He rushed us outside and we rode into the city. Russian tanks with children hanging on the sides rolled along Highway 1.

The children had red bands on their arms and were singing and shouting, "Liberation! Liberation!"

Some people were waving to them and cheering. Others stared at them with terrified faces. Still others went about their business as if nothing was happening. Dad raced along the highway, and Vinh and I pedaled as fast as we could to keep up. When we got to the airport road, we saw that no planes were taking off. The communists had bombed the runways, so we rode back home and Dad made us stay in the house for the rest of the day. The man on the radio kept saying, "Do not fear. The war is over. Our country has united and beaten the American invaders…."

I still couldn't understand why my parents were so frightened. The communists were cheering and shooting their rifles into the air, but I didn't see them shoot anyone. The man on the radio said we were free from the American imperialists. I didn't know if the Americans had been our friends or our enemies, but I knew I would find out what the communists were like. They were all over the city. I kept looking at Mom and Dad, wondering what they were going to do to make everything right. They sat with blank faces next to the radio, listening to communist songs along with the rest of us. Every fifteen minutes, the music would stop and a voice would say, "This is the Vietnamese Liberation Front. We have defeated the American invaders…."

I was tired of listening to the radio and seeing my parents so upset, so I snuck out the back door and rode my bike to the river. When I saw the first star, I wished that I knew everything. I was starting to realize the problem was too big for my father, so I asked God if He would make everything right, but he didn't answer.

When I returned home, Mom and my sisters were cleaning

the dishes. No one asked where I had been. I sat next to Dad in the living room. His eyes were open, but he looked dazed. As I moved closer to him, I knew he could sense my presence, but he still didn't speak. "What will happen now, Dad?" I asked. "Please tell me what will happen." He sat motionless, so I tried again. "What's wrong with communism? Why do we have to be scared? Why are you acting this way?"

His eyes got bigger and he looked angry, but his voice was soft. "There's no way you can understand. You're only fourteen years old. You haven't lived under the communist rule."

"But it's my life. I may be young, but I have a right to know what will happen to me." I could feel tears in my eyes, but I wouldn't let them come out.

Dad put his hand on the arm of my chair for a moment, then sat back and said, "The communists will control our lives. They'll steal our freedom."

"I know that much," I said. "But *how* will they control our lives? What freedom will they take away?" Dad looked away for a moment and then back at me. His eyes were bloodshot from lack of sleep. His short black hair, which he usually slicked back, was sticking straight up. A thin beard was growing on his sunken face. "I know you're tired," I said, "but I need to know more. I need to know why you hate the communists and why they hate us."

His face showed compassion for me, and he thought for a moment, then began to speak. "Every time we escape for-eign domination of one kind, it's followed by domination of another kind," he said. "You know that we fought the Chinese for a thousand years before the French moved in and controlled our country." I nodded as I remembered learning about the French in my history class.

"They treated us like animals," Dad said, "like tools for the promotion of French wealth and their dream of conquering China. But our people never lost hope for freedom and organized groups to fight for independence. Ho Chi Minh was the leader of one of these organizations, and his group was supported by Russia and the communist parties in other countries. People followed him because he promised freedom, equality, and a better life for the peasants. But what the people didn't understand, and what Ho Chi Minh didn't understand, was that communism was no better than French imperialism."

"But what's wrong with communism?"

"The communists take your freedom away," he responded. "You can't understand until you've lost it. They control everything about you: what you eat, what you wear, who you're allowed to talk to, what you're allowed to say."

"But why did anyone follow them if they take your freedom away?"

Dad was frustrated because I still didn't get it. He looked down and was silent for a few seconds. I thought he was going to tell me that I couldn't understand, but he went on. "Many people followed them because they promised a better life. They promised to get rid of the French landlords and give the land back to our people. But their promises were false. Under communism, no land belongs to the people. Nothing does. Everything belongs to the state, and the state is owned by the communist party. So when the communists gained control of the North, they made the taxes so high that no one could afford to own anything. Their theory was to tax the rich the heaviest and have lower taxes for the poor, but it didn't work."

"Why? Why was it bad to help the poor people?"

"Because the communists gave too much power to the peasants. They ordered the peasants to execute the landlords, but the landlords bribed the peasants and moved to the South. So to satisfy the communist leaders, the peasants executed innocent people. Instead of killing the French landlords, they killed anyone who didn't believe in and support the communist government." I still didn't really understand, and Dad saw the confusion in my face.

"The communists terrorized the villages in the North," he said. "The peasants who had been suppressed by the French were now intoxicated by their new power. When the French were beaten, instead of forming parties and voting for a new government, the communists demanded complete control. They raided villages and tortured anyone who didn't support them. My father was one of these people. He was not a wealthy man. He was as happy as anyone to see the French beaten, but he believed in democracy. He believed that everyone should have their say in the government."

"What happened to my grandfather?" I asked. "Why didn't he move to the South when you did?"

"The communists raided our village," Dad said. "They came when we were having a meeting to discuss the land taxes. My father was one of the village leaders and was making a speech about the land taxes when the communists circled around us. They looked like ordinary farmers and fishermen, but they carried weapons and ropes. I was standing at the back of the crowd with a friend. I watched them grab my father and tie him up. I ran for him, but it was too late. They were too strong and no one would help me. I was on the ground, struggling under the feet of the communists, while they humiliated my father...while they beat him in front of the whole village."

Dad's eyes became fierce. He leaned toward me and shouted, "That is what communism is about! That is what will happen to me when they find out I escaped from the North. When they discover the position I held in the American-sponsored government."

"How will they know whose side we're on?" I asked. "Mom burned your uniforms. We can pretend we're on their side."

"They'll infiltrate the South just like they did the North," he said. "They'll know everything about everyone. They will control our lives and steal our freedom!" He was shaking with anger. He sat back in his chair and took a deep breath, and I watched him for a few minutes. His eyes became empty, gazing into nowhere; he didn't seem to notice when I stood up. I went to my room and drifted to sleep thinking about what he had said, wondering if the communists would hurt my family.

Somehow I ended up at Tam's house. He was my best friend at the time. It was dark when I got there, but the door was open, so I walked inside to see if he was home. The smell of raw meat hit my nose as I walked through the shadow of the doorway. For a moment, I was in total darkness. I called for Tam quietly at first, but there was no answer so I tried a little louder. "Tam...Tam?" Still no answer.

I walked through the house to Tam's bedroom, wondering where everyone could be. My skin became cold as I walked into his room. "Tam?" I whispered. "Are you here?"

Then I saw Tam's feet sticking out from under his covers. "Tam! Stop playing games. What are you doing in bed so early?" Tam still didn't answer, so I walked slowly to his bed and pulled the covers off him. They were heavy, wet and cold. Tam was face down on the bed. I nudged him, but he didn't move. A chill shot through my bones. I grabbed Tam's shoulder and pulled him over. His body was stiff, and he had the head of a dog! It was Tam's body, but he had the head of a dog. Blood was everywhere. I tried to scream, but no noise came out. I ran from his room, and the door slammed behind me.

I ran to the kitchen to get out the back door. There were people sitting with their heads on the kitchen table. They looked the same as Tam—their throats were slashed. Blood oozed from their wounds. Long dog tongues came out of their mouths and rested in the blood on the table. I edged along the wall to the back door. It wouldn't budge. My body shook. I thought my heart would beat through my chest. I ran for the front door, and it slammed shut in front of me. Another body with a dog's head leaped from behind the door. It laughed in a deep voice and charged toward me. Its cold hands grasped my neck and shook me until I forced my eyes open. It was morning, and I realized I had been dreaming.

I threw my sweat-soaked covers onto the floor and sat on the edge of my bed. My heart was still racing as I pulled on my trousers and went to the kitchen. Mom was sitting at the table. She didn't ask why I was up so early. She just said for me to stay around the house for a while because my father wanted to talk to all of us. Everyone was awake and sitting at the table by the time I finished breakfast.

Dad's eyes sank deep into his face as he began to speak. He said he didn't expect us to understand what he was about to say, but that he had to explain it anyway. "You know for the last week we have been trying to leave the country," he said. We all nodded. "We've been trying to escape because very soon the communists will have total control of our city. And when they do, they'll take your mother and me away from you. They'll take your freedom away and teach you things that are not right. Things I have spent my whole life fighting against."

Dad was silent for what seemed to be a few minutes. We waited patiently for him to continue. "We've always saved money because we wanted to send you away from this country," he said. "We know there have been things you wanted that we wouldn't give you because we were saving as much as we could. But now it's too late to escape. We have nothing to save for. You can do what you like with the money we have. When our money runs out, your mother will cook our last dinner, and we will all go to heaven."

Tears flowed down Mom's cheeks. She covered her mouth to keep any sounds from escaping. My little brother and sisters cried. I don't think they understood what was happening, but they felt my mother's emotions. Vinh sat expressionless next to me.

"It is better to die by our own hands," Dad said, "than to die by the hands of the communists." I could see the veins in his neck getting bigger and bigger. His spirit seemed to be tearing at his body. I didn't feel confused anymore; I couldn't feel at all. My little brother Tu was only three years old. It wasn't fair that he had to die just as his life was beginning.

"What is die?" he asked. "Why do we die?" Mom looked at Dad, but he didn't answer Tu's question. His arms were shaking as he stood and walked out of the kitchen.

I stayed in my room until late afternoon when Mom asked me to bike to the market for some food. She gave me 50,000 piasters and told me to get the food and anything else I wanted. I couldn't believe she gave me so much money.

When I got to the market, it was empty except for an

old woman sitting next to a cart full of chickens. She said my money wasn't worth anything because we had a new government, but when she saw how much I offered her, she didn't refuse. I grabbed the fattest chickens from the cart and headed home. When I got there, our neighbor Mrs. Hoi was walking out of our house with a bag of rice. She said hello and asked how I was doing as she walked by. I greeted her and hurried inside to ask Mom why she had given our rice away.

"Mrs. Hoi's husband has been out of work," she said. I began to tell her we needed the rice because everything was so expensive, but she interrupted me. "The communists have taken over your father's station. They're using it as a place for people to register with the new government."

"Is Dad going to register?"

"He left a few minutes ago to see what's happening. I just hope he comes back."

I put the chickens on the counter, and Mom examined them, then she boiled some water to soak the feathers off. She had the chickens plucked, carved and frying in the wok by the time Dad got home. I listened as he told Mom he had registered with the communists. He said he had lied about his occupation during the war. He told them he was wounded in battle and had been an ordinary civilian police officer since the nineteen sixties, omitting any mention of his role as an intelligence officer. When I finished dinner, I went to my room to read. I thought about the times Dad would make me go to bed at nine, but I would stay up anyway, holding an oil lamp under the covers so I could see my book. He would come into my room, see the glowing covers, and start yelling at me. Now I could stay up all night if I wanted, but I wasn't sure how many nights I had left.

I woke the next morning to unfamiliar voices in the living room. I jumped out of bed, thinking the communists were there to take Mom and Dad away. But when I got to the living room, I saw five of our neighbors going through our house collecting our things. What are you people doing?" I shouted. "Put our things back!"

Dad told me to be quiet and pushed me to my room. "We have no use for these things anymore," he said. "The sooner we get rid of everything the better. We have to leave these things, and I want to give them to people we know and care about. I will not leave anything for the communists."

I nodded to him as though I understood, and he left me sitting on my bed. I realized then that dying meant losing everything I had. I sat on my bed for a while, feeling sorry for myself. Then I rode my bike to Tam's house. Mom had given me some money, so Tam and I rode around trying to find something to spend it on. We rode down Highway 1 to Ben Bach Dang Street, pedaled south along the river until we found a tobacco shop that was open, and spent the rest of the morning smoking cigarettes under the Highway 1 bridge. I couldn't get the thought of dying out of my head, and while we were under the bridge I told Tam what Dad had said about going to heaven.

"My father told me there's no way we can escape the communists," I said. "Our whole family is going to die together. I think my Mom and Dad are going to kill us." Tam had been my best friend since the first grade, and I could tell him anything. At first, he looked like he didn't hear what I said. He did that when he thought I was making up a story. He sat motionless, staring into the water. "I don't think I want to die," I said. "I've heard the horror stories about communism, but I don't think it could be worse than death."

Tam turned to me, looking into my eyes to see if I was telling the truth. "Are your parents crazy?" he asked. "They're going to kill you?" It sounded different to hear him say it. My parents were actually going to kill me. They were going to kill all of us. "You should run away," he said. "You can stay at my house."

We were silent for a moment. I knew I couldn't stay at Tam's house. It would be the first place my parents would look for me. I think he realized this too. "Or you could live in the banana groves across from Bach Dang," he said. "You can eat the fruit to survive. I'll visit you." I still didn't know what I wanted to do. I didn't know what death was like. I didn't know what communism was like. All I knew was what people told me, and it was starting to seem like no one really knew anything.

"I can't believe your parents are going to kill you," Tam said.

"Dad told us that Mom would cook our last dinner and we would all go to heaven. He told us it would be better to die by our own hands than by the hands of the communists."

"I don't think the communists will kill you."

"But my father was a spy for the Americans."

Tam's eyes became uncertain, and he looked toward the ground. "You shouldn't go home," he said. "Come with me to Bach Dang Harbor and we'll take the ferry across to the banana groves." I agreed to go, but I didn't think I would stay there. I didn't want to run away. I wanted to be with my family, no matter what Dad decided we should do.

When we got to the harbor, the ferry wasn't running, so we walked along the bank of the river, looking for flat rocks to skip. I had stopped to light a cigarette when Tam screeched and pointed down the river. When I looked to where he was pointing, I saw a body hanging from a tree. We crept along the bank to get a closer look. It was a man in a South Vietnamese officer's uniform—the same kind of uniform my father used to wear.

Dried blood covered the man's face and chest. His feet dangled in the water. The current had pulled the body against the rope and embedded it in his neck. My stomach turned, and I looked the other way to keep from throwing up. Then I saw another body floating in the water. It was naked and bloated up like a pale blue balloon. I heaved until my stomach felt like a small tight knot. Tam grabbed my arm and helped me up the bank to our bikes. I kept thinking I would wake up and it would all be a dream, like my nightmare about Tam. I wondered if there really was a heaven, and if there was, I thought maybe Dad was right and we should all go to heaven together.

Communist Takeover

May was long and wet. We ate or gave away most of our livestock, so I had few chores to do. Mom gave our television away and burned most of my books. The communists ordered everyone to hang the flag of the National Liberation Front on their houses and to display a picture of Ho Chi Minh in a prominent place. Each day, Mom and Dad sunk a little deeper into despair. The few times Dad spoke were usually when he cursed at the picture of Ho Chi Minh.

Communist songs and announcements seemed to emerge constantly from the radio in our house, and they blared out of loud speakers throughout the city. For the first two weeks, the voice said for all military personnel, politicians, school teachers and police officers to register with the new government. Then the first day of June, the voice said for these people to report to their local officials for three days reeducation.

The tension in our house grew. Dad hardly spoke, but I thought I knew what he was thinking. He was deciding whether he would report for reeducation or end our lives as he had said before. One morning he told me to be home for dinner because he wanted to talk to the whole family. I knew he had registered as a police officer and if he didn't report for reeducation the communist officials would come looking for him. I didn't think Dad would give in to the communists, so I thought our only alternative would be to go to heaven together.

I spent the day fishing with Tam, and when I came home, I saw that Mom had prepared a big dinner. I was hungry but couldn't bring myself to eat. We hadn't eaten dinner together since the communists took over, and I thought, *this is it—the end*. I thought my parents must have put poison in the food.

"Are you not hungry, Viet?" Mom asked as she slid the noodle soup in front of me. The smell of fresh green vegetables rose in the steam from the soup. I poured some into my bowl and stared at it for a moment, thinking the poison was in the broth. Mom watched as I dipped my spoon into the bowl. Everyone else had already eaten some, so I filled my spoon and ate the first bite, wondering how long it would take to affect me. Visions of us holding our stomachs and gasping for air flashed through my mind as Dad began to speak.

"I wanted you here tonight," he said, "because something is about to happen that concerns us as a family." He paused for a moment. "I have to go away for a while. I'm going to report to the communists."

I was confused for a moment. I thought about the dead officer that Tam and I saw. I felt like I should be happy because we weren't going to die, but I didn't want Dad to report to the communists. I thought they might kill him. I wanted to ask him why he changed his mind, but I didn't. His lips were tight, and his eyes cast down. Mom put her hands over her face. My brothers and sisters sat quietly with empty faces, waiting to see what Dad would say next.

"Viet, you will lead the family," he said. "I want you to guide your brothers and sisters. You need to help them any way you can. I don't want to leave you, but this is my only choice. If I don't return, you will live with your grandfather." Tears fell from Mom's hands.

"No matter what happens," Dad said, "you cannot forget what I've taught you. The communists will try to trick you into believing things that are wrong. Never forget the freedom you once had, the freedom to do and say what you think is right. If I don't return, you must try to leave Vietnam. It will be your only chance for freedom."

Mom was sitting alone in the living room when I woke the next morning. Dad had already left with some men from our neighborhood. I had to grow up overnight. I was responsible for the whole family now and couldn't let my father down.

After three days, some of the men who had left with Dad came home. The man on the radio called for higher ranking officers to report with paper, pens, mosquito nets, and a month's supply of food and clothes. Mom tried to find out what was happening from the men who came home, but no one would talk, not even the men who were in my father's squad. Mom said the adults in our neighborhood were suspicious of each other and frightened of the communist officials. I thought I should go looking for Dad, but Mom told me not to worry. "Your father will be home soon," she said, "We need you with us. Your father needs you to look after us. He'll be home soon."

In the evenings when the rain let up, Tam and I rode our bikes around the city. Streets that used to swarm with traffic were now blocked off. The city had been ransacked by vandals and looters. Store and restaurant windows were boarded up. Starving heroin addicts, cripples and refugees from villages outside of the city filled the streets, sidewalks and alleys. They sat or lay on the ground, holding out their hands, staring up at us with hungry eyes.

One evening when Tam and I were riding along the river road, we saw a man rip a gold chain from a woman's neck. The man ran along the street, and the woman held the front of her blue dress and ran after him. Some communist soldiers saw what was happening and chased the man and tackled him.

Tam and I watched from a distance as the soldiers took the struggling man to a nearby bridge. The woman who owned the necklace was thanking them and holding out her hand for them to give it back, but the soldiers shook their heads and said they had to keep it for evidence. In a few minutes, more soldiers came. The oldest of them, a short round-faced officer in his mid-thirties, took charge. He ordered two of the soldiers to hold the man on the edge of the bridge. Then he pulled his pistol from its holster. A crowd had formed around the bridge, so Tam and I climbed on the rail to get a better look.

"The People's Court of Ho Chi Minh City is now in session," the short officer screamed. People shifted around, and I could see the woman in the blue dress at the front of the crowd. "Silence!" The officer pointed at the captured man who was now sweating and shaking with fear, then he turned to the woman in the blue dress. "Is this the thief who stole your property?"

The woman nodded and said something, but I couldn't hear her answer over the cries of the captured man. "It was just a necklace…I was starving! Have mercy on me!" he said.

The officer raised his pistol, then stretched his arm so

that the barrel lodged in the man's thin cheek. "There is no place for thieves in our new society!"

I turned my head as the shot rang out. It silenced the crowd. The only sound was the thud of the man's body as it collapsed on the bridge. People scattered, their heads low, not wanting to be noticed by the raging officer. Tam and I rode to the top of the hill and watched the soldiers hang the body from the bridge.

As the weeks dragged by, I began to lose hope that Dad would return. I was starting to think he was gone forever. Tam and I heard rumors that the communists were killing the South Vietnamese officers but wouldn't let anyone know because they were afraid the Americans would come back. I asked Mom if we were going to move to Grandfather's house, but she wouldn't answer. "We've eaten everything in the garden," I told her. "We've butchered all of our chickens, and we're running out of money."

"Your father will be home soon," she said softly. I wanted to believe her, but I couldn't. It was as though she didn't realize what was happening. She hadn't left the house in a month. She hadn't seen how the people had changed. She hadn't seen the hungry faces, the angry faces. There was no one to help us if Dad didn't return, and there was no way for me to make money.

Around the middle of July, I heard my little brother scream, "Dad! Dad!" At first I thought he was crying to Mom, but when I looked up, I saw Dad walking through the doorway. We all ran to hug him. He usually would have held us, but he was so weak, he fell to one knee. I grabbed his arm to hold him up and could feel the bone in his arm. His body was hunched over, and his clothes hung on him like drapes.

"What have they done to you?" Mom cried.

We helped him to the table, and my sister Thanh Ha brought him some food. "They didn't kill me," he said. When he finished half the food on his plate, he leaned back in the chair and held his stomach.

"What did you have to do?" I asked.

"Give him a chance to rest," Mom said, then added, "Didn't they feed you?"

"They made us write our life histories," Dad said. "They watched us while we wrote and made us keep writing so we didn't have time to make up stories. They didn't let me stop until I had filled more than thirty pages." He grabbed a chicken leg, bit a piece off and chewed it. "They were polite at first, then they started shouting questions: 'Why did you support the American fascists? Why did you torture your own countrymen? How can you expect to be a citizen of our society?' They took turns cutting at my pride, trying to get me to answer their questions." He bit off another piece of chicken and swallowed it whole, then sat back again.

"When they gave me a chance to speak, I told them my parents had brought me from the North when I was a child. I said I was forced to join the military at an early age and purposely got wounded so I wouldn't have to fight against my own countrymen. I had to say these things or they would have kept me there."

Dad scraped the last bit of rice from his bowl, chewed slowly and gulped it down. We were all silent for a moment, then Mom told us we should get ready for bed. While she took Tu to the bedroom, I helped my father to his chair. "What did they tell you?" I asked. "What will happen to us now?"

"They said we're thirty years behind the North in becoming a socialist society, and we're sixty years behind Brother Russia. There will be a new economic scheme that's supposed to help the economy, but it will be just like the one they had in the North. Everything is supposed to belong to everyone, but in reality, it will be everything except what the communist party decides to keep." Dad's body was weak, but his mind still seemed strong.

"They said building our new society will be like building a house, a house designed by Marx and Lenin. Russia is an example of a solid but still unfinished house, and the communist party has already started to build the socialist house of Vietnam. They know how to build it, so they will be the foremen, following the instructions from Russia. The people in the South can't even be the laborers. They say we've been rotted by capitalist ideas. We're only seeds to be planted to grow new trees. These new trees will be examined and if they're sound they'll be used to build our society. After many generations we can become laborers, and if we work hard enough we may become foremen, or in other words, members of the communist party."

I didn't completely follow what Dad was saying. He seemed delirious from lack of food and sleep, and his mind was filled with communist lectures, but I nodded as though I understood so he would continue. "They said some day the whole world will follow the plan of Marxism. They said we're just the beginning and our only purpose in life is to make their dream of international socialism come true. They said when the whole world goes through the steps of Marxism and everyone on this planet is equal, we will have reached Communist Heaven." Dad was smiling. Now I knew he was delirious. After all we had been through—the escape attempt, the anger, the talk of going to heaven—now he was smiling as though the whole thing were a joke. "The communists believe the world will follow them," he said. "If they weren't so confident, I wouldn't have made it back. I wouldn't have convinced them I believed in their system, and they would have killed me." Now the smile faded from Dad's face, and he seemed to come back to reality.

"This is only the beginning," he said. "We'll be watched from now on. There are people who think they can get favors from the communists if they spy on their neighbors. We need to work as a family. We can't trust anyone, even our closest friends. The communists will try to teach you things that are wrong, and you'll have to make them believe you think they're right. The best thing for you to do is repeat the things they say. If you don't understand what they're saying, or if you don't agree with them, talk to me about it. We have to work together. Our family is all we have left."

Dad was gone when I woke up the next morning. When I asked Mom where he was, she hesitated. Then she told me he went to a Chinese suburb to see if he could find someone to buy our house. My father had spent years building our house piece by piece. When we first moved to Saigon, we lived in a thatched hut. Now that hut was our barn, and we lived in a two-story brick house with glass windows, hardwood floors and indoor plumbing. I remembered watching my father make the bricks by hand. I remembered how careful he was as he placed each one. Our home was the center of our lives, but Mom said we would have to move to a smaller, less expensive house and use the extra money to buy food until Dad decided what to do next. She said she wasn't happy about moving, and she was saying something about the communists stealing our property when a young man stuck his head through our front doorway.

"Anyone home!" the man shouted with a North Vietnamese accent.

Mom went to see who it was, and I listened from Dad's chair. I heard the man say something about a youth organization he was setting up, so I went to the door to see what he wanted. "You must be Viet," he said as he read my name from a piece of paper. I nodded. "I am a representative from the new government, and I'm organizing some activities for children in our area until school starts." I nodded again. "If you and your brother would like to participate, come to the park in your school uniforms on Monday, at nine o'clock."

"What will we be doing?"

"I'll explain everything in the park. It will be a good idea for you to be there." The young man grinned, then he turned and walked away. Mom and I looked at each other.

"I don't have to go, do I?" I asked.

"We'll see what your father says," she told me. I didn't think Dad would make us go, but when he got home that evening, he said Vinh and I would need to go, or the new officials would suspect that we were against the government.

Monday morning, Vinh and I put on our black trousers and white shirts and rode to Tam's house, then the three of us rode to the park. Several hundred young people were there, sitting in circles according to the area they lived in. We walked around until we saw the man who came to our house. His hair stuck up in the back like a rooster's tail, and a thin mustache was struggling to grow above his lip. He couldn't have been more than eighteen years old, but I thought he was trying to act like an older, respected man. He stood with his legs wide apart and his chin in the air. He didn't say a word until he was satisfied with the number of people in his group, then he held his hands high for silence and began to speak.

"My name is Le Van Tien," he said. "I am here to lead you in the good path." Le told us all to introduce ourselves, even though we knew each other because we lived in the same neighborhood. When we finished, he asked for volunteers to describe what we liked to do in our spare time. When no one volunteered, he picked a few people, and their answers were all about the same. "We like to play army games and soccer, go swimming, ride our bikes…."

Le's smile grew after each person's answer, then his face became serious. "We are the youth of the new society, which means we are the future," he said with as much force as he could. "Our parents have worked hard to provide a future for us, but they have failed in a very crucial part." A stillness swept around the circle. Le was silent for a moment. He knew he should choose his next words carefully because it's taboo for a Vietnamese to criticize his elders. When he regained his confidence, he went on.

"The education you get in school develops your knowledge," he said, "and the education you get from your parents develops your attitude. Your attitude is reflected by what you do in your spare time. By your descriptions, I can tell your attitudes are not suitable for our new society. When you're just riding your bikes or playing useless games, you are not helping society. You are only thinking of your own enjoyment, and the rest of society has to support you. Who can give me some examples of things you should be doing in your spare time?"

No one moved. I wanted to leave before he picked on me to answer a question. He waited for a volunteer for what seemed to be an hour but was really about a minute. "Since

36

you cannot think of even one way to help society," he said, "I will give you a few examples of how children your age in the North helped to liberate our country."

He read some stories about children from the North who carried supplies to the Viet Cong and told us about a girl named Nguyen Thi Sau, who was a messenger during the war. A street in Saigon was named after her a few months later. Le told us how she was used by the Viet Cong to carry crucial information because children weren't as likely to be caught by the American and South Vietnamese soldiers. He said she completed many successful missions before the Americans caught her.

"The capitalists tortured Thi Sau," Le said, "but she would not tell them her secrets. You should be inspired by her bravery and commitment to our country." I knew those children were also used to plant bombs in movie theaters and other businesses in Saigon. I was tired of him praising people who had killed many of my father's friends, but all I could do was sit and listen. When he finished with the stories, he taught us songs: "We love Ho Chi Minh because we are his children. He has a long beard and sparkling eyes that shine on us. Last night I dreamed of Uncle Ho. He cuddled me and told me I was good...." I didn't understand why those songs helped society more than playing soccer. It was just someone else's idea of what's right, and I wanted to make up my own mind.

After that day, we met in the park every morning. Le lectured us for an hour, then we had to do things to help the new society. The first week we picked up trash around the neighborhood. The second week we went house to house collecting books and other things the communists had banned, then burned them in the park. Le gained the trust of some of the children and asked them questions about their parents. After every meeting, he recorded what he learned in a little blue book. I didn't think he had the right to pry into our lives. I hated him and the control he had over my life, but to please my father I smiled at him, agreed with him, and clapped along to the communist songs.

The first week of August, Dad sold our house to a Chinese woman for less than half of what it was worth. But he did this because she promised not to tear it apart and sell it for scraps. It was important to him that our home wasn't destroyed, even if we would no longer live there. Within a week, we were living in a two-room hut on the corner of Highways 1 and 13. We all shared the bedroom, which had a bathtub in the corner, surrounded by a curtain, and a string along the wall to hang our clothes. The big room was our kitchen, dining room and living room. There was no glass in the windows, only bamboo blinds to pull down when the rains were heavy. The toilet was in a small grass building about ten feet behind the back door.

Our new house was only a few miles from our old neighborhood, across the road from Binh An Church, where I had attended Mass for as long as I could remember. There was a school next to the church, so I knew if the schools opened again I would have to go there instead of going to my old school with Tam and the rest of my friends.

Everyone in our new neighborhood weaved baskets for a living, so the first Sunday we were there, Dad went to our neighbor's house to learn the craft. When he came home that evening, he was carrying a bundle of jute grass in each hand. We all learned how to weave baskets and mattresses, but it was hard to make them look good, and we didn't sell any the first week. By the second week, our baskets were no longer lopsided and our mattresses were straight along the edges. It was tedious work, and I was relieved when a man came to our house and said Vinh, my sisters and I were to start school the first Monday of September.

I thought school would be my chance to make new friends and have some fun, so I was up early that Monday morning, eager to cross the road for my first day. Vinh and my sisters followed me to the soccer field, where about two hundred children were assembled. A man introduced himself as our new headmaster and spoke for a few minutes about the value of learning. Then he told us to report to certain rooms according to our grade levels.

Our teacher was standing on a platform when I walked into the classroom. The only person in my class that I had seen before was Phi, the son of the people who taught my father to weave baskets. I sat next to him at a wooden desk by the window and looked at my house across the road. It still didn't seem like home. It seemed like someone else's house that we were visiting. When we were all seated, our teacher introduced himself as Tan Van Houng. His huge voice filled the room and echoed off the cement walls. "I'm happy to see so many of you on the first day," he said. "We have much to learn, so let's begin."

So far, everything was like my old school. We had to introduce ourselves and tell where we lived and what we had been doing since school let out. Then we voted for a person to take roll and be in charge while Mr. Houng was out of the room. I didn't know the boy who was elected, but I could tell he was someone that everyone else could push around. We moved to our assigned seats, and Mr. Houng gave us a list of courses to choose from.

We had to take the basic courses like math and science,

but we were able to choose our foreign language. Before the communists took over, they offered only French and English, but now they added Russian. When we finished choosing our courses, Mr. Houng said we would have a basic skills test the next day. Then he dismissed us.

Mom and Dad were making baskets when I got home. I thought how old and weak my father looked compared to several months earlier, when he walked proudly in his uniform and it seemed as if everything he did was important. Now he was hunched over, not saying a word, no expression on his face, just weaving and cutting, weaving and cutting. He didn't answer when I asked if I could go out to meet some of the children from school, so I changed clothes and left out the back door. Across the road, on the steps of the school, Phi was standing with a few other boys from my class. Phi offered me a cigarette as I walked up to the steps, but I didn't take it because I thought my parents might see me.

"This is Viet," Phi told the other boys who were there. "He just moved to the neighborhood." The biggest boy had a soccer ball and was bouncing it off the back of the smallest boy's head.

"*My* name's Viet," the biggest boy told me. "We'll have to call you something else." The smallest boy stood up and walked out of reach of the ball.

"If we had one more person, we could play a game," Phi said. "You play soccer, don't you?" he asked me.

"Sure, I'll play."

"What about your brother?" Phi asked. "Go get him."

"He's studying," I said.

"Studying today?" Viet asked. "What is he, the teacher's pet?" I wanted to stick up for Vinh because he was my brother, but I also wanted to be part of the group, so I didn't say

40

anything.

"Viet and me against you three," Phi said, referring to me. "We can beat you no problem." We played the rest of the afternoon, but Phi and I didn't win. Viet would trip us or knock us down every time we got close to the goal. He wasn't bigger than I was, but I didn't want to start a fight, so I let him have his way.

At sundown, I went home for dinner. As I sat down to eat, I felt my father's eyes piercing through me, but before I could look up to see him, he started shouting. "If you think you're too good to work with the family, you will not eat with the family! Get up! You'll eat when you have earned it!"

Dad shocked me—I didn't know I had done something wrong. I got up and walked through the bamboo and straw to the bedroom. The room seemed smaller than ever. I lay on my mattress in the corner, pulled my mosquito net down, and hid my head under my pillow. It was dark when my stomach woke me. My whole family was asleep, so I went to the kitchen, ate some leftover rice, slid out the back door and walked to the river bank, where I stayed until school started. The skills test was easy, and I finished before everyone else so I got to leave early. I was still hungry but didn't want to give in to my father, so I crept along the side of our house, grabbed my bike and rode to Tam's.

When I got there, Tam was sitting on his front porch. He looked exactly the same as he did before I moved. His hair was past his ears on the sides and cut straight along his eyebrows. His skin was tanned, as he had spent all day swimming and riding his bike. As I rode up to the porch, I wished my life could be so easy. "Look who it is," Tam said as I leaned my bike against the porch. "The basket weaver from Binh An."

I walked up the steps of the porch and pushed him off his chair. "How do you know we're weaving baskets?" I asked.

"Everyone in Binh An weaves baskets. What else would you be doing?"

He was smoking a cigarette, so I knew his parents weren't home. "What do you have to eat?" I asked.

"There's some rice on the stove and some fruit on the counter. Bring me a banana." Tam's house was smaller than our old one, but as I walked through the living room to the kitchen, I thought how I would give anything to live there now. I spooned up a bowl of rice, grabbed a couple bananas, and went back to the porch.

"Where are your parents?"

"They went north to visit my Uncle. They won't be home for a few days."

"Do you have to start school?"

"I was supposed to start today, but my Dad didn't want to leave our house with no one watching it, so he said I could stay home until they come back."

"Why does someone need to watch it?"

"The communists are seizing vacant houses," he said. "If they come by and no one's here, they'll board it up and declare it the property of the people." I thought how lucky Tam was to have the whole house to himself and not have to go to school. We sat on the porch until late afternoon. He told me I could stay at his house for a few days, but I knew my parents wouldn't let me.

I rode home around three o'clock so Mom and Dad would think I came straight home from school. When I got there, Dad had gone to our neighbors to get more jute grass. I was glad he was gone because Vinh had told Mom I got out of school early. She didn't seem angry that I didn't come straight home, but she asked where I had been.

"Dad doesn't want me here anyway," I told her. "I went to Tam's so I could get something to eat."

She pushed me against the kitchen counter and stared straight into my eyes. "That is not true. Your father's upset because he can't support us alone, and your selfishness is making it more difficult for him."

I knew Mom was right, but I thought there had to be another way to make money. "Why do we have to weave these baskets?" I asked. "Why doesn't Dad do something else?"

"Your father knows what's best for us. You must be patient. Your father will take care of us."

The next day at school, there was a new man sitting in the front of the class. He stood up and smiled with bright yellow teeth when Mr. Houng introduced him. His name was Cao Than Nguyen, and he was going to be teaching us political philosophy for the next few weeks until more teachers arrived. Mr. Nguyen peered around the room as if he were judging us, then he hurried to the chalk board and wrote SOCIALISM.

"Who can tell us what this word means?" he asked with a northern accent. No one answered. "Let us try another." Then he wrote COMMUNISM on the board. "Who knows what this means?" Still no answer. He smiled and said, "It looks as if we have a bashful group here." Then he pointed to the boy in front of me. "Tell us your definition of socialism."

The boy blushed, thought for a moment, and said, "It's when the government divides everything equally among all the people."

Mr. Nguyen grinned so big that it bothered me, then he answered his own question. "Socialism is the power of the people," he said, "and communism is how the people get power. The communist party is an organization that teaches people about communism. It helps people to reach true socialism, which is the only way everyone can have total freedom. But before a society can begin the steps toward equality, it has to be an independent society. This is what our country has been fighting for, and this is what we have finally achieved."

He looked up as though he expected applause, but no one clapped. "We have beaten the Chinese…the French… and the Americans," he said. "For the first time in a thousand years, we are an independent nation! We have completed the first step in reaching our goal, but we still have much to learn. This is why I am here, to help you understand so you can all do your part." He walked around the desk and looked down at us.

"The communist party and the people from the North have fought and died to give our nation independence," he said. "They will guide us and help us to reach true equality, but each of you must also help by learning about communism and practicing what you learn. For socialism to succeed, the needs and wants of the individual person must be sacrificed. True equality can exist only if each member of our society believes in and practices socialism. When we become equal, our lives will be better. There will be no hatred, no corruption. We will all be equal. We will all be free."

Mr. Nguyen was rambling so fast that I had to ignore him so I could think. He said we all wanted to be equal, that we were happy we had independence. But the communists had brought nothing but misery for me and my family. *If communism is so good*, I thought, *then why were so many people trying to escape from it?* Everyone kept talking about equality, but I didn't understand what they meant. I had learned when things were equal, they were exactly the same, and I knew it was impossible for two people to be exactly the same, let alone a whole society. Mr. Nguyen said communism was the first stage our country would go through to reach true socialism. He said there would be greedy people who would have to be forced to turn their property over to the government. I thought about what had happened to my parents in the North and began to realize my parents were right. The communists were going to force us to give them everything we owned.

For the next two weeks, Mr. Nguyen told us how the communist heroes beat the French and finally the Americans. I had to learn about and write about how the people in the South were traitors and how we were brainwashed by the evil Americans' capitalist ideology. He didn't say why the Americans were evil, and I was afraid to ask. I wanted to understand what was right, but I remembered what Dad told me, so I wrote and said what I thought Mr. Nguyen wanted to hear.

More students and teachers arrived every week. We started the other subjects, but they were different. Instead of Vietnamese history, we studied communist history, beginning with Karl Marx and continuing through Russia, China, and finally Vietnam. Even our math books were different. Many of the word problems dealt with the war. "If the Americans sent 12 planes to bomb a defenseless village in North Vietnam, Mr. X shot down 2 planes, and Mr. A shot down 3, how many planes were left to bomb more villages?"

My normal classes were easy because I had learned most of the material the previous year, but I was getting behind in political philosophy. I could force myself to listen for the first five or ten minutes, then my mind drifted to my stomach. I would sit in class, dreaming of something sweet or some meat to sink my teeth into, and Mr. Nguyen would call on me. When I couldn't answer, he would wait, and the blood would rush to my head. Then he would tell me a day would come when I would wish I had studied harder.

When we got home from school each day, we weaved baskets until dark, but we still weren't making much money. By the end of September, we had used most of the money we made from selling our house. We were eating fish and rice soup every night. Dad's eyes grew more tired and his temper more fierce. He never hit me with his hands, but it seemed as if his eyes could kill me. Each time I asked if I could play soccer with my friends or go to Tam's house, the red veins in his eyes swelled, his neck tightened, and his jaw became tense, and I would return to my corner to weave. Every night, I told myself if I had a place to go, I would run away. Every night, I asked God if He would give me a place to go. He finally answered.

On the third Friday in October, a man came to our house to see my father. He was a representative of the government, responsible for getting volunteers to help develop the swamplands in the Mekong Delta. The program was called The Clean Water Project, and he made it clear that at least one member of each family must participate. He left a form for us to fill out and said he would return for it on Wednesday. I knew there was no way our family could survive if Dad left for another month, and that this was my chance to stop weaving baskets for a while. I told Dad I wanted to go, but he said we would discuss it later.

The next day I woke up early and finished eight baskets. After dinner, when Dad left to talk to our neighbors, I asked

46

Mom if I could go to the café to meet Phi. She said I could go for an hour, but I should be home before my father. I hurried into the bedroom and grabbed a coin I had hidden under my mattress. Then I climbed onto my bike and rode up Highway 13 to the café. The boys I played soccer with were there, including Viet, who now had a new name for me. "Kheo Leo," he called me as I walked into the café. It means clumsy.

Phi handed me a cigarette, and I sat in the booth beside him, trying to ignore Viet. I knew he just wanted to show the other boys that he was in control. But when the woman who owned the café brought us the bill, we all paid except Viet. He just stared at me. "Kheo Leo will pay my part," he said. I pulled out my coin, which was enough to pay for mine, and I started walking for the door. Viet nudged me with his shoulder as I squeezed by him. "You can pay now, or you can pay later," he said.

I followed the other boys outside and asked if they wanted to ride to the river, but Viet came out behind me and told them not to follow me. They all followed Viet in the other direction, so I rode to the river by myself. I was skipping rocks across the water when I heard Viet calling, "Kheo Leo! Kheo Leo!"

When I looked up, they were on the bank above me. Viet took a step forward and threw a rock toward me that splashed water on my feet. I picked up a rock and skipped it across the water, pretending not to notice them. Then Viet threw another rock and it hit my leg. I looked toward him and the other boys—they were all laughing. I felt my stomach flutter as Viet slid down the bank and strutted toward me.

He walked up and faced me. "If you think you can take over this neighborhood," he said, "you better think again."

The sun reflected off his gold necklace, and I thought he looked like a gangster. "I've gone to Binh An School all my life, and if you're going to be in our gang, you better get used to me being the boss."

I was trying not to shake. "I don't want to be in your gang," I said. "Just leave me alone." I was turning to walk away when Viet pushed me, and I went tumbling across the rocks. I rolled back up and kicked him as hard as I could, but it didn't faze him. He tackled me, and we splashed into the water. I came up first and landed a solid punch across his cheek that knocked him back into the water. His nose was bleeding, but he kept coming.

We wrestled across the rocks and he ended up on top of me. His hand was raised about a foot in front of my face when I felt him being pulled away. My eyes were full of dirt, but I could see him kicking. "I'll kill him," he screamed.

When I cleared my eyes, I saw a young man holding him by the back of his collar. The man looked harder than Viet, and I could tell his clothes and jewelry had come from the black market. "What's going on here?" he said. "A little boy's scuffle?" He was smiling like it was a joke.

"I'm showing Kheo Leo who the boss is!" Viet shouted.

"For a clumsy kid, Kheo Leo hit you many times," the man said, rubbing the blood off Viet's face.

"He got lucky," Viet said, and he climbed up the bank and disappeared over the top.

I was covered with dirt, and my arm was scraped and bleeding. I was relieved to see the lights were out when I got home and crept quietly through the back door, took off my ripped shirt and went to the sink to wash. Before I could finish, Dad came in and asked why I was out so late. I tried to think of a reason and kept washing so he wouldn't see what had happened. But he came closer and saw my arm bleeding.

"What have you done now?" he asked. "You've been fighting!" He grabbed my arm, swung me around and shook me. "You have to start trouble. You can't be like your brother Vinh. You leave all the work for your family and then you get in trouble and bring your trouble home!"

I wanted to tell him it wasn't my fault, that I didn't want to fight. I knew how important it was for me not to cause trouble. I knew the communists would blame Dad for my actions, but he didn't give me a chance. He turned, walked back into the bedroom, and shut the curtain behind him. I climbed into the hammock in the main room, feeling ashamed that I had let my father down. I kept telling myself it wasn't my fault, but to my father it didn't matter whose fault it was. It only mattered that I let it happen.

Everyone was up early the next morning, so I went in the bedroom to sleep some more. Mom came in at nine and told me I should get up and help weave the baskets. I was so sick of those baskets. I told Dad I could help the family more by going to the wastelands, but he ignored me.

"Why don't you talk to me?" I asked him. "Just let me go to the wastelands, then you won't need to worry about me anymore. I won't be here to cause trouble for you. You won't even have to feed me!" Mom grabbed my arm and pulled me into the bedroom, but I wasn't finished. "I can't sit in this house and weave those baskets anymore. I can't take it! I can't take seeing you like this."

I was in the bedroom for about an hour when Dad came in. I took a deep breath and prepared myself for him to scold me, but he didn't. He sat down beside me and was silent for a moment before he spoke. "Are you sure you want to go?"

he asked.

"I'm sorry," I told him. "I have to do something different. I can't stand it here."

"I just want you to show responsibility. There's no way you can survive unless you learn to control yourself. You have to learn to think before you act."

"I didn't want to fight. I tried to avoid it, but I couldn't."

"It's not just the fighting, it's your whole attitude. You have to change now. Things aren't the same. If you're going to survive, you have to listen to me. I need your help. Your family needs you." I knew Dad was right, and I didn't want to cause trouble. But everything was so confusing. My country had been fighting for my whole life, and now I was wrong because I fought to defend myself.

We spent the rest of the day weaving, and I stayed in that evening to avoid seeing Viet again. Before I went to bed, Dad said I would have to go to school for the next week, and I would leave for the wastelands on Monday.

The next morning, our teacher introduced two boys from the North who were there to tell us about our new society. He said the boys were fourteen years old, but the few black whiskers one had made me think he was older. They said the same things as our leader at the park. They told us how happy it made them to help society and how lucky they were to be raised in the North so they were not brainwashed by American capitalism.

"We are thirty years ahead of you in becoming equal," one of them said. "I am shocked at the way the children in the South act. I heard how bad life was here, but I could not believe it until I saw it with my own eyes."

They told us we were a selfish, spoiled society and we had to forget our self-importance before we could hope to become equal. I listened to them ridicule us, but I let everything they said slide through my head. I knew that in a week I would be on a bus to the wastelands, away from my parents telling me what to do, away from school, away from Viet, and away from weaving baskets.

The Wastelands

It was a cool, damp morning in Saigon. The two small windows of our bedroom threw gray beams of light that crossed in the middle of the room. I sat up on my bamboo mattress and rubbed the sleep out of my eyes. In the opposite corner of the room, I could see my parents' mattress was empty. Dad was probably in his chair, weaving a basket. I could hear Mom starting the fire in the kitchen. Just past my feet, Vinh was curled up with his head under the covers. My sisters and Tu were cuddled up next to him. I looked at the clock on the floor next to my bed. In less than an hour, I would be at the district station, getting on a bus to the wastelands.

Mom had packed my clothes and some food the night before, and I had packed my camping gear. We received a letter from the government that said my food and shelter would be provided, but Mom wanted to make sure I wouldn't starve. I got up and pulled on my favorite trousers. They were made of cotton and I had dyed them blue so they looked like blue jeans. I went to the kitchen and ate breakfast with Dad. As I ate, Mom told me to be careful and Dad told me to think before I spoke. I told them I would be fine and tried not to let them know I was nervous about going away by myself.

It was just getting light when I walked out the front door. No one was on the street, but a few people were yawning and stretching in their doorways. I walked along the side of the highway to the road that led to the district station. Where we lived in Northeast Saigon, most roads didn't have names or run in squares like they did in other parts of the city. There were two main highways that met southeast of our house. Highway 13, the one I crossed that morning, went north to Ben Cat, and Highway 1 went east to Xuyen Loc. The highways were paved, and dirt paths and gravel roads zigzagged between them. In the dry season, these roads were like brown cement, but this was late September, and most of the roads were still muddy from the monsoon rains.

When I arrived at the district station, I saw four buses parked in front of it. A few faces were staring out the bus windows, and a few people were standing on the sidewalk smoking. The district station was someone's house before the communists took over. It was one of the biggest houses in the area and must have had fifty rooms. The walls were red brick, and it was surrounded by a black cast iron fence. The road in front of it made a circle, and what had been the servant quarters was now the district post office.

I walked across the road, stepped onto the first bus, and walked sideways down the aisle to the back seat. A small gray-haired man sat a few seats in front of me, and a stocky, younger man was sitting toward the front. The driver's seat was empty, but the key was in the ignition. I sat for a few minutes, imagining myself running to the driver's seat, starting the bus and taking off. Then I imagined I was on the wrong bus and asked the man in front of me if it was the bus for National Service. He turned around and said he hoped so, then the younger man said he hoped it was going to Australia and laughed at himself. In a few minutes, other people came onto the bus. Most of them were men in their mid-twenties, probably ex-soldiers, because most men that age were, but there were also older men and women. I was obviously the youngest. I had my bag sitting next to me until the other seats filled up and a man asked if he could sit there. I moved my bag onto my lap and stared out the window.

"My name's Tu Van Tonh, what's yours?" he asked, so loud the whole bus could hear.

"I'm Viet," I said softly, turning to look at him again. He didn't seem old, but lines had already formed on his face.

"Viet! My best friend's name was Viet. Got shot in the last few days. He's luckier than you and me." I didn't know what to say. His black eyes were wide open like he had seen a ghost. He looked half frightened and half amazed, but I didn't know why. I nodded and stared back out the window. "You're pretty young to be here, don't you think?" he asked.

I answered without looking toward him. "Yes, but my father needs to stay at home to support our family. I'm the oldest son, so I volunteered."

"Volunteered? You mean you were forced to do this." I hadn't heard anyone outside my family talk so openly since the communists took over. A few of the people in front of us turned around. I thought about what my father would say.

"It's okay," I said. "I wanted to get away from the city."

He slid down and rested his knees on the seat in front of us. "Yeah, city life makes me crazy too. I've been stuck

54

in Saigon all summer, living with my aunt. No job. No money. Eating her food and not having anything to give back. For me, it was either digging dirt in the wastelands or getting my ass shot off in Cambodia."

The bus driver came on and started the bus, and we began our journey. No one told us where we were going or what we would be doing. We turned onto Highway 1 and went south through Saigon. I stared out the window, wondering where this man came from and why he wasn't afraid to openly criticize the communists. He seemed carefree. He made me curious. "What's happening in Cambodia?" I asked him as we turned onto Revolution Street. I knew there was a war going on there, but I didn't know who was fighting or what for.

"The commies aren't satisfied with ruling us," he said, meaning the communists. "They want Cambodia too, and they want us to help them fight for it. The only thing is, they won't let us carry guns—just supplies. So if I go, I'm a walking target."

I wasn't sure at the time who he was referring to when he said "us," but I learned later he was talking about ex-soldiers from the South's army. There were tens of thousands of them, and with few jobs in Saigon, the government created the National Service to keep the ex-soldiers under communist control. Whether they went to the wastelands or Cambodia, it was still part of the National Service. "Do you know where we're going?" I asked him as the bus turned onto Highway 4.

"We're on our way to the Delta, the wastelands of the South."

"I lived in My Tho when I was younger," I said. "It's just north of the Delta, isn't it?"

"Just north of the Mekong River. We'll be traveling

through it in about an hour. Do you have relatives there?"

"No, my father was stationed there during the war. We weren't there very long, and I was only a few years old. I don't remember much about it."

"I'm sure it's different now," he said. "Probably been burned and rebuilt a dozen times."

This was the first time I had been outside Saigon since I lived in My Tho. During the war, we stayed close to the city because it seemed safe. Saigon was different from the rest of Vietnam, full of electric- and gas-powered machines, movie theaters, nightclubs and indoor toilets. All I saw along Highway 4 were rice fields dotted with workers who probably didn't care who won the war. They were just glad it was over so their fields would stop being bombed and mined and their villages would no longer be burned.

It was noon when the buses pulled off the motorway and onto a dirt track. Tu had fallen asleep right outside Saigon, but he woke up as the bus bounced off the pavement. "Where are we?" he moaned, rubbing his eyes with the palms of his hands. He looked up sideways at me, and his shiny black hair hung over his face.

I told him we had passed through My Tho about an hour before, traveled east along a river, and then crossed it and headed south. Now we seemed to be in the middle of nowhere. Swampland stretched as far as I could see. The only breaks in the flat, steaming landscape were a few shanty camps set up on the high spots.

We drove along the dirt track for a few miles and came to a canal, then the bus stopped at the end of the road. To the right was a flat, wooden ferry tied to a dock in the canal. "Everyone off!" The driver shouted, looking up in the mirror above his head. Tu opened the back door and jumped off, and I followed him.

A dozen men in faded green uniforms were standing on the dock, motioning for us to get on the ferry. As we walked toward it, my eyes and nose burned from the smell in the air. People were sneezing, and a few of the women were choking and saying they couldn't breathe. It didn't seem to bother the men in the uniforms. They kept herding people onto the ferry, saying we would get used to the air.

Tu and I stood at the end of the dock, watching the people. There must have been a hundred and fifty of us, because we had filled four buses. I knew we wouldn't all fit on the ferry. It was rocking back and forth, and the thick brown water was sloshing over the sides. "What's wrong with the air?" I asked Tu.

"I'm not sure," he said. He was squinting and his face was puckered. "There's no telling what it is."

In a few minutes, when it was obvious the ferry couldn't take any more weight, a few of the uniformed men untied it and pushed it away from the dock. The engines cranked over and black diesel smoke bellowed into the sky. There were about fifty of us still standing along the canal. The guard said we could either wait for the ferry to come back or we could walk along the canal. He added that lunch was ready as soon as we got to the camp, so we all started walking. When we got there, the men in uniform directed us to sit facing a pile of lumber, and one of them climbed on top of it. He was short, with round shoulders and a round belly, and his voice was loud and full of energy.

"My name is Binh Van Nguyen. I am in charge of this project," he announced. "First I would like to thank you all for volunteering. Your task will be turning this swamp into productive farm land. We are here to help you complete your task successfully. I know you had a long trip from Saigon and are surely hungry, so let us eat!"

We all filed into line to fill the bowls we had brought from home. The older people complained about the food— it was cold fish and salt water rice. We finished eating and were called to make a circle around the pile of lumber. Mr. Nguyen stood on the lumber and explained what we would be doing. He said our first task was to build barracks so we would have a place to sleep. He asked for people who had worked in construction to raise their hands, and he picked six of them to lead crews. Then we all divided into groups and started building the barracks.

By sundown, we had two rows with three huts each built about a hundred yards from the canal. A few people had lit fires in the courtyard between the huts and were cooking food for dinner. It was the same thing, fish and rice, but at least it was warm this time. I ate with Tu and a few other men. Then Tu and I staked out our place in one of the huts. He had disappeared earlier while we were building the barracks, and I wondered where he had been, but I didn't ask him. When we finished laying out our blankets and hanging our mosquito nets, we went back to the courtyard. Groups had already formed around the fires according to age and gender, but there was no one my age, so I followed Tu and sat with the men in their early twenties. There were about ten of us circled around the fire. Everyone but me had something to say about the war.

"If the Americans hadn't left us without ammo," the man next to me said, "we would've blown the communists away."

"It wasn't the Americans' fault," another man said. "It was the greedy bastards in Saigon who used the American aid for their own benefit, like Diem in the early sixties and

Thieu in the late sixties and seventies. The officials in Saigon got rich while we were getting our asses blown off."

"The Americans wouldn't send Thieu more money because they knew his wife would spend it all," a third man said, "but they should have never given him power. They should have stayed here and run things until we beat the northern bastards."

"You're all wrong," Tu said to them. "The communists won because they had a plan to win. We never had a plan and that's why the Americans stepped in. But they didn't have a plan either. So all we had was confusion, corruption, and blood."

They argued on, and I sat and listened. None of them seemed to care if anyone overheard what they said. They cursed life under the communists and said how they wished they could move to different countries. "I think my wife is in America," the man next to me said. "She left with her parents before I got back to Saigon. I came home and the house was boarded up. A sign on my door said my house was now the property of the government. The neighbors said my family had left in April; they thought I was dead."

"My sister is in California," another man said. "I got a letter from her before the communists took over. She said everything is different there. She said the Americans are trying to forget about the war. They can walk away and forget we ever existed. All we were to them were puppets on a string, and the communists beat their ass and took control of the string."

"The war is over," Tu said. "There's nothing any of us are going to do about who pulls the strings. All I need is a stomach full of food and a woman, and the communists can do whatever they want."

"There aren't many single women around here," the man next to me observed. "You're going to be without one for quite a while from what I've seen." The men were all quiet for a moment, probably wondering where they could find some women.

"During the war we could always find a woman," the man next to me said. "We used to have a VC girl we captured up North around Hue. We kept her with us for a couple weeks. Any time we wanted her, we had our way with her." I was the only one there who hadn't said anything, so I asked him what happened when they were done with her. The men were all silent for a few seconds, then a few of them started to chuckle. "As I recall, there was an accident with a grenade," he answered.

Everyone laughed except me. I knew the man was joking and whatever had happened wasn't an accident. It made me sick to my stomach. Death meant nothing to them. Life meant nothing to them. My head felt like it was spinning and my body was numb. I thought going to the wastelands would mean getting away from the confusion of my family and the rest of Saigon, but these men seemed more confused than I was. I thought they were crazy.

I went to my spot in the barracks to lie down. The moon was full, and so bright that it seemed like daytime. Fires crackled, and voices blended together into a steady rumble. Until that time, I had always thought I had a purpose. My father raised me to believe I was important and that my actions and even my thoughts meant something. When I was younger, I pictured myself as an important man when I grew up, maybe a doctor or an engineer. I thought I would be rewarded for being a good person and punished for being evil. But as I drifted into sleep somewhere in the Mekong Delta,

I began to think that nothing mattered.

It was still dark when the bell rang for us to get up. I could smell fish cooking. Tu was already up, so I followed the line of people to the river and washed, stood in line to fill my bowl, and sat down to eat. After breakfast, we assembled in the yard between the barracks. The uniformed men were in a straight line facing us, and Binh was in the middle of them. He stood like a proud rooster, held his hands in the air, and then pushed them down for silence. "We are all volunteers here!" he shouted. Then he turned toward his men. "We are the managers of this project, and we will help you complete your task."

By this time it was obvious what our task would be. We were there to dig canals. Miles of them had already been built, and we were surrounded by other camps like ours. The officials said the canals were to drain acid from the soil so it could be used to grow rice. Everyone seemed to have a story about the acid. Some said it was from the salt water mixing with the vegetation and fermenting. Others said it was from chemicals the Americans used during the war. Everyone agreed that it was what made the air difficult to breathe. It was supposed to take ten years to clean it up, but the older men said the fields would never produce anything.

"A goal has been set for us to reach in the first month," Binh said. "If we don't complete it, we will stay until we finish." A low rumble swept across the people. He raised his hands for silence and said, "After the first month, we will no longer provide you with food. Your families will need to send it from home."

"We won't stay!" someone yelled.

Others shouted, "It's unfair! The Saigon officials lied to us!" I thought the people were going to attack Binh, then the uniformed men released the safeties on their rifles and everyone was quiet.

"There are other alternatives for those of you who do not wish to remain here," Binh said, as he held his hands out like he was embracing the swamp. "We have many other tasks! Like clearing our country of active bombs and booby traps left behind by the Americans. Or serving in Cambodia. You people have it easy compared to others—compared to the people who fought and died to rid our country of imperialism. While these people were suffering, most of you were in Ho Chi Minh City, enjoying the bribes of the capitalists. The rest of you were fighting against your brothers who were trying to save you from the Americans. Every one of you should consider yourself lucky to be here."

"He's a liar," Tu said to me. "First this was a volunteer project, but everyone had to volunteer. Then it was for only one month, but now they give us an unachievable goal and say we can't go home until we finish. Then they say we should be happy about it."

I thought it was just like Dad told me when he returned from reeducation. We were only the tools the communist would use to build their socialist house. And there were plenty of us, so they could use us until we were old or broken, then throw us away.

Tu was staring at Binh with wide eyes and flared nostrils. He looked like he wanted to kill him. I didn't see how a person like Tu could survive in Vietnam. I couldn't imagine him giving in to a communist. I thought that sooner or later he would be confronted by an official, and he would kill the man, then the communists would kill him. The war wasn't over for him, and as for so many other ex-soldiers, I thought it wouldn't be until he was dead.

Binh asked for volunteers to do the cooking and to carry drinking water to the workers. Everyone raised their hand because they thought it would be an easy job. I didn't understand until later why he picked the five strongest looking men.

They divided us into groups according to the barracks we were in, and we followed an official to get our tools and watch a demonstration on how to use them. When we all knew what our task would be, they led us across the swamp to stakes that marked where we were to dig, and we all started chopping and pounding. The earth had a light brown crust on top and was darker and moist underneath. Everyone helped to do what they could. The elderly people complained, and the younger people laughed and joked.

The five men who had volunteered to carry the water weren't happy by the end of the day. They had to work hard to get the water to all of us and cook our food at the same time. They kept trying to get people to trade jobs with them, but no one would.

The second day started off slowly. People complained about their sore muscles and limped around rubbing them. The deeper we got, the easier it was to dig, but we had farther to throw the dirt out. At three yards deep, we hit water and had to bail it out with old army helmets. It was slimy work. The first couple of days the acid burned my skin, but by the end of the week I noticed it only in the morning.

On Sunday, Tu took me to a village he had found nearby. It consisted of a small market with four coffee shops and a few grass huts, where I assumed the people who ran the market lived. The coffee shops were actually thatched pavilions, packed with people. It was the only place for miles that had normal food and coffee, not to mention rice wine. The day was bright and sticky hot. It was the kind of day you sweat even when you're sitting still. I had a few piasters my Mom had given me for emergency use, so I bought us some lemonade, and we sat in one of the pavilions.

"Good lemonade," Tu said. It was real lemonade, made with a slice of lemon and some sugar. I agreed, drank the rest of mine in two gulps, then sucked on the lemon. "You don't talk much, do you?" he asked. I shrugged my shoulders and didn't say anything. There were many things I wanted to ask him, but in Vietnam, it's not proper to question your elders until you know them very well. "I'll bet you have much to say," he told me. "You're just smart enough to keep your mouth shut." I wished my father could have heard him say that.

"I used to be like you," he said. "I kept my mouth shut and let people walk on me. But look where it got me. Now I think if I'm going to get stomped on anyway, I might as well get stomped on for doing something than for not doing anything at all." I nodded to agree with him.

"I need to get out of here," he said. "My life here ended when the communists won the war. If I'm ever going to live again, it will have to be in another country. You should think about that. You're young. You shouldn't waste your life in Vietnam. You should go where you can say and do what you want. Look at us! Sweating our asses off in the swamplands. What kind of a life is this? I have to get out of here." I nodded in agreement again, but I didn't know how to leave Vietnam. I didn't know exactly where I was or even how to get back to Saigon.

On the way back to our camp, Tu told me I was smart for keeping my mouth shut. He said his friends were either dead or had left Vietnam and I was the only person he trusted.

He said he wished we could escape Vietnam and go to America. I didn't know why he trusted me, but I was glad he did.

Two weeks of digging and bailing went by, and on the third Sunday they let us go to Saigon for the day. Tu didn't want to go, because he owed his aunt money and didn't want to see her until he could pay her back. I asked if he wanted to come with me, but he said he didn't like to be with families, because it made him miss his own too much.

The coach ride seemed long because I didn't have anyone to talk to. Dad and my brothers and sisters were at church when I got to our house. Mom was in the kitchen slicing potatoes. "Viet!" she screamed as I walked through the doorway. "You're home early. Are you well? Are you home to stay?" She hugged me, then pushed me back and looked at me. "You need a haircut. Your hair is to your shoulders, and look at you, you're filthy. Why don't you take a bath, then you can tell me what you've been doing."

I did need a bath. I grabbed a few potatoes out of the pot, and she went in the bedroom to fill the tub. When I undressed, she poked my ribs. "I've never seen you so thin," she said. "Don't they feed you?" I told her we ate plenty but worked long hours. I didn't want to tell her all we had eaten for the past three weeks was fish and rice. I knew they probably hadn't eaten much better, and she had enough to worry about. Mom went back in the kitchen, but we kept talking. "I can give you a little money if you have a place to buy food there. I don't even know where you've been. Is it south of My Tho?"

"It's in the Mekong Delta, in the middle of nowhere. But there's a village where I can get some food. Where did you get the money?"

"We borrowed some from your grandfather so we could buy a fishing boat."

"A boat! Where is it? When did you get it?"

"Your father bought it last week. He's been fishing during the day, and I've been selling his catch to the neighbors."

She told me when I got home from National Service I could help my father fish, so I wouldn't have to be in the house all day. I hadn't been looking forward to coming home, but this changed everything. I finished my bath, put on some shorts and went back to the kitchen. "Where's the boat?" I asked.

"It's tied to the dock at the end of the road. But wait until your father comes home; he wants to take you to see it."

Dad arrived, and I sat through lunch, listening to what my brothers and sisters had been doing since I was gone. When we had all finished, Dad and I walked to the river to see the boat. It was anchored with three other boats at the dock where I used to skip rocks. He pointed at the boat proudly as we walked up to the dock. "There she is," he said with a smile. I hadn't seen Dad smile in so long, and I knew this boat was his little bit of freedom. He stood strong, his feet a little wider apart than normal, his hands above his hips. Our new boat rose up and down in the water.

The boat wasn't as big as I thought it would be, but it looked sturdy. Faded red paint was peeling off its wooden planks, and it creaked as it rose up and down in the water. It was about five yards long and two yards wide. An oar hung off each side in front of a bench that went across the middle. Dad unlocked a wooden box in the front of the boat and pulled out a fishing net.

"The net fits on two prongs and we drag the river with it to catch prawns," he said. "When you get home from the wastelands, I'll show you how to use it." He was happy that I was interested in fishing because he knew it would keep me busy and out of trouble. I couldn't wait to get in the boat and row around, and before I could ask him, he smiled and told me to try. I hopped onto the bench and grabbed the oars. "Do you need some help?" he asked.

"No, I can do this," I replied.

I lowered the oars into the water and pulled back. The boat moved a few feet, and the slack in the tow line drew taut and swung the boat into the dock. Dad smiled. "Let me get the line for you. Are you sure you know how to do this?"

I had been in boats before but had never rowed one. "I can do it," I told him and dug the oars into the water and pulled back again. This time the boat glided backward, away from the dock and toward the middle of the river.

"Don't go too far!" Dad yelled as I dug the oars in again. I rowed to the other side of the bank and headed south. "Bring it back!" he shouted from the dock. "Turn her around and bring her back!" His voice wasn't serious enough for me to obey, so I pretended not to hear him. I rowed around the bend and to the bridge before I turned the boat around. Dad was shaking his head when I got back, but he was still smiling. "It won't be long before I'll have to make you keep rowing instead of telling you to stop."

It was late afternoon when we got back to the house. Mom had my clothes and some food packed in a bag, and when I looked in it I saw some money stuffed in the pocket of my trousers. She smiled and said I should go to the district station before the coaches left without me.

The next morning it was back to work. By noon, some of the people were complaining about sore muscles, and most of us were doing as little as possible. Everyone seemed to be moving in slow motion. Then I heard a woman shout, "Bomb!"

People rolled over each other to get out of the ditch and run away from where the woman had screamed. Even the old people were running, hiding behind piles of dirt and jumping into ditches. When the excitement calmed and the people crept out of hiding, the officials said the bomb was probably inactive and tried to get us to go back to work. But no one would go close to the ditch. In about an hour, two bomb experts arrived. They wore black pajamas, and Tu said they were ex-officers in the South's army. I could tell they didn't want to get close to it either. We were all watching until Binh told us they needed two volunteers to help carry the bomb out of the ditch. Everyone hung their heads and looked at the ground to avoid his stare. "The bomb is inactive," he said.

"You pick it up!" someone yelled from the back.

"I need two volunteers, and they will have the next two days off." We knew he was lying and no one moved. He picked a few people out and tried to humiliate them into helping, but it didn't work. I thought he would threaten us, but for some reason he didn't. "Go back to the camp!" he shouted. We spent the rest of the day joking about the bomb and daring each other to go take a closer look.

The next morning they told us the bomb was gone and we had to go back to work. The elderly people said there were probably more bombs and we would all be blown up. Every once in a while someone would yell "Bomb!" and people would go running through the field, but we didn't find any.

After lunch that day, Binh rang the bell for us to assemble. "Your attitudes are poor," he said. "We are not progressing fast enough to finish our goal. If we work very hard, we might finish a week late. But if we do not work hard, we will be here for another month." The mood in the camp changed at that moment. People began to argue with each other, blaming each other for not working hard enough. We all gave it our best that week, but when Friday came, we were still far from finishing our goal.

Friday at lunch, Binh stood up and said, "You are the lucky ones. You have worked hard this last week, and even though you haven't finished your goal, we feel you have finally realized the seriousness of this project. You can go back to Saigon tomorrow, after you clean the camp and prepare it for the next group of people to move in."

I couldn't believe how they twisted our minds. They treated us like children and lied to make us work harder. But everyone was glad to go home, and the people who had been arguing with each other quickly became friends again. We spent Friday afternoon cleaning the camp and mending broken tools. That night, Tu and I went to the village, and I gave him some money to buy rice wine. My father had let me have sips before on special occasions, but that night I had more than a few sips. Some of the soldiers built a fire on the edge of the village and we gathered around it, passing bottles of rice wine, singing songs and telling stories. We were at the village most of the night, and it was getting light when Tu and I got back to the camp.

People were already rushing around, getting their things ready for the trip home. A few of the soldiers were groaning because they had drunk too much, but I was still feeling good. We cooked some breakfast and sat by the fire, waiting for the officials to tell us it was time to leave.

At eight, Binh told us the coaches had been delayed, but

wouldn't tell us why. The people with money headed for the market to see if they could pay someone to take them to Saigon. Others started walking to the road to hitchhike. I was ready to go home but thought the coaches would be there soon, so I stayed in the camp. About an hour later, some people who had gone to the village came back. They said the villagers were panicking because the government had announced on the radio that the currency was changing. The officials in Saigon had said that everyone must bring their money to their district station and exchange it for new currency. The whole process was to be completed that day.

"This is part of their plan to rob the people," Tu said. "Soon the communists will own everything." Some of the men walked off from the camp, and I could hear them screaming and crying. They had left everything they owned in Saigon and didn't know if they would get back in time to change their money. "I'm not going back to Saigon," Tu told me. "There's nothing for me to do there."

"You can't stay here," I said. "Maybe your aunt can help you get a job."

"The only work in Saigon is for the communists. I have a plan to get out of this country, and now is as good a time as any." He handed me a piece of paper with his aunt's address on it and told me to find her and tell her he was leaving Vietnam.

"How are you going to survive? You have no money, no place to stay. What are you going to do?"

"Just get the message to my aunt. Let me worry about myself, and you take care of yourself. That's all we can do. You'll give her the message, won't you?" I told him I would, and he stood up and walked toward the village. I sat watching him walk away, half wanting to make him come back to

Saigon and half wanting to go with him. I had no idea how he would survive, but when I thought about him in days and weeks to come, I liked to think he made it to America.

The hours dragged by, and the tension in the camp made my body tired. I was in my hut, about to drift to sleep, when a low rumble of voices grew into a roar. By the time I rolled to my feet and went outside, people were running for the canal. The ferry had arrived and people were swarming onto it. It was full by the time I got to the dock, so I walked along the canal toward the road.

I sat in the back seat of one of the buses, leaned against the side of the seat, and tried to block out the voices. When the buses started to move, the people calmed and I drifted to sleep. When I woke, we were pulling off the motorway and heading into Saigon. The coach stopped at the district station and we all got off. There were no goodbyes. People were in a hurry to get home and see what had happened. I walked along the dark street to the field that led to my house, wondering if we had any money left and if we would need to sell the boat.

"Viet!" My sisters cried as I walked through the door, and they rushed over to hug me. My little brother was right behind them, and I picked him up and twirled him around. Vinh nodded from my father's chair.

"What's to eat?" I asked as I headed for the kitchen. "What happened to the money today?"

My youngest sister, Minh Ha, fixed me some rice and vegetables left over from dinner, while Vinh told me about the money changing. "We have a hundred fifty piasters, but they're supposed to be worth more than the old money, and the government is supposed to give us basic things to live, like soap and food." He showed me the stamp book the government gave us to record how much food we received, then he quoted Mom, saying, "They figured up what we needed, promised us half of that, and will give us a quarter of it."

Mom and Dad walked in while he was talking. They didn't seem excited that I was there. Dad sat at the table and looked through the stamp book, and Mom put my sisters to bed. When she came out of the bedroom, I asked her if we had any money left. "We've been very lucky," she said. "We have more than we had before."

"What happened here today?" I asked her. "How did we get so much money?"

"I was at the corner market this morning when they announced the money was changing. I ran home to see if I could catch your father before he went fishing, but he was already gone. Then shortly after I got home, Mrs. Ngo, the woman who bought our house, came by and asked if I could change some of her money. We had only thirty thousand piasters to exchange, which was less than the maximum allowed per family, so Mrs. Ngo gave us some money to change for her, and she let us keep almost half of it."

"We should be better off than before," Dad said, "but we won't be certain for a few days."

"What happened to the rich people who couldn't exchange all their money?" I asked.

"Most of the rich people have their money in gold," he said. "This whole thing was designed to abolish the wealthy class by taking their money and redistributing it, but most of them don't keep it in cash anyway."

"What about the stamp books? Where do we go to get our food?"

"The store that was boarded up down the road is now the co-op shop," Dad responded. "We're supposed to give them the baskets we make in exchange for food and essentials. But we don't make enough baskets to meet their quota, so I don't think they will give us much. The communists know if they control our food supply and living essentials, they'll control us. We have to take part in their system or they'll send us all to the wastelands, but we can't rely on them. We'll need to make enough baskets to keep them happy, and we'll sell and trade prawns to survive."

"There's nothing we can do about it now," Mom said. "Let's get some sleep and see what happens tomorrow."

When I woke the next morning, my family was getting ready for church. I rolled over to cover my ears, and Dad asked if I was going with them. I pretended not to hear him, and he grunted and left the room. I listened to their footsteps leaving the house but still heard sounds in the kitchen, so I knew Mom was fixing something to eat. I lay in bed, half dazed, thinking about what I would do for the next few days. I saw a half-made basket sitting next to the door and was dreading having to weave it. Then a vision of our new boat floated through my mind. *The boat!* I thought. *We have a boat!* I jumped up, pulled on my trousers, and headed for the door.

"You were too tired to go to church, but now you're racing out the door," Mom shouted. "Where are you going?"

I told her I wanted to see the boat again, and she smiled. "But don't get in it until your father comes home," she said as I ran out the door, "and be back before church lets out! I want us all to eat together!"

I got my bike from the side of the house, jumped on, and rode to the dock. Our boat was rising up and down in the water. I looked it over proudly, thought for a second what Mom said about not getting in it, then jumped in and untied the rope. The water was calm by the dock, but when I paddled to the middle of the river, the current picked up and pulled me downstream. I paddled with the current, and the boat cruised easily. I stuck the paddle down, turned to the left, then to the right, then pretended I was in a race and paddled on both sides until I was floating under the Highway 1 bridge.

On the other side of the bridge was a park where I used to fight my cocks. I had been there many times before, but I was always on the land, looking across the river. It seemed like a different world from the boat, like I was part of the river, in constant motion. I passed the park, passed the boats that lined the docks, and drifted between rice fields on my left and warehouses on my right. The ripple of water against the boat was the only break in the silence, and I lay back, letting the river show me my new world.

After a while I started to wonder how long I had been gone and how hard it would be to paddle back. I wanted to keep riding the current, but I knew church would be letting out soon and pictured Dad on his way to the dock. I stuck the paddle down on the left side until the boat turned halfway around, then dug into the water on the right side as hard and fast as I could. The current pulled the boat backward, then to the left. I paddled on the left side and straightened it out, then the boat slid to the right. I paddled as hard as I could, right, left, right, left, and the boat moved slowly upstream.

Thoughts of my father standing on the dock, shaking his fist, went through my mind, and I paddled harder, but the boat hardly moved. I was out of breath, but every time I stopped paddling, the boat floated backward. I wanted to give up and wait for the tide to slow the current, but that wouldn't be until evening.

I challenged the river and told myself I was stronger,

dug the paddle deeper, and breathed in rhythm with my strokes. I made it back to where I used to fight my cocks. I thought about their strength—how they fought to the death. My arms were throbbing and my heart was pounding. I changed my grip, kept paddling, and made it under the bridge and around the bend. I saw the dock, and seeing it gave me a boost to pick up speed. I made it. I tied the boat and collapsed on the dock, smiling.

In a few minutes, when my muscles loosened, I got up and rode back to our house. I looked at the sun, guessed it was between nine thirty and ten o'clock, and wondered if Dad had been to the dock already. Everyone was home when I walked in, but lunch was still on the stove, so I knew I wasn't late.

I walked quickly into the kitchen and saw it was ten. I was home safe until my sister Minh Ha asked if I had taken the boat out. I thought as quickly as I could: *Church lets out at nine thirty, I was on the dock for five minutes, it took me two minutes to get back, Dad could have been there and seen the boat was gone, everyone is looking at me, I'll take a chance….* "No," I lied. "Mom told me I couldn't until Dad was with me."

Minh Ha smiled at me. They were all smiling at me. They knew me better, but no one said a word. I finished lunch first and asked Mom if I was supposed to help do anything. She told me I could leave, but I waited until everyone finished eating so I could get her alone and ask her for some money. She had known what I wanted when I offered to help with the dishes and gave me enough for a cup of coffee. The new money didn't look real, but I took it and left before Dad found something for me to do.

I was going to go to Tam's house but decided to bike by

the café first. I knew sometime soon I would have to face the boys in my neighborhood, and I wanted to get it over with. I wasn't frightened of Viet anymore. He was nothing compared to the soldiers I had been working with for the past month, and Mom said Phi had asked about me while I was gone, saying he hoped I would be home soon so we could play soccer again.

I rode to the dock and made sure I had tied the boat solidly, then headed for the café. When I got there, Viet and Phi were sitting on the steps sharing a cigarette. They both smiled when I stopped in front of them. Phi's was a genuine smile, and Viet's was sarcastic. "Where is everyone?" I asked.

"No one comes to the café anymore," Phi said. "Most people are in school during the day and have to help their parents in the evening and on weekends."

"Does your father have a new boat?" Viet asked. "I've seen him heading out to fish in a boat—is it yours?"

Now I knew why Viet was smiling at me. He wanted a ride in the boat. "It's ours," I told him. "They bought it while I was away."

"When can we go for a ride?" Viet asked.

"I don't know," I said. "Maybe in a few weeks."

"Your Mom told me you were in National Service," Phi said. "What was it like?" I told them about the soldiers' stories and finding the bomb. "Everything's the same around here," Phi said, "except people are starting to spy on each other."

"And Crippled Thanh is in charge," Viet said.

"Who's that?" I asked.

"He's in charge of the co-op," Viet replied.

"And the Bureau for Public Security," Phi added.

"The what?" I asked.

"It's the communists' new spy organization," Phi answered. "The children have the Red Scarf Youths, and the adults have the Bureau for Public Security. Crippled Thanh is in charge of both. If you see your neighbor doing something wrong, you're supposed to tell him, and he reports it to the district station."

"Why do you call him Crippled Thanh?" I asked.

"Because he walks with a limp, stupid," Viet said.

"He moved into the house by the pavilion," Phi said. "No one knows where he came from, but he has a northern accent."

Viet floated some of the new coins in his coffee to show us how light they were and rubbed some ink off the corner of one of the bills he had. "This money looks fake," he said. "We could make it ourselves if we wanted to.

How about a boat ride, Viet? Let's take the boat for a ride."

"No," I said, "we'll take it out sometime when my parents go to my grandfather's. Then we can go for a long trip."

"You probably don't even know how to row it," Viet said.

"I know how to row it," I told him. "I took it out this morning."

"Then let's go now."

"Where did you get all the money?" I asked, trying to distract Viet from the boat.

"I sold a few things on the market today."

"What did you sell?"

"Some things my brother gave me. Now let's have one more coffee and go for a boat ride."

"No. I need to go into the city to deliver a message for someone."

"What kind of a message?"

"It's for a friend I met at National Service. He didn't come back and he wanted me to let his aunt know he's okay."

"We'll go with you," Phi said. "Where do you have to go?"

I pulled the directions out of my pocket and looked at them. "Binh Minh Café," I told them. "It's on Tu Do Street, close to the river."

"Let's go," Viet said, and we raced to our bikes. We rode to Highway 1, across the bridge, and south onto Ben Bach Dang Street, which ran along the Saigon River. Tu Do Street was a few miles further south. It was called Freedom Street during the war and was the place American soldiers went on their time off. For ten years, it was like a wild party twenty-four hours a day. But the communists boarded up most of the hotels, and the others were used to house their soldiers. Vendors still lined the broken sidewalks, and the communist soldiers walked along the pavement, admiring stereos and motorbikes. But it was a mild scene compared to a few years before.

When we got to the café, I asked a young woman if Hoa, Tu's aunt, was there. "Who wants to know?" the woman asked.

"My name is Viet," I said. "I have a message for her."

The woman eyed me from head to toe. Her face was lean and her hair was long and unbraided. She wore bell bottom trousers and a shiny purple blouse. She was beautiful and hard looking at the same time. "Viet—how patriotic." She seemed amused by me. I had never seen a woman act like her; her movements were open, not withdrawn like most Vietnamese women. "And what is this message about?"

"It's about her nephew Tu."

"I'm Hoa," she said abruptly. "Is Tu in trouble?" I told

her he was fine, but he wasn't coming back to Saigon. "What's he going to do?" she asked. "Stay in the swamplands and dig mud?"

"I think he's trying to leave the country."

"Great!" she snapped sarcastically. "He's going to get himself in trouble, and he sends a boy to tell me so I can worry about him."

"He said for you not to worry."

She looked away from me, and I looked at Viet and Phi. They were smiling because she had called me a boy. "Thank you for bringing the message," she said. "Now I have to get back to work." I didn't know what else to say, so I got on my bike, and Viet and Phi followed me.

"That woman was strange," Phi said as we rode away.

"Did you see that tattoo on her arm?" Viet said. "I'll bet she's a prostitute."

We rode back to Binh An, and I was home in time for dinner. Dad didn't seem angry that I was gone all day. He asked me about National Service, and I told him how they set goals for us and told us we couldn't go home until they were finished. He listened to me like I was an adult, and I took the opportunity to ask if I was going fishing with him the next day.

"I've talked to the headmaster," Dad said, "and he agreed to let you work with me instead of going to school. But you're supposed to study with Vinh in the evenings and help the Ho Chi Minh Youth group on the weekends."

"Why do I need to help the Red Scarfs?" I asked. "They'll just want me to spy on you and listen to their communist stories."

"You can study at home and help the Red Scarfs," he said, "or you can go to school every day. We have no other choice."

I told him I would rather fish than go to school. I think he already knew that would be my answer. He told me to get some sleep because we were leaving at four the next morning.

Fishing

It seemed like I had just shut my eyes when I felt a shiver run from my ankle up my leg. My foot was sticking outside the mosquito net, and Dad was shaking it to wake me. "Get up if you're going with me," he said and shook it again. I pulled my foot under the net, tossed the blanket over me, and tucked in the sides. "It's past four," he said before he walked out of the room.

I rolled onto my side and tucked the blanket tighter for warmth. Raindrops pitter pattered on the roof and splashed onto the bamboo gutters. Golden lantern light flickered through the doorway. Mom was scraping the wok in the kitchen—long steady scrapes of metal on metal. Dad's silhouette appeared in the doorway and stared down on me. I pushed myself up and crawled from under the net. "How does it feel to be a fisherman?" he asked as I pulled on my trousers.

I forced a smile and walked slowly past him to the stove. The fire crackled, and blue flames curled around the wok. I rubbed my hands by the flame and smelled the eggs Mom was cooking. "Eat a good breakfast," Dad said. "We have a long day ahead of us." Mom packed our lunch while I ate. Dad told her to expect us home around seven, and I calculated how many hours we would be gone. "Let's go," Dad said, the moment I finished eating. "Get a shirt and let's go."

It was dark when we left the house. No lights were on because the government shut the electricity off from nine in the evening until five in the morning. As we walked along the path to the river, cold mud seeped between my toes. My body shivered from the rain. We arrived at the boat, and I sat in the rower's seat, not because I wanted to row, but because I wanted to show Dad that I could. "Are you rowing the whole way?" he asked.

"How far are we going?"

"About two hours south of the city," he said with a grin. "Row as far as you can, and I'll take over."

Dad sat on the net box in front of me, and I put the oars in the water. Just before I pulled back, he untied the rope, and the boat glided away from the dock. The tide was going out, so I had a slow current with me. I rowed under the Highway 1 bridge, past the park and along the east edge of the city. Tiny raindrops speckled the black river and circles swelled around them. Warehouses and factories lined Ben Bach Dang Street to the west. Rice fields rolled into the dark gray sky to the east. White light and loud crashes of clanging iron escaped the giant windows of the tire factory, but there were no people on the docks in front of it—just a huge mass of concrete glazed with water.

A few months before, when Tam and I rode our bikes into the city, we saw the docks lined with shanties of Styrofoam, plastic and cardboard. They were the homes of the homeless, the ex-soldiers, the thousands of refugees who fled in front of the communist army, the orphans and the diseased. It was like a leper's village. Children wandered along the pier and streets with abandoned looks on their faces. Women held deformed babies in their arms. Men with missing limbs hobbled between the blue plastic shanties. There had been thousands of people, but now they were gone. The pier and streets were empty, except for two communist soldiers in khaki uniforms. They stood at the edge of the pier watching us pass.

"Where have all the people gone?" I asked Dad.

"I'm not sure," he said. "The communists got rid of them somehow." Spirits seemed to hang in the gray mist above the pier. We floated by silently, like we were passing a graveyard. "Let me take the oars," Dad said, and we switched places. We passed Bach Dang Harbor, where Tam and I saw the dead soldiers. I saw the tree they were stuck in and looked for bones, but didn't see any.

"Where did the communists take those people, Dad?"

"I don't know," he said again. "One day they were there, the next they were gone." He kept rowing and didn't look back at me. I knew he didn't want to tell me what he thought happened to the people, but I persisted.

"What do you think happened, Dad?"

"At says the communists dumped them into the sea," he said, watching my reaction. I tried not to look startled. At was Phi's father, and my father's best friend at the time. Dad liked him because he was against the communists, but didn't trust him because he talked too much. "At could be right," Dad said, "but don't talk to Phi about this. You have a right to know, but talking to other people will only get us in trouble."

He rowed out of Saigon without saying another word. The rain stopped and the sun broke through the clouds as we passed a small fishing village called Nha Be. On the wooden docks, fishermen rushed around, loading and fueling their boats. "Everyone's rushing to get the good spots," Dad said.

We passed the village and went right at a fork in the river. The farther we went, the wider the river became. Dad rowed in the shadows of the jungle on the east side, so it still seemed dark. To the west, past the shadows, the mist had risen and the water was gold in the sun's reflection. "This looks like a good place to start," he said, pointing ahead of us. "It's shallow along this bank and there aren't many trees in the way."

He rowed the front of the boat onto the mud bank and told me to tie the rope to a tree. Monkeys screeched high above us. They sounded close, but the vegetation was so thick I couldn't see them. Giant trees hung over the river and vines dropped like snakes from their branches into the water. Dad got the nets and colander out of the box and set them on the bank, and then he sat on a fallen tree and loaded his pipe.

"I like a smoke to warm up before I start," he said. I sat next to him and looked across the river. "I'll do most of the fishing today," he told me between puffs. The cherry scented smoke curled around his pipe then drifted in front of me. I inhaled the sweet smell and held it inside. "Watch what I do. When you think you can do it, I'll let you give it a try."

He finished his pipe, straightened the nets, and pulled two bamboo rods out of the boat. The rods were connected at one end, and he laid them on the bank in the shape of a V. Then he attached the net to the rods and straightened it out. "Tie this to the front of the boat," he said, handing me a rope. He tied the other end around his waist, picked up the net, and waded into the water. "Grab the colander and untie the boat. I'll pull you away from the bank."

Dad waded through the waist-deep water against the current, pushing the net in front of him and pulling me and the boat behind him. We had gone about thirty yards when he pulled the net up and shook it. I could see a few prawns, but not as many as I expected. I held the metal colander out, and he shook the prawns into it. "Tie the colander onto the boat and throw it over the back," he said. "The water will keep them fresh until we get home."

The prawns clicked inside the metal colander until I lowered them off the back of the boat. "How much will we make, Dad?"

"It depends on the river. Not much if we keep going at this pace."

He scooped along, and about every thirty yards he pulled the net up and shook it. I sat on the boat, day dreaming and gazing into the jungle. The morning turned to afternoon, the pale gray sky turned bright blue, the sun rose above us, and my stomach began to growl. "When do we eat?" I asked Dad when he came to the boat to empty the net.

"I want to keep fishing while we can," he said. "When the tide comes in, it will be too deep." He told me to eat if I wanted, but I didn't want to seem weak so I asked if I could use the net. I thought it would be easy—just push the net along and pull it up every once in a while. I got into the water and situated the net in front of me, then Dad climbed in the boat.

"Push it slow and steady," he said," and keep it out of the mud." The net got heavier with every step. I pushed it

85

about ten yards and couldn't push it anymore. "Pull it up," Dad said. "Pull it up!" I used all my strength to pull it out of the water. It was full of mud. "Shake it out. You're pushing it too hard and sinking it into the mud."

My next attempt was about the same, but I kept trying and on my fourth attempt came up with a few prawns. We had about fifty in the colander when Dad said he would take over the net. I was wrinkled and tired, and I thought how strong he must have been to fish all day alone while I was in National Service. Dad got about a dozen with his first attempt, but after that he didn't get any. We rowed to the other side and tried again, but still no prawns.

"The river is too high," he said. "We won't catch anymore today." We tied the boat to the bank, washed the nets and laid them out to dry. Dad changed into the dry clothes he had brought. Mine were already dry from the sun. As I looked into the basket to see what Mom packed for us, I said I thought we'd had a good day.

"We caught enough to feed ourselves," Dad said, "but we'll have to catch more so we can save money." We ate the rice cakes and dried pork Mom had packed, and he loaded his pipe. The tide was coming in, and he said we should go while the current was with us. He had a smoke while I loaded the nets into the boat, then I started rowing back to the city.

The brightness of the day was gone when we passed Nha Be. The sun had become a huge red ball on the horizon. Pink clouds streaked the pale blue sky. When we got to the southern edge of the city, Dad took the oars, and I lay against the back of the boat. A slow steady breeze blew against my face, and I slept until our boat bumped against the dock.

"We better get these prawns to your mother," Dad said. I grabbed our lunch basket and walked with him to the house.

"A good first day," he said as we walked along the road. It was dry now and covered with a thin layer of warm dust. "When we get you your own net, we should be able to save money and buy an engine. Maybe a bigger boat."

I couldn't wait to get home and show everyone what we caught. By this time, the market was closed, so Mom would take the prawns around the neighborhood to sell or trade them. Phi's mom had introduced my mom to other people in the neighborhood, and she was the one who helped us learn how to weave baskets. Mom would go to her house first to see if they wanted to buy some prawns. If they didn't have money at the time, Mom would give them some prawns and Phi's mom would help sell them.

Fishing was the same for the rest of the week. We left early in the morning and came home late in the evening, so all I did was fish, eat and sleep. On Sunday, we stopped at the market in Nha Be, and Dad bought me a net. I was getting pretty good with it by the end of the next week, but we spent four to six hours each day just getting to the fishing spots, so we still weren't saving any money. Then the first week in December, our luck changed. We had just finished for the day and had put our nets out to dry. Dad was sitting on the bank, smoking his pipe, and I was getting our lunch basket when a boat about the size of ours, but with an engine, stopped next to us.

"Are you having any luck!" the man in the boat shouted as he killed the engine.

"Enough to get by," Dad said. "We only started a month ago, so we're still learning."

"My name is Quang," the man said. "I started last summer."

"My name is Vu, and this is my son, Viet."

The man nodded at me. His skin was weathered and tanned, as dark as the cotton trousers he wore. They were rolled up to his knees. "My propeller got caught in some grass," Quang said. "The grass is tangled around it, and I wonder if you have a wrench so I can take it off."

"I have a crescent wrench in the box," Dad said. "Will that work?"

"Can I try it?" Quang asked.

Dad got the wrench, and I helped Quang pull the propeller out of the water. "Are you from the North?" Quang asked, recognizing Dad's northern accent.

"I moved from the North many years ago," Dad said as he handed Quang the wrench.

"Did you fight in the war?"

Dad hesitated, "I was in the army in the sixties."

I wondered why the man asked so many questions and thought he might be a communist. A year before, it would have been normal for a stranger to ask questions, but lately the only people who talked to strangers were people preaching communism. I knew Dad was thinking the same thing.

"I fought for the South," Quang said, easing my father's concern. "It's all I knew how to do until the communists took over. My father bought two boats last summer, and my family has been fishing ever since."

"Had your father fished before?" Dad asked.

"He was a fisherman in the North before Uncle Ho started the land reform." Quang strained to unscrew the nut that held the propeller on, then he twisted it off with his fingers.

"Do you know what village he's from?" Dad asked.

"I'm not sure. I think it was about thirty miles south of Hanoi."

As Quang untangled the grass, they talked about the war.

Dad told him about the battles he was in around My Tho and about being wounded in Saigon during the Tet Offensive. Quang said he spent most of the war in the North, but he fought in the Iron Triangle for the last few months. "It was a worthless war," he said. "Look at us now. All that bloodshed for nothing."

Quang finished untangling the grass and put the propeller back on. "Where do you live?" he asked, and Dad told him Binh An. "We live this side of Highway 1," Quang said, "on the east bank of New Port." Just south of the Highway 1 bridge the river makes a circle at high tide, and the island in the middle is called New Port. It's the same area where I used to fight my cocks, next to the park.

"Are you hungry, Quang?" Dad asked, as I pulled our lunch out of the basket.

"I've eaten, but I'll wait until you finish, and I'll give you a tow back."

"That's okay," Dad said. "We can row with the current."

"It's no trouble. It's becoming rare to meet generous people, and I would like you to meet my father."

"We can eat on the way back," Dad said, and we tied our boat to Quang's. It was great, cruising up the river without having to paddle. Quang towed us past the warehouses to the first dock on New Port. Dad told me to take the prawns to Mom so she could sell them, then he got into Quang's boat, and I rowed back to our dock.

When I got home, I asked Mom if I could go to Tam's house for a while. She knew I hadn't seen him in two months, and she said I could go if I promised to be home for dinner. I promised, then grabbed my bike from the side of the house and pedaled to our old neighborhood. I rode by our old house on the way to Tam's. It seemed abandoned. The plow sat idle in uncut grass, rusting and rotting into the ground. There were no animals in the barnyard, and no garden. On the front porch, a dusty hammock swayed in a light breeze. It used to be my favorite place for an afternoon nap, but now it was abandoned, serving no one. I wanted to take a closer look, but when I started up the drive I saw the old Chinese woman staring out the window, so I turned back.

When I got to Tam's house, I parked my bike in the yard and walked up the wooden stairs to the porch. A small, middle-aged man in a khaki uniform met me at the doorway. He startled me. "Is Tam here?" I asked.

The man sensed my fear and stepped toward me. I hadn't greeted him respectfully. His lips were tight and his face was irritated. "There is no Tam here," he said.

I looked to my left, then to my right, making sure I was at the right house, even though I had been there a hundred times before. Then I looked back at the man. He stared up at me, bothered by my height, judging my appearance. I pulled my hair back and sucked in air for courage. "Do you know where Tam is?"

"The family moved away," the man said with a heavy northern accent. "I live here now."

"Do you know where they went?" I asked too abruptly.

"Why do you ask so many questions, boy?"

"Tam was my best friend."

"Then you should know where he is," the man snapped.

I lowered my head, turned, and walked to my bike. I didn't look back, but I could sense the man staring at me as I rode off. A knot formed in my chest. I should have gone to see Tam sooner. As soon as I got back from the wastelands, I should have gone to see him. I pedaled as fast as I could until I was out of the man's sight, then I stopped and threw my bike in the grass on the side of the road. I stood staring at the sky.

When I got home, I leaned my bike against the house and walked across the soccer field behind the school, then toward the river to Phi's house. He and Viet were sitting on the front porch. "How's fishing?" Phi asked as I walked toward them. "I wish I could be fishing instead of weaving baskets all day."

"It was fun at first, but now it's becoming more like work."

Phi's house was similar to ours. It was framed with bamboo and sided with pine planks. A covered porch with bamboo rails stuck out six feet and ran halfway across the front. Clay shingles covered the roof and bamboo gutters ran along the sides. Viet was sitting on the porch rail, and Phi was sitting sideways on the hammock. "When are you getting your own boat?" Viet asked. "I want to go cruising."

"Not for a while. We just make enough to get by."

"I've been weaving baskets ten hours a day," Phi complained. He held his hands out so I could see his calluses.

"*I* wouldn't weave those baskets," Viet said. "We make enough money in one afternoon to feed ourselves all week."

"How do you make so much money?" I asked.

"My brother gets rice from the country every week," he said. "We sell it on the market for ten times what he pays for it."

"Why do people pay so much for it?" I asked.

"Because people need to eat," Phi said. "Last week, the co-op ran out of rice, and we had to buy it on the market."

"The only people who have anything," Viet said, "are the communists and the people who sell on the market. You have to take risks to make money."

"What do you mean?" I asked.

"It's dangerous business," he said. "My brother only buys from the farmers he knows because some people would turn him in. Sometimes he gets caught, but he outsmarts the officials or bribes them. The whole system is corrupt. You just have to know how to beat it."

From inside the house, At yelled, "Phi! What are you doing?" Phi didn't answer quickly enough, and At came through the doorway. "Are you done for the day?" he asked. "You've hardly done anything."

"I finished eight baskets," Phi said. "I'll do two more before I go to bed."

"Hello Viets," At said, referring to Viet and me at the same time. We nodded, then he looked at me and asked why I wasn't fishing.

"We got a tow back from a man we met today."

Mom walked up to the porch while we were talking to At, and Phi's mom came outside. Her long gray hair was braided and wrapped in a spiral on the back of her head. She was taller than At and almost twice as wide, but she was solid and quick. One time I saw her chase down Phi's younger brother after he pulled her onion plants up. She had him by the back of his shirt in five steps. I introduced Mom to Viet. She had seen him around our neighborhood but hadn't met him before. Viet was polite, but Mom saw through him and quickly turned to Phi. "I hope my son isn't keeping you from your work," she said. Phi smiled, embarrassed.

"He promised to work hard later," At said, then grunted and went back in the house.

"Can we take the boat to the bridge and back?" I asked Mom. "Phi and Viet want to go for a ride."

"I thought you were going to Tam's house."

A lump formed in my chest. "He's gone."

"What do you mean, gone?"

"Some communist lives in his house now. He was rude to me and wouldn't tell me where Tam was." Her face showed her sorrow for me. I wanted to tell her how I would miss him, but I didn't want to seem weak in front of my new friends. "Can we take the boat out, Mom?"

She turned to Phi's mom and asked, "Is it okay with you?"

"I guess," she said, looking at us with suspicion, "but don't be gone long."

"And be careful," Mom said. We raced off before they changed their minds.

"I thought this was your boat," Viet said when we got to the dock. "You shouldn't have to ask your Mom if you can take it out."

"Just get in if you want a ride," I said.

I rowed north, toward the Highway 13 bridge. We could see Phi's house from the river. We passed the pavilion and the bamboo racks where they dried the jute grass. "There's Crippled Thanh," Viet said. A thin man in loose black pajamas limped along the side of the pavilion. When he got to the corner, he saw us floating by and stopped to look at us.

"Great," Phi said. "Now if we don't make quota, he'll tell my mom it's because I'm riding in boats when I should be working."

"What's this quota you keep talking about?" Viet asked.

"If we don't make quota, we don't eat," Phi answered. "We get our food from the co-op, and Crippled Thanh is in charge."

I rowed to the bridge and turned around. "Go under the bridge," Viet said. "Let's go to the end of the river."

Past the bridge, the river went another half mile north

during high tide. There were no houses on the other side, just fields of head high jute grass and strips of trees for as far as I had ever gone. "I want to get home and eat," I said. "We'll go further next time."

Crippled Thanh watched us as we passed the pavilion, and we pretended not to see him. In five minutes we were at the dock. Viet tried to make me row to New Port, and I told him maybe next time. Phi went back to his house to finish his two baskets, Viet said he was going to the café, and I went home to eat. I wondered if Viet really made a lot of money or if he was just talking. He lived in a different neighborhood, and I had never seen his house. Phi said Viet's father was killed in the war and he lived with his mother and two older brothers. I assumed the man who pulled Viet off me the day we fought was one of his brothers, but I never asked him. I didn't want to remind him of that day. They lived a couple of miles east of Highway 13, and the way Viet made it sound, there were no other houses around them, so there were no neighbors to spy on them.

After dinner, I sat with Dad on our back porch. My brothers and sisters were studying, and Mom was hoeing in the garden. Looking west from our porch, we could see the skyline of the city. A dirty gray haze hung in the sky and sagged between the buildings. Beyond the haze, layers of red, yellow and orange streaked the sky. Dad looked at his watch as the sun set below the horizon. "Eight fifteen," he said. "The days are getting longer."

"What time does the tide go out tomorrow?" I asked.

"Not until nine, but we're meeting Quang and his father at five. They're going to tow us out."

"It's nice of them to help us. Are they going to teach us how to catch more fish?"

94

"They told me the fishing is better closer to the sea. Quang's father's name is Mr. Vi," Dad said, showing respect for him because of his age. "He's from a northern village not far from where I was born, and his life has been much like mine."

In front of us on Highway 1, cars and mopeds raced in and out of the city. Two-stroke engines screamed by, blowing trails of smoke, interrupting the calm of the evening. "If we catch more fish, will we get an engine for the boat?" I asked.

"They offered to tow us out until we can save enough to buy an engine. Mr. Vi says he doesn't want anything in return, but I would like to help them some way if we can."

"We were lucky to meet Quang today," I said. "I'm glad there are still people we can trust."

I went to bed early and fell straight to sleep. The next morning, Dad rowed us to New Port and took the river around to the east side of the island. He stopped at a wooden dock with three boats tied to it. "These all belong to Mr. Vi," he said.

We walked across the dock, through a gate and up the stairs to their house. The front of the house rested on four poles and the back was set halfway into the hill. Under the house, fishing nets, poles and rusty buckets hung from nails in the rafters. The door was open, so we walked in. Quang and three men were sitting at a long hardwood table. A young woman was stirring something in the wok on the stove.

"Good morning, Vu," The oldest man said to Dad. "This must be your son Viet."

"Hello, Mr. Vi," I said.

"This is my youngest son, Loc," he said. Loc was about twenty, maybe older. "This is my oldest son, Minh," Minh looked as old as my father. "And you met Quang yesterday.

Would you like something to eat?"

"That's okay," Dad said. "We had a good breakfast."

"Then we should get started," Vi said, and all four men stood up together.

"The fishing should be good today," Vi said when we got to the dock. He looked up to the sky and breathed in the fresh morning air. "The moon was full last night."

Dad and Quang tied the boats together, and Loc and Minh fueled the biggest boat. Vi watched them from the dock, and I stood beside him. "How long have you been fishing, son?" he asked.

"About a month, Mr. Vi," I said bashfully.

Vi was about my height. His hair was gray, but he had the body of a thirty-year-old soldier. His face was too hard to wrinkle. His eyes were almost black, but they sparkled when he looked at me. He spoke slowly, as though he always thought about what he would say before saying it. "When the moon is full," he told me, "the tide stays out longer, the river stays low, and we catch more fish. You'll catch more today than you ever thought possible." Vi reminded me of how people in Vietnam were before the communists took over, before everyone was afraid to trust anyone. I was happy there were still people who would help others instead of just trying to get ahead themselves.

We cruised along the river, past where Dad and I fished before. Many streams and canals ran into the main channel, and we turned west onto a stream about a hundred yards across. "The Coast Guard Station is a mile ahead of us!" Quang yelled, pointing up the main channel.

The channel was a mile wide, wide enough so the still blue water blended with the horizon of the pale blue sky. A northern wind carried the smell of the sea past us. "Do sharks come in this far?" I asked Dad.

Before he could answer, Quang yelled from the other boat, "No big ones," and they all laughed. We followed the stream west. The sun rose behind us, and to the south, white puffy clouds rolled over the trees. "If we go any farther on the main channel, the Coast Guard will stop us," Quang said.

The jungle became thick on both sides of the river. Birds cheeped and shrieked and fluttered out of trees. Fish flew from the water and curled in the air. We stopped along a sand bank and tied the boats. "This will be a good place for Viet to start," Vi said. "The bank isn't too steep and the current is slow."

I had never fished alone and was a little nervous. They had a raft for me to keep my colander attached to. Dad would take the boat to the other side of the river, and Vi and his sons would fish upstream. My stomach did summersaults as I climbed into the water, but I hid my fear. "Stay in the water," Vi said. "There are tigers around here, but they won't come after you in the water. And watch out for snakes."

He was serious, but Quang and Loc saw the fear in my eyes and smiled. "You'll be okay," Quang said. "Just keep your eyes and ears open." They untied the boats and pulled away. By the time I got my net situated in front of me, Dad's boat looked like a small dot on the other side of the river. By the time I started fishing, he had pulled out of sight.

The sun was bright, but trees hung over the edge of the river, and I was shaded in darkness. The bushes and vines were so thick I couldn't see into the jungle. I tried to keep my mind on fishing, but visions of snakes slithering into the water and hanging off vines behind me kept going through my mind. I couldn't believe how many prawns I caught each time I pulled the net up—big fat ones, three or four inches long. It was hard work though. Trees hung in the water and snagged my net, and I had to swim around some of them. My body shook from fear and the cold water. After a few hours, I wanted to find a place to dry off, but Vi's words about tigers were etched on my mind, so I kept fishing.

The tide came in and the water was up to my chest. Past the shadows of the trees, I saw the reflection of clouds on the river. The sweet, stale smell of rain filled my lungs, and big drops began falling from the trees overhead. In minutes it was pouring. The rain was warmer than the river, but a cold wind swept along the top of the water. It had been too long since breakfast, and I wished I had eaten more. My hunger had come and gone three times, and now I had a constant throb in my stomach. I wanted to find a spot to sit down, but I didn't want to have worked hard all day then have them find me sitting on the bank like a lazy little boy. Finally, I heard an engine behind me. Vi and Quang were in the first boat, Loc and Minh in the second, and Dad in the third. They were smiling.

"You look like a drowned rat," Quang said, and their laughter broke out. I forced a smile to show them I was tough enough to take it, then tossed my colander onto my father's boat.

He opened the top and looked inside. "Look at this," he said, holding the colander toward Vi.

"That's a good day's work," Vi said. "A good day's work."

I climbed in my father's boat, embarrassed by the compliment. We went up the river to the first open spot and tied the boats so we could sort the nets and clean everything. When we finished, the rain had stopped and we all started to eat. I rested against the engine in Vi's boat to warm up and when I woke, we were at Vi's dock. "Are you sleeping here?" Dad asked.

I staggered to our boat as they smiled at me, and Dad paddled home. Mom was excited about how much we had caught. Dad had about twice as much as I had. I told myself it was because they gave me the hardest part, but really it was because I hadn't learned to use the nets with the least amount of effort and I wasn't as strong as Dad. Mom hurried out to sell the prawns. I didn't stay up to see how much she made, but I knew we were on our way to an engine.

A New Beginning

Christmas came, but it wasn't like the years before, when the whole community celebrated together, even the Buddhists. Every year, on the twenty-third of December, Dad would take Vinh and me to the soccer field in our old neighborhood. There would be at least a hundred other Boy Scouts from our area. We would make a camp and assemble a stable with the baby Jesus, Joseph and Mary, the animals and the wise men. We would spend the day building our camp and playing games, then at night we would build a huge fire and circle around to listen to stories and sing Christmas carols. At twelve o'clock, the priest would say Mass, and we would sleep that night in the camp.

The next day, the women would join us. Mom and my sisters would have spent the week preparing food. Each family brought what they could, and everyone shared. The men gambled, the women kept the food coming, and the children played games. It was a time to talk about the previous year, for courting, and for families to get together and be thankful.

But this year we no longer had Boy Scouts. The man on the radio said people must limit their celebrations and continue working to build the new society. The bonds that used to tie the community together were now broken. Bonds were forming for the people who supported the new government, the Ho Chi Minh Youth groups, and the co-ops, but I had fished every weekend so I still wasn't a Red Scarf, and we didn't make enough baskets to be members of the co-op.

An eerie feeling lingered in our neighborhood and throughout the city—the feeling of walking alone on a dark path, thinking someone is watching you. The hair rises on the back of your neck. Your skin crawls. You want to look behind you, but you don't want to show you're afraid. I felt it when I walked with Phi to get grass from the pavilion and when we were at church. Someone was always watching, but we didn't know who. We had an idea, but couldn't ask questions, because if you ask questions, you must be guilty of something.

On Christmas Eve, we crossed the road to Binh An Church for the ten o'clock Mass. People came from all parts of the city to hear Father Quyen's sermon, so we left early to get a seat. Father Quyen was Saigon's head priest, advisor to President Diem and President Thieu before the communists took over. During the war, he traveled around the country saying Mass for our soldiers. Dad said Father Quyen was one of the most respected men in the city and the communists were frightened of his influence over the people. But Father Quyen never said anything against the communists. In his sermon that evening, he told us to pray to God when our lives were troubled and to turn the other cheek when evil passed our way.

On Christmas day, we took the bus to Grandfather's

house. Gas for the mopeds had become too expensive, so they had been rusting behind our house since the summer. Grandfather still lived in western Saigon, so we traveled along Highway 1 until it turned into Red Cross Street, then circled around the north edge of the city. No Christmas decorations hung from the light poles or palm trees. The billboards that used to advertise Coca Cola and Marlboros had been taken down or changed to advertise the communists' programs and philosophy. "Justice in Labor, Power to the People," they said in black letters on white backgrounds.

Before the communists took over, Saigon was like a colorful European city, but located in the tropics, so it was even more beautiful. The French had built Saigon with wide streets like the boulevards in Paris, and the streets were lined with cafés, villas and stone cathedrals. But since the communists had arrived, the sparks of the city seemed to have been extinguished by a cold, gray mist. People's faces even seemed to have lost their color. It was late morning when the bus stopped at a market along Red Cross Street. The market was closing for the day, and as we stepped off the bus I watched people making last minute purchases. There was a steady rumble of voices and above us on the electric poles loud speakers screeched, "The journey has just begun. Much work is to be completed. Everyone must join in the struggle for equality. . .."

We walked between small brick houses, along a paved street that led to Grandfather's house. "My children," he cried as we walked through the doorway, "Merry Christmas!"

My cousins stood bashfully behind him. Doan was ten, Kim was six and Dinh was three. My uncle stepped out of the bedroom, wearing his best black trousers and a loose white shirt. His eyes were bloodshot and dark circles hung below them. "Merry Christmas," he said. We all bowed.

Aunt Nhu came from the kitchen to greet us too—a small, stocky woman with full cheeks and a worried smile. She grabbed Tu from my mother's arms. "You're so big!" she said. "Look at those chubby cheeks."

Grandfather reached out for Tu. "Growing like a water buffalo."

Mom and Aunt Nhu went to the kitchen, Dad and Uncle Houng went outside to sit on the porch, and the children all followed Grandfather to his chair. We gathered around him, Tu and Minh Ha on his lap and the rest of us cross-legged on the floor. "Tell us a story?" Minh Ha asked him.

Grandfather told us several stories about kung fu heroes, then Mom called us for dinner, and we sat in a circle on the living room floor. In the middle of the room was a large bowl full of rice; bowls of vegetables, pork, and chicken; a spicy soup we called pho; water chestnuts; egg noodles; and my favorite, spring rolls. Grandfather said a prayer, Mom filled the bowls with rice and passed them around the circle until we each had one, and then we piled the meat and vegetables on the rice. With hungry faces, bowls in one hand and sticks in the other, we scooped and chewed until all the food was gone.

When we finished, the women and girls cleaned the dishes. Mom put Tu and Dinh in the bedroom for a nap, Vinh and Doan played kickball in the back yard, and the men went to the porch for a smoke. I went with them to lie in the hammock. The men sat quietly at first, Dad and Uncle Houng on a wooden bench leaning against the front wall of the house, and Grandfather in a bamboo chair with a cushion. On the white wicker table in front of them was a red tin can of tobacco. They dipped into it—Grandfather first, then Dad, then Uncle Houng.

"I don't know how we'll make it," Uncle Houng said as he packed the tobacco in his pipe. Dad was lighting his, and Grandfather was already puffing. "No one has money to buy new clothes, and most people mend their own now, so they don't need tailors."

"Have you thought about a different business?" Dad asked.

"There's nothing else I know how to do," Uncle Houng said.

"Nothing you can do without them knowing your position in the army," Grandfather said. They were all puffing steadily now. The sweet smoke drifted across my face.

"Ten years," Uncle Houng said. "Ten years as an electrical engineer, and now I'm worth no more than a bum. I can't even feed my family."

"What about fishing?" Grandfather said. "It seems Vu is getting along."

"Just barely," Dad said. "It takes money to buy a boat and more money to buy nets."

"I have some gold," Grandfather said. "Maybe we should buy a boat. You could fish together." I knew Dad didn't want to fish with Uncle Houng. My uncle was a good man, honest and a hard worker, but like many people, he wasn't suited for physical labor. "Maybe business will pick up for Tet," Uncle Houng said.

They puffed their pipes with hopeless expressions. I lay in the hammock, drifting in and out of sleep. When I listened, the conversation was about no money, no future for the children and no hope for a good life under the communists. I thought they were overreacting. My life was okay—fishing was better than going to school, we had chicken and pork for dinner, and we had our own boat. We didn't always eat well, but we weren't starving. At least we weren't taken away like the people on the docks.

For the next two weeks, we worked every day. After fishing I ate, listened to the radio and fell asleep. Then I awoke the next day and did it again. It was the second week in January when Mom told us the government was taking people's businesses away. She had heard it on the radio and seen flyers announcing a new government program. All private business was officially banned.

When we got home after fishing the next time, Mom said Crippled Thanh had come by. She called him that too. "He was very rude," she said. "He came right into the house and looked around before I knew he was here. He startled me. He said we were to be at a meeting tonight."

"What's the meeting about?" Dad asked.

"I don't know," Mom replied. "He left before I could ask him."

"It's probably about the co-op," Dad said.

Mom made dinner as they talked. Fish sizzled on the open grill. She turned them, buttered them and turned them again. Tu pulled on her long blue shirt. "What's dinner?" his tiny voice asked.

Mom ignored him. "The meeting is at nine. Why do you think it's so late?"

"They need to wait for people to finish work and dinner," Dad said. "Don't worry. I'm sure it's about the co-op."

After dinner, Mom and Dad went to the meeting. Tu didn't cry anymore when they left. He was starting to realize that when they were gone, he could do what he wanted. I was left in charge, but my sisters looked after Tu and cleaned the dishes and Vinh studied, so I lay in the hammock until

Mom and Dad returned.

"That man is the devil," Mom said as she came through the doorway. I opened my eyes and saw her angry face. "He has no right to take our boat."

I jumped from the hammock. "What! They took our boat?"

My brothers and sisters had gone to bed. Dad sat at the table, and Mom sat beside him. "Sit down, Viet," Dad said.

"What's happening?" I asked.

"Thanh declared our boat government property," Dad said.

"What does that mean?"

"From now on," he said, "we're supposed to give our catch to the co-op, and it will be distributed equally among everyone."

"But what about our boat?" I asked. "Will they take our boat?" Mom's eyes watched Dad closely, asking him the same question.

"They will not take it," he said, and his eyes emptied. "No, they will not take it."

Dad moved to his chair next to the window. From there he could see past the school and down Highway 13. Sometimes when he sat there alone, peering out the window, he looked like a guard, watching and waiting for the enemy. Mom pulled the chair from the kitchen table and sat facing him. I stayed in the hammock.

"So what happens now?" I asked. "Do we keep fishing?"

I could see Dad was thinking, and he collected his thoughts before answering. "Nothing has changed," he said loudly, then was silent for a moment. "We're still in control of the boat. No one else is allowed to use it. The only dif-ference is that we give all the prawns to the co-op."

"But how do they know how much we catch?" I asked.

Mom's tight lips almost smiled. Then she stood up, her

eyes huge and fixed on the doorway. "Father," she said. I looked to the doorway and saw Grandfather. His gray hair was uncombed. His face was troubled.

"They have taken Houng," he said. "The bastards have taken my son."

"What do you mean?" Dad asked, getting up from his chair.

"They took the whole family."

Mom clutched her face then looked up, trying to be brave. Terror showed in her eyes, and I felt it run through my skin. Dad looked confused. Mom went to Grandfather, and they stood holding each other, shaking. "They were supposed to be back for dinner," he said. "They didn't come, and I was worried, so I went to the shop. It was boarded up, and a sign said 'Property of the People.' The bastards took them."

"Where?" Dad asked. "Where did they take them?"

"I don't know," Grandfather answered. "I went to the district station, but they wouldn't tell me. I said my clothes were in the shop and I wanted to get them. If I had told them I was Houng's father they would have taken me too. The bastard said I should mend my own shirts. He told me one pair of clothes is more than many people have and my clothes would be donated to the new society."

Mom helped Grandfather to a chair, and they sat around the table. "What will we do?" she asked, looking at Dad.

"We have to find them," he said.

"I think they've taken them to one of those zones," Grandfather said. "The New Economic Zones."

"Why do you think this?" Dad asked.

"It's happening all over the city," Grandfather cried. "Thousands of families have been taken away. They announced it on BBC." The BBC was a British radio station that broadcasted from a ship in the South China Sea. It was illegal to listen to it, but people did because it was one of the only ways to find out what the communists weren't telling us.

"We'll use the money we saved," Dad said, "and we'll get them out of the country."

"How can we do that?" Grandfather asked. "Do you know someone who can help us?"

"I think so," was Dad's response. "There's nothing we can do tonight, but tomorrow I'll find a way."

"Stay here tonight," Mom said to Grandfather. "They may be looking for you."

"I'll go to the station tomorrow," Dad said, "and find out where they took them."

"You can't do that," Grandfather said. "They won't tell you, and they might take you too. Houng will find his way back. We need you to organize their escape. I have some gold; I'll get it tomorrow. That's all we can do." They were silent. The air in the house was filled with their terror. When Mom noticed I was still awake she told me to get some sleep, so I went to the bedroom and crawled under my net.

The next morning, we went to Vi's. The men were all sitting at the table when we walked in. Quang was reading a newspaper. *The Truth*, it said in bold letters across the top. I hadn't seen it before. "What is that?" Dad asked Quang.

"An underground newspaper," Quang said. "They were scattered at the fish market yesterday."

"Read the article about the women," Vi said. "The women with the curtain shop."

"Yesterday morning," Quang read, "a woman set fire to her linen shop and burned with the building. Her daughter was also killed in the fire. The shop had been seized by government officials the day before and declared the property of the people. The owner of the shop, Mrs. Lan Giap, was beaten by the officials and forced off her property. The next morning she poured gasoline on the fabrics and set fire to them."

"That's enough," Vi said. "It's awful."

"Daylight robbery," Dad said.

Vi stood up from the table. "Before long, they'll declare our boats belong to the people."

"They already have," Dad said. "They seized ours last night."

Vi sat back down. "Those bastards."

Quang slammed his fist on the table. "They can't do this!"

"Control yourself, boy," Vi said.

Quang's lips were tight. "We should have left this country long ago."

"Settle down, boy," Vi said. "We will be fine."

"They took my brother-in-law yesterday," Dad told them. "They took his whole family. We think they'll be sent to a New Economic Zone."

"Oh God," Vi said. "Do you know where they are?"

"The officials won't tell us," Dad said. "I only hope they can make it back to Saigon."

"But then what will they do?" Quang asked. "The communists will send them back or put them in prison."

"My father has gold," Dad replied. "Do you know how we can get them out of the country?"

Vi didn't hesitate. "It will take much gold," he said, "but I can help you."

"I've heard many stories," Dad said. "Stories about men taking people's money, sometimes turning them over to officials, or dumping them at sea. Do you know someone we can trust?"

"I know a man in Nha Be," Vi said. "I haven't known him long, but I think he's an honest man. He wants to get his own family out and needs money for supplies. I think you can buy seats on his boat for your brother-in-law's family."

Dad looked ashamed. Vi had helped us so much already, and there was no way for us to repay him. "I hope my brother can make it back in time," Dad said. "He doesn't know how to survive in the jungle and he has the whole family."

We took three boats and the raft and headed for Nha Be. When we arrived, Vi said he should go alone. We left him at the village, fished until late afternoon, and picked him up that evening. He had found the man, and the escape could be arranged. But we had to pay half the money right away and we still didn't know if Uncle Houng could make it back in time for the trip. We didn't know if he could make it back at all.

Quang let me take *The Truth* home to read. Dad saw it in my back pocket on the way home. "Burn that after you read it," he said, "and don't let your brothers and sisters see it." I stuffed it a little farther into my pocket.

When we got home, Mom took about half our catch to the co-op. The rest she would take to a market in the city early the next morning to avoid being noticed by Crippled Thanh. That would be her routine for a while. The rest of the time, she worked in the garden, weaved baskets, cooked our meals, made and mended our clothes, and worried about our future. Tu was always by her side—not a burden anymore. He helped her when he could and was learning when to stay out of the way.

The Truth was a five-page newspaper. I thought it was probably printed in some dark basement in the middle of the night. Most of the stories were about victims of communism. One article said the same thing my father had told me about the people on the docks—that the communists dumped the diseased and the crippled into the sea. There was an article about pirates who attacked those who were trying to escape from the communists in boats, referred to as *boat people*. It said the pirates stole their money, raped the women, and threw the men into the sea.

There was an article about the reeducation camps that compared them to the concentration camps in Germany, and another about the New Economic Zones. "Nazi Zones," the headline read. The article said they were set up to redistribute the population and to solve unemployment. But it said the communists were sending city people into the swamplands where nothing would grow and telling them to farm. Some were sent with no tools, no seeds and not enough food to survive. It said many people died of snake bites, malaria and malnutrition. Cadres from the North were in charge of the zones and many of them were corrupt. They kept what little food there was for themselves, so most of the people tried to come back to Saigon. Some made it; others died on the journey. I thought about Uncle Houng and my cousins. I prayed for them to make it back, but the article gave me little hope.

February came and brought Tet, the new year, the time to respect the past and plan for the future. We had seen Grandfather several times. He gave Dad the gold, and Vi gave half the gold to the man in Nha Be. There was no word from Uncle Houng.

In past years during Tet, Mom would make or buy us new clothes. We celebrated with feasts, parades and dances. Mom and the girls would prepare food, and Dad, Vinh and

I fixed things around the house. One year we built a fence around the garden and planted banana trees in the back yard. The celebration would last two weeks, and on the last evening every family stayed in their house to honor their ancestors. We would open all the doors and windows and ask our ancestors to grace our lives with luck in the upcoming year, then we would light firecrackers to scare evil spirits out of our house. Many people still believed this practice would work, but for us it was more of a tradition. My parents' faith was Catholicism, but we still took part in the older traditions of our country, just as many Buddhists took part in celebrating Christmas.

This year few people celebrated, because the government condemned the waste of time and money for a Chinese holiday. "We have more important tasks," the man on the radio said. "We must produce goods to strengthen our country and learn how to be better citizens."

Our family had no celebration. The river was low, so Dad and I fished every day. Mom couldn't afford to buy material to make us clothes, so she made me some trousers from Dad's old ones, and made Vinh's trousers from mine and the girls' dresses from hers. It was an empty feeling, going into the new year without preparing. It was bad luck.

On the last day of Tet, we went to Grandfather's house. It was the second week in February. Uncle Houng had been gone for a month. Mom and Dad and Grandfather talked about the escape, but there was little hope in their eyes. The boat was leaving in five days.

Grandfather had a copy of *The People's Press*—this was the communist party's newspaper. I lay in the hammock reading "Success in the New Economic Zones." The article said co-ops had been formed in the New Economic Zones and many were now self-sufficient. It said the program was helping ease unemployment and many people were now volunteering to go to the zones. I showed the article to Dad, and he said it was a joke with no humor. "The communists lie to our faces," he said. "They take our property and steal our hope."

We took the last bus home, east on Red Cross Street, past the Highway 1 bridge, and got off behind our house. The electricity was off, but the windows of many houses flickered with candlelight. Our house was completely dark, and I was the first one through the doorway, ten steps in front of Vinh.

"Viet," a man whispered as I walked into the kitchen. I looked around frantically, but couldn't see in the darkness. Vinh and Mom came in behind me. "Viet, it's me, Houng."

"Thank God!" Mom cried. Houng crawled out from behind the stove.

"I didn't know if it was you," he said weakly. "I'm sorry I frightened you."

Dad came through the doorway, "Are you okay? Where are the children? Where's Nhu?"

Uncle Houng's voice was excited but weak. "We all made it. They're hiding under a bridge. The one just north of here."

Dad lit a lantern and Mom wiped Uncle Houng's soiled face with a towel. "Where did they take you?" Dad asked. "How did you get back?"

"They took us to an Economic Zone north of Bien Hoa, but we escaped. We've been walking for three weeks." Uncle Houng spoke without taking a breath. "We must have walked sixty miles. We left the zone with another family, but they didn't make it. Their boy was bitten by a snake and died in

113

the jungle. The family turned themselves over to the officials in a village. We have malaria—the children are very sick."

"We have to get them inside," Mom said. "Girls, there's some rice left. Mix in some vegetables and make soup for your uncle."

"I will go after the children," Dad said.

Mom helped Uncle Houng to a chair. His body was slouched, he had no shirt, and his trousers were soiled and ripped. I could see the bones of his face. His lips were dry and stuck together, and his eyes were yellow with malaria. Mom wrapped a blanket around him and fed him the soup.

In fifteen minutes, Dad returned with Aunt Nhu and the children. He carried Kim, wrapped in Uncle Houng's shirt. Her eyes peered out, too big for her face, watery and yellow. Aunt Nhu carried Dinh. She was in better shape than Uncle Houng, and she took Dinh to the bedroom. Doan stood by the stove, shivering. They all shivered, and the golden lantern light reflected the beads of sweat on their sunken faces. Dad carried Kim to the bedroom, and Doan followed. We wrapped them all in blankets.

Mom cooked rice and vegetables and more soup. They ate little, chewed slowly, and gulped hard. When Uncle Houng regained a little strength from the food, he came to the bedroom to see about the children. Mom gave us blankets and sent us to the living room to make beds, and Dad and Uncle Houng came out of the room and sat at the kitchen table. "We have organized your escape," Dad said.

Uncle Houng looked puzzled, "What do you mean?"

"We're getting you out of the country."

Uncle Houng's face was blank, helpless. "How?"

"We know a man who's escaping, and we bought seats on the boat."

"Is Father going too?" Uncle Houng asked, but he already knew the answer. Grandfather would never leave Vietnam. He would die first.

"It's the only way," Dad said. "If they find you, they'll send you to reeducation. You need to leave now, when you have the chance."

"I know you're right," Uncle Houng said, "but the children are sick. They'll have to get stronger before they can travel."

Mom and Aunt Nhu came out of the bedroom. Aunt Nhu had taken a bath, but she still looked dirty. Her hands and feet were swollen and bruised. Her body moved slowly, but her eyes were still bright and strong. Vinh, Tu, and the girls had fallen asleep on the covers Mom gave us. They would go to school the next day with a secret, and Mom had talked to each of them, making sure they knew not to say a word. I was worried. I thought at any minute the officials would come and they would take us all away.

Mom and Aunt Nhu sat at the table. I sat beside Dad, knowing I could sit there because I would be a part of the escape. "Kim is very sick," Mom said. "She can't travel for a while."

"The boat leaves in five days," Dad said.

"What boat?" Aunt Nhu asked.

"We've organized an escape," Dad said.

"We can't stay in Saigon," Uncle Houng said. It was his position to tell his wife. "They'll find us and send us back to the jungle or put us in prison. It's the only way."

"What about pirates?" Aunt Nhu asked. She braced herself, holding onto the arm of the chair. "What about the children? We could die."

"It's our only choice," Uncle Houng repeated. "We could

die if we stay here. We could have died already."

"Houng is right," Dad said, "it's the only way."

"How will we escape?" Aunt Nhu asked.

"A family in Nha Be has organized an escape," Dad replied. "We bought seats for you on their boat."

"How big is the boat?" Aunt Nhu asked. "I refuse to die in the ocean. That frightens me. And what about the children? They won't survive the trip." Dad was out of answers. We all knew the risks were great. We had all heard the stories of pirates and of boats sinking. If the officials caught them, we knew they would be sent to labor camps that were much worse than the New Economic Zone. Everyone was silent.

"I know we have to do it," Aunt Nhu conceded. "I'm just frightened. I'm frightened for the children." Aunt Nhu was a strong woman. She said she was frightened, but there was no fear in her eyes, only determination. She had survived the trip through the jungle, a trip that killed many people. They had foraged for leaves and fruit and snuck into farmers' bins and stolen rice. Their chances of making it across the ocean were about the same as their chances of making it back to Saigon had been, but they were already weak and there was only so much luck.

"We will go fishing in the morning," Dad said.

We were all quiet for a moment, and then Mom said, "We should get some sleep. It will be a short night." But it wasn't a short night; I lay awake until morning, scared to sleep. Visions of communists spun through my mind. Sometimes they were monsters, sometimes men with black painted faces. During the war, there were billboards showing the communists as wolves with babies in their mouths. A story book I had read depicted them as dragons. The anti-communist propaganda was not as bad as the communist propaganda, but it was still disturbing. The combination twisted my mind into a whirlwind of confusion.

The next morning we dropped Vi off at Nha Be and fished until late afternoon. When we got back to the wooden dock where we had left him, Vi was standing at the end with another man. We tied the boats to the dock, and Vi walked toward us. The man he was with looked like a peasant; he wore black cotton trousers and a loose gray shirt. The knees of his trousers were patched with gray flannel. "This is Mr. Nguyen," Vi said when they got to our boat.

"A pleasure to meet you, Mr. Nguyen," Dad said.

"We can't talk long," Mr. Nguyen said. "People will notice. Mr. Vi has the plan. We'll leave Monday morning."

"What should my brother bring?" Dad asked.

"We have everything," Mr. Nguyen said. "You just have to get to the boat. I know you must be worried—I'm worried myself. But we have a solid boat with a good engine. We've been taking it past the Coast Guard for three months now. They know we're fisherman and they haven't stopped us in the last month. Your money has helped us leave before we expected. The supplies and boat are ready—now all we need is luck."

Dad thanked Mr. Nguyen, Vi boarded our boat, and Quang started the engine. "It's a good plan," Vi said as the tow rope stretched and pulled us upstream. "We'll hide your brother and his family in our net boxes. We'll meet the big boat on a small stream south of Nha Be. If the Coast Guard doesn't stop them, everything should be fine." Vi was trying to ease Dad's mind.

There were many things that could go wrong, but Monday morning came and my sisters hadn't told their secret. Doan and Kim were nourished and even excited about moving to a new country. Uncle Houng told them they were going to California. Dinh was still sick. He had gained a little weight, but he was weak and his eyes watered constantly. Mom had bought some medicine for him, and every night before dinner she had prayed that he would get well.

We left before light. Uncle Houng and Doan waited under the Highway 1 bridge. Dad and I floated under, and they climbed into our net box. Aunt Nhu, Dinh, and Kim had stayed the night at Vi's. They would be hiding in the net box in Loc's boat. Only Loc, Vi's youngest son, would be going with us. Dad had talked Vi and Quang out of going. That way if we were caught, there would still be someone to take care of Vi's family.

We traveled in tandem down the river, trying to think of it as just another day fishing, but Loc had the engine wound a little tighter than normal. He was anxious to get it over with. As we passed the docks, communist soldiers stood watching us and my heart skipped. A Coast Guard boat was docked at Nha Be. *Probably looking for us*, I thought. Loc turned left into a small channel, and we went a few miles east.

The morning turned from black to gray. A cool mist covered the river, but you could still see a few hundred yards. Loc spotted a boat, and Dad moved toward the net box but didn't open it. The boat was anchored just off shore. It was about ten yards long, bright blue with a yellow stripe along the wooden stern. I could see a few faces peering out the window of the cabin.

We came within fifty yards, and Mr. Nguyen waved to us from the back deck. Loc guided us up to the boat and we both tied on. He opened his net box and helped Aunt Nhu, Kim, and Dinh climb aboard. We opened the net box and

Uncle Houng and Doan crawled out, wide eyed and stiff. There was no time for introductions. Doan climbed up, but Uncle Houng hesitated.

"Go," Dad said. "Write to us when you get to California."

Uncle Houng smiled nervously, and we boosted him up. Mr. Nguyen pushed them into the cabin as they stared back at us, their eyes still too big for their lean faces, their bodies and souls scarred by the communists. They were risking their lives to escape their own country, risking their lives for freedom, for a new beginning.

Grandma

In March, the mail service between North and South Vietnam was reinstated. Dad mailed a letter to his old address, never expecting to get a reply, but in early April we received a letter from his mother.

"My father is alive!" Dad cried after opening the letter. We crowded around him, and he read it aloud. His mother and father were still living in the Red River Delta. His older brother and his family lived with them now, and his sister had gotten married. I had never seen Dad so happy. A tear formed in the corner of his eye, but he wiped it off before anyone else noticed. "For twenty years, I have hoped they were alive," he said.

After Tet, there were many people in Saigon who received letters from long lost relatives. The government began a program to allow people from the North to visit their southern relatives. At dinner one night, Mom told us about a neighbor who had relatives visiting from the North. She said the northern relatives couldn't believe the high standard of living in the South. They wanted this and wanted that because they thought the people in the South owed them for giving our country independence.

Dad said the communists' propaganda in the North caused this by convincing people that the southerners were the main cause of their poverty. The communists said if it wasn't for the South trying to split the country and follow the Americans, there would have been no war and all of Vietnam would be prosperous. The communists believed the people in the North paid the price to teach us what was right and now we owed them for what we didn't want in the first place—communism.

I believed the stories about other people's relatives, but I knew Grandma couldn't be that way. Dad told me his family hated the communists, and Grandma's letter didn't say anything about how bad it was in the North or how good we must have it. Her letter said she was happy my father was okay and she hoped to see her grandchildren someday.

The first week of May, we received another letter. Dad's whole family was pitching in to send Grandma to see us. She would be coming from Hanoi in a government bus and was to be in Saigon by the end of the month.

Throughout this time, we worked hard to save money for the engine and to buy gifts for Grandma and Dad's family. Sometimes we fished three days at a time, put our catch in ice boxes to keep it fresh, and camped in the boats at night. We worked as a team with Vi and his sons. Most mornings, Vi took our catch to China Town and sold it to a Chinese man whom Dad had worked with during the war. The man bought our catch with dollars and gold so we didn't risk losing our savings if the communists changed the currency again.

Dad and I made one to two dollars for three days' work

and still had enough fish and prawns to give to the co-op. Dad never said how much money we had, but I tried to keep track, and by the last week in April I thought we should have enough saved for an engine.

It was during that same week in April that my sisters met us at the doorway as we got home from fishing. "Grandma's here!" they cried, "Grandma's here!" Dad hurried past them and I followed. Grandma rose from Dad's chair as we walked in.

She wore black trousers and a dark gray shirt that hung to her knees. This was the traditional ao dai dress that many women wore. Grandma's body was small and her skin dark and wrinkled, but her eyes sparkled like polished black jewels. Her white hair was wrapped in a circle on the back of her head. I was too old for her to kiss, so I bowed to her. "What a big boy," she said. "I thought you were only fifteen." In Vietnam, no one celebrates their own birthday. At the start of the new year, everyone is a year older, so I turned fifteen after Tet.

"It's an honor to meet you, Grandma," I said.

"And look at you," she said to Dad. "A grown man with a family now. You were Viet's age when I last saw you."

Dad nodded, "I have missed you, Mother."

"Enough of that," she said. "Did you have a good day fishing?"

"It was fine. How is Father?"

"He's fine. We're all fine."

"You must be exhausted from the trip."

"It was the easiest five days in twenty years," Grandma said. She called to Mom, who was starting the fire in the stove, "You have hungry mouths here. Better clean these fish while they're fresh." I had a basket in each hand, one filled with prawns and the other with snapper and bass. Grandma took them from me and said, "You wash and prepare yourself for dinner."

Before Dad could stop her, Grandma took the baskets to the sink and dumped them. She was amazed and confused at all the fish. "We can't eat all of this," she said.

"We have to give the catch to the co-op," Dad explained.

Mom looked up from the stove with no expression. "Viet, take the catch to Thanh. You can wash when you get back."

I scooped the fish back into one of the baskets and put all but three snapper and three bass in the other. Grandma's strong presence seemed to fade and she returned to Dad's chair. I hated taking the catch to Crippled Thanh. This time was like all the rest. He and his family, which consisted of two small boys and his wife, were in the pavilion sorting the grass for each family to use. Like always, Thanh was perched cross-legged on a wooden table, reining over his kingdom of grass baskets and mattresses.

I took the two baskets to him, and he looked down on me, waiting for me to open them and show what we caught. He responded his usual way. "I hope you can catch more next time or we will need to send Mr. Quoc with you." Mr. Quoc was Crippled Thanh's best spy, who claimed to have been a fisherman many years before. Dad had already told me not to worry, because Mr. Quoc was too old to fish.

Thanh pushed himself along the table and off the side. I followed him to the co-op shop next door. The building was a general store before the communists took over. It used to be painted bright blue, but Thanh painted it gray and took the sign down. Inside, the dusty shelves were sparsely stocked with bags of rice, cans of coffee, and dried fruit in clear plastic bags. There was a wooden ice box in the back left corner, and I walked directly to it and dumped the catch. Crippled Thanh stood at the counter watching me. "I hear you have a visitor," he said so abruptly I shook.

"My grandmother's visiting from the North."

"Can you tell me why your father did not fill out the proper papers?" Crippled Thanh limped around the counter holding a clipboard in his hand.

"I don't know. I don't think Father knows about the papers."

He limped by me to the cooler and started counting the fish. "Where did you catch the bass?" he asked.

"I'm not sure where we were. In a canal close to Nha Be."

"Out for three days again?"

"Yes."

"You should get home now. Tell your father I will call on him later about your visitor."

"Yes, Mr. Thanh." I bowed and hurried out the door.

When I arrived home, dinner was ready. Every piece of china we had was on the table. We even had spring rolls. Dad apologized to Grandma for not having more to eat, and Grandma said we all had more than enough.

Grandma didn't say much at dinner. I thought it must be strange for her to be with us—strange to see her son after so many years without seeing him change gradually, but instead, all at once. Grandma was a traditional woman. Like all the older people in Vietnam, especially those who never lived in Saigon, she believed strongly in the family order. She was used to the oldest man being the boss and the parents being in total control of their children. It was strange for her to see Dad married to someone she and Grandfather hadn't chosen. Our southern accents were sometimes hard for her to understand, and sometimes she corrected Mom's speech.

She even told Mom I needed a haircut.

After dinner, Vinh and my sisters studied, Mom gave Tu a bath, and Dad and Grandma sat on the back porch. I was going to the porch to listen to them when Crippled Thanh walked through our doorway. I had forgotten to tell Dad he was coming. "Where is your father?" he asked.

"He's on the back porch," I said, and Thanh followed me through the kitchen and out the back doorway. I knew Dad was irritated to see him, but his face didn't show it.

"I hear you have a visitor," Crippled Thanh said.

"Yes, my mother. She's visiting from the North."

"You have not registered her with me. You were supposed to tell me she was coming."

"I didn't know," Dad responded.

Before Dad could introduce him to Grandma, Crippled Thanh handed Dad the clipboard he was carrying. "Fill this out," he said. "Return it to me tonight. You could be in serious trouble for not filling this out ahead of time. I will not report you this time, but in the future, you will give prior notice when you have visitors." Thanh limped around the side of the house, first looking at our mopeds, then at the garden, and then adding a quick glance through our bedroom window. Finally, he disappeared around the corner.

"That man is rude," Dad said to Grandma. "He's the leader of our solidarity cell, and his position has gone to his head."

"You should have reported to him," she said, "then you wouldn't have had the trouble." Dad didn't reply, but I knew what he was thinking. The communists made new rules every day. Before, you only had to report if more than two people were visiting. He didn't know about the new rule, but he nodded to Grandma as though she were right, then asked about his father.

125

"Your father was kept in prison for three years. It was a very hard time but now it's over."

"How did you survive?"

"Your brother and his family moved in with me. Everything changed after you left. The communists took our whole farm. Eight families live there now, and we work the small field next to the house. We give our rice and poultry to the co-op, and they give us points for the work we do. Then we use the points to get food at the co-op shop."

"Did Yung have to fight in the war?" Dad asked, wondering if he might have fought against his brother.

"No, they said he was unfit to fight for our country. Instead, he had to work four extra hours a day to accumulate enough points to support a soldier."

"What about Minh Ha?" Dad asked. Minh Ha was Dad's sister, whom my youngest sister was named after.

"She was married shortly after your father returned. Her husband was wounded in the war. They gave him a medal and a management position in a co-op across the river." Dad's eyes sank to the ground, and Grandma seemed to sense Dad's feelings about his sister being married to a communist. "They give us the extra portions of food they get," she said. "We're lucky they're part of the system. Eventually, the only way to survive is to go along with the system. It's more powerful than you. And as you know, it will follow you wherever you go."

I knew it hurt Dad to hear her say this. He had always told me how strong his family was, how his father wouldn't give in to the communists. He didn't disagree with Grandma; he nodded, and stared at his feet. "All we have left is the family," she said. "The family is my only happiness. I hope someday we can all be together."

126

Black clouds hung over the city, ready to burst and begin dumping the evening rains. I followed Dad and Grandma inside. My brothers and sisters were already in bed, and Mom went to the bedroom as soon as we walked inside. "Your grandmother will sleep in your bed while she's here," Dad whispered to me.

They sat at the kitchen table, and I went to the hammock where I would sleep. I waited for Grandma to tell Dad that we should move to the North, but she didn't speak. A tense silence filled the air until they went into the bedroom.

The next morning, we all went to church. It was another rainy day, as the days would be until August or September. At nine o'clock we walked across the muddy road to the church. Mom had spent the morning fixing our breakfast and getting my sisters and Tu ready for church. By this time, she knew how to make them look good enough to be proud of, but not so good that our neighbors would suspect us of having too much.

Binh An Church was a white brick building. The windows were tinted a faded purple color and covered with black iron bars. It was the sturdiest building in the area, and during the war it was used as a bomb shelter. The main entrance was on the Highway 13 side, and a graveled path made a circle from the highway to the entrance. Wet bicycles and mopeds stood in the gravel path and leaned against the white brick walls.

"Hurry," Mom said as she pushed the girls in front of her. Dad carried Tu, and Grandma walked briskly beside him in her faded ao dai. Vinh and I walked in the back of the group.

Inside the church, the smell of rain-soaked cotton lingered along with a whisper of voices. Most people were still standing. I slid my feet along the slippery hardwood floor, between

127

the lines of people who stood along the ends of the pews. Dad introduced Grandma to people as we walked to our usual seat, the third pew on the left. Binh An was a big church, the biggest in northern Saigon, and people came from all over the city to hear Father Quyen's sermons. Church was the one thing that remained the same even after the communists took over. At least until this day.

We moved between the second and third pews, first Mom and Tu, then the girls, then Grandma, Dad, Vinh and me. Father Quyen had come to the wooden podium that was elevated three steps above us. He opened his Bible, and everyone took their seats. I looked across the rows to see if Phi was there, and to my right, across the aisle and four rows back, I saw Crippled Thanh. It was the first time I had seen him in church and he seemed out of place, sitting straight and proud in his black pajamas, alone at the end of a pew.

"It is a joy to see so many of you on this first rainy Sunday," Father Quyen said. His voice was not as powerful as it used to be—not that he spoke differently, not that his tone or volume was different, but just that his words seemed to come from his lips instead of his heart. I looked around at the faces and saw many eyes focused on Crippled Thanh.

"Before I start the sermon this morning," Father Quyen said, "I must tell you that services are canceled next week because of the Independence Day celebration. Those who live in district nine are to meet at the pavilion to prepare for the celebration. Those from other districts should consult your solidarity cell leaders about the activities in your area."

A low rumble of protest scattered the damp air. It ceased when Crippled Thanh looked around the room. Grandma's face was one of the few that didn't look puzzled. "They can't cancel church," Mom whispered to Dad.

"Today's sermon is on the value of the family," Father Quyen said, trying to move along with the service like nothing major had just happened, but his words felt empty. "I would like to talk about the value of family and its extension into the community."

Father Quyen had never used the word *I* before in his sermons. He had always used the word that meant *servant of God*, until today. For the first time, he seemed like a man, a normal man. He went on to say how we should respect our mothers and fathers and how important it is to love our neighbors. It was a simple sermon, similar to one Father Quyen's assistant priest might have given. It was short—only twenty minutes instead of an hour or more, about God being the creator and us owing our lives to him, working for the church, and studying hard to become good Christians.

When the sermon was finished, Father Quyen left through the back door instead of standing at the front to greet the congregation. Crippled Thanh stood at the front doorway instead, examining people's faces as they left. He seemed to be checking for dissent.

Everyone left the church silently, the same thought on their minds. Father Quyen used to be the leader of the community. He used to have the final word on all important matters. Church was God, and God was first, the family second, the community and country third. But everything changed that day. The state was now first—the communist state, led in our community by Crippled Thanh. The state would tolerate the family and God only as long as they didn't interfere with the state's activities.

For some time, the men had no longer congregated in circles outside the church. Groups of more than three would be questioned by Crippled Thanh. This was the communists' way of keeping people from organizing groups against the government. But this day, there were men circled around the assistant priest. Our friend At was the most vocal of the group. I couldn't hear what he was saying, but he gestured wildly with his hands, and I knew he was upset about church being canceled. Crippled Thanh glanced at him and made a note on his clipboard.

Tu cried, "I'm hungry," as we walked back across the muddy road, and my sisters asked in unison, "What's for lunch?" suspecting a treat because Grandma was there.

Mom didn't answer them. "Wipe your feet before you go in the house," she said.

When we got home, Grandma took Tu to the bedroom and put him in dry clothes. The rest of us changed, and Mom came to the bedroom to make sure we hung our clothes properly. "How can they cancel church?" I asked her.

"They can do whatever they please," was her reply, and she went to the kitchen. She was starting the fire and Dad was standing above her when the argument started. Their nerves were on edge already because of the situation at church, and Dad said we should have chicken for lunch instead of fish. In most situations, Dad was in charge and Mom wouldn't question him. But when it came to the children or the meals, Mom was usually in control. "We don't have enough to satisfy our children's hunger, and you want me to buy food to indulge your mother's tastes," she said.

It was unbelievable and unacceptable for Mom to say something like that, especially in front of Dad's mother. My sisters and Tu were still in the bedroom. Vinh and I looked at each other with amazement. Grandma got up from her chair and charged toward the kitchen. "How can you talk to your husband like that?" she asked. "Have you no respect?"

Mom was a little surprised at herself. She tried to pretend she hadn't spoken and fanned some air on the coals. I thought Mom was right to question Dad. It was not only a waste of money we didn't have, but it was also a risk, because if our neighbors smelled chicken cooking they would tell Crippled Thanh and he would be over to question us in a matter of minutes. But Mom had no choice. She was obligated to do as my Dad said and to respect Grandma. Mom cooled down instantly, but then Grandma added, "Sometimes the night is long, young lady." This was a common expression used to tell someone they needed to be stronger. It was an insult.

"Don't tell me the night is long," Mom said back to her. Vinh and I looked at each other. We couldn't believe what was happening. It seemed Mom had abandoned her principles and denied her place in the family. "Don't tell me the night is long when I've been through a thousand sleepless nights," she said. "I have children to care for."

"Be quiet, woman," Dad said. He never talked like that. I was shocked. He pointed, and Mom followed his command and went to the bedroom.

"That's what happens when a son doesn't marry the wife chosen by his parents," Grandma said. "You will return with me to the North."

Vinh and I looked at each other again. "Get to the market," Dad said to us. He handed us some money and told us to buy a fresh chicken and some fruit. We left without speaking.

"Is Dad going to leave us?" Vinh asked as we walked toward Highway 1. I knew to go to the market by Vi's house so no one would know us. I didn't want anyone we knew to see us and question our actions.

"He won't leave," I said, "but this is crazy."

"Why? Why is Mom acting that way?"

"Because Dad is going to give everything to Grandma." Mom had told me that Dad was giving Grandma our radio, a moped, and the money we saved for the engine. She told me because she thought I could talk to Dad. But there was no way. He was the head of the family, and even though I helped make the money, Dad was still in control. He felt guilty about leaving his family in the North, and it wasn't my place to question him.

"But Grandma told Dad he was going back with her. If he goes, will we all have to go?"

"Be quiet, Vinh," I said. I was always too blunt with him. "No one is going anywhere."

When we arrived home, Mom was in the kitchen. Her eyes were puffy. Anyone else would say she had shamed herself, but I knew she wasn't being selfish. She only cared about us and wanted the best for us. She spent more than an hour preparing lunch, which would have been normal before the communists took over, but since we moved to the new house it had been fish and rice most every day.

Grandma seemed to sit a little straighter at lunch that day. She had established her dominance. She felt she had set Mom in her proper place. Halfway through lunch she shocked me again. "I will give Viet a haircut after dinner," she said. I looked up from my bowl.

"Thank you," Mom said. "He needs one." I felt like I was the one who lost the battle that day. After lunch Grandma cut my hair in a bowl shape, so I looked like a little boy.

Grandma then took every opportunity to ridicule Mom's values. She condemned Uncle Houng for leaving his father in Vietnam, which I knew made Dad feel guilty about leaving his family in the North. "Doesn't he value his family?" she asked. Then she told Mom if she worked harder, I could be in school. "How can you sacrifice your son's education?" she asked. "That's the most important thing in a man's life. If he has no education, he will get no respect. You're no better than the communists if you don't value your family and respect your position in it. How can you live like this?" Mom kept her head low and didn't speak.

The rain fell all day. Mom and the girls wove, Vinh studied, and I kept Tu entertained by throwing coins against the wall and seeing how close I could make them lie. Dad went to Vi's for the afternoon but didn't say why he was going. Grandma sat in Dad's chair and stared out the window. It was a slow, damp, endless day.

That night when we had all gone to bed except Dad and Grandma, I lay on the hammock pretending to sleep. They sat at the kitchen table, whispering so Mom couldn't hear them from the bedroom. I listened.

"You can't remain with that woman," Grandma said. "She's no good. She doesn't act Vietnamese. She has no respect, and she has influenced the children, corrupted them. You deserve better."

"I'm not a boy," Dad said. "She is my wife, and these are my children. It's different in Saigon. You're right—we don't have the same values as people in the North, but that doesn't mean we're wrong."

"But the family—a person cannot exist without the family."

"I've lived without my family for twenty years, and I've survived and changed. I've learned there are possibilities for my children that don't exist in our country. Possibilities for a good life—a free life—like you and Father told me to find when you sent me from the North."

"But the communists will follow you wherever you go. They're too strong. They'll be everywhere. The world is changing, and the only hope for happiness is to keep the family together."

"I know I'm being selfish. I know I'm not the man you expected to find after all these years. But this is my family now. I want to give you what I can, but I must take care of my family too."

"Then the whole family will move to the North. I'll arrange it with the officials."

"You can't do that, and even if you could, my children wouldn't have a free life. The only way for them to have a free life is to leave Vietnam."

"Leave Vietnam!" Grandma shouted. Mom must have heard her. "You're going to leave the country! I'll never see you again. You can't go—you can't abandon your country."

"But for most of my life, my country has been South Vietnam," Dad said, "and South Vietnam no longer exists. I'm not abandoning my country; I'm escaping from the communists, who have stolen my country. Stolen my children's freedom."

Dad and Grandma were silent for a while. I had no idea Dad was still planning to leave Vietnam. All the time I thought we were saving for an engine, we were actually saving for our escape. I thought Vi must be a part of it. Mom didn't even know Dad's plan. She was upset that Dad was spending the engine money on herbs for Grandma.

"If you try to escape, your family could be killed," Grandma said. "And how will you pay for it? Where will you go? How will you survive in another country?"

Dad had answers for all her questions. "This is why I became a fisherman. We're able to save money for our escape, and we have a boat to take us to the ocean. I'm planning the trip with another family who has three boats. Working together, we can buy a boat capable of taking us across the ocean. We'll go to Singapore first. The United Nations has programs to help us resettle in the United States. Maybe California."

"California!" Grandma almost shouted. "Your head has gone crazy. You're dreaming, son. The Americans have twisted your head. Your place is in your country, and your country is Vietnam. Your family is in Vietnam."

"I don't want to leave you," Dad said. "I want you to come with us."

"No, that's out of the question. Your father will never go, and there's no way we could all get out of the country. You'll come to the North with me. We need to keep the family together." Grandma wouldn't budge. I rolled over and peeked out of one eye. She was sitting straight in her chair.

Dad's head hung low, ashamed. But he made one more attempt to make her see his side. "Twenty years ago, you sent me to find freedom. I didn't want to go, but you said this was what Father wanted. What would Father want me to do now? Has twenty years of communism changed him so much? Has he lost hope for freedom? Has he lost hope for his grandchildren?"

Dad had chosen the right words. Grandma took a deep breath, sat back in her chair, and closed her eyes. When she opened them she said, "Your father would want you to go."

Dad was silent. He didn't seem relieved to have Grandma agree with him. He seemed ashamed for persuading her. I was in shock. How could Dad keep this secret from us? But I knew why: because he couldn't risk one of us telling someone. But how could he be so strong as to keep it inside?

Dad blew out the lantern, and Grandma went to bed. The last thing I saw before going to sleep was Dad sitting in his chair, watching the sheets of rain falling from the roof. In six days it would be one year since the communists took over, one year since Dad used to come home in his police uniform, check the livestock, and throw the ball with me and Vinh. In that time we had lost our house, all of our livestock, our best furniture, our television, and almost everything we owned.

The next morning, Dad and I went fishing, and he told me he was going to give Grandma the money we had saved for the engine. "In the South, we have a better chance for a good life because the communists don't control us as much. But my family in the North has no hope of a good life without our help. This is why I have to give them all I can." I nodded, knowing anything I said wouldn't make a difference. "We can save more money," Dad said. "Grandma needs medicine for my father, and my brother's children need food. I have to help them every way I can."

"I understand," I said.

"I want you to know this because you help to make our money. Your mother doesn't understand now. She wants the best for you and your brothers and sisters. So do I, but we'll be fine. It seems like we're suffering because we used to have so much more, but we'll be fine." I nodded again, and nothing more was said.

We fished by ourselves that week and went home every evening so Dad could spend time with Grandma. On Sunday, April 30th, 1976, we all went to the pavilion to prepare for the Independence Day celebration. Everyone in our solidarity cell was there, thirty families and the assistant priests. Father Quyen didn't come.

Vinh and my sisters knew children from their classes and joined them in a circle on the floor in front of Crippled Thanh's table. He was standing on the table directing us all to sit down and listen to him. I found Phi, and we stood at the back of the crowd.

"I am happy to see you all here on this joyous occasion," Thanh said. "Today we celebrate one year of independence!" His family clapped their hands and everyone else followed. "As you can see, there are sheets of cardboard, wooden posts, and paint in each corner of the pavilion. Each of us will make a sign to carry in the Independence Day parade, which will go from the school to the district station. The children who are members of the Ho Chi Minh Youth Organization will help you with slogans to write on your signs. Please form lines to get your materials and return to your places."

Lines formed at each corner, and the Red Scarf Youths passed out the materials. Most of the children in our neighborhood were members, but I still hadn't participated enough to earn a scarf. There were many people there whom I hadn't seen before. New families moved into our area every week to replace the families who were sent to New Economic Zones. Phi had told me before that he thought it was only a matter of time before his family was sent away too.

We spent the morning making signs and learning communist songs, which we were to sing during the celebration. It was strange to watch my father sing, "Long live Uncle Ho, he is in our hearts and in our souls…." When we finished making the signs, we followed Crippled Thanh along the streets leading to the district station. We chanted the whole way, "Long live Uncle Ho, he is in our hearts and in our souls. Independence we have won, we'll build our country free and strong…."

The rain held off until we reached the district station, but then a heavy rain began to fall. The roadside gutters ran full of muddy water, and the wind whipped the palm trees above us. The parade continued slowly behind Crippled Thanh, around the circle in front of the district station, where the officials stood on the porch inspecting us and then joined the parade and led us back to the soccer field. We congregated in front of an army tent, and from the tent the officials made speeches to the rain-soaked crowd. Crippled Thanh introduced the speakers, who all talked about the same things. "My fellow comrades. This is a great day, marking the first anniversary of our independence…."

Cheers for Uncle Ho echoed through the crowd. Crippled Thanh looked around to see who was cheering the loudest. People competed to make the most noise and seem the most enthusiastic so they could possibly get an extra portion of rice or a toothbrush. One person would say to the next, "This a great day. I am so happy we have our independence." And the other person would say, "Uncle Ho was such a great man. He will live in my heart forever."

Some people had tears of joy in their eyes. I watched Dad say those things. He had to; there was no way to tell who the spies were. People would turn in their own relatives for an extra portion of rice. The communists were in complete control now. They controlled our food supply, and when people are hungry they will do anything or say anything for something to eat.

Red cotton flags with a yellow star in the middle waved in the gray mist. People held banners with portraits of Ho Chi Minh. "Long live the communist party," we chanted. Each new speaker was guaranteed an extended standing ovation. The officials stood in the tent with huge smiles. It was their day, their victory, not the people's victory, as they said in their speeches, but the communist party's victory. They soaked up the fake energy from the crowd, just like they soaked up our wealth.

The speeches ended around two o'clock. They told us the Ho Chi Minh Youth Band would be playing at the soccer field at seven and we were all invited to attend, which meant we had to be there. It was a relief to go home. Dad was exhausted and went to the bedroom to lie on his bed. Mom started dinner, and my brothers and sisters sat on the floor making fun of the whole day. "We love Uncle Ho," they sang. "He steals our money and burns our homes…."

Grandma shook her head and told Mom she shouldn't let the children act that way. "It's better to let them get it out of their systems here," Mom said. But it really was because she enjoyed the chants they made up that she didn't tell them to stop. It was the only release for her hatred of the system. Our only happiness was to make fun of the communists behind their backs, because when they were around all we could do was agree with them.

School was closed the next two days for the celebration, and we were not allowed to fish because we had to attend the events. On Tuesday, we walked with Grandma to the bus station and said goodbye. She hadn't said much since her talk with Dad. She even seemed to accept Mom and the fact that we were Dad's family now. But that didn't stop her from agreeing to take the gifts of all the money we had saved, one of our mopeds, our radio and Dad's watch. Now all we had was the house and each other, and with Crippled Thanh watching us I knew it could take a year to save enough money for an escape.

Tuesday night was the last night of the Independence

Day celebration. We all went to the soccer field behind the church for a play entitled *All Saints Day*. I sat with Phi toward the back of the audience, and halfway through the play Viet showed up. I hadn't seen him in a month. His hair was still long, and he was wearing a new gold necklace. "Where have you been?" Phi asked him.

"On a mission with my brother," Viet said. Then he whispered so only Phi and I could hear, "We killed a communist official." Phi and I looked at each other with disbelief and continued watching the play.

All Saints Day proved to be the most wretched attack on religion the communists had come up with. The play began with a communist cadre warning the people against having faith in something besides the state, and it ended with a priest attacking a woman in the confessional. At walked out before the play was over. I thought he was brave to take a stand, but I knew Dad would say he was putting his family at risk.

After the play, I walked with Phi and Viet to the Highway 13 bridge. It was a wooden bridge about ten yards long, and it was the best place to get away from the adults and out of the rain. Giant flat rocks had been piled underneath to keep it from washing out when the tide came in, and we sat on one of the rocks, listening to the rest of Viet's story about killing the communist official.

"We snuck into his house late in the night," he told us in a slow, mysterious voice. "My brother told me to watch the door, but I could see him creep to the bastard's bed. First he covered his head with a towel so he couldn't scream, and with one swift slice he cut his throat. We were out of the house and the village before anyone knew what happened." Phi and I looked at each other and smiled. It was hard not to believe Viet with his crazy eyes.

"I can't believe your father walked out of the play," I said to Phi. "I hope he doesn't get in trouble."

"That's all you worry about," Viet said, "getting in trouble. It's the communists who cause the trouble. If no one takes a stand, they'll do whatever they want."

"They'll do whatever they want anyway," I said. "The only way to beat them is to outsmart them."

"And you're the smart one, huh?" Viet and Phi both laughed.

"They had no right to cancel church," Phi said.

"They canceled church?" Viet asked. He never went to church anyway, but he acted like cancelling church was an offense against him.

"Then they made us watch that play about the priest attacking a girl in the confessional," Phi said. "I wonder what Father Quyen would have done if he were there."

"He would want you to do something about it," Viet said. "We can't let the communists get away with it."

"What can we do?" I asked.

"You're the smart one," Viet said. "You think of something."

I knew he was testing me, trying to make me feel inferior. We sat on the rock for a few minutes, and I tried to think of a plan. "There's extra paint at the pavilion," I said. "We could paint something on the co-op shop."

"That's a stupid idea," Viet said. "What good will that do?"

"It's not a bad idea," Phi said to Viet. "What do you want to do, kill Crippled Thanh?"

"I guess it's not a bad idea," Viet said. "Okay, smart one, what should we paint?"

"How about *Communism Is Hell*?" I suggested.

"That's not bad," Phi said. "Let's do it."

Viet smiled. "Not a bad idea at all. But we need to wait until everyone goes to sleep. Can you little boys get out of the house without your parents catching you?"

"I can," Phi said.

"I can," I said, even though I wasn't sure I wanted to go through with it.

"We'll meet here at twelve o'clock," Viet said. "Don't be late."

Viet curled off the rock and darted up the bank and out of sight. Phi and I looked at each other. "Are we really going to do it?" we both asked at the same time.

"I'll do it," Phi said. "We have to do something. No one else has the guts."

"I'll do it too," I said, and we snuck along the river bank to Phi's house, then I walked along the path to mine. Dad was the only one awake when I got home. He didn't ask where I had been, but he told me to get to bed because we were fishing with Vi in the morning. It was a hot, sticky night, so he believed me when I said I would be more comfortable sleeping in the hammock. When he went to bed, I took the wind-up clock from the kitchen and put it next to the hammock, then fought for two hours to keep my eyes open. At ten before twelve, I pulled on my trousers and snuck out the door. Viet and Phi were under the bridge when I got there.

"I didn't think you would come," Viet said. "Let's hear your plan, smart one."

I had no plan but made one up as quickly as possible so I could be the leader. "We'll sneak along the river bank to the pavilion. The paint is in the back left corner. I'll get the paint, and you two wait in the bushes. I'll get a brush for each of us. I'll paint *Communism* on the top. Phi, you can paint *Is* underneath, and Viet, you'll paint *Hell* under that. We'll be in and out of there in five minutes."

"Why do I have to paint *Hell*?" Viet complained.

"Because you're the smart one," I said. "Let's go."

We crept along the river bank and up to the pavilion. We waited in the bushes for a few minutes to make sure no one was around, then I crawled like a soldier to the back left corner of the pavilion. The paint was there. I grabbed a bucket and three brushes and scampered back to the bushes. My heart raced, but I tried to act calm. "I got them," I said. "Now be quiet so we don't wake Crippled Thanh."

Visions of Crippled Thanh catching us filled my mind. I could see him stringing us up, having all the neighbors come by to spit on us, and then burning us at the stake. We stayed low and crept along the side of the pavilion to the co-op shop.

"Where should we paint it?" Phi whispered.

"Be quiet. Follow me." I was in charge now.

We crept to the northeast side of the building, the side everyone passed to get to the pavilion. As we crawled under the window, the hinge creaked, and I froze. Phi bumped into me, and Viet bumped into him. "It's the wind," Viet whispered. I rose on the other side of the window, dipped my brush, handed the paint to Phi and began writing. I finished *Communism* before Phi handed the paint to Viet, and I ran back to the bushes. Phi finished Is and was halfway to the bushes when I heard the yell.

"What's going on here!" It was Crippled Thanh, limping along the side of the co-op shop with a lantern in one hand and a stick in the other. Viet dropped the bucket of paint, threw his brush at Crippled Thanh and ran the other direction. Crippled Thanh limped after him with the lantern flickering and his stick waving in the air.

"What do we do now, smart one?" Phi whispered.

My mind was spinning. "Get home before they come looking for us."

We darted out of the bushes and along the river. I didn't look back until I passed Phi's house, and then I saw him run in the back door. He made it. I kept running and made it to the hammock, pulled my trousers off and shut my eyes. My heart pounded. My muscles trembled. I could still see Crippled Thanh's angry face as he came around the side of the co-op shop. Thinking about the look on Viet's face almost made me smile. He had only finished *Hel* when he threw the brush at Thanh. But the message was clear, and I wondered if Crippled Thanh saw us and knew who we were.

Summer of Terror

Dad hurried me through breakfast while Mom packed three days worth of clothes for our fishing trip. We stepped out of the house and into the rain. It was a cold rain, the kind that makes your joints ache and your body shiver. I jumped over the puddle at the bottom of the porch and stopped. Across the street in front of Binh An Church, two gray vans were parked along the circled path. They were guarded on each side by four communist police officers.

"Look in front of the church," I said. As soon as Dad saw it, he grabbed my arm and pulled me into the house. We both watched from the east window.

"What are you looking at?" Mom asked as she walked from the kitchen, put her hand on my shoulder, and peeked around me. Before I could answer, the doors of Binh An Church flew open. Out stepped more officers carrying Father Houng Quyen. Two of the officers held his arms, and two others held his legs. His white cotton robe was pulled up, showing the bare flesh of his thighs.

"Let me go!" Father Quyen screamed.

"Shut up, old man!" an officer snapped back at him.

Father Quyen struggled as they carried him to the first van, then went limp with exhaustion. Two officers opened the back doors, tossed him in, and slammed the doors. The assistant priest stood at the doorway of the church, watching the officers as they climbed into the front of the van. I heard the engine turn over, then the grinding of the gears, and then the van jolted forward. My first thought was that Phi, Viet and I had caused the whole thing by painting the co-op shop. The officials must have thought Father Quyen put us up to it, and I thought they would be at our house to get me next. Mom and Dad looked at each other in shock. Again, there was nothing they could do.

"Let's go," Dad said to me. "We don't want to keep Vi waiting."

While we fished, I thought about telling Dad what I had done. I thought it might be best if I hid in the jungle south of the city. Dad could say he didn't know what had happened to me and bring me food when he came fishing. But I didn't tell him. I didn't have the courage.

After the first day of fishing, in the evening when we were sitting around the fire cooking our dinner, Dad told Vi what had happened to Father Quyen. He said Father Quyen had been on the communists' black list for some time, and they were after him because of his influence in the community. Dad said Father Quyen was probably taken because he didn't participate in the Independence Day celebrations. This gave me hope that Crippled Thanh didn't know I painted the co-op shop. All I could do was keep my mouth shut and wait. We had a good three days and made a record four dollars, but then a heavy storm hit, and we were stuck at home for two days.

The sky remained black, except when the lightning cracked. Thunder shook our house and the rain poured down. Mom, Dad and I wove baskets. Tu tried to weave. Vinh and my sisters went to school and wove when they got home. The first evening, Mom told us the story about someone painting the co-op shop. I fought to keep the fear out of my face when she asked if I knew anything about it. She told me Crippled Thanh said he knew who painted it. After dinner, I went to Phi's house, but he wasn't home, so I walked to the café. Viet and Phi were sitting at the back table.

"Look who it is," Viet said when I walked in. "It's the smart one." I smiled when I saw him, remembering how he had thrown the paint brush at Crippled Thanh. I sat with them, and Viet bought me a coffee and gave me a cigarette.

"Home because of the storm?" Phi asked.

"Yeah, I've been weaving baskets all day."

"I know how you feel," Phi said.

We drank our coffee and smoked cigarettes, then we headed for the Highway 13 bridge. We were walking along the North Road when Crippled Thanh spotted us, and before we could escape he waved us down. "What are you boys up to?" he asked as he hobbled toward us. He wore his usual black pajamas, which hung on his thin frame like drapes. "Do you not have anything productive to do?"

Viet didn't flinch as Crippled Thanh approached us. "We're not causing any trouble," he snapped.

"Who are you, boy?" Thanh snapped back at him.

"I'm Viet Quang Tranh."

"And what brings you to our neighborhood, boy?"

"These are my friends. We just went for a coffee."

"A coffee? And where do boys get money for coffee?"

"My brother gave it to me."

"You run along, boy," Thanh said to Viet, and we all started to walk away. "Not you two!" he shouted. "I'm not finished with you yet."

A lump formed in my throat. I tried not to shake, but it was useless. How could Crippled Thanh not know it was Viet who threw the paint brush at him? There were no other boys in our neighborhood with long hair like Viet. Thanh's bulging black eyes watched my shirt sleeve shiver. "Why do you shake, boy?" he asked. "Do you have something to hide?"

"No, Mr. Thanh, I'm cold from the rain."

"I thought you were a fisherman. I thought fishermen were used to being wet."

I shrugged my shoulders, and Thanh turned to Phi. "Your family has not met quota for three weeks. Is it because you are wasting time when you should be working?"

Phi was calm. "Yes, sir. I should be working. You're right, sir."

Crippled Thanh smiled for the first time. His teeth were large and yellow. "Then I will not catch you wasting time again. And you, Viet—this is not the first time I've seen you wasting time. Have you been doing your school assignments?"

I had gained my composure. "I haven't had any assignments, sir."

"Get home now," Thanh said. "I will deal with you later."

We scampered off, not looking back. "He's out to get us," Phi said before he turned at the road leading to his house.

"Do you think he knows we painted the co-op shop?" I asked.

"I don't know," Phi said. "If he knew, I think he would

have said something about it."

Phi walked toward the river, and I walked across the soccer field behind the church. When I got home, Dad was sitting in his chair, staring at the circular drive where we last saw Father Quyen. "Where have you been?" he asked.

"I was with Phi. I wanted to see what he knew about Father Quyen being taken."

"Does he know anything?"

"Nothing. No one knows why he was taken. It's terrible, isn't it, Dad?"

"It is terrible, and you should learn from what happened. You should learn to keep your head down and your mouth shut."

We wove the next day, and after dinner I went to the café again. Phi wasn't there, so Viet and I sat by ourselves. He told me stories about planning escapes for people, and stealing valuables from communist officials and selling them on the black market. I didn't believe him until he showed me the money he was carrying. He had as many dollars as he had piasters. There must have been twenty of them. Viet folded the bills in half and pushed them into the front pocket of his trousers. "You don't get money like this weaving baskets," he said, handing me a cigarette.

I was lighting the cigarette when I saw Dad walk into the café. I choked, coughed and dropped the cigarette under the table. Dad's eyes burned through me. He took four steps across the café, grabbed my arm and pulled me to my feet. "Are you having a good time?" he asked, squeezing my arm tighter. The woman who ran the café watched from the cash register. Viet said he had to go, slid from his chair, and darted out the door. "What have you done now?" Dad asked me.

"What are you talking about? I haven't done anything."

149

"Thanh just came to our house. He wants to see us. What have you done?"

Dad shook me until I answered, "I haven't done anything. I don't know what he wants."

My stomach turned and my neck stiffened. He let go of my arm and pushed me out of the café. "If you haven't done anything, why does he want to see us? Do you think he wants to give you a medal for smoking with that hoodlum?"

As we walked along the road to Thanh's house, I found the courage to tell Dad what I had done. "I painted the co-op shop."

He took a few steps before he realized what I was talking about, then he grabbed me by the shoulders and shook me again. "Dammit!" he shrieked. "You have killed us all. You've shamed our family and ruined us for good." I wanted to run—I knew he was right. He had told me many times not to cause trouble. I felt ashamed for doing such a stupid thing. There was no hope for us now. They would blame Dad for my actions, and we would be sent away. There would be no escape.

"I don't think Crippled Thanh knows," I pleaded. "He didn't see me. Phi and I hid in the bushes. I can deny it. There's no way he knows."

Dad erased the anger from his eyes and regained his composure. "I have been a failure," he said. "This is my fault for letting you have too much freedom. We'll have to pay the price."

We walked along the road to Crippled Thanh's house. The sky was clear. The moon was just above the palm trees that lined the road. Its yellow light reflected off the tin roof of the pavilion. We walked up to the house, and Dad called for Thanh. He came to the doorway, clipboard in hand. "We will sit outside," he said. "It's a beautiful evening."

Thanh was as calm as the night. There was no way he could think I painted the co-op. If he did, I knew he would have been screaming by now. Dad and I sat along the wooden bench, and Thanh pulled up a chair to face us. "We have a most important matter to discuss. I have met with the district cadre, and Viet's name was brought up along with some other boys in the area." I breathed easier, and my bones stopped shaking. "Their names were brought up because we feel they need more encouragement to become useful members of our new society." Dad even smiled at this point. I wished I hadn't told him I painted the co-op shop. "When Viet was allowed to quit school," Thanh continued, "the agreement was that he would study with Vinh and participate in community activities. Have you been doing this, Viet?"

They both stared at me, waiting for my answer. There was a long silence—long enough to make the hair rise on the back of my neck. "I - I helped with the Independence Day celebration," I said. Dad smiled with approval—he seemed relieved that I had said something after the long pause. Thanh was not so impressed.

"That is all you have done!" he shouted, surprising us. "What did you do today, boy?"

I looked at Dad, but he offered no assistance. "I wove baskets all day, finished four, and had a coffee with a friend."

"A coffee with a friend," Crippled Thanh smirked. "Did I not talk with you about that yesterday? Did I not tell you to stop wasting time?"

"Yes, sir," I said, before Dad could ask about Thanh's talk.

"Where did you meet this Viet?" Thanh asked. "And where does he get money to buy coffee?"

"He was in my class when I started school. I don't know

him well. I don't know where he gets the money."

"First, you are not to see this boy again," Thanh said. "He is not in our solidarity cell, so I have no authority over him, but you are not to see him. He is a hoodlum, a bad influence, and I will see that he is looked after." Thanh looked at Dad, and Dad nodded in agreement. I nodded and said I would not see Viet again.

"Second," Crippled Thanh snapped, "you will begin studying the political philosophy text that your brother Vinh has. Third, you will write weekly reports on what you have learned. What other things do you think you can do to improve yourself?" He had stumped me again. My head was empty now. What difference did my answer make? He was going to tell me what I had to do. I was silent. It was a long silence—too long for Dad.

"I will help Viet organize his activities," he said. "We'll do it tonight and give you a report tomorrow. Will this be okay, Mr. Thanh?"

"I want ten goals in writing tomorrow. I will trust your judgment this time. But this is your last chance. If you fail, there will be consequences." I felt like an animal that Thanh was training. I had no say in my life, and if I didn't follow his rules he would not only punish me, he would punish my whole family.

"I take full responsibility," Dad said. "I'm sorry for not being a better father. There is no excuse for my actions. Thank you for helping us, Mr. Thanh. We will give you our report tomorrow." Crippled Thanh smiled widely. I felt guilty because Dad had shamed himself to give me another chance. I told myself I would stay out of trouble, but I didn't think it was fair that I couldn't see Viet.

"Then I will see you tomorrow," he said. He stood up,

leaned on his cane, and hobbled to the edge of the porch. "A beautiful night, isn't it?"

"Yes," Dad said, "it's a beautiful night."

When we got home, the whole family was lined up by the doorway to examine the family criminal. I stared at Vinh until he returned to the table to study. The girls sensed my anger and went to the bedroom. "What happened?" Mom asked.

"Everything is okay," Dad said. "In the future, Viet will stay home unless we're fishing. We're lucky this time." Dad told Vinh to go to bed, and we sat at the table writing my goals to improve myself. *First, I will not see Viet. Second, I will work harder with the family. Third, I will study political philosophy and outline what I learn. Fourth, I will attend Mr. Thanh's meetings every Wednesday. Fifth, I will go to school when I have extra time. Sixth, I will help the Ho Chi Minh Youth....*

I had to include an apology for my previous actions and say it was because of my greed that I had put myself above the other members of our new society. Dad made me use communist words and phrases he had learned in his reeducation. He said I must learn to convince them I believed in their new society, and at the same time keep enough pride to believe in myself. I felt strange writing those things. For my whole life, Dad had taught me not to lie and now he was helping me do so. It seemed to bring us closer together, and I began to realize that my Dad was a real person, a person who felt fear and suppression, and that he would do anything to free our family. Mom gave my report to Crippled Thanh the next day. Dad and I were gone three days to fish and returned Wednesday evening in time for the weekly meeting.

The meeting was held at the pavilion. All the adults in

our solidarity cell were there. Crippled Thanh began by lecturing people who hadn't met their quotas and praising those who had surpassed them. Then he read a story about a communist hero who had sacrificed his life for our equality. Everyone had to write a summary about the story, and then Thanh asked if anyone had questions about improving themselves and the community.

"I have a question!" Phi's father, At, yelled from the back row. He stood up and stared right into Crippled Thanh's eyes. "I want to know why Father Quyen was taken away."

Thanh glared at him angrily. "You know I have no control in this matter. But if you wish to make more trouble, you can direct your question to the district officials!" A military officer stepped from the darkness surrounding the pavilion. Four soldiers stepped behind him. Crippled Thanh must have expected questions about Father Quyen, and now he would use At as an example.

The officer was short and stocky. As he stepped into the light, I recognized him. He was the man who had shot the thief on the bridge. I remembered how his beady black eyes twinkled before he pulled the trigger. I felt a shiver as I remembered the sound of the thief's body when it fell to the bridge. The officer's cold eyes were now fixed on At's face. "Is there a question?" he asked.

At's eyes sank to the ground then rose fiercely. "You have taken our priest. You have stolen our leader!"

"Mr. Thanh is your leader now!" The officer took a step toward At. I thought I felt the ground shake. "It is your failure to recognize this that got your priest taken away. He disrupted the advancement of our new society." The officer took another step toward At and raised his fist. "Disruptions will not be tolerated!"

I thought At should be quiet; he was in enough trouble already. All eyes in the pavilion focused on him. He took a deep breath and shouted, "Bring our father back! He has done no harm!"

The district official nodded to his soldiers and they moved toward At. The people cleared out of their way, and At turned and ran out of the pavilion. But At was no running match for the soldiers. They caught him, tackled him to the ground, pulled his arms behind his back, and carried him the way the soldiers had carried Father Quyen.

At screamed, "Murderers! Murderers!" They dropped him to the ground and gagged him. Mrs. At ran after them. The head officer swung his rifle, and I saw the wooden part hit her face. Her head jolted back and she fell to her knees. Then they carried At into the darkness as Mrs. At crawled toward them, sobbing.

"This meeting is adjourned!" Crippled Thanh shouted, and people scattered to their homes.

Dad and I helped Mrs. At to her feet. Blood ran from her swollen cheek. "They can't take my husband," she cried. "Don't let them take my husband!" We walked her back to our house because Dad said her children shouldn't see her in so much pain. Mom cleaned her face and covered the wound with a white bandage, but there was nothing Dad could say to stop her sobbing. At was gone.

The next day Dad and I went fishing. He was more motivated now than ever to save money, but he still said nothing of his escape plans. We fished for four days but caught little because the rains kept the prawns out of the shallow waters. When we returned home, Mom was sitting with Mrs. At on the front porch. Mrs. At's whole face was swollen, and tears filled her eyes.

"At is dead!" Mom exclaimed as we approached the porch.

Dad stopped at the steps and leaned against the rail. I sat on the steps below him, and a heavy silence lingered. "They won't let us bury him," Mrs. At cried. She covered her face and her huge body shook.

"She went to identify his body," Mom said, "and they made her sign a document that said he committed suicide."

Mrs. At looked up. "They killed him! I saw his face. I felt his ribs. They said they would take my children if I didn't sign their papers." Mom moved to Mrs. At and put her arm around her shoulders. "The children," Mrs. At cried. "What will I do with the children? How will we survive?"

"You will be fine," Mom whispered, trying to calm her.

"Do the children know?" Dad asked.

"Yes," Mom said. "The little ones are inside. Phi is at home."

"Get the catch to Thanh," Dad told me, "and stop at Phi's on your way back. Tell him his family is having dinner with us tonight."

When I got to Phi's house, I called for him from the front doorway. He didn't answer, so I walked in. He was stretched out in the hammock, not moving. I could sense he knew I was there, and I sat on the floor beside him.

"I'm sorry about your father."

Phi didn't answer, probably because he couldn't without crying and didn't want to seem weak. He was the head of his family now. I sat for a few minutes before he looked at me. When he did, his eyes were wide with fear. His hair hung below his eyebrows. It was long enough to make him look young—too young to be so afraid. "Is my mother okay?" he asked.

"She's fine. My mom is making dinner. My dad told me to have you come to our house."

"I'm not hungry. I want to be alone."

I left Phi sitting in the hammock with his hands over his face. As I got to the porch, I turned to go back inside and talk to him some more, but then I stopped again at the doorway. There wasn't a sound in the house, not a breeze through the curtains. The air stood still. It would be Phi's last moment of solitude for some time. I left him with it and returned home.

By the end of the evening, Mrs. At had calmed down, and she and the children went home. The next time I saw Phi was a few days later during At's memorial. Only our family and At's relatives were there, except for two men in black pajamas who stood at the back of the church. I guessed they were spies for the district station, there to make sure no revenge was planned against the state. At the last weekly meeting, Crippled Thanh had declared At an evil force against the people. Our neighbors, some who had been At's friends for years, had condemned his name and boycotted his funeral. During the service, I noticed Phi looked different. His face was troubled, and his hair was cut above his small pointed ears. When he looked at me, his stare was empty. There was no joy, no laughter. The few good memories we shared seemed to have faded from his mind. Only worry remained.

After the service, I saw Phi only when I passed his house on the way to the co-op shop. He would be sitting on his porch weaving, smiling when I approached him. He would ask me about fishing, and I would sit with him for a few minutes, watching him weave the grass into rows and tie the corners. Then I would carry the catch to Crippled Thanh, and another fishing trip would be completed.

My life had changed too. When I wasn't fishing, I wove baskets or studied political philosophy and wrote reports. The political philosophy text was a series of stories about communist heroes who had either killed a large number of American invaders or set up co-operatives in jungle villages. I read the stories, then outlined them in my reports, describing how I longed to be like the communist heroes who killed the people who fought for my freedom. Dad made me attend school every few weeks. In the morning, the whole school met on the soccer field for calisthenics, led by the new children from the North. Then there was an hour of listening to the political philosophy teacher.

"We are the roots of equality," he would say, "and we must learn to become the new socialist men of the future. We must practice what we learn, and we must set an example for the world to follow."

History class was next. It wasn't the history of Vietnam but of communism, beginning with Karl Marx, then Stalin, then Chairman Mao, then Ho Chi Minh. We learned how the spirit of our people brought the evil Americans and their war machines to their knees, and how the North won the war because communism is the right path to equality. We read Vietnam's new Declaration of Independence, which began, "All men are created equal; they are endowed by their Creator with certain inalienable rights; among these are Life, Liberty and the Pursuit of Happiness…." Our teacher said these words were written by Ho Chi Minh.

The studies were easy because the children from the North kept the pace slow. I don't know if they weren't intelligent because many of the teachers in the North were killed in the war, or if it was because their minds had been closed by so many years of communism. When I wasn't fishing, weaving, writing reports or in school, I had to help the Red Scarfs pick up trash.

It was early September when our new priest announced Father Quyen's death. By this time, few people were attending Mass. The main attraction at our church had been Father Quyen. His sermons on nonviolence had helped people to cope with the communist suppression, but the new priest seemed afraid to address the problems of living under the communists, so people no longer came.

The new priest said Father Quyen had died of malaria and his body had been cremated. A delegation, including my father, went to Crippled Thanh and asked if they could build a monument in Father Quyen's name, but Thanh refused them. Father Quyen had been declared an enemy of the people. We were allowed a small ceremony, guarded by the district officials, and Father Quyen was erased from Vietnamese history like everything else the communists condemned.

After At's and Father Quyen's deaths, I became more frightened. Since the communists had taken over two of the people I knew who had openly stood up against them had already been killed. Father Quyen was killed because he was a powerful man in Saigon. He was a role model for many people, and the communists were afraid of his power. He had never openly condemned them, but he never supported them either. Dad said Father Quyen didn't support the communists because they limited people's freedom to worship God. He preached and practiced passive resistance to evil. He said in his sermons that we should turn the other cheek, but when he turned the other cheek the communists killed him.

At was the opposite. He had little power and no followers.

But At spoke out against the communists, and even though he could do little harm, the communists considered him a bad seed. Because one bad seed can spoil the crop, the communists killed him too.

Another person I knew who was against the communists was my father. He was still alive because he took a slower, more subtle approach, not letting the communists discover his contempt for them. He pretended to support their efforts, and at the same time he planned to escape. But I thought my father's approach was too slow—the communists were becoming stronger each day. Stories about fishermen escaping the country circulated around the city. This prompted the Coast Guard to tighten their grip on the channels south of Nha Be. We didn't have the papers to fish in the southern channels anymore, so we had to stay north, where the prawns weren't as big or as plentiful. Each day I watched the hope fade from my father's eyes. I wanted to ask him about his escape plan but I couldn't. I couldn't tell him I had listened to his talk with Grandma.

But I felt like I had to do something. I knew we had to get out of the country. Life in Vietnam seemed hopeless, and from what I had seen it would be only a matter of time before the communist officials discovered my father's contempt. I thought they would kill him too or they would send us all to a New Economic Zone. At night I lay in bed trying to think of a way to make more money. I dreamed of being at the wheel of a giant boat, sailing across the sea, taking my family to freedom. But how could I make that kind of money? Who did I know who could help me? My thoughts led me to the only person I knew who wanted to rebel against the communists and could actually help me—Viet.

Viet always had money. He always seemed to get what

he wanted. He remained inconspicuous, unaffected by the communists. If anyone knew how I could make a lot of money in a short period of time, it was Viet.

Every day that I was home, Mom would send me to the post office. Many people had received letters from relatives who had escaped, and Mom kept hoping we would receive one from Uncle Houng. I was on my way to the post office when I saw Viet for the first time in months. He was strolling up Highway 13, wearing bell bottom blue jeans and a red silk shirt, puffing on a cigarette, his long hair blowing in the wind. I motioned for him to follow me into the bushes so no one would see us talking.

"Well, if it isn't the new socialist boy," Viet said to me. "Where's your red scarf?"

"Shut up, Viet," I said.

"I saw you picking up trash with the Red Scarfs last week. Are you spying on your parents now?"

"You know I help them only because I have to."

"You should only do what you want to." Viet smiled at me, knowing I was embarrassed. "I can't believe you switched sides."

"I haven't switched sides. I'm just trying to stay unnoticed until I can get out of this country."

"What do you mean?" Viet was interested now.

"I'm going to help my family escape. I need you to help me."

"Why should I help you?"

"Because you'll do anything against the communists."

"What are you talking about?" Viet looked at me like I was joking.

"The only way to beat the communists," I said, "is to get out of this country and organize an army against them."

"You're crazy. What's happened to your head?"

"I have to get out of here." My voice was desperate. "I *am* crazy. This place and these people are driving me mad. I need to make some money, and you're the only one who can help me."

"But why should I help you?" Viet asked again. "What's in it for me?"

There was nothing in it for him. I had nothing to give him. "I don't know. I thought you could help me, but I guess you're like the rest of the people around here. The communists control you too."

"They don't control me!" Viet snapped. "But it takes hundreds of dollars to escape. There's only one way to make that kind of money."

"Just tell me how. I'll do anything."

Viet smiled. His smile made me nervous. "Meet me here tomorrow," he said.

"I can't tomorrow. I'm going fishing."

"Then when can you meet me?"

"Thursday. I'm supposed to help the Red Scarfs, but I'll meet you here instead." Viet wouldn't tell me what I would have to do. He just said to meet him at nine o'clock.

The next day, I went fishing with Dad. The rice fields had turned from bright green to gold and were now filled with thousands of workers, chopping and bundling the stalks. The jungles crawled with life, and fish jumped and splashed. We caught enough prawns to save two dollars, but I knew at this pace it could take us a year to save enough money for an escape. On Thursday morning I rode my bike to the spot where I was to meet Viet. He was there when I arrived.

"Look at this," he said, holding out a gold watch and some jewelry.

"Where did you get it?" I asked.

"You let me worry about that. Your job is to sell it." My stomach jumped. I thought we would be selling rice for his brother, not stolen jewelry.

We rode along a path through the woods so my parents wouldn't see me, then we took Highway 1 into the city. Viet said we were going to China Town. That was the only place where people had money to buy expensive jewelry. It was a long journey, down Ben Bach Dang Street to the Saigon Pier, then west along Am Nigh Street to the central market. A mile before the Presidential Palace we turned south, and I followed Viet through narrow aisles between food stands, pushcarts, and old ladies sitting on blankets covered with merchandise.

We came to the streets of China Town, which ran south from the central market. They were lined with Chinese restaurants, tailor shops and fish markets. Booths were set up along the sidewalks, and freshly killed chickens and sides of bacon hung from their rafters. There was a low rumble of haggling over prices, butchers slamming their mallets onto cutting boards, clanking chains of bicycles and the pop-pop sound of two-stroke moped engines. Viet and I wove through a swarm of people until he stopped at a corner restaurant.

I couldn't read the Chinese letters on the front of the restaurant, but I could read the poster on an electric pole in front of it. "Curfew in effect September 1st," it read. The fine print said anyone caught on the streets during business hours would be checked for documents from their solidarity cell leaders. Anyone without the proper documents would be prosecuted. I pointed to the poster, and Viet chuckled. "It's just a communist scare tactic," he said. "The communists have more to worry about than prosecuting two boys."

"Yeah, like thieves selling stolen jewelry," I said.

Viet laughed. "Look at this," he said, holding out his arms to the crowd. "Does it look like there's a curfew around here?" It didn't. It looked the same as a few years before. Pushcarts lined the streets. People were selling everything from bananas to calculators. China Town was like a separate city from Saigon. The communists didn't control it yet, but we would soon find out they were beginning to. I followed Viet into the restaurant, and he bought us lunch. I watched greedily as he pulled out his money and flipped through the green dollars to pay our bill. Then we walked along the crowded street, and he explained what I was to do.

"This watch is worth a thousand dollars," he said, holding it in front of me. "It's a Rolex, solid gold. Look at the diamonds by the numbers." It was a beautiful watch, glittering in the afternoon sun. "All I want is two hundred dollars. The gold is worth that much. You keep whatever more you can get." I wondered what kind of person would have that much money.

"It's better if you work alone," Viet said. "People get suspicious if too many people are involved." We stood on the corner, outside the restaurant, and he handed me the watch. "I'll stand back and keep an eye on you. Just stay on this corner and wait for wealthy looking Chinese men to walk by. Don't say anything to them. Just hold the watch where they can see it. If they want it, they'll motion for you to follow them out of the crowd. Don't go too far with them. Just step into the alley so I can still see you."

My heart pounded as Viet walked away, and my chest tightened so much it was hard to breathe. Two wealthy looking men were walking up the street toward me. I cupped the watch in my left hand and held it in front of them. "How much?" One of the men asked.

"Two hundred fifty."

"Piasters?" the man asked.

"Dollars." The men chuckled and walked on. After a few more attempts, Viet motioned for me to follow him, and we went to another part of China Town. "There's no way we can sell it," I said. "No one has that much money."

"Sure they do," Viet said. "There are men around here who have a million dollars. We just need to find the right one."

Viet left me standing on another corner to try again. It was late afternoon when the right man finally came along. He was dressed in a black suit and a white silk shirt. It was unbuttoned at the collar, and I could see thick gold chains hanging from his neck. "Two hundred fifty?" the man asked. "Let me take a look at it."

I walked into the alley, and the man followed me. I handed him the watch, then looked to make sure Viet could still see me. Viet was waving his arms frantically. "Get the watch!" he shouted. "Get the watch and get out of here!"

I heard someone scream, "Police!" and everyone started scrambling. When I turned back, the man was running into the crowded street. He still had the watch! I acted on instinct and ran after him, tackling him from behind. People swarmed above us. I was on top of him, trying to roll him over and pry the watch out of his hand. I felt a thud across the middle of my back, and then a hand grabbed my wrist and wrenched my arm behind me. I was pulled to my feet.

My eyes focused and I saw people running in all directions. Communist soldiers were tackling people and dragging them to gray vans parked in the middle of the street. I couldn't see who had me, but I was being dragged too. The man with the watch was running through the crowd, and Viet ran after him. I was thrown into a van with about twenty others, then the door slammed shut and left us in the dark. The engine strained and the van jolted forward. I tried to stop my mind from spinning so I could think of an excuse for being in China Town, but before I could, the van stopped and the doors were flung open.

"Everyone out!" the guards shouted, and people moved slowly onto a wooden loading dock. The sun's white glare filled my eyes until I rubbed the darkness of the van out of them. We were surrounded by a concrete wall about five yards high. "Move it!" the guards shouted.

They marched us across the dock and into a building, through a large office filled with communist police, and down a narrow hallway to the end cell, which was already half full of people. They packed so many of us into the cell that there was no room to sit down. I leaned against the cold concrete wall next to the cell door. The place smelled of sweat and urine. People argued about what would happen to us next. One man said it was his third arrest. He said they would check our papers, take our valuables, and let us go. I reached into my pocket, looking for the papers I knew I didn't have, wishing I had picked up trash with the Red Scarfs and let Dad worry about making money.

We had been there for a half hour when the cell door flew open. A guard in a khaki uniform grabbed me by the collar and pulled me into the hall, then he grabbed four other men and marched us to the office. Some of the officers who arrested us were standing in a circle laughing. The guard motioned for us to sit down on a wooden bench, and I maneuvered into the middle, thinking I wouldn't have to go first. An officer sat at the desk in front of us, war medals hanging from the left pocket of his uniform. A thin beard grew around his tight lips. His black eyes moved from one side of their sockets to the other as he examined each of us, then came back to the middle and stared straight through me.

"Get up, boy," he said. I stood up and walked to the front of his desk. "Empty your pockets." I pulled my pockets out to show him they were already empty. "Where are your papers?"

"I am only fifteen," I said. "I don't have papers."

"Then why aren't you in school?"

"I need to help my family fish."

"Then why aren't you fishing!" he shouted. "You should have papers to fish! Where is your home?"

"Binh An."

"Why were you in the market? Why are you so far from home?"

I had thought of my excuse. "I needed bearings for my bike."

"Then why don't you have money? You are lying!" He stood up and shouted over his desk. "Tell me what you were doing in China Town!"

"I - I must have lost my money when they dragged me to the van."

"Sit down. We will deal with you later."

I sat on the bench and watched the other four men go to the desk, one by one, and dump their money out of their pockets. Each time, the officer smiled and scraped their money into his top desk drawer. The officer had them each sign a form, then he let them go. When he was finished with them, he called me back to his desk. "I will give you one more chance. What were you doing in the market?"

"I was looking for bike parts."

"You are lying! Take him back," he said to the guard.

"His cadre will deal with him."

I spent the rest of the day waiting, watching the door, praying for the guard to tell me I could go, praying that Dad wouldn't find out what had happened, and praying that the officer wouldn't contact Crippled Thanh. Almost everyone had been let go when the door flew open and the guard pointed toward me. My skin crawled as he led me into the office. I could hear Dad's voice. He was apologizing for me again. I walked into the office with my head down, and when I looked up, Dad glared at me. The officer made me sign some papers, confessing to my crime of breaking the curfew, and he let me go. Dad didn't speak to me until we were out of the station.

"This time you are in serious trouble," he said as we walked down the steps in front of the station. I didn't say anything. My throat was too tight to speak. I knew Viet must have told him to come looking for me, so Dad knew I had disobeyed him again. When we got to the bottom of the steps, he asked where my bike was, but I still couldn't answer.

"Did you lose your bike?" I nodded. "You lost your bike, and now I have to pay for your bus fare home." My chin sank to my chest. "Look at me! You have shamed yourself enough."

I looked up with watery eyes. "I thought it would be okay to see Viet away from the neighborhood," I said. "I didn't know this would happen."

"Of course you didn't know," Dad gritted his teeth. His eyes were more sad than angry. "But if you had obeyed me, you wouldn't be in trouble."

"I'm sorry Dad. I will never do it again."

"It's too late to be sorry," Dad said, and I knew he was right.

Arrested

Dad and I went fishing the morning after my arrest. When we returned Sunday evening, Mom had some bad news. Crippled Thanh had come to our house, and I was to be at the district station Monday morning. I didn't know what to expect. Crippled Thanh didn't say what the meeting was about. He didn't say he knew I was arrested, but I sensed that serious trouble was on its way.

Monday morning, Mom made breakfast, and the whole family stared at me while I ate. Dad's eyes looked the same as when Uncle Houng was taken—helpless, hopeless. Mom hugged me and mumbled a small prayer before I left. I took the short-cut and walked across the field that led to the road the district station was on. At the end of the road, in the middle of the circle drive, a red flag with a yellow star in the middle flapped in the wind. On the left side of the circle drive, a rock wall surrounded the station. The black cast iron gates were open. I walked through them, along the sidewalk and up the stairs. A small gray-haired man sat at the desk inside the doorway. I told him who I was, and he directed me down the hall to room 12.

As I walked to the room, the only sound was the squeak of my sandals on the tile floor. Room 12 was the last room on the left. I knocked softly on the door, but there was no answer, so I opened the door and peeked inside. The room was empty except for a long foldout table and some metal chairs. Iron bars ran across the open window, and a clock hung on the white plaster wall. I sat in the chair at the end of the table and waited. It was ten o'clock when the door opened and Crippled Thanh walked into the room. Another man walked in behind him and shut the door. I lowered my eyes to show respect.

"So this is Viet Nguyen," the man said. I didn't look up. Thanh sat on my left, and the other man on my right. "My name is Minh Van Loc," he said as he put a folder on the table. "I have been reading your reports for the past three months."

I glanced up and saw his full cheeks and dark serious eyes. A black beard grew around his mouth, making him look like a well fed copy of Ho Chi Minh. He wore black pajamas like Crippled Thanh, except his were of thicker cotton. Thanh put his clipboard and pencil on the table, and Mr. Loc cleared his throat. "Do you know why you are here?"

I shrugged my shoulders. Thanh looked at me with disgust. "Is it because of my reports?" I asked.

"That is one of the reasons," Mr. Loc said. "The smallest reason." My stomach jumped. "Is there anything you have done that we should know about?" he asked.

The question seemed to float into my mind from a distant place. They shouldn't know about my arrest, I thought. They shouldn't know about me painting the co-op, and they shouldn't know how much I hate them. There was nothing about me that they should have known. I took too long to answer.

"Tell us what you did," Crippled Thanh said. "You will not be punished if you tell us the truth."

My mind raced. Was he telling me the truth? Or was he tricking me so I would confess? "I have done nothing wrong."

"You are lying!" Crippled Thanh shouted. Mr. Loc glared at him, and Thanh looked away from me.

"Let us start over," Mr. Loc said. "Let us begin with your reports." He pulled the top report off the pile and glanced over it. "You said in your first report that you would spend one hour each evening studying political philosophy with your brother. Have you been doing this?"

"Yes."

"Tell me what you have learned."

My mind was blank. Even if I had been studying every night, I would have been too nervous to answer. I tried to think of what Dad would say. "I have been studying with Vinh every night, but it is hard for me to understand everything because Vinh is not a skilled teacher."

"Then you should have gone to school," Thanh snapped.

Mr. Loc glared at him again. "Your reports have shown improvement throughout the past two months. This tells me you are learning what is expected of a good member of society. But your actions do not represent your understanding. Your actions represent the selfishness of the American capitalists."

I tried to look ashamed. Mr. Loc leaned over the table, lecturing as close to my face as possible. He seemed to be trying to force his words into my brain. "A member of our society must move forward with the other members, not alone. If you attempt to stand still as the wheel of society

171

moves forward, you will be crushed."

There was a long pause, and Mr. Loc sat back in his chair. They both stared at me, waiting for me to defend myself. "I want to be a good member of society," I said, "but I am not always sure what to do."

"Do you think we are blind!" Thanh snapped. This time Mr. Loc let him continue. "Do you think you can trick us? We know what you have done. We know you were arrested. We know you vandalized the co-op shop. You think you are clever, but we know. Your reports are full of lies."

My stomach tied itself into a knot. My face went numb. They knew everything.

"Let us begin with the co-op shop," Mr. Loc said. "Is it true that you painted the co-op?"

I still didn't know if they knew or if they were trying to trick me into confessing. I wondered if they had talked to Phi and Viet. I wondered if one of them had confessed. "I didn't paint the co-op," I said.

"You are lying!" Crippled Thanh jumped to his feet, and his chair hit the wall behind him. He had forgotten about his weak leg and he almost toppled over the table.

"We know you painted the co-op," Mr. Loc said. "Lying will only get you in more trouble. Now admit what you have done so we can get on with this."

"Say it!" Thanh shouted. He leaned over the table. His eyes pierced through me. "Say what you have done."

I shook my head to answer no. Mr. Loc leaned toward me. They were both within inches of my face. "Should we involve your parents?" Mr. Loc asked.

They moved away from me and watched my expression. I couldn't stop shaking. I imagined my father walking into the room, the look of disappointment on his face. My throat was tight, but I squeezed the words through. "I did it. I painted it."

"And who were you with?" Crippled Thanh asked.

"I was alone."

"You lie again," he said. "You are not worth our time."

"We know who you were with," Mr. Loc said. "They have already confessed. They did not hesitate to include your name in the crime." I didn't want to believe him. I could believe that Viet would tell, but not Phi. He would never tell.

"This leads us to the black market incident," Mr. Loc said. "Why were you in China Town?"

"I was looking for bicycle bearings."

"Lying again," Thanh snapped. "This boy is a waste of our time."

"Tell us why you were in the market," Mr. Loc commanded.

"I am telling you the truth," I said.

"We already know the truth," he said. "Now we want you to tell us."

I wondered if Viet had told them I painted the co-op and I decided he had. "I was with Viet." I had gotten myself in deeper. Crippled Thanh sat down, looking at me with interest and wide open eyes. I don't think they knew I was with Viet until I told them. I should have stuck to my story.

"Why was Viet there?" Crippled Thanh asked.

"He didn't have anything else to do."

"You are lying again, boy. We know what you were doing. Now tell us!"

This time I called their bluff, "I was looking for bicycle parts."

Mr. Loc and Thanh looked at each other. Mr. Loc nodded and said, "Take him home. Get his clothes. Inform his parents of his crimes against the people."

Crippled Thanh grabbed my arm and pulled me to my feet. He was smaller than I was, but I didn't resist. He led me out of the station and told me to sit on the back of his moped, then he zoomed out of the gate. When we turned onto our road, I saw Mom sitting on the front porch weaving a basket. Her jaw dropped when she saw us. She put the basket next to her, stood up and walked quickly inside. By the time Thanh rode across our yard and up to the porch, Dad was standing in the doorway and Mom was standing behind him. I wanted to run, but I didn't know where to go. I still didn't know what would happen. I didn't think the communists would kill me, but the thought crossed my mind. Thanh held my arm as we walked up the stairs and onto the porch.

"Your son has been charged with crimes against the people," he told Dad. He pulled a piece of paper from his pocket and held it so we couldn't read what it said. "Viet Quoc Nguyen is hereby charged under the criminal act issued in 1968, by the Vietnamese Communist Party, to serve two years reeducation."

Tears fell from Mom's eyes. Dad held out his hand for the paper, but Thanh put it back in his pocket. "What is he charged with?" Dad asked.

"I am acting under the authority of the district station. If you have questions, you can direct them to the district officials."

Dad wouldn't look at me. There was nothing he could do. There was no way for him to help me. Mom was pushing him from behind, trying to break through. "You cannot take my son!" she cried. "He has done nothing wrong."

"Control that woman," Crippled Thanh said. "Have her get Viet some clothes and food if she wants to help him."

Mom disappeared from the doorway. Thanh swung me around and tied my hands with a piece of leather. Tu came to the doorway in time to watch his big brother being tied up. Mom came back with a bag full of clothes and food. She hugged me until Dad pried her away. Crippled Thanh pointed toward the moped. I got on the back, and he zoomed us out of the yard. Tu held onto Mom's leg and waved as we rode out of sight. Dad didn't look up.

We rode for fifteen minutes west on Highway 1, then turned north and traveled another ten minutes to the jail. It was a huge compound, used to hold communist spies and terrorists during the war. I thought they must have interrogated the communists there, trying to turn them into capitalists. Now the table was turned, and they would try to turn me into a communist.

Barbed wire curled on top of the concrete wall surrounding the prison. Guard towers stood at each corner with black machine guns mounted and ready to fire. Crippled Thanh rode up to the gate and showed the guards his papers, and they directed us into the compound. Inside the wall was a courtyard, big enough to accommodate ten trucks lined up side by side and five hundred or so prisoners. Two concrete buildings with three-inch wide slits for windows stood side by side, stretching about fifty yards ahead of us.

Thanh led me into the west building, and I stood in the front office while he filled out the papers. Two guards came into the office, frisked me, went through my bags, checked my head for lice, and untied my wrists. Thanh finished the paperwork, and the guards led me down a long empty hallway. When we came to the third door on the right, they opened it and pushed me inside. A hot stench of ammonia hit my face. The air was a mixture of sweat, smoke, and urine. It burned through my nose and into my lungs. The rumble of a hundred voices vibrated in my ears.

The metal door slammed behind me, and the lock clanked above the voices. The cell was dimly lit by a few light bulbs hanging from the ceiling. Dusty beams of light shot through the slits in the outside walls. Men stretched along the floor, others leaned against the walls. It was hard to tell how big the cell was because the smoke distorted my vision. I squeezed and twisted through the men, taking small breaths, trying to filter the foul air with my lips. No one moved to let me sit down, so I tried to squeeze between two men.

"The new men sit by the toilet," one said. I felt like an animal in a cage. I tripped over a man's leg, fell on top of someone and was pushed onto the floor.

"Get up, boy. Get away from me."

I was pushed around until I found my feet and stumbled toward the toilets. There was no more room around the toilets than anywhere else. I stood gazing around for a place to sit.

"Viet," I heard. It was a familiar voice. My name never sounded so sweet. "Viet."

The voice came from behind me, and when I turned around to look, I saw Phi and Viet sitting cross-legged under the haze. Phi was waving his arms. Viet was withdrawn like a captured animal. I twisted through the bodies, and Phi moved to give me a place to sit.

"Did you bring anything to eat?" they asked at the same time. I handed them my bag, and they devoured the dried pork and rice cakes. The men sitting around us looked at me with greedy eyes. I was ready to offer them the food when Viet tied the bag and put it between his legs.

"Don't be stupid," he said. "We'll need this."

"How long have you been here?" I asked.

"Two days," Phi said. "Crippled Thanh arrested us. He knew we painted the co-op."

"They took Phi and me the same day," Viet said. "They tried to make us confess, but I lied the whole time. I would have killed those bastards if I'd had the chance."

"Did you put up a fight?"

"Of course I did. I was in the café when Crippled Thanh came to get me. As soon as he told me to follow him, I kicked him and ran out. I would have gotten away, but he brought soldiers with him. I hit them a few times, but they pinned me down and tied my hands."

"Where do you think they'll take us?" I asked.

"No one knows," Phi said. "I just hope they take us soon. No place could be worse than this."

For the rest of the day, we talked about our arrest and questioned each other to see who confessed. I decided neither of them had said anything about me that I wouldn't have been tricked into saying about them. Being in jail seemed to make Phi a little bolder and Viet a little calmer.

As the day progressed, the beams of light that shone through the slatted windows grew dimmer. My body cramped. People started to maneuver around for space to sleep. The three of us pushed out at the same time, and then curled on our sides. We lay like hogs in a pile. My sweat mixed with the urine on the floor. It soaked my clothes until they stuck to my skin and burned like acid. We lay like that for fifteen minutes, and then we sat up. It was a long night of bone-aching, sticky, hot ten-minute naps.

It seemed like days until the gray morning light beamed through the slats. The door clanked open, and a guard called for volunteers to get breakfast. Three men who were close to the door got up with stiff legs, hobbled out, and returned later with five gallon buckets of boiled flour cakes. I was nauseated from breathing the rotten air, but when the bucket passed me, I grabbed one of the cakes and forced it down. After breakfast, a few men had to carry the toilets to be dumped. The noise in the cell steadily increased and the light through the window turned from gray to yellow to white.

It was mid-afternoon when the door opened again. The cell went quiet as the guard stepped in. He held a few sheets of paper in his hands, and he said for everyone whose name was called to get their things and line up in the corridor. As he called the names, people started wagering who would be called next. Packs of cigarettes, tiny morsels of food, watches and necklaces changed hands as the people were called. I didn't know where the men would be taken but I prayed my name would be called next. In fifteen minutes, when a quarter of the room was emptied, the door slammed shut without any of the three of us being called. Viet said we would be there until the room filled up again and they had to let more people go.

Thoughts of terror flew through my mind. What if they forget I'm here, and I never get out of the sewer? What if they leave me here until the urine rots my bones? People maneuvered for new territory, and we spread out as much as we could. I was able to lay back against my bag and fell into a daze, trying to pretend I was already dead and nothing mattered anymore. I was almost asleep when I heard the rumble of truck engines through the slats. The room fell quiet as we all sat up to listen. Men crowded around the slats, and those who could see through announced what was happening in the courtyard.

"There are four trucks. They're lining up the men in the courtyard. There are women out there!"

In minutes, the cell door opened and a guard stepped in. "The following people report to the corridor."

The list went on until Phi and Viet were called, one after the other. They both smiled and walked for the door. My stomach sank; I was alone again. But the list went on, and in another ten minutes, when the room was almost empty, my name was called. I couldn't wait to get outside and take a deep breath, to see the sun, and to stretch my legs. I found Phi and Viet in the hall and squeezed between them before the guard could put me in my proper place. The guards marched us outside and told us to sit in lines on the dusty ground. There must have been two hundred men sitting in rows, and twenty guards lined up in front of us. The women had already been loaded on one of the trucks, and we could see their eyes peeking through the slats in the back doors.

A man with medals on the chest of his khaki uniform stood in the center of the guards. He held his hands up for silence and began to speak. "You are being transferred to a camp where you will be taught to become better men, better citizens of our new society. You now have a chance to learn, a chance to become an asset instead of a burden to your fellow men. Work hard, study hard, do not let your country down."

The guards loaded us, line by line, into the trucks. I felt like an animal being taken off to slaughter. I sat against the metal wall of the trailer, the doors slammed shut, the engines roared, and the trucks jolted forward. As we traveled, the people in the back told the rest of us where we were going. "There's Hang Xanh Market. We're going onto the M1. We're heading north. We must be going to Vinh An."

The man sitting next to me said his brother was in Vinh An, and he had visited him a few times. People began asking him questions. "How big is the camp? What kind of work will we do? Are there women? Do they feed us?"

The man said he never saw the camp because it was back in the jungle and they kept the visitors in a pavilion next to the road. He said his brother was fed two times a day, but it was never enough. His brother became very thin, and the main reason he visited was to bring food.

The truck bounced along the highway for a few hours, then it slowed down and turned onto a dirt road. The people in the back said we were going through the jungle, and the man sitting next to me said we would be there in less than an hour. I pulled the last four pieces of fruit from my bag, gave one to Phi, one to Viet, and one to the man sitting next to me. He was an older man, not wealthy looking, but with a look of intelligence. I thought he would be a good person to know, so I introduced myself as I handed him the fruit.

"My name is Doan," he said, and he asked why I was arrested. After I told him about painting the co-op and being arrested in the black market, he said he was also arrested in the market. "I had to deal goods in the market to make enough money to take food to my brother," he said. "With both of us in prison, there will be no one to bring us food."

"What is the camp like?" I asked. "What will they do to us?"

"My brother works twelve-hour days, clearing the jungle and planting crops," he said. "The only way to survive is to get food from your family."

The truck came to a halt, and the doors swung open. People jumped out, and we moved toward the door. There were guards in blue uniforms pointing their rifles at us and telling us to sit in lines on the grass. Doan pointed toward a grass pavilion on the edge of the trees and said it was where he visited his brother.

There were about forty women in the front row, and most of the men were staring at them. Some of the women looked tougher than the men, and they stared back at us with hard, tanned faces. The road and the pavilion were the only signs of civilization. The rest was jungle. Two of the guards talked with the truck drivers and exchanged papers. The other guards strutted around, telling us to straighten our lines. When the guards finished their paperwork, they came back and ordered us to get up. The two with the papers told the women in the first line to follow them and headed into the jungle. Phi and Viet and I were in the second line and followed them in single file.

"Move it!" the guards ordered. "Keep close!" Some fired rifles into the air, while others used the butts of their rifles to knock people forward. We walked single file along the path, huge mosquitoes buzzing around our heads. Every few seconds, one zoomed down to take a chunk from my arm. We could hear monkeys howling and birds singing. The guards kept shooting and cursing.

We had walked for almost an hour when a woman stepped out of line and squatted down beside the path to relieve herself. As I walked past her, I heard one of the guards scream at her, and when I turned around, I saw him swing his rifle. The butt of the rifle caught her in the jaw, and she flew into a bush with her pants still down. About twenty of us stopped and watched as she crawled to her feet, pulled up her pants and stumbled back to the line. The side of her face was covered with blood. "Walk, you bastards!" the guard screamed. "What are you looking at?" Then he fired a shot into the air.

We walked for another hour, and the jungle opened into

Vinh An. A river, orange from the sun's reflection, circled around the far edge of seasoned grass buildings and disappeared into a dark green jungle. As we walked, I thought there must have been more than a hundred buildings, most of them set up in squares with courtyards in the middle. Lines of people in black pajamas moved around the camp with hoes, rakes and bundles of grass on their shoulders.

The path led us into the west side of the camp. To the right were two rows of barracks, framed with bamboo and sided with mud and grass. The river ran alongside the barracks, then there was a sand bank and more dense jungle. To the left was a grassy area the size of four soccer fields, then more barracks as far as I could see. On the opposite end of the field were a stage and two grass buildings on each side. I never dreamed the place would be so big.

Lines of men and lines of women were walking from the jungle into the camp, filling up the courtyards. The men's heads were shaven, and I could see red blotches on some of their scalps. The guards led us across the grassy area and told us to line up facing the stage. I counted heads and estimated there were more than two hundred of us. A man and a woman in blue uniforms walked out of a hut on the corner of the field. I could tell by the way they strutted onto the platform that they were the leaders. One of the guards walked up to the man and handed him some papers, and the rest circled around us. The two leaders held their hands high for silence, then the man began to speak into a microphone.

"I am Thounh Van Nguyen," he said. "I am here to guide you through your reeducation. At home, you were charged with two years, but you will be released when you prove you are ready to function as a productive member of society. Some of you will be here for six months. Others will be here much longer." I thought to myself, this will be like our goals in the wastelands. They'll let us go when they feel like it.

"This is not only a place to work," Mr. Nguyen continued, "it is also a place to learn. You must first learn the importance of labor, then you will learn self-criticism and self-motivation."

He stepped back, and the woman stepped forward. "My name is Lan Su San," she said. "I will be in charge of the women's company. It will be hard work for all of us to reach the goals that Mr. Nguyen has told you about. Right now you are a burden to your families, your communities and our society. But you are lucky. You have been provided with food, this camp, the tools you will work with, and your clothes. Our first step is to make ourselves independent. The next step will be to make ourselves useful to society."

The woman stepped back, and Mr. Nguyen told the guards to issue our supplies. We followed them to a warehouse behind the stage and next to the river. We were each given two pairs of black pajamas, a hat and mattress—both made of grass—a mosquito net and a blanket. The sun was below the horizon by the time we got everything. The women were taken away, and the guards took us farther into the camp. We walked by a kitchen, and I could smell cooked fish. I hoped they were taking us to eat, but they led us past the kitchen, past two rice bins and along the river to the third set of barracks.

They told us to form sixteen lines facing the water. Viet counted sixteen rooms and told Phi and me to get in the same line with him. We sat in the courtyard for a few minutes until Mr. Nguyen came out of a small building next to the east barracks. Sixteen men in black pajamas followed him. They marched in front of us like soldiers and when they were even with our lines they did a military turn so they faced us.

"The line you are in now will be your squad for the time you are here," Mr. Nguyen said. He walked up and down the lines, examining us. "The men in front of you are from the Young Men's Voluntary Scheme. They have accomplished the steps of labor, self-criticism and self-motivation. They will be your cadres."

I could still smell the fish cooking, and my stomach growled so loud that Viet turned around and smiled at me. Mr. Nguyen saw him turn around, and he stopped in the line next to us, staring at Viet for a few seconds. Then he continued around the front end of the line.

"These men are here to help you achieve these goals," Mr. Nguyen said as he walked up our line toward us. "They will live with you, work with you, and be responsible for your progress." Now he was right in front of Viet, and he stopped. "They will also report to me when you are not progressing with your goals." He stared at Viet. "If this is your case, we have other ways to educate you."

I held my eyes low but I could see Mr. Nguyen's feet moving toward me. I could sense his eyes staring through the top of my head. I didn't look up until he took another step forward, and as soon as I did, he stopped. I was frozen. I could feel him staring at me, and everyone was silent. There was no sound until my stomach growled again—a long, slow rumble that could probably be heard for a few yards.

"Look at me, boy," he said. I looked up to the bottom of his face. "Are you hungry, boy?"

I didn't think I heard him right. I sat for a moment, thinking I was in a dream. "Yes," I said. A few words of agreement swept through the rows of men.

"I need two volunteers from each squad to go with the

cadres for dinner."

We all volunteered, and Viet and I were chosen from our squad. We followed the cadres behind the barracks and along the river to the kitchen. The smell of boiled rice and fish grew stronger, and my mouth began to water. We walked beside the rice bins and lined up behind some men from other companies who were getting food for their squads. They were thinner than the other men I had seen. They moved slowly. Viet asked one of them if the work was hard, and the man looked away without answering.

When we got into the kitchen, I noticed that the cooks looked healthier than everyone else. A cadre told Viet to follow him to get the bowls, and I stood in line, watching guards strut through the kitchen, pick chunks of fish out of the pots, and shove them into their mouths. "How many in your squad?" the cook snapped at me when it was my turn. I told him eleven counting our cadre. He scooped rice into a large bowl and handed it to me. I stood there for a moment, thinking he would give us some fish. He looked at me with hard, serious eyes. "Is there a problem, boy?"

I said no and started to walk away. The cooks and guards laughed at me. "Come here, boy," another cook said. I walked to him, and he threw a whole fish on top of the rice. "Now get out of here."

The fish the cook gave me was smaller than what I would normally eat myself in one meal, and now I had to go back to the barracks and share it with ten people. On the way back, we saw more men walking through the camp with hoes and shovels on their shoulders. They looked like walking zombies. Some were so thin I couldn't believe they were walking at all. I wondered how long before I would look like them.

The sky was dark when we got back to the barracks, but there were torches lit at each corner. Guard towers were set up every couple hundred yards around the camp, and their spotlights searched through the trees and along the river bank. I thought they must have been searching for people who were trying to escape, but I didn't think escape would be possible. We were surrounded by a thick dangerous jungle. It would take days to walk to the nearest village, and weeks to walk to Saigon.

When we put the food down at the front of the squad, the men circled around us and grabbed bowls. There was no order. The biggest men pushed their way to the food and filled their bowls. The fish was gone after five men tore at it, and the ones who didn't get any argued with the ones who did. The cadres watched us argue but didn't say anything. When we finished eating, they told us to get back in our lines. Mr. Nguyen came to the front of the squads.

"For the last fifteen minutes, I have watched you display the greed that put you here!" he said. "Fighting to get more than the person next to you, comparing how much each of you took from the bowl, and not being satisfied unless you took more than someone else. This is not the right attitude of a person in a socialist society! There can be no jealousy, no envy, no greed! I can see you have much to learn."

I thought about the guards in the kitchen who were stuffing their faces with fish, and I thought how Mr. Nguyen looked much fuller and healthier than the prisoners. The cadres were lined up beside Mr. Nguyen. He held his hand toward them and said, "These men have volunteered to help you. They have given part of their lives to make your lives worthwhile. Listen to them, and learn from them. You are dismissed."

Our cadre led us to the room in the right corner of the barracks closest to the river. It was about five yards wide and ten yards long, with a table and chair inside the doorway to the left, and a cot against the far wall. To the right were two bamboo platforms raised above the dirt floor, with an aisle down the middle. A rope ran along the end of each platform, and there were hooks on the wall to hang our mosquito nets. There were no windows.

The cadre told us to lay out our mattresses and blankets, and Viet threw his on the spot next to the door. Phi took the spot next to Viet, and I took the one next to Phi. On the other side of me was a boy about my age. I noticed right away how pale he looked, and I thought he must have been sick. Next to him was an older man who hadn't said a word since we arrived. Across the aisle, on the other platform, was a huge man with a pitted face, a man with a shaved head next to him, and three men that Viet said were drug addicts because they were thin and their eyes were red and glassy.

When we finished laying out our blankets and tying up our mosquito nets, we sat on the edge of our beds, waiting to see what would happen next. The cadre sat on his desk and motioned for us to gather around him. Viet, Phi and I sat on the side of Viet's mattress, the big man sat on the corner of his space, and the others slid down so we formed a half circle around the cadre.

"My name is Binh," he said, rising from his desk to stand in front of us. He was a young man with a boyish face and round wire rimmed glasses. His hair was shaved around the sides and longer on the top, making him look like a young army officer. He had a small, solid frame, and his alert eyes darted around, looking at us each individually as he spoke. "I will be your cadre for the time you are here. First, I want you all to introduce yourselves. Tell us how old you are, where you are from, and the events leading up to your being brought here."

Everyone looked at each other, wondering who would start, then Binh told Viet to go first. "My name is Viet Quang Tranh," he said. "I'm seventeen years old." Phi and I looked at each other with surprise. I thought Viet was just a year older than me. "I'm from the Binh An area in Saigon, but I don't know why they sent me here."

There was a long silence before Binh told Phi to go next. "My name is Phi. I'm sixteen years old and I'm also from the Binh An area in Saigon."

"Did you know Viet before?" Binh asked. Viet was shaking his head no, as Phi said yes. "Were you arrested together?" Phi looked at Viet, then they both said yes. "What were you arrested for?"

"We don't know," Viet said before Phi could answer. "One minute I was having a coffee, and the next minute I was sitting in jail." Binh looked confused, then told me to go next.

"My name is Viet Quoc Nguyen. I'm fifteen years old and I'm also from Binh An."

"Were you arrested with Viet and Phi?" Binh asked.

"I knew them before, but we weren't arrested together."

"Why were you arrested?"

"I was arrested in a market." Binh nodded and wrote something on his clipboard. I thought he would say that Viet and Phi and I would be separated, but he didn't. He looked up at the boy next to me and told him to introduce himself.

"My name is Danh Vu Minh," the boy said with a small, weak voice. He was wearing black trousers and a white, button up shirt. He looked like a schoolboy. "I'm sixteen years old and I'm from downtown Saigon. I was arrested in a market when I went to get food for my family." Binh nodded, made a note, and looked up at the quiet man.

"I am Dan Cu Nguyen," he said, slowly. His legs were crossed, and I could see holes in the bottom of his sandals. "I am around forty-five years old. I was living in a New Economic Zone north of Saigon, but my family was starving so I went back to the city. I was looking for a job in the market when I was arrested."

Binh made another note, then looked up at Dan with concern in his eyes. "If you work and study hard, you will be with your family in a little time," he said. Dan bowed his head and stared at the floor.

Now we were to the first of the three red-eyed men, the smallest and best dressed. He wore black bell bottom trousers and a blue silk shirt. Two faded gold chains hung from his neck. Viet had told me before that they were fake. "My name is Qui," he said. "I'm from Saigon and I used to be a soldier for the South's army. I guess that's why they arrested me."

The second man had a gold tooth that reflected the lantern light. The rest of his teeth were black. He was thin, and his hands trembled as he spoke. "My name is Loc. My story is the same as Qui's."

The third had hair to his shoulders, a dragon tattooed on his left forearm and a serpent on his right. He had crazy eyes; they were bloodshot, but they were powerful. He looked to be the toughest of the three—in fact, the toughest of the whole squad. "My name is Tu," he said in a raspy voice. "Same story."

Binh nodded, made a note and looked up at the man with the shaved head. "My name is Cu Tan Dzu." He spoke slowly, with the authority of a priest. "I'm from Tay Ninh. I was arrested in Saigon because I didn't have travel papers."

Binh looked at the man with the pitted face. "I am Manh," he said with a kind, deep voice. His skin was as black as his peasant's trousers. "My friends call me Big Manh. I was a fisherman south of Nha Be. I was arrested selling prawns in the market."

"It seems as if everyone knows why they are here," Binh said. His eyes twitched around the room. He seemed to be searching for someone to agree with him. When no one did, he turned to his desk and picked up a piece of paper. "These are the rules of the camp. In a few days, you will all be given a number. At night, if you need to leave the barracks to relieve yourself, you will stand by the door, state your name and number, and say where you are going. When you return, you will state your name and number again, and you will say what you are returning from doing. Are there any questions about this?"

There were no questions. Binh read silently for a moment, and continued, "Until further notice, you are not allowed to speak to or gesture to anyone outside our company. You will not leave the company barracks by yourself for the next few weeks, and after that, you will get permission from me first. If you disobey these rules, you will be accused of attempting escape, and you will be put into the discipline company."

He looked up again and asked if there were any questions. Viet raised his hand. "What happens in the discipline company?"

"If you would like to know," Binh said, "I can arrange for you to be transferred immediately." Viet was silent and lowered his eyes to the floor. Binh smiled, then continued with a stronger voice. "At no time are you allowed to talk with people from the discipline company. You will see them walking to the river. You will know who they are because their heads will be completely shaved. If they gesture toward you, ignore them, or join them."

We all smiled nervously. Binh looked at each of us. I thought he was trying to guess who would be the first man sent to discipline. "I am sure you noticed there are women in this camp," he went on. "You will eventually be allowed to meet them, but at no time will there be inappropriate physical contact. Failure to comply with this rule will result in you being sent to the discipline company. Are there any questions about the rules?" No one had questions. Some of the men had been in the cell for almost a week, with very little sleep, and we were all ready to curl up in our blankets and get some rest, but Binh wasn't finished.

"We will spend the next few weeks learning the procedures of the camp and restoring our barracks. I will give you instructions to follow for our daily activities. On Sundays, you will be given time to wash clothes and clean the barracks. Every night, when our labor is completed, we will have a meeting to discuss our progress. In the next week, I will teach you the procedures of these meetings, and you will learn the basics of self-criticism and self-motivation."

A bell rang three times, and Binh said it was the nine o'clock bell. "Curfew time. No one is allowed to leave except to use the latrine. Remember to state your name and why you are leaving."

We could hear people singing in the other barracks, and Binh listened for a moment. "They are singing the Vinh An theme song," he said and started singing with a squeaky high voice. When it was over, he told us we would need to learn it for the camp meeting on Monday. He sang it line by line, and we had to repeat after him.

"Vinh An is our new land. In this land we will grow. In this land we will stand, until everybody knows…." It went on to say what a wonderful place Vinh An was and how fortunate we were to be given a second chance to prove ourselves worthy. I thought it was foolish, but we sang along until we learned it word for word.

When Binh was satisfied, he applauded us. "You have accomplished your first goal. Now let us sleep. We have a big day tomorrow."

We hung our mosquito nets and he blew out the lamp. I lay back in my space, listening to the Vinh An theme song echo around the company. I wondered if I would ever get out of the camp and what I would be like when I did. Would they turn me into a communist? Would they brainwash me? I was frightened and confused. I was afraid the communists were going to fill up my mind with something I didn't want to be.

After hearing the rules, I felt isolated. I was glad to be out of the cell, but I still felt trapped because I couldn't go anywhere without permission. I couldn't even go to the toilet without asking first, like a dog that has to stand at the door and bark.

Two years would be a long time. I would be seventeen when they let me out, if they did. I thought my life would be wasted; it wouldn't be worth living if it wasn't mine. I would just be existing. But why? Why would I keep living? I asked God why he let the communists win the war. He didn't answer, and I told myself God didn't exist, then cursed Him for letting this happen to me. I forced my mind to go blank, then filled it with dreams of faraway places. For the rest of the night, I was free.

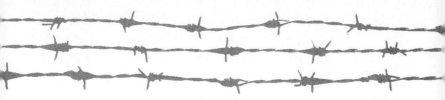

Vinh An

The bell rang. I opened my eyes and saw Binh, black pajamas on, a red band tied tightly around his bicep, eyes alert and hair slicked back. "Everybody up!" he screamed. Moans and yawns circled the barracks. The lantern on Binh's desk flickered dim, yellow light. I stretched my arms and rolled from under the net. "Get your uniforms on. You have a half hour for a bath and the latrine."

We staggered out of the barracks. The stars were fading, and the moon was setting over the trees on the far side of the river. Slumped-over bodies in black pajamas moved across the courtyard and around the east barracks to the latrine. Spotlights still searched through the trees. The line for the latrine was fifty men long, so Phi and I walked to the bamboo platform that floated on the river. I splashed some water on my face, and my eyes jolted open, then I used my finger to brush three days of scum off my teeth, and we walked back to the barracks. Big Manh had given Viet a cigarette, and he shared it with us. The rest of the men came back to the barracks, and we sat on the platform until a bell rang.

Binh stuck his head through the doorway. "Line up in the courtyard," he said, then darted outside, and we staggered behind him. "Come on, men, move it! You look like tired old ladies. Motivation! Self- motivation!" He jogged circles around us then headed for the far side of the courtyard. "Let's go, line up behind me. Move it! Move it!"

We all shuffled into line. Mr. Nguyen was standing in front of the company, his legs wide apart, hands on his hips, chin in the air. The cadres stood in front of the squads, and one by one they stepped forward. "Squad number 1, all present, Squad number 2, all present…." They went down the line, and everyone was there.

"We will begin this morning and every morning with exercises to clear our minds," Mr. Nguyen said. Before he could continue, three shots rang out from up the river and echoed throughout the camp. A low rumble of voices swept across the company as we wondered what the shots were for.

"Silence!" Mr. Nguyen screamed. "We have our own business to attend to. Breathe in and raise your arms." He lifted his arms slowly. "Now breathe out and let them down, slowly…slowly!" We followed along. "I can't hear you breathe! I want to hear those lungs stretch. Now lift!" Men coughed as the cool air hit their tobacco-soaked lungs. "Okay, now jumping jacks…1,2,3,4…1,2,3,4…I cannot hear you!" The cadres counted as loud as they could. "Toe touches! 1,2,3,4…."

A man in the squad next to me sat down. The rest of us counted, moaned and bent as far as we could. Mr. Nguyen walked over to the man who was sitting. "What is wrong with you?"

"I'm not hopping up and down like a monkey when my

stomach is still empty," the man said.

"What is your name?"

"My name is Ut."

"Well, Mr. Ut, perhaps you would like an alternative to exercises." Mr. Nguyen turned away and walked to the cadre at the front of Ut's squad. "Report to my office with Ut. Everyone is dismissed."

We were in the barracks long enough to fold our mosquito nets and blankets when the next bell rang. "Breakfast," Binh said. "I need a volunteer to help me get breakfast." All the men raised their hands, and Big Manh was chosen. He came back with a bowl of pickled white radish and some rice. Binh handed out bowls and told us to help ourselves. Big Manh went first, filled his bowl to the top, and then handed the spoon to Binh, who filled his halfway and laid the spoon in the bowl. We all grabbed for the spoon at once. Viet came up with it and filled his bowl, smashing the rice so it looked half full. He handed me the spoon, and I did the same thing. I handed the spoon to Phi, who also filled his bowl and smashed down the rice, and then he handed the spoon to Danh, but there was less than a spoonful of rice left.

"I cannot believe your greed!" Binh shouted. "We are here to work together, not to take from each other, or to compete. That is the way of the capitalists, not the way of the socialist man. Now put the food in the bowl." We dumped the rice back into the bowl.

"You need to learn self-motivation in everything you do," Binh said. "Your competitive ways put you here in the first place, and you will not leave until you change, until you learn the principles of equality." We eyed the food like a pack of hungry dogs ready to tear at one small rabbit.

"You are no longer single men," Binh said. "You are

brothers in this squad. If you cannot function in a small group like this, how do you expect to function in society? Now we will try again." Binh's expression was that of a father whose children had failed him. We passed the bowl, we each got a piece of radish and some rice, and there was some left in the bottom. Binh sat at his desk, beaming like a proud parent who had taught his children to share. I looked at his plump face as I ate, knowing he got all the food he wanted. In less than a minute we were finished and all staring at the rice left in the bowl.

Viet broke the silence. "Would you like me to take the bowls back?" he asked.

"That is a good gesture," Binh said, "but there is rice left, and we should not waste it."

"I'll take care of it."

"You do not learn fast, do you, boy? The rice is for all."

"I meant that I would divide it into eleven portions," Viet said. Big Manh chuckled, and the rest of us smiled. There was enough rice for a teaspoon apiece.

"We will not divide the rice," Binh said. "You each know how much to take. Pass the bowl!"

Big Manh grabbed the bowl, put his sticks in and came out with a small clump of rice. He waived it in front of his face, following it with his huge black eyes. He held it under his nose, smelled it, then opened his mouth, rolled it onto his tongue and smiled. Everyone laughed except Binh. He smiled, but it was an evil, devious smile. When we had each eaten a teaspoon of rice, Binh told Big Manh to collect the bowls and stack them on his desk. His smile grew as Big Manh stood up and walked up the aisle. Binh seemed to enjoy the power he had over us. When Big Manh put the bowls on his desk, Binh grabbed them and headed out of the barracks. The red-eyed men went to their bunks and whispered. The rest of us stayed in a circle.

"We'll starve in a week if this is all the food we get," Viet said, and Big Manh agreed with him.

"We will not starve," Cu said. He sat on the platform next to Big Manh with his legs crossed, staring straight ahead. "You must train your body to live on less food. You must train your mind, and you will survive."

Big Manh looked at him and chuckled. "Religion won't help you here, Mr. Buddha. If you train your mind to live on less food, the communists will give you even smaller portions."

"I didn't say anything about religion," Cu said.

Another bell rang, and Binh ran into the barracks. "Assemble! Move it!"

We jogged to our places. Mr. Nguyen stood in his same spot. "Squad 1, all present, Squad 2, all present."

"Sit down," Mr. Nguyen said, gesturing downward with his hands like Father Quyen used to do in church. He stood looking around the company for a moment, then walked up the first row. "You have already lost one member of your company," he said. "Mr. Ut has chosen the discipline company instead of ours."

Mr. Nguyen turned and walked down the second row. "You will be getting your hair cut now. But first, we need to collect your personal items. These items will be kept in storage and will be returned when you are released."

He turned and walked up the third row. "Some of you are drug addicts. If you turn in your drugs now, you will not be punished. If you are caught with them later, the punishment will be severe." He eyed a few men in the third row, walked to the middle of the cadres, turned and faced us. "Get your belongings, and assemble in ten minutes."

We walked back to the barracks. The three red-eyed men hurried ahead, and the rest of us walked together. "Why didn't Mr. Nguyen tell us to bring our belongings before?" Viet asked Binh. "Then we wouldn't have to go back and forth."

"It is good for you to ask questions," Binh said, "but questioning our commandant will only cause you trouble."

We collected our belongings, the bell rang, and we assembled. There were now three men with clippers in their hands, standing by stools at the front of our squads. Binh gave us tags to identify our belongings. Mr. Nguyen strutted around the courtyard and gave orders to guards to search the barracks. The barbers pointed at the three closest men, who walked slowly to the chairs and sat down. As the barbers' shavers glided closely along the men's scalps, I saw Viet run his fingers through his hair.

They were halfway through our squad when Mr. Nguyen led the guards in front of us with arms full of jewelry, money, and all the other things we were supposed to have turned in. The barbers kept shaving. My hair hadn't been cut since Grandma's visit and was almost to my shoulders. I sat on the ground rubbing it, knowing it would be gone in a matter of minutes. The cadres emerged from the office and began teaching us a new song. "We will learn to trust our brothers. We will earn our brothers' trust. We will live and work together so our nation will not rust…."

The barber pointed at Viet and smiled as he walked to the stool. "You've needed a haircut for a long time," the barber said. Viet didn't answer. I had thought it would be humorous to watch him get his hair cut, but it wasn't. I was next. "Two girls in a row," the barber said as I sat on the stool. When he finished, I walked back to my place and sat down. Viet turned around and rubbed the stubble on my head. I tried to do the same to him, but he pushed me away.

We sat watching Phi's hair fall to the ground and sang, "Vinh An is a new land, in this land we will grow…." We kept singing until everyone's hair had been cut.

Mr. Nguyen came out of the office as the barbers were walking away and motioned for us to stand. "We gave you a chance to motivate yourselves! The result of this was carried from your barracks a few moments ago." He walked through the middle of the squads, staring at certain men. "We know who you are! Your mistakes will be recorded in your file." He walked back to the front of the company and turned around slowly. His forehead wrinkled; his eyes lit up. He smiled just like Binh smiled. "The following people, report to the office." He read a list of about twenty names, including Dan and Tu from our squad. The men whose names had been called hung their heads and walked to the office. "The rest of you have work to do," Mr. Nguyen said and strutted off to the office.

Binh led both squad seven and ours to the warehouse and talked to the men in charge, who then stacked bundles of hoe, ax, and machete blades by the door. We each carried a bundle back to our barracks. Everyone else was eating when we got back. Phi went with Binh to get our food— boiled flour and a fish in salt water gravy for our squad. After the feast, we divided our tools. Each squad received two machetes, an ax, and a shovel, and each person was issued their own hoe. Another squad had gone to get bamboo to make handles, a cadre demonstrated how to tie the handles on, and we constructed our new tools.

When we finished, Binh told us to go to the barracks,

then he arrived there a few minutes later with Dan and Tu. They walked directly to their bunks and sat down with expressionless faces. Binh passed out paper and pencils without speaking, then sat on his desk. "The number in the top left corner of your paper will be your number while you are here." Mine was 26-6-3, which meant the 26th company, squad six and person number 3. We had to write our life histories starting with when and where we were born, to when and why we were arrested. We had to write about what we thought of the arrest and why we should be given a second chance. I thought of what Dad would write and made it brief in case I had to write it again. I said I was glad to be given a second chance at Vinh An and was sorry for my previous actions.

We spent the rest of the day perfecting our handles and building a tool rack. After dinner, Binh showed us the proper way to make our beds, then we built a fire ring to boil our water and a clothesline to dry our clothes. He gave us a half hour to bathe in the river. The day turned to night and we met in the barracks for review.

Binh sat on his desk with the lantern next to him, and we sat in a half circle around him. "Every night," he said, "we will spend time evaluating our progress." His voice was quiet and serious. "We will help each other by pointing out our improvements and failures. We will start by explaining our three goals. Who knows what these are?"

Phi raised his hand. "The goals are labor, self-criticism and self-motivation."

"That is very good," Binh said, and he clapped his hands silently. "Who can explain self-criticism and self-motivation?"

Tu raised his hand, and Binh nodded at him. "Self-criticism is pointing out faults in yourself and in your brothers.

Self-motivation is recognizing your own fault and not making the same mistake in the future."

"That is very good," Binh said, "but there is more. When a person points out someone else's fault, they should do so in such a way that does not put the person down, but enables them to learn. A good way to do this is to point out something good you noticed about the person, then point out the fault, then suggest a way that we can all learn from the experience." I looked around the group of men. It was a sticky hot evening, but Loc had a blanket wrapped around him. He shivered and his face was pale. I thought Binh had to notice that Loc was sick, but he ignored him.

"Self-motivation is more than not repeating your mistakes," Binh said. "It is also learning to anticipate what is right and wrong and acting accordingly. You will learn more about our goals as you learn about the philosophy of our new society. Self-criticism will help you learn these things, but self-motivation will have to come from within you. Let us start by evaluating each other's actions today. Who would like to begin?"

Everyone looked at each other. No one wanted to start because we knew the first one would be criticized for what he said. I stared at the floor, hoping he would not pick me. The silence sent a chill up my back. "Let me give you an example," Binh said. "First, I would like to congratulate the squad for the improvements you made on the barracks. The shelves and clothesline will be a benefit to all of us." Binh stared around the room expecting us to say something, but no one spoke. He held his hands in front of him and clapped silently. No one moved.

"I gave you a compliment," Binh said. "Applaud." We applauded, and when Binh looked away, Big Manh clapped silently, and twirled his huge black head like a school girl. Binh leaned against his desk and continued.

"Because there are so many people in this company, each individual in our squad will be looked upon by others as a member of squad six. We will be viewed as a group, not as individuals. This is why self-criticism and self-motivation are so important. Each member of our squad is no better than the squad as a whole, and the squad as a whole is no better than its weakest member." Binh stood solidly, staring around the group.

"Earlier today, some members of our squad acted in such a way that made our whole squad look bad. You were all given a chance for self-motivation, and some of you failed." We tried not to stare at Dan and Tu, but everyone did.

"Mr. Nguyen asked to hold your valuables while you are here. It was a simple request. The only reason for not turning these things in, is if you plan to leave this place without our releasing you. Maybe you did not trust us to keep your things. But without trust, we cannot achieve our goals." Binh leaned against his desk.

"No one was punished for their actions today. We are giving you a chance to learn, a chance to trust. We are confident that once you learn why you are here, and trust that we are helping you, our country, and eventually the whole world, you will not have thoughts of escaping. You will be thankful for this opportunity to improve yourselves and to become a real asset to our great country." He paused for a few seconds, and his eyes rolled back in thought. "When you criticize someone, you are not criticizing an individual, but yourselves as a group. Who would like to begin?"

There was another long silence. Dan raised his hand because he was the oldest. He sat for a moment, collecting his words, and began, "I would like to compliment the group's improvement during meal time. The greed we all showed, grabbing at the rice the first meal, was not good." I thought to myself how Dan didn't grab at all. He seemed to know that Binh would dump the rice back in. "I hope we will not make the same mistake in the future," Dan said. "We are only as strong as our weakest member, so we should take only what we need and save the rest for those who need more."

Binh clapped silently, while we clapped out loud. "Very good criticism. I am very happy with the accomplishments you have made on your first day." He smiled proudly and sat on the desk. "By your words tonight, I can tell you are learning." His smile faded into a determined straight face as he leaned toward us.

"But you all have much to learn, or you would not be here. You have been given a second chance to make yourselves worthy of our great nation. First, we must make ourselves better to make our squad better. Second, we must make our company better to make our camp better. Third, we must make our camp better to make our country better. Some day we will teach the world the ways of socialism. Some day the whole world will reach the goals we are pursuing. Now we must rest, and think about our goals."

We hung our nets and got into bed. Binh blew the lamp out, and I lay in the dark with the events of the day bouncing through my head. I thought about what Cu said earlier. I wondered if I could train my body to live on the food the communists gave us.

The clanging of the bell started another day. The first thing I saw was Binh, bouncing around the barracks, clapping his hands, yelling…"Let's go, another day, everyone up, move it! Move it!" All of us but Loc crawled out of bed and got dressed. He had his blanket over his head, and Binh was shaking his foot. "Get up Loc. We have a busy day." Loc didn't move. Binh pulled his covers back and shouted "Let's go!" Beads of sweat covered Loc's face; his body trembled. He reached his arm toward the blanket, and Binh covered him back up. "Loc will be fine," Binh said to us. "Fifteen minutes until assembly, move it!"

My stomach cramped and my head spun during exercises. The whole company was in slow motion. Men coughed and groaned, and a man in squad five passed out when he tried to touch his toes. I thought if they didn't feed us a good meal soon, men would begin to get sick. When we were dismissed, we went back to our barracks to wait for breakfast. Loc was still lying in his bed, and Dan asked if he could get him some water from the kitchen. Binh told him to wait for the bell and then bring some back with the food. Loc's body shook his blankets; he pushed his face into them to hide his pain. Watching Loc had made me forget about my own hunger, but breakfast came and reminded me of it. They gave us cooked cabbage and red rice, the kind of rice you feed cattle.

After breakfast we assembled. "Today we will learn to march," Mr. Nguyen said. "Tomorrow we will be introduced at the camp meeting, and I want you all looking sharp." He threw his hands up, and we stood. "When I say forward, you move forward with your right leg first. When I say left face, you turn left. When I say right face, you turn right. When I say halt, you stop. Are there any questions?" There were none and the marching began.

"Left face!" We turned left. "Forward march!" Half the men started with their left foot. A few men tripped over themselves trying to switch to their right. We marched around the courtyard like a group of army recruits, out of step, turning the wrong way, not paying attention. The cadres ran around us, telling us we were misfits, and making men do push-ups when they turned the wrong way. We marched around the courtyard, down the river, into the assembly area, up the river, around our courtyard and back to the assembly area.

It was noon when we finished, but the lunch bell didn't ring. Mr. Nguyen said the rest of the day would be spent planting a garden, and we were dismissed for five minutes to get our tools. While we were walking to the barracks, Viet asked Binh when we would eat, and said he answered that we wouldn't get lunch until we started our real labor. We spent the rest of the day planting a garden, perfecting our hoe handles, sharpening the blades and complaining about how hungry we were.

When we returned to the barracks, Loc was gone. No one asked where he had been taken. We ate dinner and washed our bowls, and Binh passed out more paper and pencils, saying, "We will now write letters to our families. In these letters, you can explain the procedures your family will follow to visit." He finished passing out the pencils and paper and sat on his desk.

"You can tell your families about our camp, and about our goals. You must let them know you are happy to be here and you have everything you need. You must create a good image of our camp so our countrymen will know we are working to become better men. Any complaints you have should be brought to my attention, not thrown at your families to burden them. Are there any questions?" There were none, and I started my letter.

Dear Mom and Dad and family,

How is everything at home? I hope you are all okay. I have been doing well. I'm at Vinh An Labor Camp. Phi and Viet are here, so I'm not alone. I'm sorry I let you down and am not there to help the family. We are learning the value of labor, so when we get out we will be useful members of society. I have only been here two days, so there's not much to say, but I have already learned much. Living and working with other people is helping me to lose my self-importance and realize the greater importance of helping other people. It's hard for me because I have been selfish for so long, but I'm glad to have this chance to improve myself. I'm allowed to have one visitor, and you can find out the procedures at the district station. Tell them I am at Vinh An Labor Camp, Company 26, Squad 6, Number 3. Don't worry about me. They said if I show good improvement, I can come home soon.

Viet

When I finished the letter, I read it to myself, and couldn't believe what I had written. I wanted to tell my family the truth. I wanted to tell them the food was horrible and we didn't get enough. I wanted to say I was scared and yearning to go home. It seemed someone else had written the letter, someone who believed in communism. I hoped Dad would know I was trying to trick the communists so they would let me go.

Binh was helping Dan write his letter when I finished, and Viet handed me his to read. He wrote that we were starving in the camp, and he gave his Mom a list of things to bring. I told him the cadres would read the letters, but he said I was a coward and the only way we would survive was if our families brought us food.

We gave our letters to Binh, and he left to take them to the office. While he was gone, Danh, the boy next to me, asked me what had happened to Loc. It was the first time Danh had said anything except when he was asked a question. "He's going through withdrawal," I said.

"Withdrawal from drugs?" Danh asked in a tiny voice. "I thought it was dysentery."

"It's probably both," Big Manh said. Danh sat back with a worried look. "Don't worry," Big Manh told him, "if you train your mind, you won't catch it."

This got Cu into the conversation. "You'll survive, son," he said. "If you want to live, you will live."

"Have you done physical labor before?" I asked Danh.

He held out his hands in front of him. They were blistered and cracked after what I thought was an easy day. "My feet are worse," he said, "and I have never eaten rice like this. It hurts my stomach." The rice burned my stomach too, but I told Danh he would have to get used to it if he wanted to survive.

Binh returned from the office and said it was time to review the day's progress. He moved the oil lamp to the front of his desk and sat cross-legged next to it. "Let us review," he said, and we gathered around. The light flickered on one side of his face, lighting one serious eye and leaving the other dark. "Who has criticism to offer tonight?"

Phi raised his hand, and Binh nodded at him. "Everyone did a good job planting the garden," Phi said, "but we all need to work on our marching."

"Very good." Binh clapped silently, and we clapped out loud. "I'm happy to see you have all your tools ready. I looked at them earlier, and you did a good job. Who else has criticism to offer?"

Dan raised his hand, and Binh nodded at him. "I noticed that many people helped each other construct their tools. This shows that we are working as a group."

"Very good," Binh said. We clapped until Binh held his hands for silence. "Let us move along. Who else can offer some criticism?" No one raised their hand, and Binh looked at each of us. "Tu, do you have any criticism?"

"I think we have covered everything," Tu said. He looked at Qui and chuckled.

Binh jumped from his desk and charged up the aisle. He stood directly over Tu. "We lost a brother today!" he screamed. Tu glared up at him with a fierce look; his body tensed with anger. I thought Tu was going to tear Binh apart. Viet nudged my back and smiled.

"Loc was sick today because of drugs," Binh said. He walked back to his desk, turned around, and lowered his eyes with disappointment. "I know there are others in our group who are also drug addicts." He looked up and stared around the group, trying to make us think he could tell if we were or not. "If you tell us of your drug habit now, we can help you before you are as sick as Loc. Loc was selfish for not telling me sooner. Now he will contribute nothing to our squad for days or maybe even weeks."

I wondered how Binh could say he didn't know Loc was sick—Loc had been shaking for a day and a half. There was a long, tense silence as Binh stared at each of us, giving us a chance to confess. He stared at Tu and Qui the longest, but neither budged.

Then Binh sat on his desk and his serious smile grew into a happy grin. "Tomorrow is our monthly camp meeting. Let us practice our songs so we can show our brothers and sisters that we are ready to join them." I had never seen any-one change moods so fast—it seemed as if Binh had no real emotions. He thought and did everything like a robot. "Let's start with the Vinh An theme song." He leaned forward and made a motion with his arms like we were his children and he was gathering us.

"Vinh An is a new land…." he started slowly, opening his mouth wide when he sang, thinking it would help us learn faster. We all mouthed the words a step behind him and sang every few words out loud. When the song was fin-ished, he began the labor song.

"We love labor, labor will help us grow. We love labor, the first of our three goals. Our path begins with labor, to build our bodies strong. Self-criticism follows and our greed will soon be gone…."

After exercises and breakfast the next morning, we as-sembled for the camp meeting. Mr. Nguyen said we looked good in our uniforms. I thought we looked like ascetic monks. "Many of you will be seeing people you know," he said. "Do not gesture toward them in any way. Everyone here is a representative of this company. You will show respect and discipline. There will be no laughing, no stepping out of place. This is a chance for you to motivate yourselves. Now march!"

We marched out of the courtyard in double file, with the cadres beside us, and Mr. Nguyen out in front. We marched along the river, past the kitchen and warehouse to the as-sembly field. I couldn't believe how many people were there, all wearing black pajamas, all looking like zombie-robots, acting on the commands of the cadres. We stumbled into place, and I gazed around the field. Each company looked like a huge black square, and they were all singing the Vinh

An theme song. Binh was singing loud enough for all of us, so I clapped along and mouthed the words. When the singing stopped, a man came to the podium at the middle of the stage, tapped the microphone, and began singing the national anthem. When the anthem was finished, he introduced the camp leader, Mr. Cao Vu Trung.

Mr. Trung wore a khaki uniform, black army boots, and an officer's hat. He was a short, stocky man with a round stomach and full cheeks. He strutted to the middle of the stage, smiled with thick red lips, and gestured for everyone to sit. "I would like to begin this morning by introducing a new addition to our camp." He held his arms toward our company. "Welcome Company 16!" We stood, and everyone applauded, then he had us sit down. "Next, I would like to congratulate the carpentry company. They have surpassed their goal for the last six weeks!" The cadres stood to applaud, and the rest of us followed. Mr. Trung indicated for us to sit, then cleared his throat into the microphone.

"As I am sure you have noticed at meal time, the fishing company has also passed their goal!" The cadres stood again, applauding wildly, and we followed. Mr. Trung named a few other companies who had reached their goals of production, and he said the other companies would need to work harder so they wouldn't be a burden to society. When the criticism was finished, he introduced the camp doctor, who told us there had been many cases of dysentery reported in the last few weeks. He said drainage ditches should be cleaned and the bushes around the camp should be trimmed to cut down the mosquito population.

After more introductions and information about the camp, we were dismissed. The other companies filed out in order, following the commands of their cadres. Right turn, left turn, march . . .. We walked out, trying to act like the other companies, but we were out of step. When we got back to the courtyard, we assembled.

"A good first meeting," Mr. Nguyen said, "but we will have to work hard so we can learn all the songs, and so we can march in disciplined order. Today we will clear the drainage ditches and cut the bushes back like the doctor suggested."

Our squad was assigned to clean the ditch from the toilets to the river. These ditches were a half yard wide, and two yards deep, and they ran between each set of barracks throughout the camp. Each company had their own latrine, which was a grass hut built over the ditches. We spent the afternoon shoveling the sewage and leaves out of the ditch, throwing them into pushcarts and dumping them down the river.

When we finished our section, Viet and a few other men jumped in the river to wash. My legs and arms were covered with the black stinking mud, and I was walking to the river to join them when Phi stopped me. "The cadres are watching us," he said. "We better help the other squads." I looked toward the east barracks and saw Binh and another cadre staring at the men in the river. Phi and I walked to our barracks, grabbed our hoes and joined a squad that was cutting bushes.

We were exhausted by the end of the day. My skin burned from the sun and the sewage, so I went to the river to wash. The dinner bell made me angry when it rang. Dinner wasn't going to fulfill my hunger, only remind me of it. As I ate my bread and salt water gravy, I wondered how long before Mom would visit and what she would bring me to eat. I gulped my food down in three bites and watched Danh fumble with his. His face reminded me of my little brother Tu's face

211

when we didn't have meat.

"Things will not get better," I told him. "You'll need your strength. The real labor starts tomorrow." He looked at me with sad, swollen eyes, and his blistered hands cupped the bowl in front of him. His soft cheeks were scorched by the sun. I didn't think he would last a week after labor started.

We had just finished dinner when the bell started ringing. It wasn't a normal ring, but a constant clang! clang! clang! We walked out of the barracks, and I looked across the courtyard. Mr. Nguyen was at the bell, ringing it like a madman. Binh was running from the office yelling, "Assemble! Move it! Move it!"

We jogged into place, and Mr. Nguyen strutted to the front of the company. "We have read your letters. They are full of greed! Full of requests to burden our society." He walked down the third row. "You are already a burden to society because you have not produced anything." He stopped at the middle of the row and stared at an unlucky man.

"Society has provided you with shelter, with food, but you are still not satisfied. You expect more. You expect your families to bring you food!" Mr. Nguyen continued up the row, turned and walked down the fourth. "This tells me two things." He stopped, holding one finger in the air. "You expect your families to go hungry, so you can have their co-op portions." Now he held two fingers. "Or you expect your families to deal on the black market." He continued down the row and chose another man to stare at. "You are asking them to commit crimes, crimes that put you here in the first place." He walked back to the middle of the cadres, turned, and faced us with legs wide apart and chest out. "You will write new letters tonight!" he shouted. "This time you will show consideration for your families. Respect for society.

212

And self-motivation! You are dismissed."

We walked back to the barracks, and Binh stood in front of his desk until we gathered around him. "I am disappointed that you chose to burden your families. You have everything you need here and you still ask for more. We will write new letters tonight, but first, I want to hear some criticism. I hope you have at least thought of criticism."

We all gave small nods that we had, and he asked for a volunteer to start. There was a long silence, then Dan finally spoke. "I'm glad we are getting second chances to write our letters, but as Binh told us before, we should look ahead, and not need to be told what to do."

We all nodded in agreement. "We should think of society instead of ourselves," Phi added. We nodded, and Binh smiled; we were silent until he asked for more criticism.

I had been thinking about the people who went swimming instead of helping the other squads but I didn't want to say anything. I thought the whole review system was awkward, and knew that Binh was going to use it to turn us against each other. I kept my eyes lowered so he wouldn't choose me to speak, but it didn't work. "Viet," he said, "you haven't offered any criticism. Have you been thinking about ways to improve our squad?"

Everyone stared at me, and blood rushed to my face. "I would like to say we all did a good job clearing the ditches and cutting brush today," I said, "but some of us went swimming when we finished our section instead of helping the others." The men nodded in agreement.

"That is very good criticism, Viet. I am glad to see you were aware of this. But your criticism will do us no good unless you point out the people who failed to help the others." I thought the criticism was to help the whole group, not to

213

punish certain people. Pointing out people would only embarrass them and make me feel guilty for turning them in. I wished I had kept my mouth shut. "We need to know who went swimming, Viet," he said again. "This is the only way we can grow." I felt myself shrink to the size of a child, and my throat tightened. "This meeting will not continue until you tell us who went swimming."

I looked around at the men. Dan and Cu were nodding for me to answer. I swallowed and said, "It was Tu, Qui, Viet and Big Manh." Tu's eyes penetrated my flesh. Why did I have to be the first to name names? I knew these men would be watching me now, waiting for me to make a mistake so they could get me back. I lowered my eyes.

The meeting continued, and someone said we should be more motivated to learn the songs and how to march. I was relieved when Cu said Viet and I should be more enthusiastic in marching. Before it was over, everyone had said something about someone else. When we ran out of the smallest of things to criticize, Binh added a few more. "No one tonight said anything about themselves. No one thanked the people who gave them criticism. No one showed appreciation for those who noticed them and took the initiative to help them with their faults. This is something I want you to think about tonight, and we will practice it tomorrow."

He stood up and grabbed some paper from his desk. "I think we have made much progress today," he said as he passed out paper and pencils. "The ice is now broken, and we can move forward with some real progress. Now let us write our letters."

I wrote the same thing I had before, and when I finished, I read over Viet's shoulder: "We have everything we need," he wrote. "Vinh An is a wonderful place, and I know I will be happy here…."

Binh collected our letters. We sang, and he blew out the lamp. I lay with my eyes open, staring into the darkness. In the room next to us, men were still singing, "We love labor, labor will help us grow."

Labor

"Everyone up! This is the day we have waited for. Move it!" Binh was walking up the aisle, banging on our bed posts with his clipboard. "Move it! Everybody up!"

We staggered out of bed, washed, went to the latrine, and assembled for exercises. Mr. Nguyen was pumped full of energy, strutting back and forth in front of the company. "Hard work builds a strong mind. Without a strong mind, there is no hope for self-criticism and self-motivation...." He walked up the middle of the squads, chest out, arms swaying stiffly, hard khaki hat tipped forward. He stopped at the back of the company, and we all turned to face him. "Labor is the first step in reaching our goals. Are you ready for labor!"

The cadres screamed, "Ready!" Everyone else was silent.

Mr. Nguyen walked back to the front of the squads, then turned slowly to face us. "I will ask you one more time. Are you ready for labor!"

"Ready!" we replied.

"Fall out!" he shouted, and we walked back to the barracks for breakfast.

After breakfast, we assembled with our tools. Mr. Nguyen was still pumped. He marched back and forth in front of our squads. "Labor will help you to become better men," he exclaimed. "Labor will tune your bodies for the great task you have taken upon yourselves. Labor will contribute to our society…." He stopped at the front of squad one, "Are you ready!"

"Ready!" we shouted.

"Fall out!"

Mr. Nguyen made a military turn to his left and marched forward. Squad one followed, and we filed out in single file. He led us down the river, up the bank and along a narrow trail into the jungle. Monkeys screeched and ruffled the leaves in the tree tops. Birds chirped above the constant hiss of insects. Small beams of morning light shot through the cool, damp air.

We walked for a half hour and came to an open field. The sky was now pale blue, streaked with long white clouds. Steam rose from shoulder high grass ahead of us. As we walked, I saw the field was divided into squares: some were of freshly tilled red earth, others of sweet potatoes in different stages of growth, and still others of wild jungle grass. Lines of men in black pajamas moved slowly across the fields, scraping, chopping and digging the earth. Our cadres told us to line up along the edge of the jungle an arm's length apart. Mr. Nguyen walked to the middle of the line, ten feet in front of us.

"Your job is to chop the grass and clear this field." He motioned toward the field with his hoe, then walked to the grass and took a few whacks before turning around. "Okay, men. Get to work!" The line of men moved forward and most of us began whacking the grass with our hoes. Others stood looking at the grass like they didn't know what to do. The cadres gave more demonstrations, and in minutes, we became a giant human machine moving across the field.

Mr. Nguyen was twenty men to my left, chopping the grass like a madman axing his victim. The back of his shirt was soaked with sweat. His eyes were wide, his lips tight. He was ten feet in front of everyone, showing us how much he valued labor. The cadres were right behind him, setting the example for the rest of us to follow. We had moved thirty feet into the grass when a man screamed. I looked to my left and saw him hopping on one leg. I stopped chopping and looked closer. The man had fallen to the ground with his leg in his hands. He had sliced himself with his hoe. "Get back to work!" the cadres shouted, then two of them carried the man to the shade.

We chopped for an hour. Danh was to my right, struggling to keep up. His hands bled and his pale face glowed with sweat, but his lips were drawn tight. His face was determined. He put all his energy into whacking at the grass, but only a small chunk came out each time. I tried to chop as much on his side as I could, but my hands were hurting too.

The sun rose to the middle of the sky. My black pajamas melted into my back. The work was harder than fishing, and the heat and lack of sufficient food were wearing on me. I thought I would get used to it in time, but I didn't think Danh would. His determined look was fading with every chop. "Ask to relieve yourself," I told him. "Sit in the shade and rest."

Danh kept chopping. His movements slowed until he was hitting the grass and none was breaking. Dan was on the other side of him, and we both chopped at his section, trying to keep him up with the line. My arms became raw from the grass ripping at them. My trousers were soaked with sweat. My head spun until the grass became a green blur, streaked with white rays from the sun.

"Water break!" Mr. Nguyen shouted. I leaned against my hoe and wiped my forehead with a wet sleeve. Up and down the line, men collapsed onto the ground. The cadres told us to move into the shade.

Dan and I helped Danh to the edge of the trees, leaned him against a stump, and collapsed on the ground next to him. Viet and Phi were right behind us. "This isn't right," Viet said. Phi and Dan went to the water tube and came back with a few bowls of water. I gulped half a bowl, and the water crashed in my stomach like it was an empty bucket.

"Can you make it?" Dan asked Danh.

"I have no choice," he said, and Dan bowed his head because he knew it was a stupid question.

We had been sitting in the shade for too short a time when Mr. Nguyen yelled, "Back to work!" He was first in the field, chopping and pulling the grass, but his example was not inspiring. Watching him made me angry because I knew he was getting more food than we were.

The human machine moved slowly into the grass. I counted whacks, added everyone's together and estimated our machine was whacking six thousand times a minute. It was an overwhelming sight. Being just one person in more than twenty companies advancing across the fields for as far as I could see made me feel small and useless. I thought about what the district official had said: "If you do not move forward with the wheel of society, you will be crushed."

Even the cadres suffered from the heat. A few hoes broke, and I hoped mine would too, so I could take a break. Men

219

passed out, and others gouged themselves and were taken to the shade. Danh and some men from other squads were chosen to rake the fallen grass. The rest of us kept chopping.

Lunchtime came but it was just a tease, not enough food to thicken the water in my stomach. The whistle blew and our machine moved into the grass, slower than before. By the end of the day, we were almost at a standstill. The sun fell over the trees, a cool breeze swept into the valley, and our sweat dried into salt.

"Company halt!" the cadres screamed. I peeled my hands from the hoe and they curled back, cramping, until I pried them open again. A few men raked the rest of the grass into piles, then the cadres lit the piles on fire. We stood at the edge of the trees, watching the flames and smelling the green smoke. Companies of men walked single file along the edge of the field, then disappeared into the jungle like ants going into their hill.

We assembled at the edge of our field, and Mr. Nguyen strutted to his position in front of us. "Congratulations on your first day of labor. You have worked hard, but you will work harder. You will become stronger, and with this strength you will accomplish the rest of your goals." Then he led us along the path and into the jungle.

When we got back to our barracks, we headed straight for the river. The sun was gone, and the sky was dark blue, lit by a full moon and clusters of tiny stars. I jumped into the river with my clothes still on. The water cooled my skin, and I was still soaking when the dinner bell rang. I didn't want to move, but I didn't want to miss my portion, so I climbed out, wrung my clothes and headed for the barracks. I swallowed my pumpkin soup in a few gulps, and then looked into Danh's full bowl. He sat next to it, cross-legged

220

on his bed. His chin sunk into his chest, and his body swayed back and forth as if he were asleep.

"You need to eat," I said, but he didn't hear me. He was somewhere else, or nowhere at all. I spoke louder and nudged his arm. "Eat," I said. "You have to eat."

"Leave me alone." Danh pushed his bowl toward me and curled up in a ball. I wanted to eat his food, but I couldn't. I covered it and put it on the shelf, hoping he would eat it later. I lay back on my blanket and shut my eyes. In two breaths I was asleep, and in two more Binh's voice pierced my mind. I thought I was dreaming but when I opened my eyes he was sitting on his desk, the lamp next to him, flickering gold on the side of his face.

"Let us review."

What could we possibly criticize each other for today? I thought. *We worked as hard as we could. We were too busy chopping to do anything wrong.*

We pulled ourselves into a half circle, and review began. "First I would like to compliment you on your first day of labor," Binh said. "I saw many of you helping others. This shows you are pledging yourselves to the group and not just thinking of yourselves. Who has criticism to offer tonight?"

Dan raised his hand. "I was inspired by the courage Danh showed today," he said. "He has not done this kind of work before, but he pushed himself past the point of exhaustion. He refused to give up. But in the future, if Danh continues to push himself too far, I'm afraid he will damage himself and will not be able to help our squad."

Binh applauded and smiled with joy. I knew this was Dan's clever way of getting Binh to tell Danh not to work himself to death. "That is very good criticism. We cannot lose any more brothers. As Dan said, if someone hurts themselves, they hurt the group as a whole. What counts is our attitude toward labor—not only how much we accomplish physically, but also mentally." Binh asked us to applaud Danh, and we all clapped. There seemed to be some compassion behind Binh's smile.

Danh looked at Dan like he wanted to say thank you, then stared at the floor. "Do you have anything to say?" Binh asked him.

"I would like to thank Dan for his criticism," Danh said weakly, still staring at the floor. "I'm sorry for not considering how my actions could affect the squad."

Binh clapped silently as we clapped aloud. "Would anyone else like to offer criticism?" He gazed around the barracks, and as he looked at each of us, we looked at the floor. I thought he was going to criticize us for not having more to say, but he didn't. "A very good job today, men. Now let us show as much enthusiasm in our singing as we did in our work."

He began singing "We love labor…." and we followed, "Labor will help us grow…." Then we hung our nets, Binh blew out the lamp, and we all lay down to sleep.

I chopped grass in my dreams the whole night and woke up exhausted and hungry. Binh was walking up the aisle, banging on the posts, "Everyone up!" I rolled over and cleared my eyes with the heels of my palms. "Everyone up!" he yelled again.

My eyes cleared as Binh raced to Qui's bed and pulled the covers back. Qui's bed was empty. Binh pulled the covers off Tu's bed. Tu's bed was empty. He turned around and caught me staring at him—his eyes seemed to be on fire. He raced toward me but stopped short and pulled the covers off Danh's bed. Danh was curled up in a ball, shivering.

"Get up!" Binh screamed at him, then he darted out the door.

With all the excitement, I didn't notice Viet wasn't up yet. As soon as Binh left, Phi nudged me and pointed toward Viet's bed. I peered around Phi and saw Viet's mattress rolled under his blanket. Phi looked as shocked as I felt; Viet hadn't said anything about escaping. Cu and Big Manh lay back in their beds, and we heard three shots ring out. Big Manh groaned and pulled the covers over his head.

Danh sat up. "You should stay in bed," I said to him. Dark circles were swollen under his eyes. He didn't look like he would make it through the morning.

"I'm fine," he said, and he forced himself up and got dressed.

In another moment, the assembly bell rang. I pulled on my trousers and walked outside. Guards and cadres were running around in a frenzy. We lined up and they counted heads: "Squad 1, two missing. Squad 2, one missing. Squad 3, one missing…" I kept adding as the reports went in: thirty-four men had escaped.

The rest of the morning was normal, except that we got a little more food because Big Manh didn't tell the cooks we had three less mouths to feed. Danh forced down half a bowl of the red salt water rice, then ran behind the barracks, and we heard him choke it up. The work bell rang, and we assembled with our hoes on our shoulders. "Your brothers have deserted you," Mr. Nguyen said, "but worse than that, you have shamed yourselves. Who would like to tell the rest of the men what I am talking about?" There was a tired silence. "You can criticize yourselves, or I will criticize you. You all know what I am talking about. Who will offer the criticism?"

A man from squad three raised his hand. "We took more

than our share of food," he shouted.

"Who took more than their share?" Mr. Nguyen asked. A few men from other squads raised their hands. Everyone in our squad stood still. "We know who took more than their share. You think you are clever. You think you can eat the deserters' food." He walked along our squad. When he got to Cu, he screamed, "You ate the deserters' food. Now you will do the deserters' work."

We marched along the river and through the jungle and lined up along the edge of the uncut grass. "Move it!" Mr. Nguyen bellowed, and the human machine moved forward.

We all seemed to be working as hard as we could, but the cadres walked up and down the lines screaming at us, "Your brothers have deserted you! You must work harder to make up for them."

There was no break in the morning. The sun rose over the trees, and the afternoon became sticky hot. Men collapsed from exhaustion, and when they recovered they were used to carry water up and down the line. Every time I took a drink, my head spun and my muscles froze. Danh collapsed right after lunch. He fell to the ground face first. I reached down to turn him over, but Binh shouted, "Work! There is no time for you to stop." He and another cadre carried Danh to the shade.

We chopped until the sun sank to the tops of the trees, then we raked the grass, lit the piles and walked single file into the jungle. When we got back to the camp, Phi and I soaked in the river, then we sat with Cu and Big Manh on the bank. I watched the moon climb above the trees and the stars grow brighter. The spotlights turned on and their white circles swept through the trees. The river rippled quietly below the banging and scraping of metal as men sharpened their tools for another day of labor.

Big Manh rolled the last of his tobacco into three cigarettes and gave one to Phi and one to me. We were silent for a few minutes, too tired to speak. A few men were still soaking in the cool river, but most had returned to the barracks to wait for dinner. When the last man within hearing distance stood and walked up the bank, Big Manh asked about Viet. "Where will Viet escape to?"

"I don't know," Phi said. "He didn't tell us anything, but I suppose he'll go back to Saigon." I imagined Viet running through the jungle, ducking in and out of bushes, hiding from guards who were right on his trail.

"It's a long walk to Saigon," Big Manh said. "Maybe he'll get a ride."

"If he doesn't want to be turned in," Cu said, "he'll walk."

"At least he's out of this prison," Big Manh said.

"This whole country is a prison," Cu said. "The only way to escape the prison is to escape the country."

"I want to escape this place," I said, "and when I do, I will leave the country. I'll organize an army and kill all the communists."

"Those are big dreams," Cu said. "Admirable dreams, but not realistic."

"Don't you think about freedom?" Big Manh asked Cu.

"I used to think about freedom," Cu said with a sad grin. "Now I think about survival."

Clang, clang, clang. We pushed ourselves up with our tired arms and walked to the barracks for dinner. Danh was asleep on his bed. I woke him, but he wouldn't eat. After dinner, the assembly bell rang. We lined up, and Mr. Nguyen came out of his office, followed by fifteen prisoners and a couple of guards with rifles. The prisoners' heads were bowed, so we couldn't see their faces, but I could tell that Tu and Qui were among them. Viet wasn't there. I looked at Phi, and he smiled. I wondered if Viet was still sneaking through the jungle or if they had killed him.

"As you know," Mr. Nguyen said, "these men were once a part of our company. But they no longer want to be with us. They were unable to motivate themselves, so they will be sent to a place where they do not need self-motivation, a place that will do the motivating for them." He walked along the row of prisoners, poking them in the chest with his finger. "Only one day of labor, and they gave up. They abandoned us."

He turned toward the company. "Would anyone like to speak on these men's behalf?" There was silence. Everyone knew if they spoke up they would be going to the discipline company with them. "Who would like to speak about sending them to the discipline company?"

A cadre raised his hand and walked to the front of the squads. "These men have committed a serious act. They have showed no self-motivation. They will slow our progress. They should be given the most severe form of criticism."

Mr. Nguyen walked up and down the squads, staring at us until we raised our hands to vote for sending the men to the discipline company. Then he walked to the front of our company. "On your knees!" he screamed at the fifteen men, and most of them fell to their knees. The guards pushed the others down with the butts of their rifles. "This morning your brothers ate your food," Mr. Nguyen said. "Tonight, they have sentenced you to the most severe form of criticism. What does this tell you of your brothers' feelings about you deserting them? Contemplate this question in discipline!"

The head guard told the men to stand, then they marched

out of the courtyard, and we were dismissed. On the way back to the barracks, Big Manh told me he hoped Viet made it, but during review that night we all said how awful it was that the men had tried to escape. Binh said for us to save our criticism for when the men returned from the discipline company. I wanted to ask him what had happened to Viet, but I didn't want to seem concerned.

We criticized each other for taking more than our share of food. I waited for Dan to say something about Danh working too hard again, but he didn't. Danh barely had enough energy to sit up at the meeting, but no one said anything, and Binh smiled at him like nothing was wrong. We finished review and sang a few songs, Binh blew out the lantern, and we got ready for bed.

I wanted to sleep and dream—it was the only way to relieve my aching body. But before my head hit the mattress, Binh told Phi and me to follow him outside. He led us across the courtyard and before I knew what was happening, we were at Mr. Nguyen's office. We walked through the doorway of the small grass hut, and Binh pointed for us to stand in front of Mr. Nguyen's desk. My knees shook. Mr. Nguyen sat back in his bamboo chair, folded arms, stern tanned face, white hair trimmed close like an officer. "Were you friends with Viet Tranh?" he asked. Phi said we were. "Which one of you would like to tell me where he is?"

We looked at each other and shrugged our shoulders. Slam! Mr. Nguyen's fist hit the table. He stood up, leaned over his desk, and stared into my eyes. "I will rip the truth out of you, boy! Now where is he?"

I thought Phi would do the talking because he was older, but he didn't speak. His body trembled, and his eyes were huge with fear. "I don't know where he is," I said. "He didn't tell us he was escaping."

"You expect me to believe that?"

"It's the truth, sir."

He shifted his eyes to Phi. "Maybe you can tell me?"

"I don't know, sir. He didn't tell us he was escaping. We woke up this morning and he was gone."

Now he looked at Binh, who seemed almost as nervous as we were. He was standing behind us with lowered eyes. "These are your men," Mr. Nguyen said to him. "Should we believe them, or should we help them to remember?"

My heart stopped. My skin froze. Binh took his time answering. "I know these boys come from the same area, and I know they are friends. It is hard for me to believe that Viet would not tell them of his plans." Visions of the discipline company flew into my mind—of communists tying me by the thumbs, beating me like they did my grandfather. "But I have already lost three members of my squad," Binh continued. "So far, Viet and Phi have showed good improvement. If they are lying, we will find out soon enough, then we can punish them accordingly. Until then, I suggest they remain members of our company."

I breathed for the first time since Binh started his long-winded answer. I glanced toward Phi. We kept our faces blank and stood as still as possible, praying for Mr. Nguyen to agree. "That is all," he said, and sat back in his chair, calm as the night. What could mean life or death for us was a small decision for him.

The next week dragged by. Sometimes after work I was too tired to wash and would lie on my bunk until dinner. Every day, more men who had tried to escape and had been caught were lined up in front of us, and we voted to send them to the discipline company. I wondered what they did to them there, and what had happened to Viet. By the end of the week, all but three had been caught. Binh said the others had died in the jungle, but we hoped that Viet had made it back to Saigon.

Danh became weaker each day. Monday, he started off as quickly as any of us, but in a half hour he was barely moving. Tuesday, he passed out after lunch. Wednesday, he carried water all day. On Thursday, he walked to the field, turned pale and hung on his hoe for fifteen minutes. Then his eyes lit up, he chopped for fifteen minutes, then hung on his hoe again. During review, Dan criticized him for working too hard. Binh clapped his hands silently, and we clapped out loud. Danh said he was sorry for not thinking of the group, and we clapped again. It was obvious that he couldn't do physical labor and that he was sick. He wouldn't eat, and his face was sunk in, making his eyes look too big for his head. During review, Binh told him not to work too hard, but during the day, he walked up and down the line telling us to work harder.

Friday morning, Danh didn't get out of bed. I could tell by his eyes he had given up. When we returned from work Friday night, he was gone. Binh said they took him to the hospital and he would be well in a few days.

At review Saturday night, Binh told us that tomorrow would be the first regular Sunday, which meant that when we finished working in the garden, repairing our hoes and doing our laundry, we could have visitors from other companies. "What about Danh?" Phi asked. "Is it okay if a few of us visit him?"

"I will check with the commandant," Binh replied. "If he allows it, I will give you a pass."

Sunday morning, after working in the garden and washing

our clothes, we reminded Binh about the pass. He went to the office to ask Mr. Nguyen, and he returned in a few minutes with yellow bands for us to tie on our arms. This way the guards knew who the visitors were.

Phi and I walked past the kitchen and across the bridge to the hospital, which was two bamboo barracks structures like ours, but longer. Two huts and an office stood between the barracks. We walked into the office to ask permission to see Danh, and the nurse directed us to the east barracks. Danh was sleeping when we got there, so Phi nudged his arm and he woke up. He smiled when his eyes focused on us, like a child who smiles at his mother when she comforts him. Black circles surrounded his bulging eyes, and his lips were dry and stuck together. "Thank you for coming to see me," he said weakly.

"Are you feeling better?" Phi asked.

"The doctor gave me an injection, but I still can't eat the food." He mumbled something about his family, then hid his face, crying behind his hands. We gave him a few seconds to collect himself.

"You will have to be strong," Phi said.

I didn't know what to say, so I stood next to his bed and felt sorry for him. We were ready to go back to the barracks when Loc walked up the aisle. He looked like he was somewhat recovered, but his hands and voice quivered like he was cold. "How is the labor?" he asked.

"Harder than we imagined," I replied.

"I'm not looking forward to going back," Loc said. "Not after seeing what they did to Danh."

"When will they send you back?" I asked.

"As soon as they think I'm well." His face began to sweat, and his eyes were still yellow.

"You don't look so good," Phi told him. "You should get back to bed."

Loc walked slowly down the aisle, and we said goodbye to Danh, then walked back to our barracks. When we got there, we saw skinny men in faded pajamas, some of them with red blotches on their scalps. Most of the men were sitting in circles in the courtyard; others were wading in the river or resting in the shade of the trees that lined the bank. Phi and I went to the barracks and lay down for a nap. It was late afternoon when the assembly bell rang, and Mr. Nguyen told us he had a surprise.

"You have worked hard this week," he said. "The weak men have deserted, and now our company is strong, ready to proceed with our goals. To reward your efforts, we have planned a party for you. Company 16, a female company, will join us tonight for song and dance." Everyone cheered, but Mr. Nguyen held his hands in the air. "Silence! If you cannot act like gentlemen, the party will be canceled." We all quieted, and he continued, "This will be a time to learn. Company 16 has been here for more than a year. They have proven themselves in labor, self-criticism and self- motivation. They have accomplished their goals, and they are coming here to help you learn. I expect you to participate in the activities we have planned, and I expect you to show self-motivation."

I thought how embarrassing it was going to be, acting like a dog on my cadre's leash in front of women. We spent the rest of the day collecting wood for a fire, and after dinner we formed a circle around the fire and practiced our songs. When the women arrived, they made a circle outside ours. We sang the Vinh An theme song, and as we sang, the women moved into our circle, so it was male, female, male, female.

231

However, about thirty men on the far side were left without enough women to go around. I glanced at the woman to my right. She had a scorpion tattoo on her forearm. The woman to my left had a scar from her lip to her ear. I thought that either one could have beat me in a fight.

Our cadres began dancing with the women cadres. They danced far apart, eyes lowered, picking their feet up high, waving their arms out of beat as we sang. I guess it was a communist folk dance. Binh motioned for us to start dancing. He tried to waive his arm with the tempo and looked like an idiot.

I turned to my left and looked at the woman with the scar on her face. Luckily, Big Manh asked her to dance. I swallowed deeply and turned to the scorpion woman. She looked me in the eye, and I swallowed again. "I don't want to dance to these songs," I said shyly, "but I have to."

"Don't worry." Her eyes opened wide; she was surprised at my honesty. "I don't want to dance either, but we must put on a good show for the cadres." I felt better that she knew I wasn't as stupid as I looked, dancing around like a school boy. When we finished the song, she told me her name was Chau. "You're so young," she said. "Are you alone here? Do you have any friends?"

I told her about Viet escaping, and said Phi was still here. "Visit me next Sunday," she said. "My number is 16-8-3."

Chau's cadre called for her squad to assemble by the fire, and I watched her walk away. She was a tall, lean woman. Her serious face seemed to hide a thousand stories. Big Manh nudged me from behind. "A little old for you Viet," he said, then chuckled and danced like the cadres.

Chau's squad performed a skit about a group of sisters who saved their village from a capitalist attack. The skit began with the girls working in a field. Then they killed the American invaders by luring them into pits, and then continued with their labor. After the skit, we sang and danced to a few more songs. Then the women were taken away, and we assembled. "You showed discipline and self-motivation tonight," Mr. Nguyen said. "Now go to your barracks for review. Tell each other what you have learned tonight, and continue with your enthusiasm in labor tomorrow."

We were about to begin review back at the barracks when the bell started ringing. As we jogged into place, I saw Viet standing between two guards. His head wasn't down like the others' had been, and his eyes were on fire. He struggled until Mr. Nguyen slapped the side of his face with his open palm, then the other side with the back of his hand. Blood ran from Viet's mouth, but his eyes were still fiery. I remembered fighting with him a year before and wondered how I survived. He looked like a crazed beast. "Do we need to discuss what to do with this traitor?" Mr. Nguyen asked.

A cadre yelled, "Let us vote!" so I had to raise my hand to send Viet to the discipline company. I didn't raise it as high as the others, but Viet's crazy eyes were staring through me, and I felt as though I were the traitor.

The next week was harder. Our bodies shrank and we moved slower each day. When I stood up, my head spun and I thought I would pass out. We craved food. We craved sugar. The cigarettes were gone. In the evenings, men searched the ground for bits of tobacco, and more tried to escape. More men were caught, and we voted to send them to the discipline company. Review became more critical, usually centered around people's greed for a little more food. By the end of the week, we had finished chopping the grass and began breaking the hard red earth.

On Sunday, I got another pass to visit Danh. I went alone this time because Phi wanted to sleep. When I got to the hospital barracks, the doctor told me Danh had been sent to Saigon for better treatment, so I went to Loc's bed to see if he knew what had happened.

"They took Danh away yesterday," Loc said. "They took him away with a blanket over his head. He wasn't moving."

"Was he dead?" I asked.

"I think so."

I sat on the corner of Loc's bed. He told me he had been trying to act sick, but he was better, and they were sending him back to our squad before the end of the day. I stayed with him for a few minutes and told him about Qui and Tu being sent to the discipline company, then I went to Company 16 to visit Chau.

It was the only time I had been on the other side of the assembly field since the first day. It was the old section of the camp. The bamboo buildings were seasoned, dark and raveled. The men there moved slower than we did. The women seemed to be in better shape, but I never found out why. I was nervous, walking to Chau's. I didn't know if she would remember inviting me. I wasn't going to visit her, but I made the mistake of telling Phi and Big Manh about her invitation. They would have made fun of me and called me a coward if I didn't go.

Company 16 was next to a wooden bridge that crossed the river. I found Chau sitting with some other women on the bridge. They all giggled when I walked up. Chau smiled at me, and sensing how embarrassed I was, asked if I wanted to walk along the river. This made the women giggle more. "How was your week?" she asked as we walked away from the bridge.

"It was okay." We walked up the river to the edge of her courtyard and sat on the bank. She looked at me with dark, serious eyes. I glanced at her, then looked away. "How long have you been here?" I asked.

"Long enough to know how to stay out of trouble. This is why I invited you to see me." I was confused. I had been thinking about her all week. I had never had a girlfriend, and I knew she was too old for me, but she seemed to be my only chance. "I asked you to come here because I want to help you." I was ashamed that Chau had invited me because she felt sorry for me. I didn't think I needed a woman to help me. I looked away as she spoke to me, but I listened.

"You shouldn't have told me you didn't want to dance," she said. "You didn't know who I was—I could have been a cadre. You have to take this place seriously. The communists are playing a game, so you think this is a game. But this is a game of life and death. People disappear from this place for no reason. If you're singled out, you're as good as dead. Someone you think is your best friend will turn you in for a few extra grains of rice. You shouldn't have trusted me. You can't trust anyone here."

We were silent for a few minutes, and I stared across the river. Guards patrolled along the bank with black rifles slung over their shoulders. Women's voices mixed together, and a cool breeze blew along the river. "I knew I could trust you," I said. "I knew you weren't a communist."

Chau grabbed my arm; her grasp was tight. She tried to shake me, but I resisted. "You don't know anything. You must realize this: you cannot trust anyone except yourself."

"Can I trust you?" I asked.

Chau smiled gently. "You were lucky this time," she said. "Now go."

When I got back to the barracks, Loc was already there. He was sitting with Qui and Tu, who were back from the discipline company.. They stopped talking when I stepped in. Tu looked up, and I saw the power was gone from his eyes. His head was shaven, and sores covered his arms and feet. "Where have you been?" Loc asked.

"I went to visit a friend. Have you seen Phi?"

"He and Big Manh are by the river. They're trying to catch fish with their mosquito nets."

I pulled my net from the hook and walked to the river. Phi, Big Manh and Cu were dredging the water with their nets. When Phi saw me, he held up a string with three small river bass on it. "We will eat tonight," Cu said with a big smile. I waded into the water and took over Cu's section as he watched us from the bank. We fished for a half hour but didn't catch any more.

The assembly bell rang and we lined up. Tu, Qui and the other men who had tried to escape were lined up in front of us. Mr. Nguyen motioned with his hand toward them."The deserters have returned from discipline. Tonight we will decide if they are ready to join us again." He walked along the line of men and stared at them with his hard eyes. "When these men were sent to discipline, they were asked to ponder a question: why is it wrong to desert your brothers? Tonight in review, they will answer this question for us. If we are satisfied with their answers, we will vote to give them a second chance. If we are not satisfied with their answers, they will return to discipline."

He dismissed us, and we went to our barracks for dinner. As we ate, Binh passed out letters. Phi and I both got one. Mom said everyone was fine at home and she hoped I was studying and working hard so I could come home soon. She

236

and Mrs. At had signed up on a waiting list, but she wasn't sure when they could visit.

After dinner, review began. "This is an important night," Binh said. He stood solidly in front of his desk and his eyes traveled from one man to the next. "Who would like to offer the first criticism?" We all looked toward Dan. Tu and Qui shuffled nervously as their eyes darted back and forth. "Viet," Binh said, "you have not offered criticism for some time. You will start."

All eyes focused on me. I stared at the floor and tried to think. "We've all been working very hard," I said, "but we should not have eaten Tu's and Qui's food."

Binh gave me a disappointed look. "Your criticism is good, Viet, but you are avoiding the most important criticism of the night." He stared at me, waiting for me to say something against Tu and Qui. The silence sent a chill up the back of my neck.

"Tu and Qui worked hard for the first day, but they should not have deserted us."

Binh smiled. "That is closer, Viet, now continue." I didn't know what else to say. My skin stiffened. "The question, Viet. Ask the question."

"Why is it wrong to desert your brothers?"

"Who are you asking? Criticism must be directed at the individual, or no progress can be made."

I looked up at Tu and Qui. They looked back at me with swollen, tired eyes. I could feel the pain in their faces. "Tu, why was it wrong for you to desert us?"

Tu was sitting on the platform, but his legs were curled up to his chest. His voice was tired; he seemed to be talking in his sleep. "It is wrong to desert our brothers because our strength comes from working together. I'm sorry for deserting you. I know it was wrong. Please give me a second chance. I'll work hard to make up for my mistake."

Binh gave the signal for us to clap. "Manh, would you like to continue with criticism?" Big Manh asked Qui why it was wrong to desert his brothers.

"Our squad is only as strong as the weakest member," Qui said. "Our country is only as strong as the weakest citizen. We have been given a great opportunity at Vinh An. We have been given the opportunity to help our country. I deserted this opportunity because I was ignorant. But for the last two weeks, I have had much time to think. I want to be a part of this squad. I want to accomplish the goals of labor, self-criticism and self-motivation. I want to help our country."

Binh clapped again, and we followed. I couldn't believe how two weeks of discipline had changed Tu and Qui. They had been South Vietnamese soldiers before. Even though they were drug addicts when I first saw them, I could tell they had pride. The discipline company had stripped them of their pride in two weeks.

"Is there any more criticism before we vote?" Binh asked.

Loc raised his hand. "Tu and Qui have been punished for their wrong actions. From their answers tonight, I can see they have realized their mistake. I think they're ready to help our squad."

"Is there any more criticism?" Binh peered around the barracks, and no one moved. "Let us vote. Who is in favor of taking Tu and Qui back into our squad?" We all raised our hands. Binh's smile didn't change. "Welcome back, gentlemen. Now let us continue with criticism. Tu, would you like to start?"

Tu had some criticism ready. "I noticed today that Manh,

Phi and Cu were fishing. I think it is good that they are doing this, but I wonder what they did with the fish."

Binh's eyes lit up. "Where were you fishing?" Big Manh pointed toward the river, and Cu smiled. "Did you catch any fish?" Binh asked.

"A few snapper," Big Manh said.

"And what did you do with them?"

"They are on a stringer. We were going to ask you if we could cook them tonight."

"Why do you need more fish?" Binh asked.

Big Manh didn't answer; his eyes were angry. Binh stared at him until he lowered them. "No one was given permission to fish," Binh said. "We cannot have everyone wading through the water, catching the fish that are meant for the camp as a whole. Manh, go release the fish."

"But they will die anyway. They will be wasted."

"Do you disobey me?" Big Manh lowered his eyes and walked out of the barracks. "Enough criticism for tonight," Binh said. "We have accomplished much. Tomorrow, we will continue with labor."

Self-Criticism

I was sitting on the river bank with Phi, Big Manh and Cu when Viet returned from the discipline company. It was a Sunday evening, two weeks after they took him away. His head was shaved, and dry red blotches covered his scalp. The fire that raged in his eyes as the guards had taken him away was now a faint flicker. "You look terrible," Phi told him.

Viet sat down, folding his stiff legs in front of him. "I've been in a hole for two weeks," he said with a weak, raspy voice. "They tried to kill me, but I wouldn't die."

Big Manh and Cu glanced at each other with a serious look. "What did they do to you?" Big Manh asked.

"First they made me sign a document confessing to my crimes."

"You signed it," I said. "The way you were struggling here, I'm surprised they got you to sign anything."

"I struggled until I got to the discipline company. The first thing I saw was a row of men strapped to a rail. Their feet dangled just above the ground, and their faces were covered with dried blood. I couldn't tell if they were dead or alive. When I saw that, I decided to do whatever the bastards told me."

"What did they make you do?" Phi asked.

"Nothing. That was the point of it. They said they gave me a chance to motivate myself, and since I failed, they would show me what non-motivation caused. The first week I was there, they put me in a cage just big enough to squat in. Every morning, they gave me a bowl of red rice. The rest of the day and night, I squatted. During the day, the guards wouldn't let me sleep. They walked by every ten or fifteen minutes and rattled the cage."

"Where did you shit?" Phi asked.

"I didn't need to much, but when I did, I went in the cage." We all looked toward the ground, not wanting to acknowledge the same thing could happen to any one of us. "After the first week, they let me out, but I couldn't stand. Two guards stretched me out on the ground and pulled on my arms and legs. The muscles in my legs felt like they were ripping. They made me and five other men hobble around the courtyard. The head guard asked us why we deserted, and I told him my family would starve if I didn't get back to Saigon. I thought it was a good answer, but he flew into a rage.

"They threw me into a hole in the ground that was even smaller than the cage, and I landed in a few inches of slime. I didn't know what it was at first, but when the smell hit me I knew: it was the piss and shit from the men who were in there before me." Viet pulled up the back of his shirt; black holes with red rings covered his back. "The sores are from leaning against the side of the hole. Worms dug into me

241

while I slept. At first I tried to stay in the middle, but after a few days I passed out."

Viet lay back, resting on his elbows and trying to stretch his legs. We were silent for a moment, then he rolled over and looked at me. "Remember when you told me you wanted to leave this country? You should leave now. If you wait, it could be too late. You should leave now while you have the strength."

"But you tried to leave," I said, "and they caught you."

"They were lucky. I would have made it, but I was in a hurry. I tried to get a ride, and some guards spotted me." Cu smiled at Big Manh—he had told us that would happen. "I know how to get out of here now," Viet said. "It's simple. You just have to steal some food and walk." He rested his head against a rock and shut his eyes.

I walked back to the barracks and collapsed on my bunk. I thought about escaping, but I knew I wouldn't try. It wasn't worth being thrown into a hole full of piss.

After dinner, we all criticized Viet for deserting us, then we voted to take him back into our squad. Before Binh blew out the lantern, he told Dan and Qui to borrow knives and axes from the other squads. "We will cut bamboo tomorrow," he said with a happy grin. "It will be a nice change from working in the field."

After exercises the next morning, Binh led us along the river bank, up a path and into the jungle. We walked for more than an hour before we saw any bamboo; the trees closer to the camp had already been cut. We chopped our way through the brush, slapping off mosquitoes and dodging branches. Finally, we came to a group of bamboo that stood ten to twenty yards high. They were grown together in clusters, so they were solid at the bottom then branched out at the top like giant shoots.

"Who has cut bamboo before?" Binh asked. No one had, so we stood waiting for him to show us how. "Cutting bamboo is simple," he said. "Cut the dead shoots on the outside first, then cut the green ones from the middle, so they won't spring out." I knew that cutting bamboo was dangerous. Every child in Vietnam was told to stay away from the bamboo trees because the shoots could spring out with enough force to kill a person.

Binh told us to get to work, then he went to a fallen log and sat down. It was the first time I had seen a cadre sit while the rest of us were working, but it was also the first time we had worked away from Mr. Nguyen and the other cadres. I thought how I would like to offer Binh some criticism about how he should get up and help us. Dan and Big Manh began chopping at a ten-yard-high tree, and Phi and I dragged the dead shoots back. The others stood a safe distance away. When we got to the green part, Dan told us to stand back, then chopped as hard as he could. His ax bounced off the bamboo like a rubber ball.

"You have to cut from the middle," Binh said from his log. "Boost Big Manh up. Stop looking like a bunch of misfits." We boosted Big Manh to the middle of the cluster, and Binh looked on nodding his head and smiling. Big Manh whacked at one of the middle shoots.

"That one is too big," Dan said. "Start with a smaller one until we figure out how to do this."

"If you just chop the smaller ones," Binh said, "we will never finish. Keep chopping, Manh." Big Manh gave it another whack, then another. The giant shoot creaked under the strain. "Hit it, Manh!" Binh shouted. "Show us how strong you are."

Big Manh reared back and axed the giant shoot again. This time it sprung loose, catching him under the arm and catapulting him into the air. I never saw anything like it. His body sprung upward, flipped over halfway, and fell into the middle of the cluster of shoots. It looked like a circus act. Binh walked toward us, laughing. Dan climbed into the cluster, and I went in after him. When I got closer I saw one of the small pointed shoots in the middle had pierced Big Manh's chest. Blood ran down the shoot.

"Manh!" Dan screamed. "Talk to me!"

Big Manh lay limp, motionless, face down. The point of the shoot had ripped through the back of his pajamas. Time stood still as the two of us looked at him, knowing anything we did would be too late. Big Manh's huge spirit surrounded us, then faded away.

Phi and Cu boosted Binh into the cluster. "Is he hurt?" Binh asked us.

"He's dead," Dan said.

Binh told us to get down, and he told Phi to hand him an ax. He began whacking at the shoot that pierced Big Manh's body. Then he whacked at the shoots around him. Bamboo flew in every direction, and huge shoots fell like clockwork. It was obvious he knew what he was doing. We stood watching him, thinking that Big Manh would still be alive if Binh had helped us. When he had finished chopping, he pulled the shoot out of Big Manh's chest. It was thick with blood. Dan and I were still closest, and Binh handed his body down to us. I had never touched a dead person before.

"Cut the shoots in ten-foot sections," Binh commanded. Everyone stood motionless, staring at him. "Cut the shoots!" he screamed.

I thought of running. Now would be our best chance. We stood in a half circle around Binh, machetes and axes in our hands. We all leaned slightly toward him. Cu was behind him and was slowly raising his axe from the ground when Binh sensed our anger and pulled the pistol from the back of his trousers. He stood firm; his eyes glared. "Cut the shoots!"

Cu lowered his axe and we all turned away. We began cutting the shoots, and when we finished, Binh tied the sections together with vines. As we lay Big Manh's body on the shoots, I noticed the jungle was quiet. No birds were chirping, no insects were hissing. Dan and Cu carried Big Manh's body to the river. The rest of us carried more shoots and tied them together to make a raft. Binh pushed the raft into the river, and we grabbed onto the sides and floated downstream with it.

Big Manh's body lay stiff on its makeshift raft, a symbol of what my life was worth to the communists. His face was gray; his blood mixed with the water and ran over my hands. When we got back to the camp, we carried him to the office. Mr. Nguyen came out, and he and Binh stared at the body for a few seconds. "Go to the barracks," Binh told us. I thought he didn't want us there while he explained what had happened. We spent the rest of the day breaking up the raft and making stakes. Some were stained with Big Manh's blood.

After dinner, Binh told us he would not be there for review and left Dan in charge. I had never respected Binh and now I hated him. He was a hypocrite, a coward. Not only was he responsible for Big Manh's death, but he wouldn't even criticize himself for what had happened. Because he was in charge, he only practiced his communism when it favored him.

We gathered around Dan that evening and were silent for a few minutes, staring at the ground. Dan asked if anyone had criticism, but no one spoke. A heavy pall hung in the barracks until Viet moved to the edge of his bunk. "I have some criticism," he said. "I criticize all of us for not avenging Big Manh. We should have rushed Binh when we had the chance. No one here has any pride."

"Without life," Cu told Viet, "pride cannot exist. Therefore life is more valuable than pride." Viet lay back in his bed. When Binh came into the barracks, he blew out the lantern and left without speaking. He never mentioned Big Manh's name again.

November passed, and the camp grew. During the camp meeting in December, I counted fifty-three companies with a hundred people each. When new prisoners were brought in, we watched them walk by, fat and soft, as we had been a few months earlier. Every day I did my work, said my criticism and clapped for Binh. Viet's sores healed and scarred. We broke the earth and planted potatoes, then moved to another field and chopped the grass.

It was January when Mr. Nguyen announced we would be having visitors. He read a list of names, including mine, Cu's and Phi's. "You will be taken to the visitors' area on Sunday," he said. "You will have your pajamas washed, smiles on your faces and good things to tell your visitors about Vinh An."

I didn't sleep Saturday night. I lay awake wondering what Mom would bring me to eat. After breakfast, the bell rang, and the people who had visitors were assembled. There were about thirty of us. "You are looking good this morning," Mr. Nguyen said. "I am sure your attitudes will be as good as your appearances."

He finished a lecture about appropriate things to tell our visitors, then two cadres and six guards escorted us through the camp, up the path and into the jungle. I was anxious not only to see Mom, but to have contact with the outside world. Our suffering had brought the men in my squad closer in a way, but had also caused us to think only about ourselves and our own survival. I walked as fast as I could, rushing to see someone who wasn't too tired or too hungry to care about me.

It was noon when we got to the visiting area. Men and women from other companies were already lined beside the pavilion, but no coaches had arrived yet. My first thought was that the communists were only teasing us. There would be no visitors, and this was their way of teaching us not to rely on outsiders. We sang "I love labor…Vinh An is a new land…." We sang every song they had taught us, until someone yelled, "Coaches! They're coming!" We began to cheer, but the guards told us to be quiet or the visitors would be sent home.

Three coaches pulled up with a cloud of dust and stopped. The cadres walked through the dust and met the drivers as they got off. The drivers handed the cadres a few sheets of paper, which they brought back to the pavilion. The head guard told us to wait for our name to be called, then to find our visitor and return to the pavilion. The visitors unloaded from the coaches and some of the prisoners stood up, trying to see their relatives. "Sit down!" the guards screamed.

My name was called before Phi's, and I ran to the crowd and found Mom and Mrs. At. Mom cried when she saw me. We hugged each other, and she pushed me back, holding my shoulders and staring at my face. Then she cried again.

"You're so thin. Don't they feed you?"

"I'm fine," I said.

"Where's Phi?" Mrs. At asked. "Is he okay?"

"He's fine," I said, and I led them to the pavilion and pointed toward Phi. When his name was called, he jumped up and ran toward us.

"My son!" Mrs. At cried. Tears rolled across her full cheeks. They hugged each other, then Mrs. At turned to Mom. "They're very thin," she said. "They look sick." She rubbed the top of Phi's head. "What happened to your hair?"

Phi and I both grabbed for the bags our moms were carrying. "What did you bring us to eat?" I asked.

"Slow down," Mom said as I grabbed the bag from her hand. Before she could say anything else, Phi and I were sitting on the ground, eating chicken legs and white rice. We sat outside the pavilion, close to the trees. Mom kept stroking my face. "My son, what are they doing to you?" Mrs. At was doing the same to Phi.

We had eaten all the chicken when a woman screamed, "What have you done with my son!" Two guards were holding her, and another was trying to cover her mouth. "Murderers!" the woman screamed. "Devils!"

Three more women and two men circled around the guards. "Where is my daughter?" one of the women asked.

More guards came over to the group, cocked their rifles and pointed them at the distraught parents. "On the bus!" one of the guards commanded, and the people moved slowly to the bus.

Mom and Mrs. At looked on with terrified eyes. "Those men are animals," Mom said. "Are you safe here? Will they hurt you?

"We'll be fine," I said. "How is our family?"

"Vinh quit school to help your father fish," Mom said, gaining strength as she talked about the family. Her eyes dried, and her voice became strong. "Tu can spell your name," she said, smiling for the first time."

"I wish I could be home for Tet. I wish I could be there to help the family."

"We won't have much of a Tet this year. We have many new neighbors who watch us closely."

"Will Dad come to visit next time?"

"Your father cannot bear to see you in here, but he sent a message for you." Mom looked around to make sure no one was looking, then leaned over and whispered into my ear, "He said for you to be strong. He said to act like you believe everything the communists say, and do what they tell you to do. He was proud of your letter. He said it showed you have the intelligence and strength to make the communists trust you."

I reached for a new bag of food. "Don't eat this," Mom said. "It's from Viet's mother; she asked me to bring it to him." Mom wanted to know how Viet was doing, and I told her about his escape."His mother's very worried. She hasn't received a letter from him, so she thought that he may have caused trouble."

"He's well. He was in the discipline company for a few weeks, and they made him squat in a hole for trying to escape. He was sick for a while, but now he's well."

"They put him in a hole!" Mom's face lit up with terror. "Will they do that to you? Will they torture you?"

"I don't think so."

"We should have escaped this country a long time ago." Mom's voice quivered again. "We should have left before the communists took over."

249

"Why didn't we, Mom?"

"Because your father wouldn't leave his country. As long as South Vietnam existed, your father wouldn't leave. You have to be strong, son, and do whatever they say to survive. In time, we'll escape this terrible country."

We ate most of the food our mothers brought, and then I lay on the ground. My stomach felt like a soccer ball pumped with too much air. I fought to keep the food down, but I had eaten too much. I ran to the side of the trees and lost the only good food I had eaten in four months. When I returned to the pavilion, the coach drivers began honking their horns and the guards went around telling the visitors it was time to leave. Mom hugged me and told me to be strong, then she and Mrs. At walked to the coach.

"Line up!" the guards ordered as the coaches pulled away. We lined up, and they marched us back into the jungle. When we got back to the camp, we assembled, and Mr. Nguyen came out of his office.

"I see most of you have brought food back with you." He walked up the middle line, grabbing bags from the men and looking through them. He held up a whole cooked chicken. "Your family must be doing very well at home," he said to the man he had taken it from. He walked to the next man, pulled his bag open and looked inside. "What do we have here?" He pulled out a carton of filtered cigarettes. "Capitalists' cigarettes!" He poked the man's chest with his fingertips. "Where did you get this?"

"I don't know where they came from."

"You lie!" Mr. Nguyen poked the man again, and then slapped his face. "Who brought these to you?"

"I don't know where they came from."

Mr. Nguyen slapped the man again. He was a small,

helpless man, but he was determined not to tell. "To discipline with him!"

The guards took the man away, and Mr. Nguyen continued up the line. I was holding Viet's bag, but I hadn't looked in it. What if his mom had sent something she bought on the black market? Mr. Nguyen would think it was mine. I would either have to claim it, or turn Viet in. Mr. Nguyen moved down my line. "What do you have in your bag?" he asked Phi.

"Just some food, sir."

He opened Phi's bag, looked in it, closed it and gave it back. Now it was my turn. "Are these your bags?"

"Yes, sir."

He opened Viet's bag first. My heart stopped. He reached his hand inside the bag, then his eyes lit up. Slowly he pulled his hand out of the bag—it was covered with rice pudding. Shaking the pudding off and licking his fingers, he said, "Not bad," and continued down the line.

The rest of the squad was eating dinner when we got back to the barracks. When I handed Viet his bag of food, he quickly opened it and started eating. "Everyone stop what you are doing!" Binh shouted. "Does anyone see the wrong action taking place?" No one said anything.

"We now exist as a group, so the gifts we receive are gifts to the group." Viet almost spat the chicken out of his mouth. Binh paused and stared at him. "The food should be divided equally. Do you agree, Viet?"

Viet swallowed his chicken and tried to smile. "I'm sorry, Mr. Binh, I should have thought of that myself." He dumped his bag onto the bed. Phi, Cu and I dumped the food we had left.

"You should not apologize to me," Binh said in a soft

voice. "You should apologize to the group."

Viet apologized to everyone, then I did too, then Phi, then Cu. The men who didn't have visitors helped themselves to the food on Viet's bunk, watching to see what everyone else took. Binh said he didn't want any because we were getting enough food already. I didn't see how he could act like he was getting the same food as we were when he was so much fatter.

"I know some of you are not happy about sharing the food," Binh said. "You think since your family brought this food, you should keep it for yourselves. You think you own it. You think like this because you still put yourselves above the group—above society." He sat on his desk and smiled, and I braced myself for a lecture.

"Your families sent you this food, but other people's families work just as hard as yours. Whether they are working in factories or farms, or producing goods to sell abroad, they all contribute to society, which in turn supports us. Without society you would not have this chance to learn and grow. You should consider yourselves lucky that society is giving you this chance to improve yourselves. Society supported you. The little amount of food your families brought today is nothing compared to the sacrifice many have made to provide you with this camp and the food that we eat each day. You are dismissed. We will continue this discussion in review tonight."

Viet, Phi and I walked to the river and sat on the bank. I thought about all the food we ate. It seemed like more food than our whole squad had eaten since we were brought to Vinh An. The bell rang, and we returned to our barracks for review. "Who would like to offer the first criticism?" Binh asked.

Qui raised his hand. "I would like to thank the men who shared their food," Qui said, "but they should have done so without regret. It was obvious that some of the men didn't want to share the food with their brothers."

"Who did not want to share?" Binh asked.

"As far as I could tell," Qui said, "no one wanted to share."

"That is very good criticism. Who would like to accept this criticism?"

"I will," Viet said. "I didn't want to share my food, and this was wrong."

"I will also accept the criticism," I said. "We were greedy, and we thank you for pointing this out to us." Phi and Cu agreed as well.

Distrust

The first potatoes we planted sprouted, and we finished planting the second field and moved to a third. Binh never criticized himself for what had happened to Big Manh, and of course, we never said anything about it. But the criticism of ourselves was never-ending. Review wasn't finished until each person had criticized someone else. If we didn't have criticism for others, we had to have some for ourselves. We were always watched—if not by the cadres, then by each other.

Cu was the only one who got used to living on the food they gave us. I thought he was amazing. Physically, he became the ultimate communist tool. He was thin, but never looked unhealthy; his eyes were always clear and alert. He never worked too hard, and he never worked too little. He seemed to be in rhythm with something bigger than any of us could see or feel.

Dan was not as clever as Cu. His intentions were just as good, but his talent was lacking. He suffered but did not complain. Lines formed on his face and worry showed in his eyes, but he never confided in anyone. One time, I asked Dan about his wife and child, and he didn't answer. He didn't trust any of us, but I trusted him. He was the master of criticizing without making a person look bad, and I respected him for that.

Qui became the weakest member of our squad. He never recovered from the discipline and was always being criticized for not working hard enough. He watched us closely, making sure he would have criticism of his own to offer.

We found out in review that during the war, Tu's job was to go into the communists' tunnels and flush them out. In Vietnam, these men were called tunnel rats, and they were some of the most respected men in the South's Army. Tu gained his strength back after discipline, but his attitude had changed. He no longer questioned Binh and became one of the hardest workers. I respected him, but I never got to know him. He thought of me as a child, and compared to him, I was.

Loc was either sick or faking being sick most of the time. If we weren't working or criticizing, he was sleeping.

Phi got weaker and his movements slowed. Like me, he existed moment to moment. There was no reason to look ahead, and we were too tired to remember the past.

Viet had the most energy of any of us. When he recovered from discipline, he stole paper from Binh's desk and made cards so he could gamble with other men in our company to win food and tobacco. He had a card game going every night for two weeks until someone turned him in. I thought they would send him to discipline, but instead Mr. Nguyen slapped him a few times, and made him burn the cards and stay up all night cleaning the latrine.

But this wasn't the end of Viet's schemes. The first week

in February, he invited Phi and me for dinner. When we asked him what he was talking about, he said he was cooking dinner for Tet. He led us to the fire where we boiled our water, and looked around to make sure no one was watching. "Come close," he said. He lifted a rock from the coals, and underneath was a pile of burnt potato ends. Phi and I looked at each other with disbelief.

"Where did you get them?" Phi asked.

"From the trash dump behind the kitchen," Viet said proudly. "I got them last night."

Phi put the rock over the potatoes. "If they catch you creeping around at night, they'll shoot you."

"Relax. Do you think you can live on the food they give you?" Phi was silent. Viet uncovered the potatoes again, wrapped them in a towel, and led us behind some bushes. Phi said again that he thought Viet would get caught sneaking around at night, but when Viet offered us some of the potatoes, neither of us could refuse.

Three days later, Viet asked me to go with him to the garbage pit. I was afraid to go, but I was hungry, and knew I wouldn't feel right eating what he brought back unless I helped him. After review that night, we told Binh we were going to the latrine, and instead we sneaked behind the barracks, through the bushes and along the river to the garbage pit. It was a dark night, but the spotlights searched through the bushes. We lay flat on the ground, letting the light pass above us, then ran to the next bush and hid again. When we got to the bushes behind the kitchen, we saw guards and cadres through the window, eating and laughing.

We crept along some high grass to the pit. Viet crawled in and started picking through the trash while I stayed in the grass. I could smell the rotten food. I didn't want to crawl in, but Viet motioned for me to help him. As I did, two guards came out of the kitchen. We crawled farther into the pit and covered ourselves with garbage. They threw chicken bones and cabbage on top of us, and walked back into the kitchen. I felt like a hungry rat. We grabbed the chicken bones and some more potatoes, and crept back along the river. The lanterns were out when we got back, but the fire was still burning in the middle of the courtyard. We hid the food in some bushes behind the barracks.

"Binh is probably looking for us," I said. I was shaking with fright.

"He isn't looking for us," Viet said.

"What about our clothes? We smell like rotten food."

"We need to wash in the river."

"You're crazy. Then we'll be soaked."

"I'll tell Binh you fell in the latrine, and I had to help you wash." It was a poor excuse, but luckily, Binh wasn't there when we got back to the barracks. We climbed into bed and hung our nets. I whispered to Viet that I was never going back to that place. "That's okay," he said. "Phi can go next time."

Phi did go the next time, and I went the time after that. We became expert scavengers. We could be out of the barracks, into the pit, and back to the barracks in seven minutes, with no smell on our clothes and no sweat on our foreheads. The extra food made our labor easier. All we had to do was act like we were as tired as the men who were getting half the food we were getting.

In review one night, Qui complimented Viet on how hard he was working. "But I don't understand why you have so much more energy. I think you're getting food from some-where." This was nothing out of the ordinary. Qui was always accusing us of things we didn't do, and Binh usually didn't pay attention.

Two nights later, it was Phi and Viet's turn to get the food. I told them they shouldn't go. I had a bad feeling about it, but Viet said I worried too much. "I can be in and out of that pit before they know I'm gone," he said. Phi looked at me with a worried smile, and after review, they left for the latrine. As soon as they left, Qui said he thought they were going to steal some food. I thought Binh would ignore him, but instead he darted out the door. I wanted to go after them to warn them, but there was no way. In minutes, the bell started ringing—the constant clang! clang! clang! that told us someone was in trouble.

We put on our trousers and assembled. Two guards led Phi and Viet in front of us, and they were forced to their knees, one on either side of Mr. Nguyen. "We have rats among us!" he exclaimed, and grabbed Phi by the chin. "These rats are not satisfied with our food. They would rather eat garbage!"

He shook Phi's head, then pushed him to the ground. Viet cringed and looked away, not wanting to give him a chance to slap him. A guard came with a bowl of rotten fish and handed it to Mr. Nguyen. "If they would rather eat garbage," he said, "let them eat garbage." He emptied the rotten fish onto the ground, then pushed Viet's face into it. "Eat!" He pushed Phi's face into it. "Eat, you little rat!"

He held their faces in the garbage until they had eaten most of it, while the guards laughed quietly. Phi vomited the fish back onto the ground and was coughing, but Mr. Nguyen pushed his face back into it. The cadres looked on as though an important lesson were being taught. When Phi had eaten his vomit, we were dismissed. They kept Phi and

Viet up the whole night cleaning the latrine and running circles around the courtyard. The next day, it was back to work.

In March, the rains became heavy; it rained every afternoon. The cool showers were better than the scorching sun, but the earth was wet, and it was harder to dig with the mud sticking to our hoes.

They brought the barbers back to cut our hair again. Because of the lack of nourishment, our hair had taken five months to grow to the middle of our ears. We were sitting in our squads, waiting our turn, when three shots sounded. I looked to the river and saw two men swimming across. Guards ran to the bank, shooting their guns in the air, but the men kept swimming. The guards ran up the other side of the bank. There was no way the men could get away, but the guards fired into the river, and bullets splashed around them. One of them stopped and waved his arms in the air. "Don't shoot!" he screamed in terror, but they kept shooting. They took bets on who could hit the men first. Bam! One man went down. Two guards claimed to have hit him, and they argued over a pack of cigarettes. The other man made it to the edge of the river, and the guards pulled him out of the water.

Silence and tension pervaded our company for the rest of the day, and more guards were posted around the courtyard. Phi said they were there to keep us from revolting, but Viet laughed. "Are you serious? These cowards would never revolt." I knew Viet was right. The distrust our captors created among us kept us from planning a revolt. Like at home in Saigon, we couldn't trust anyone, so the communists had complete control.

After review that night, Viet told Phi and me he was going to escape. Phi laughed at him, but Viet insisted. "They don't think anyone will try to escape now," he said. "Not after what we saw today. They think we're frightened, but I'm not. This is the perfect time to go."

Phi and I looked at each other. We knew Viet was serious. "What is your plan?" I asked.

"We have bread for breakfast every Monday. I'll volunteer to get breakfast and then escape with the food."

"You're crazy," Phi said. "You'll never get away with it." I had been worried before that Viet might try something stupid, but I knew he wasn't crazy enough to escape in the light of day—not after we saw the guards shooting at the men in the river.

The next morning Viet volunteered to get breakfast. He smiled at us before he left, and we smiled back, thinking he was bluffing. Phi and I waited outside the barracks so we could call his bluff when he returned with the food. We saw the first man return to his squad with their breakfast, then the second, then the third. Everyone came back except Viet. "He's bluffing," Phi said. "He's taking his time, trying to make us worry." We went back into the barracks and waited with the others.

"Where's Viet?" Qui asked. "Why is he taking so long?" We waited another five minutes before Binh left to find him. In another five minutes, we heard the three shots. My heart jumped, then it began to race.

"That fool," Phi whispered. "He'll never make it." I sat on my bed, waiting for Binh to come back and question me, but the assembly bell rang first, so we lined up and they counted heads. I thought Mr. Nguyen would pull me out of line, but he didn't. We were dismissed and returned to the barracks.

"Circle around," Binh said, and we made a half circle

around his desk. "Viet has deserted us again. He will be caught, and this time the punishment will be severe. We will not take him back into our squad. He has proven to us that he is incapable of learning." He walked up the aisle, and stood above me. "Did you know Viet was planning to escape?"

"No, Mr. Binh. Viet has disappointed me with his actions." I don't think Binh believed me, and I wasn't sure why he didn't question me further.

"I suppose you knew nothing of his escape either," he said to Phi.

"No, Mr. Binh," Phi said, "I didn't know."

Binh walked back and sat on his desk. We were so weak that missing one meal would make it almost impossible to work all day. We watched Binh, wondering if he would take pity on us and let us get breakfast. He sat on his desk, staring at Phi and me. "Viet was everyone's responsibility," he said. "Because we did not pay attention to him, because we did not know of his plans to escape, and because we did not stop him, we will not eat this morning."

Self-Motivation

The monsoon storms hit Vinh An hard. Sheets of water whipped in the wind, and the river rose until the current was swift and clouded with mud. The first week of April, we dug ditches around the fields, trying to stop the flooding water. The second week, we dug up the potatoes we had planted so they wouldn't wash away. It rained for six days straight. On the second day, there was no assembly bell. Binh said we would not be working because the fields were flooded. We waited for the breakfast bell, but it didn't ring. Cu asked why we didn't have breakfast, and Binh said they were running low on food. "What about the potatoes?" Cu asked.

"We piled them too close to the river," Binh answered. "They washed away."

"Why can't they bring more food in?" Tu asked.

"The river is too swift," Binh replied, "and the roads are too muddy. Our food will be rationed." For the next two days, we got a bowl of rice soup once a day. By the third day, we had no energy to move. Binh was only in the barracks to bring our food and to sleep. He still had plenty of energy, and smiled like nothing was happening. When he left the barracks, I imagined him and the other cadres stuffing their faces with the potatoes he said had washed away.

On the fourth day, the water rose into the barracks. Binh waded in and told us all the food was gone. On the fifth day, I began to feel my body eating away at itself. I dreamed constantly, not knowing if I was asleep or awake. No one moved from their beds. On the sixth day, the rain stopped, and that evening, Binh gave us each a handful of peanuts. I ate them one by one. The next day the water receded from our barracks. Binh told us food was on the way, and we should have it by evening. I didn't have the energy to be excited. I was existing like a plant, not able to move, hardly conscious.

The dinner bell rang, and Binh came into the barracks with a bucket of rice, some fish and some vegetables. It was the first time they had ever given us more than two things in one meal. We rolled to our sides and slowly scooped food into our mouths. I was so weak, I could barely chew. My head spun, my body went numb, and I fell asleep.

I woke to the breakfast bell the next morning. I knew they wouldn't let us die; they needed us to replant the fields. We stayed in the barracks all day, gaining our strength back. When Mr. Nguyen assembled us the next morning, I thought he would say something about the flood and about us doing a good job of surviving on no food, but he didn't. He said we would have one more day to rest, and then we would restore the camp.

There was much to do. The sewer ditches were clogged with wood and other debris from the flood. Both bridges and some of the latrines had washed down the river. We cleaned the sewer ditches during the days, and in the evenings, we restored our tool racks and chopped wood. A camp meeting was held, but little was said about the flood. We returned to the fields, dug canals and planted rice.

They fed us well for two weeks, and when we had gained some weight, they said we would have visitors again. It was the same routine, but this time the coaches were there when we walked out of the jungle. We assembled, and by the time they counted heads, Mom had picked me out of the men and was waving at me from the edge of the pavilion. When we were dismissed to meet our visitors, I led her to the edge of the trees where we could talk in private. She told me that Mrs. At didn't have the money for the bus fare, so she had sent food along for Phi. "Did Viet make it home?" I asked.

Mom was stroking my face; her eyes were full of pity. I grabbed one of the bags from her hand before she answered. "Yes," she whispered, and then looked around to see if anyone was listening. "You're thinner than before. Have they been starving you?"

"The valley flooded and we ran out of food," I said. She stroked my cheek again, but I pulled away so I could bite into a chicken leg.

"Viet came to our house one night," she said. "He told me it was easy to escape and brought me a map to give you. But I don't trust him. He seems crazy to me."

"Did you bring the map?"

"Yes, but there's still nowhere for you to go." She was quiet for a moment, and seemed to be deciding if she would tell me the next part. I grabbed another piece of chicken. "Your father is organizing an escape for some people," she whispered.

"An escape from where?" I asked between bites.

"He and Mr. Vi are using their boats to taxi some people

south of Nha Be. He can get paid for it in gold, or he can have a seat on the boat."

"When is the boat leaving?"

"Not for a few months. They need to get more supplies."

"Will Dad take the money or the seat on the boat?"

"That's up to you, son. Do you want to escape?"

"What about you?" I asked. "Is everyone going to go?"

"We will go later," she said. "You must escape first, so we know you're safe."

"Where will I go? What will I do?"

"The boat is going to Singapore; they have refugee camps. Maybe you can go to America and live with your uncle."

"Uncle Houng made it." I began to smile, but Mom kept a serious face.

"We haven't heard from him. I pray that he made it."

"How will I know if the trip is still planned? What if they don't let you visit again?"

"I'll write you. I'll tell you someone is getting married. The date of the wedding will be the day the boat is leaving."

"How will you know if I can escape?"

She looked away, and wiped her cheek. "I don't know," she cried. "This is crazy. I don't want you to escape. I don't want to lose my son." She hid her face in her hands.

"I will go," I said. "I can't stay here. I'm a burden to you here. Someday we'll be together where we can be free."

The guards yelled for us to assemble, and Mom grabbed my arm. "How should I give you the map?" she whispered.

"I have nowhere to hide it. It will be too risky." She looked at me with worried eyes. "Don't worry," I said. "I'll find my way home."

When I returned to the barracks, Loc and Qui were both sick. The monsoon had brought dysentery, and our resistance

265

was low. I was the only one in the squad who had a visitor, so Phi and I shared our food with the others. Loc and Qui groaned with pain all night, and Loc was at the door every fifteen minutes. "Tri Loc Dung, number 8, going for a shit."

At assembly the next morning, twenty men were reported sick. During the day, more people said they couldn't work. The guards walked up and down the line, telling the men to keep chopping. No one was dismissed until they soiled their pants.

When we returned to the barracks that evening, Loc and Qui were still there. The air was thick with the smell of dysentery, so we stood outside the barracks until the dinner bell rang. Binh came out of the barracks, and Cu asked him why they didn't quarantine the sick men. "The hospital is full," he replied. "They will stay in the barracks until the carpentry company finishes the new building."

"How long will that take?" Cu protested.

"It will take as long as it takes," Binh said.

The dysentery hit Phi early Tuesday morning. He was in the latrine during assembly and barely made it back to his bunk. When I returned from the field that night, he was too weak to walk, so I had to carry him to the toilet. His legs and pants were soiled. He was too cold to wash in the river, so I carried water to the barracks and sponged him off. That night he slept curled up in a ball, holding his stomach. Every half hour he woke up screaming for me to take him to the toilet.

By Thursday, the new hospital had been built. Qui and many others had recovered from the dysentery, but Phi and Loc had become worse, so Dan and I took Phi to the hospital. The place smelled sour. I tried not to breathe so the dysentery wouldn't creep up my nose. We carried Phi through the rows of bamboo beds. Holes were cut in the middle of them, so people could relieve themselves without getting up. We pulled Phi's trousers off and laid him on the bed. I didn't want to leave him. I couldn't see how anyone could get better in those conditions. There was no medicine and only one doctor. As we walked back to the barracks, Dan said God would save Phi, and I wondered why God let this happen to us in the first place. The next Sunday, Dan and I went to the hospital to see Phi. He was still weak, but he smiled when he saw us.

"You look like you're getting better," I said.

Phi sat up and smiled bigger. "I want to come back to the barracks. I would be well by now if I didn't have to stay in this place."

Dan looked around to see if anyone was listening. "When will they let you come back?" he asked.

"They won't tell me. I only see the doctor when he walks by my bed. All I do is lie here. If I didn't have to breathe the sickness, I would get better." Phi's face began to sweat, and his body quivered like a cold wind had hit it. We stayed with him for a few minutes, and then Dan said we should let him rest.

When we returned to the barracks, Binh told us we were having a special assembly. "This is the day you have worked for," he said before we assembled. I didn't give what he said a second thought, and jogged into place, thinking we would have to dance with the women again.

Mr. Nguyen stood front and center, legs apart and chin in the air. He held a clipboard in his right hand. "The names I am about to call are the men who have proven themselves in labor and self-criticism," he announced. "These men are ready to move on with self-motivation." I wondered what kind of trick they had in store for us. He had an amused look on his face—the same look he would get before he inflicted punishment on someone. He waived the clipboard in front of us and said, "These men will be sent to a new camp. In this new camp, they will spend less time in labor and more time developing their knowledge of our new society. In this camp, they will discover their roles in helping our society to become stronger."

He read the list, and mine was the fifth name called. I didn't know if I should be happy or scared. I didn't know what to expect. Dan's and Cu's names were read, but Phi's wasn't. I would be alone again; I thought there would be no one for me to trust. Mr. Nguyen dismissed everyone who wasn't called. The men who weren't looked happy, and the men who were looked worried. We had learned from the past that what our captors considered good usually meant more pain for us. Mr. Nguyen told us to gather around him in a half circle. He smiled and held his arms wide apart like he was embracing us, then he motioned for us to sit. "This is a great accomplishment," he said. "I believe each of you will contribute to our new society. This is why I have recommended you for promotion."

He knelt on one knee. I had never seen him like that before. He talked to us like we were one of them, like we had changed overnight. I was confused. *Did I trick them,* I wondered, *or are they tricking me*? I had so much to think about and so little energy. *What about the escape? What if they take me to the North? I might never see my family again.* Mr. Nguyen's words mixed with my thoughts.

"Your new camp will be totally self-sufficient. You will live near a village. You will acquire money and will be allowed to spend money in the village. You will have more time to practice self-criticism and to prove your self-motivation. Does anyone have any questions?" Someone asked where we were going. "To Xuyen Moc."

Someone else asked how long we would be there. "It depends on your improvement. If you continue accomplishing your goals, you could become a cadre. Many of your cadres came from Xuyen Moc after being there only one year. They were exceptional students and proved their worthiness. Now they are teaching others." I wondered what they did in Xuyen Moc that turned people into communists in such a short time. "Congratulations again, men. Tomorrow after the camp meeting, you will report to the main office. They will return your valuables and take you to the coaches."

We were dismissed and went back to our barracks. Cu, Dan and I were the only ones chosen from our squad. Cu and I wondered out loud what the camp would be like, and Dan sat on his bunk with worry in his eyes.

Later that day, I went to see Phi in the hospital. The place still reeked with sickness, but Phi said he was feeling better. I told him right away what had happened, and he looked at me with confusion. "What do you mean?"

"They picked Cu, Dan and me for a new camp. They say it's a promotion, but I don't know what to expect."

Phi looked worried. His eyes squinted, and he looked away. "All three of you are going?"

"Yes." I felt terrible. I had thought I would have no one, but it wasn't true. Dan and Cu were good men, and they would help me; they would be my friends. Phi was the one who had no one, and he had to continue with labor. I sat on the end of his bed, and we were silent for a few moments.

"I'm happy for you," he said. "I wish I could go with you."

"I wish you could go too. I think the reason you weren't chosen is because you're sick. Maybe if I talk to Binh, he'll let you go too."

"You know better than that. If they were going to let me go, they would have. They never change their minds."

I knew he was right. "Then I could stay here," I said. "I can fake sickness and stay here with you. We can escape together." I told Phi in a whisper that Viet had made it home. Mom had made me promise not to tell anyone about my plans for escape, and telling him would be risking my life and my family's lives, but I thought I could trust him. "My father has a seat for me on a boat," I whispered directly into his ear. "Maybe we can get another seat and escape the country together."

Phi smiled and pushed me away. "You're crazy. You're crazy enough to make it. I need to stay in this country. I have to get out of this place, but I have to take care of my family. They'll call me on the next round. I'll get into the new camp, and I'll get back to Saigon. It's my only choice."

I spent the night thinking about the promises Mr. Nguyen had made. I was longing for contact with the outside world, with people who led normal lives and weren't constantly controlled by others. If what he told us was true, I thought I would have more freedom in the new camp. Then I thought more and realized I would still have to follow the communists' orders and listen to their criticism. I still wouldn't be free. I was just climbing the ladder like everyone else, knowing I could never reach the top.

I thought about the letter Mom was going to send. I wondered if she would know I was sent to a new camp, and if I would ever receive the letter. It could be my only chance to escape, and now I could miss it because I had been promoted. My mind raced the whole night as I tried to think of a way to let my family know where I would be. But my life was out of my hands. All I could do was go to the new camp and hope Mom would find me.

The next day, I gathered my things and walked with Dan and Cu to the office. Binh and the rest of the men were at the field. There were no goodbyes. A guard led us to the warehouse, we turned in our tools and blankets, and they gave us back what we turned in on the first day. The guards led us along the path to the visitors' pavilion. We loaded onto cattle trucks, and they took us to Xuyen Moc to begin self-motivation.

Xuyen Moc

After traveling for most of the day, the trucks came to a halt. The doors were flung open, and we stepped down to our new home. We were at the edge of Xuyen Moc, a village about one hundred miles east of Vinh An and two hundred miles north of Saigon. The road we had traveled on met with a path that led through a small village. Dark, skinny, oily-haired children with no shoes or shirts ran up the path toward us, then stopped a safe distance away to stare with wondering brown eyes. One held a soccer ball; another held a stick like it was a gun, pointing it at us and giggling.

Wooden houses with tin roofs lined the path on both sides. The first one was set up like a café, with tables on the front lawn, surrounded by a bamboo fence. Old men sat at the tables, smoking pipes and sipping coffee. In gardens behind the houses, women stood with their hoes at their sides. Everyone watched as we lined up, counted off, and marched down a path, away from the village. A cool breeze blew across a golden peanut field to our left as the sun set over a small, swift river to our right. We walked for fifteen minutes and came into the camp.

The smell of pigs drifted in the breeze, the sky had turned dark, and the camp was lit by yellow lights on tall bamboo poles. Speakers hung on some of them, screeching with a woman's voice: "Welcome, company F, our new company arriving from Vinh An." People in black pajamas were circled around fires in the courtyards to our left, and others were walking out of barns to our right. They greeted us with smiles and nods. We passed five barracks and marched into the courtyard of the sixth, the last one. While we were lining up, a man came out of the end of the barracks and stood under a light at the far end. He motioned for us to sit.

"I am Trung Van Tu," he said with a commanding voice that scattered the hot, thick air. He was the biggest Vietnamese man I had ever seen; his shoulders were round like an American soldier's. "Congratulations on your promotion. Welcome to Xuyen Moc!" The light behind him made a circle on the red dirt. He paced from one side of the circle to the other, moving with power and arrogance. "You are now members of company F. Along with companies D and E, we are responsible for planting, maintaining and harvesting the crops."

Trung pointed toward the barracks we had passed when we walked into the camp, then he walked to the other side of the circle. "Company C is the craft company. They harvest the grass from the field in front of you and make baskets for our country to export. Company B is the livestock company. They help the field companies during harvest, take care of the livestock, and prepare our food. Together we have become the first self-sufficient camp in the South. We are proud of this accomplishment, and we reward the efforts of those who work and study hard to contribute toward our goals."

He walked to the center of the light and stood with his legs wide apart and his arms behind his back. "Company A is our graduation company. It consists of the people who have shown great promise in helping our society. These men and women spend most of their time studying the philosophy of our new society so they can become leaders and teach others about our goals. Many of your cadres at Vinh An were taught in Company A, and in time, each of you will be evaluated and possibly recommended for the company."

He looked around the group, checking our reactions, and then continued. "Vinh An taught you the value of labor. In this camp, you will practice labor, and you will learn more about socialism. Those of you who prove your worth will be chosen to teach others."

A bell rang in the courtyard next to us. People with bowls in their hands walked from the courtyard to a building behind Trung. He noticed us watching the people and said we would eat after we formed our squads. He counted the women and told them to make three lines to the left of him, and then he counted the men and told us to make seven lines beside the women. Cu lined up behind Dan, and I lined up behind Cu. Trung walked through the lines, moving certain people and asking people's names. When we were in our places, he walked back to the circle of light and turned to face us.

"You have all shown the ability to motivate yourselves," he said. "In the next few weeks, each of you will lead the squad for one day. When everyone has led the squad, you will choose the best leader."

Every squad except ours had ten people, which had only nine. I thought they must have planned the exact number of people, and one man didn't come for some reason. Trung assigned each squad a number and pointed to our room in the barracks, then he asked for two volunteers to go with him to get our food. Dan and another man were chosen from our squad, so I took Dan's bag to the barracks for him.

The barracks was five rooms long and two rooms wide. Trung's office was at the end, next to the path, and our room was on the south side, next to the office. A small wooden desk stood in the left corner of our room. Three bunk beds lined the right wall and two bunk beds were next to the desk on the left. Mosquito nets and blankets were stacked neatly on each bed. I noticed them right away and took the top bunk next to the door. I laid Dan's bag in the bunk under mine, and Cu put his things on the bottom bunk next to me. I thought I was the youngest one in our squad, probably the youngest in the company. There were two boys in our squad who looked to be around eighteen, but they didn't seem to notice me. They put their things on a bunk across the room and only talked to each other.

Dan brought the food back, and we helped ourselves. We got twice the amount of food that we got at Vinh An. We all put on a good show, making sure we didn't take more than our share, practicing our self-motivation. After dinner, we assembled, and Trung explained more about the camp. "You will be allowed to spend money in the village," he said, "but you will only spend the money you earn. Everyone here is equal, and no one will take money from their friends or family."

He spoke from the center of the circle, and we sat in our squads, legs crossed in front of us, faces glowing in the yellow light. Trung said we would be paid thirty piasters per month, then he subtracted for rent, food, clothing, soap, toothpaste…even our tools. When he finished, we had three piasters left per month, enough for a pack of cigarettes and a few cups of coffee.

"Tonight you will get acquainted in your squads and write letters to your families," he said. "Tomorrow morning, you will supply me with a list of your names, home addresses and the order of your leadership trials. The first leader will wake the squad at the first bell. You will have your squad fed, washed and ready for assembly in one half hour. During the day, you will watch over your squad to make sure each one is learning and performing the tasks of the day. In the evening, you will lead review, and the next day, a new leader will begin. Are there any questions?"

There were none, so Trung dismissed us, and we returned to the barracks. One of the older men asked if we would like him to lead our first review, and we all agreed. "My name is Cao," the man said. He sat on the desk and told us to circle around. He was a small man with receding hair and thick eyebrows who took charge without hesitation. He told us to introduce ourselves and tell where we were from and why we were sent to Vinh An. He even told us to say why we were promoted. He seemed like he'd had the meeting planned the whole time. I thought he might have been a communist, planted in our squad as a spy.

Cao introduced himself first, saying he owned a butcher shop in Saigon before the nation was united. "I was arrested for not turning my business over to the new government," he said. "I was promoted because I now realize my greed. I want to help the new society." Cu said he was put in Vinh An because he traveled without papers, but now he realized why the government had to keep track of people. He said he wanted to help the new society. Dan told about his wife in the New Economic Zone, and said he was promoted because he believed in the new society. I said I was arrested in the black market, but I didn't know why I was promoted. Cao made notes as we spoke.

No one had taken the bunk above Cu, so the two older men on the bunk opposite him went next. "My name is Vu," the first one said. "I'm from Saigon, and I was sent to Vinh An because I refused to stay in a New Economic Zone. I have since realized the importance of everyone taking their proper role in our new society, and this is why I was promoted." I didn't believe Vu had changed; there was no way they could change an old man like him. I thought he was just playing the communists' game.

The second man's name was Khanh. He was from a village in the Mekong Delta, and he was arrested for refusing to turn over his farm to the communists. When he finished his introduction, he asked if one of the younger men would let him have a bottom bunk because he had a bad leg and couldn't climb to the top.

"My name is Dinh," the next man said with a northern accent, and he told Khanh he would switch bunks with him. "I'm from Hanoi, but I lived in Ho Chi Minh City the last few years of the war. I was a prisoner there, and I was accused of offering information to the Americans. I've been a follower of the new society my whole life and proved this by my actions at Vinh An."

Quan and Tri were the younger ones. They were both from Nha Be and had stories similar to mine: they were arrested in a market and sent to Vinh An. Neither said why they had been promoted.

We spent the rest of the evening writing our letters. Cao suggested we take turns leading the squad in alphabetical order with him going first. No one disagreed. At nine o'clock

Cao blew the lantern out. I lay in bed wondering how long I would be in Xuyen Moc, whether Mom would write soon, and how Phi was doing at Vinh An.

We woke up the next morning to the bell. Cao jumped out of bed and yelled, "Everyone up!" I pulled on my trousers and stepped outside; the sun hadn't come up yet, but the sky was bright gray. It was a cool, misty morning, and steam rose from a river about two hundred yards in front of the barracks. The smell of livestock mixed with the morning air. Cu came outside, and we followed the rest of the people who were walking toward the river. Beside a rope bridge were wash docks, and we waited our turn, then knelt at the edge of a dock to wash our faces and scrub our teeth. When we returned to the barracks, Cao had our breakfast. "Hurry, hurry," he repeated until the bell rang again.

We assembled for exercises, and then Trung explained more about the camp. "The building next to the kitchen is the library," he said. "During your free time, you will be allowed to check out books. These books will help you learn more about our struggle to win independence, the goals of our new society, and the leaders who made it possible. As you learned at Vinh An, we are only as strong as our weakest member. This fact will be demonstrated more here because we are self-sufficient. If someone does not pull their own weight, it affects us all directly. If one member fails, we all fail. If one person must be punished, we are all punished. We are responsible for each other."

We spent the rest of the day putting handles on hoe and shovel blades, and sharpening old tools. Trung stayed in his office most of the day, and every once in a while he stepped out to observe us. After dinner we assembled.

"Most of you did a good job today," Trung said. "I noticed

many of you taking leadership roles and teaching others the tasks we needed to accomplish." His voice became stronger and louder as he walked toward the women's squads and leaned his huge frame toward them. "There are some of you who think this is going to be easy!" He pointed toward a woman in the first squad: "You!" The woman flinched. "What did you do to help our progress?" The woman was still, stunned. She had no answer. "You let others do your work for you," he said. "You sat waiting for the work to be done."

Trung pointed toward another woman. "You fumbled with your hoe until someone else assembled and sharpened it for you." He pointed at a young man next. "You are the one who sharpened it. Instead of showing her how to help us, you reinforced her weakness. Everyone is at fault!"

Trung's body was pumped with anger and he seemed bigger than before. He paced back and forth in front of the company, and I thought at any second he would lunge at one of us. "We cannot give each other the opportunity to become lazy. We have much to do here. We have no room for parasites. They must be criticized until they become productive members of our company."

He spoke to us like we were children. One of the women he had criticized began sobbing. "Now you cry!" He moved toward her. "You beg for sympathy. Our society has no use for you. Your brothers and sisters fought to give you this opportunity. They were tortured by the American invaders. They did not cry! They gave their lives to give you freedom, to give you equality, to give you a country. And you cry for no reason. You cry for yourself!"

He turned and opened his arms to the group. "You are all to blame for this. You will all be punished!" His voice powered through me, and a chill swept through my bones.

"Squad 1, fall out! Squad 2, fall out!" He made us run around the barracks, and ran next to us, showing off his strength. He pushed the slow ones and screamed, "Move it!" We ran for what seemed to be an hour. The older men and women fell to their knees, and Trung pulled them up and pushed them forward. Cu and I ran side by side. It was easy for us to keep up with the group, but it was humiliating. When Trung was satisfied, he assembled us in the courtyard.

"Your punishment was easy this time," he said. "I am giving you a chance to learn. We will take our goals one step at a time." He paced back and forth in his circle of light, his voice echoing over the heavy breathing of the older people as they fought to catch their breath. "The first goal is to become one as a company. You showed potential at Vinh An, and this is why you are here. But this is not going to be easy." He walked to the first squad of women, then he strolled in front of each squad, picking certain people to stare at. When he reached our squad, he stopped. "Who will tell the company what we learned here today?"

A few of the older men raised their hands, and Trung pointed toward Cu. "We have learned to put the company above ourselves," Cu said. "We have learned that we do not succeed as individuals. We can only succeed as a group."

Trung smiled and held his hands in the air. "You have learned!" he shouted. "You have learned well." He lowered his hands and walked back to the light. He was quiet for a moment and seemed to be deep in thought. "But this is a small part of our goals," he declared. "We are starting small, showing you how socialism works in a small group. In time, you will understand that even our company has no importance in itself. We are only a model for the rest of society to follow. In time, our society will become a model for other societies to follow. We will teach others what we have learned: the value of labor, self-criticism and self-motivation, the tools we use to reach equality. In time, all societies will follow our model. All societies will become one. We will have reached Communist Heaven!"

Trung had pumped himself up again. He paused until the veins in his neck sank back into his flesh. "It will take time and effort for you to learn the ideas and dreams that Uncle Ho gave to us. This plan is described in the books we have in the library. They begin with the philosophy of Marx and Lenin, and they show how our society can make this philosophy work. I can only offer you these ideas. I can only show you how they work in our company. You must read, and you must learn how our dream of equality will come true. You are dismissed."

Everyone seemed to take a deep breath at once. We walked to our room, and Cao started review. "Who would like to offer criticism?" he asked. No one spoke. Khanh pulled his covers back and lay in his bed. "Review has just begun," Cao told him. "It is not time for bed yet."

Khanh sat up in his bunk and glared at Cao. "I ran around these barracks for an hour," he said. "My legs hurt, my back hurts, and I have been criticized enough for one day."

Cao's face lit up with anger. "You will do as I say, or you will answer to Trung." Khanh sat up and moved to the end of his bed. "Now who will offer the first criticism?" Cao smiled, and peered around the group. Dan raised his hand and said we did a good job constructing our tools, then he said we should try harder to work as a group. "This is very good criticism," Cao said. "Who will offer the next criticism?"

Vu raised his hand. "There should be no fighting among ourselves," he said, "and no need to report each other to Trung."

We all nodded to agree, and Cao seemed a little embarrassed.

"Is there any more criticism?" he asked. There was none, so he started singing, "We love labor…" and we all joined in.

When we finished, Cao blew out the lantern, and the older men crawled into bed. Quan and Tri walked out the door, and Cao asked them where they were going. "To the latrine," Tri said, and added sarcastically, "should we check with Trung first?"

"No." Cao didn't notice the sarcasm in Tri's voice. "Make sure you're back in five minutes."

The running had worn out the older men, but I was wide awake. I lay in my bunk for a few minutes, and when Tri and Quan returned, I walked outside. Cao didn't question me when I left. I walked to the latrine, but I didn't need to use it. I stood in a daze for a moment then walked to the fence that surrounded the cattle yard. I climbed the fence next to the barn and sat on top of it in the shadows. The night was clear and quiet. The cattle stood in pairs, threes and fours, leaning against each other, scratching each other's backs with long tongues. I sensed someone walking toward me and turned around. It was Cu. He walked up to the fence and looked into the corral. "The cattle get along better than we do," he said.

I had been thinking the same thing before he spoke. "Was Cao looking for me?" I asked.

"He's asleep," Cu replied. "The running was hard on the older men." Cu wasn't a big man, but he was one of the strongest men in our squad. He climbed the fence and sat next to me. "Do you miss your friends?"

I looked toward him. I had never been alone with him before, and I never remembered him talking only to me. He always seemed to live in his own world and only spoke when something of great importance needed to be said. I felt honored that he came to talk with me. "I was thinking about Phi," I said. "I wonder if he recovered from the dysentery."

"Phi is well. He could be better off than we are."

"What do you mean? Aren't you happy to be here?"

"I'm happy to have more food, but I'm not happy to be here. The communism is starting to seep into me."

"Are you talking about Trung's lecture?"

"Yes, and this is just the beginning. He'll lecture us until he pounds the communism into our minds."

"But I thought you could block it out," I said. "I thought you had total control of your mind."

"Everything around you affects your mind," Cu responded. "You can block most of it out, but some will still get through."

"Will they brainwash us here?"

"They'll try. They'll fill our minds with Uncle Ho's dream."

"It all confuses me," I said. "I don't know if Ho Chi Minh was evil or good."

"He wasn't evil," Cu said. "He was like Buddha and Jesus and all the other men who developed great followings. I think he wanted the best for the people. The problem is, when great men harness so much power for something good, evil men capture some of that power and use it for their own benefit."

"So who's right?"

Cu looked toward me, and the moonlight caught his eyes. They were bright, powerful eyes that made me think he must know everything. "They all have good points and bad points. What matters is that people should have freedom to choose. Trung doesn't have the right to humiliate us, to punish us in the name of Ho Chi Minh or Karl Marx or anyone else. No one knows which religion or government is right, but they're all wrong when they believe only in themselves."

"Do you think there will be Communist Heaven?" I asked, still thinking about Trung's lecture.

Cu chuckled. "Communism won't survive; equality of people won't exist. It's a wishful theory that's not possible. Can you imagine a world where everyone is equal?" I tried, but I couldn't. "Our world is constantly changing," Cu said. "The only governments that will survive are ones that allow for change. Men must be able to discuss how things are changing and criticize the government so it can adapt intelligently. In time, the rest of the world will move ahead and communism will fall behind." I was relieved to hear Cu's words. Not just because he helped me understand, but because he seemed to be on my side. We watched the cattle for a few minutes and walked back to the barracks.

The next morning, it was Cu's turn to lead. I helped him get our breakfast, then we assembled with our tools. Trung stood in front of us with a young man at his side. "This is Phong. He is my assistant, and he will be in charge of the company when I am called to other duties." The young man wore wire rimmed glasses and was dressed in black pajamas like ours, but his hair was to his collar. He stood very much at ease and didn't seem to have the proud attitude of most communist cadres.

After exercises, Trung led us across the bridge by the washing docks to a flooded rice paddy. The east half of the paddy was a shallow lake of thick red water. The west half was above water, but the canals that used to distribute the water were now filled with soil and debris from a flood. We walked through ankle-deep mud to the middle of the paddy and assembled around Trung. "Our job is to clean the canals so the field is ready to plant when the water recedes," he said. The earth was darker where the canals used to be, and the brown lines formed squares across the paddy. Trung drove a stake at the end of one line, and Phong unrolled a string along it for about one hundred yards. "This is your goal for today," Trung said. "You will dig a canal two yards wide and one yard deep. Is there anyone who does not know how to dig?" No one dared raise their hand, but no one looked motivated to dig. Khanh whispered to himself that it was too muddy to dig. I thought he was right. It hadn't rained in a week, but it was still the middle of the rainy season. We could dig for a month and another flood could fill the canals again.

"Squad leaders!" Trung said. "It will be your job to help the members of your squad. It is your responsibility to make sure we reach our goal." We lined up on each side of the string and began digging. The red slime stuck to our shovels and hoes. It was miserable, standing ankle-deep in the mud, scraping our shovels with our hands. Trung marched up and down the line. "Who will be the leaders among you! Who will show how they value labor!"

We dug for an hour, and a man asked Trung if there was any water. "You want water!" he screamed. "Then why did you not bring water? Self-motivation! That is what this camp is about. Do you expect me to bring your water?" He pulled the man out of line. "Stop digging!" he commanded. We stood watching Trung, wondering if we would have to dig the whole day with no food and water. "This man wants water!" he shouted, then turned to the man. "Who is your squad leader?"

The man pointed to his squad leader, and Trung strode to the man and stood directly in his face. "You bring your squad to work with no water!" The man was small—he almost fell backward when Trung shouted at him. I looked toward Cu; he hadn't brought water either. Trung turned away from the man and walked to where we could all see him. "Today's leaders have shown no self-motivation," he declared. "None of them asked what our task was for today. How would they know what their squads needed if they did not know the goals of the day? I hope tomorrow's leaders will show more motivation."

Trung chose three men and three women to go with him for water and food. He left Phong in charge and we continued digging. Phong walked up the line talking to people, telling exhausted, older people to take breaks. When he came by us, Cu asked him if there were containers at the camp for us to use to carry water to the field.

"There must be containers somewhere," Phong said. "Trung probably forgot them, and that's why he got so angry." I couldn't believe what I heard. Phong walked on like nothing had been said. He seemed too honest to be a communist. He was putting in his time like the rest of us, but he said what he wanted to say. I wondered how someone with an open attitude like his ever became an assistant to someone like Trung.

By sundown we reached the end of the rope, and Trung congratulated us for finishing our goal. We were covered with mud, and on the way back to the camp many of us swam across the river instead of walking over the bridge. When we returned to the barracks, Phong moved into our room. He took the bunk above Cu, so he was right next to me. After dinner, Cu went to the desk and told us to circle around for review. He tried to be serious, but I could see in his face that he didn't care about leading. He asked for the first criticism, and Cao raised his hand.

"We all worked hard today," he said. He looked around the group like Binh used to do, smiling, wanting us to applaud. When no one did, he continued. "I do think that Viet could contribute more to the group if we teach him the proper way to shovel."

I thought Cao was picking on me because I was the youngest. I wanted to criticize him for something, but instead, I played the game. "I'm sorry for not shoveling properly," I said. "Thank you for pointing this out to me." I smiled at Cao, but inside, I hated him. I knew he was only trying to make himself look better so he would be voted as the leader. I was glad when Phong offered the next criticism.

"You have offered good criticism," he told Cao, "but I was in the field all day, and I watched Viet shovel two loads of dirt for every one you shoveled. Maybe it would be best if Viet showed *you* the proper way to shovel." Cao had no reply; he had been humiliated again. Cu tried to keep a straight face, but a smile forced its way onto his lips. "Who will offer the next criticism?" he asked.

We went around the room, criticizing each other for not working hard enough. Cao was silent for a while, then he criticized Cu for not bringing water. Everyone accepted the criticism they knew they didn't deserve. Trung stepped through the door as Vu criticized Quan for eating too much at dinner. Trung didn't speak to us, but he smiled victoriously: his students were being programmed as planned.

At nine o'clock, Cu blew out the candle, but the day wasn't finished yet. We sat in the dark singing, each one trying to be a little louder than the next, showing more en-thusiasm, hoping they would be picked as the leader. When the singing was done, I lay in my bunk and pulled the blanket over me. I was angry at Cao for criticizing me, but at the same time, I knew it wasn't his fault. He was caught in the same system as me, and he had to scratch other people as he tried to climb to the top of the pile.

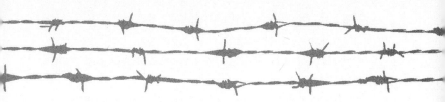

Dan

For the first two weeks of June, we chopped, shoveled, ate
and slept. My day of leadership came, but it was uneventful.
Dan was voted as our squad leader, probably because Cu
and I voted for him and everyone else voted for themselves.
I thought Dan and I would become friends, but he didn't
speak to me unless I asked him a question. I imagined he
didn't speak to me because I was young, but Cu told me
Dan kept to himself because he missed his family so much.

In June, Mom visited. It was during the middle of the
week, and we were digging canals in the rice paddy when
Trung told me she was there. He looked at me with suspicion
and asked why she was visiting unannounced. I was nervous
that she might have brought the money for my escape. My
voice quivered as I told him I didn't know she was coming.
Trung told Phong to take me to the visitors' pavilion. It was
the first time I had talked to Phong without other people
around. As we walked along the path toward the visitors'
pavilion, he spoke to me like we were friends. "You don't

seem happy that your mother is here," he said.

"I'm not sure why she's visiting.'

"She's probably visiting because she misses you. You're lucky. I've never had a visitor."

I smiled at him. "You can go home any time you like. You're a cadre."

He looked at me with surprise. "I'm not a cadre," he exclaimed. "I'm a prisoner like you."

I smiled at him again. "Then why does Trung call you his assistant?"

"Because my father is a party official. He's the one who put me here. It's his idea of drug rehabilitation."

I was shocked by what Phong told me. I didn't know him well enough to trust him, but he seemed to trust me. "Were you a drug addict?"

"I used to take drugs," he said. "I had to."

"Did someone make you take them?" I asked.

"No one forced me to, but my father left my mother and me during the war. He was in the South's army, but he was a communist spy. We never knew until he left, and when the war ended, he returned to regain control of our lives."

"But why did you take drugs? Didn't you know they were bad for you?"

"They didn't seem bad at the time. They were an escape from my family."

I wanted to hear the rest of Phong's story, but we came to the main road, and I could see Mom standing next to a taxi by the café. When she saw us coming, she came to meet us. I introduced her to Phong and asked him if he wanted some of the food she brought.

"I'll let you talk in private," he said. "Take your mother to the visitors' pavilion. I'll wait for you at the café."

Mom and I walked to the pavilion. Two guards sat next to us until I offered them some chicken, then they went outside. "They weren't going to let me see you," she whispered when the guards were out of hearing distance. "I told them a man came to our house and said you were being tortured. I told them I wouldn't leave until I saw you."

"Why did you come?" I asked. "Do you want me to escape?"

"The boat isn't leaving. I came to tell you not to escape. The officials caught the people with the big boat."

"Is Dad in trouble?"

"He isn't worried about himself. Mr. Vi had arranged everything. But if the officials torture the people, they may turn in Mr. Vi." I was both worried and relieved. I hated Trung and the control he had over my life, but I could survive in the camp. I told Mom I was getting enough food to eat, and I didn't want Dad to organize another escape. I knew the communists would send him to prison if he was caught, and he was my family's only chance for survival. She said my brothers and sisters missed me, and when I told her I wished we could all be together, her face grew long and sad. "Your father misses you too," she said. "He's become ill and hasn't been able to fish. Vinh tries to meet the quota, but Thanh is never satisfied."

I finished the chicken I was eating, but couldn't eat any more. I was ashamed because I knew Mom had used money that my family needed so she could come to see me and bring me food. "Will Dad get better soon?" I asked.

"I don't know. He has no energy. It seems as if he's lost hope." She began to cry, and I put my hand on her shoulder to comfort her. "I shouldn't have told you this," she said. "I know you're suffering here. I shouldn't have made your suffering worse."

"This camp is better than Vinh An. We get more to eat here."

"But you're still so thin," she exclaimed, handing me another piece of chicken.

"I get enough to eat. Take the food back with you. Tell Dad that I'm fine. Tell him I will escape from here and I'll be home soon to help the family."

"You can't escape," Mom cried. "It's too dangerous. There's nowhere for you to go."

"But I want to be home to help the family. I miss you."

"Crippled Thanh will see you if you come home. If you can survive here, you need to stay. I'll tell your father that you're well. If he knows you can survive, he'll get better."

The guards came into the pavilion and sat next to us. I knew they wouldn't leave until we gave them some more food, so I told Mom to come with me to the café. As we walked along the road, I told her that Trung was suspicious of her visit, and I should go back to the field. "I'll write you a letter as soon as I can," I said. "Tell Dad not to worry about me. Tell him I'm in the new camp because the communists believe I'm on their side. They'll let me out of here soon, and we can all be together." She smiled, but there seemed to be little hope in her eyes.

We walked to the taxi and said goodbye, then Phong and I walked back to the camp. "What happened to the food your mother brought?" he asked. "It looked like she brought enough to feed an army."

"I didn't want to seem selfish. I told her to take it back."

"You shouldn't try so hard. You don't have to make yourself miserable. Even if you get out of this place, even if they make you a cadre, they'll always say you're greedy. You need to make yourself happy *now*; there's no way to know what they'll do to you next."

I didn't tell him about my family. I nodded to him and we continued walking. When we got back to the barracks, there were only a few hours of daylight left. I took my hoe from the stand, but Phong told me to put it back."By the time we get to the field," he said, "it will be time to come in." He looked around to see if anyone was looking. "Follow me," he said. He walked close to the barracks and slid into Trung's office. I hesitated, but he waived me inside with his arm. It was a small room with a desk in one corner and a bed in another. There were no windows, but light seeped through the grass walls. Phong sat in Trung's chair and put his feet on the desk. "We can stay in here for an hour, then we'll rake the courtyard so it looks like we've been working when the company comes back."

I sat in a chair next to him and pulled a book from the shelf. The title was *New Socialism in Vietnam*. "What are you looking at that for?" Phong asked. "It's all communist propaganda." I put the book back on the shelf. "I'd like to burn those books," he said, "just like my father burned my books when he returned from the North."

"What about your father?" I asked. "When will he let you go home?"

"He'll never let me go home. I used to think he cared about me, but he doesn't. He's just like Trung. All he cares about is communism."

"But he's your father—he must care about you."

"I tried to please my father," he said angrily. "I worked hard in the fields here and studied hard too. I learned every-thing I could stand about communism, and then I went home to visit after I'd been here a year. I had changed. I no longer used drugs and I did everything they told me to do, but my father still wasn't satisfied. I had proved to him that I had changed, but it wasn't good enough. He said I had to prove my worth to society."

We smoked a cigarette, then we got our tools and raked the courtyard. When the people came back from the field, they circled around me, thinking I would have food and cigarettes to give them. I told them my family needed food as much or more than we did. It was obvious they didn't believe me, but Phong told them I was telling the truth.

The next Sunday, I went to the library with Cu. Most of the books were about heroes from the North who had sacrificed their lives to free our country. The book I checked out was about Ho Chi Minh. It explained that he traveled the world to learn how our country should be governed, and gave his life so our country could be liberated from imperialism.

I had respect for Ho Chi Minh because he had lived in poverty, even though he was the leader of North Vietnam. He used himself as an example for others to follow, instead of governing from a white castle. But Cu said that Ho Chi Minh didn't sacrifice his life for our country. He said that Uncle Ho's studies and political work was what gave him a reason to live, just like money gives a businessman reason to live, and spreading the word of God gives a missionary purpose, and children give a mother's life meaning. He said most people care for others because it makes them feel better. We love others so they'll love us back. I wasn't sure if I agreed with Cu, but he always seemed wise.

A few weeks passed, and Trung announced that one of the women's squads and two of the men's would get to visit the village on Sunday. He said we should decide among ourselves who would go, and someone asked if we would get the money he promised so we could buy things in the village. "You will get your salary when our goal is finished," Trung said, and no one was brave enough to protest.

We decided the first women's squad and the first two men's squads would go this time, and we would rotate each time we were allowed to go. We went back to our barracks, and Cu and I got our books to take back to the library. We were about to leave the barracks when the bell rang. It wasn't lunch time, so we knew someone was in trouble.

When we assembled, Trung paced in front of us. "You have failed again!" he shouted. "You were given another chance for motivation and you failed." He pulled two women out of the first squad, dragged them by the backs of their arms and made them face the company. "These women think they are better than we are," he said. "They have painted their faces because they think they are better." The women had put on some lipstick. I don't know where it came from, but Trung had it now. He held their faces and painted their cheeks.

"You have had time to change yourselves," he said. "You have had time to rise from whores to useful members of society. The only purpose of makeup is to hide your true self, to make others think you are above them. We are equal here! No one is above anyone. We are laborers. We have no time for beauty. Our efforts are to help society, not ourselves. Your actions show that you have not lost your self-importance. The only way to make yourself better is to work harder. Tomorrow, we will all work harder. Today we will learn from our mistake. Now run!"

He kept us running and marching for the rest of the day. When the lights went out, he had Phong light torches, and then he lectured us. By ten o'clock, people's heads began to nod. He went over the same lecture on self-motivation. "I do not care if you are male or female," he said, "sixty years old or sixteen years old. You are all equal here…." I fought to keep my eyes open, but many people fell asleep. When Trung saw someone's chin drop, he would rush to them and knock them over. "Run!" he screamed. "Wake up and run."

The next morning, Trung led us to the field, but halfway through the day, he left Phong in charge. I thought he was probably returning to the barracks to sleep. Everyone was dragging all day. Phong didn't say so, but I knew he felt sorry for us. He told Quan to watch for Trung, and he told some of the older people to rest. It was a long, exhausting day, followed by weeks of digging in the thick red mud.

In August, the water receded, the rains let up, and the dry season was upon us. We continued digging canals, and company E began planting rice. Trung gave us another chance to visit the village, but our squad was last in line, so we wouldn't go until October. The days blended together until September, when we had our first official visit.

On a Sunday morning, Trung read the list of people who had visitors. Dan was the only one from our squad whose name was called. I was surprised because he had never had a visitor before. Trung said the visitors would be arriving at noon. He reminded us that our camp was proud to be self-sufficient, and no one was to accept gifts from visitors. Before noon, Phong led the lucky ones to the visitors' pavilion. Phong's father had contacted Trung. He wanted to see how his son was improving, so Phong was going back to Saigon on the visitor's bus.

I spent the afternoon in the library, reading about the battle of Dien Bien Phu, where the communists had beat the

French. I stared at the pages, but I wasn't paying attention to what I was reading. I kept wondering why Mom didn't visit and worried that Dad was still sick. I imagined Crippled Thanh coming to my house and arresting my father. I pictured Tu in my mother's arms, crying as communist guards beat my father and carried him away. I was still daydreaming when I felt a hand on my shoulder, and I turned around.

"I am glad to see you are reading." Trung was standing over me. My body shook with fear. I wondered if he knew what I was thinking. "What is your name, son?"

"I am Viet Quoc Nguyen."

"A patriot," he said with a smile, because my name means *patriot of Vietnam*. I started to close the book, but he stopped me. "Read," he said. "There is much for you to learn if you are to become a leader of our new society." Then he picked a few books off the shelf and walked out the door.

I read until the dinner bell rang and then walked back to our room. When Dan came with our dinner, I asked him who his visitors were. "My wife," he said, but he didn't seem happy. His eyes were still full of worry.

We finished dinner, had review, and sang our songs. We were usually the last squad singing, but this night, Dan blew out the lantern early. I lay in my bunk, wondering if I would ever see my family again. When I woke up the next morning, Dan was gone. Cao was waking everyone, asking if they had seen him. "He probably went to the latrine," Cu said, but Cao was suspicious. He pulled on his trousers and rushed out the door. In minutes, the bell rang, and we assembled. Dan wasn't there.

"You have failed again!" Trung screamed. "You have lost a member of your company!" He chose one of the squad leaders to be in charge, then he told us to run around the

297

barracks until he returned. He was gone for an hour, and when he returned he led us to the field. We worked all day with no breakfast and no lunch. Trung marched up and down the line, telling us to dig faster. When the sun set below the trees, he led us back to our courtyard and lectured us. "Escaping is the worst crime one can commit," he said. "Dan was a leader among us. He was given a chance to help our society, but he refused. When he is captured, his only use will be labor."

The next day, Cao tried to take charge, but no one would listen to him. The older men were discussing who should be the next leader, but their discussion stopped when Trung walked through the door. His presence filled the room, and he stood enjoying his power for a moment before he spoke.

"You have failed," he said. "You chose a leader, and this leader deserted you. Dan is a coward. He was given a great opportunity, and he failed." Trung walked to the far wall, inspecting our bunks, looking for fear in our faces. "Because you failed in choosing your own leader," he said, "I will choose a leader for you. I will choose one who not only knows the value of labor, but who also knows the value of knowledge."

He walked back to the doorway and turned to face us. "Since you arrived here, I have monitored your progress in labor, self-criticism and self-motivation. You have all made progress in labor and self-criticism, but there is one of you who has showed outstanding progress in self-motivation. Even though he is the youngest member of your group, he is the best example for the rest of you to follow." My heart stopped. Was he talking about me, or did he think Quan or Tri were younger than I was? Cao glared angrily at me, Vu and Khanh seemed confused, and Cu smiled.

"Viet will be your new leader!"

There was a long, numbing silence. Trung stared around the room until the men applauded. I sat wondering what I should say when the applause stopped, but it stopped too soon, and Trung looked toward me. His eyes pierced through me as he waited for me to speak. I cleared my voice and forced words through my mouth. "Thank you for this opportunity," I said. "I will try hard to be a good leader and to make myself worthy of our new society."

As I spoke, I felt like my words were someone else's, the words of a communist. I felt guilty. When I finished, they applauded again, and Trung nodded at me and walked out the door. I felt like I was being punished. I believed that he had picked me only because I was the youngest. I thought he was using me to make a point to the rest of the company, to show that we were all equal and age didn't matter.

Squad Leader

For the next few days, I felt like I was living under a spotlight. I had to try harder than the older men. I knew they would be watching and waiting for the moment when they could criticize me. The first morning after I was appointed as leader, I saw Cao peeking around the corner of the barracks. He was watching me walk back from the kitchen with our breakfast, making sure I didn't pick at the food.

When Dan was leader, he would take his portion of food last, making sure the rest had enough before he filled his bowl. I thought I would do the same thing, but the first day when I tried it, there was no food left when the bowl came to me. The next day, I broke the rules of self-motivation and divided the food for everyone.

That evening, Trung rang the bell for us to assemble. He stood in front of us with Dinh at his side. "This man has reported misconduct in his squad," Trung said. "Instead of letting each member take the food he deserves, his squad leader is dividing the food himself." Dinh smiled at me sarcastically as Trung spoke. "Why did this man report to me instead of offering the criticism to his squad?" Trung asked, opening his arms to the company.

He turned his eyes sharply toward me. He was asking me the question, but I had no answer. More than a hundred eyes were focused on me as I felt the blood rushing to my face and my skin quivering. "Tell us the answer!" he commanded. He walked to our squad and stood in front of me. My mind was blank with fear, and I answered without knowing what I would say.

"We have not had review yet." As soon as the words left my lips, my body tensed, preparing for Trung's attack. I had seen him lunge at many people and had feared the time when I would be his victim, but his attack didn't come. He turned away from me, strode over to Dinh, and poked him on the chest.

"Precisely," Trung told Dinh. "You have not had review yet. Instead of criticizing Viet for his actions, you came to me." He poked Dinh's chest again. "This matter could have been solved among your own squad members, but instead you wanted me to know. Why did you do this?"

Trung turned to the company. They all knew the answer, but Dinh was silent and lowered his eyes. "I know the answer!" Trung shouted. "You reported this because you thought I would punish Viet. You thought I would take his promotion away, and you hoped I would make you the leader!"

His eyes surveyed the company, stopping when they reached me. They seemed to penetrate my skin. "Dinh has demonstrated his greed and his lust for power," he said. "This is not the way of our new society! We need leaders who want the best for the people, not the best for themselves."

He was speaking directly to me as though he knew I

were on his side. My mind spun with confusion. If it had been another squad leader I thought Trung would have congratulated the man who turned him in and demoted the squad leader. I didn't understand why he wanted me to lead. Had I tricked him, I wondered, or was he tricking me?

We spent the rest of the day running around the barracks and listening to Trung's lecture on leadership. That evening, I led my first review session. I felt strange standing beside the desk asking for criticism, as though I were in a dream in which I was a communist. Tri offered Dinh the first criticism, saying it was wrong for Dinh to tell Trung about us dividing the food, and that he should work and study harder if he wanted to become a leader. Dinh gritted his teeth and admitted he was wrong.

After review, Cu left for the latrine. I waited a few minutes then left too, so I would meet him as he was coming back. I was confused about how I was feeling. It frightened me to watch Trung from a distance and now I would have to meet with him once a week to discuss my squad's progress. I was becoming part of his scheme to train our company, and it frightened me. I met Cu on the path and asked him if we could talk. "We'll sit by the river," he said and proceeded to the river with slow, graceful steps, as I followed. He sat on a rock, and I sat on the ground beside him.

"I don't understand why Trung chose me," I said.

Cu looked at me with disbelief, "It's obvious to me. Trung chose you because you're the youngest."

"That's what I thought at first, but it's a contradiction. If it doesn't matter how old one is, why did he choose me because of my age?"

Cu's disbelief became disappointment. "Communism is full of contradictions. It's like religion, except in this case,

302

Trung is God. He determines our destiny."

"What do you mean? How does he determine our destiny?"

"He controls our lives," Cu said abruptly. "He controls when we sleep, how much we eat, and whether we live or die."

I realized it was a stupid question, and I was quiet for a moment, thinking of my next words before I said them. "It isn't right for me to lead those who are older and more experienced than I am."

Cu looked at me with more patience than before. "If you respect the older men, they will know that by your actions. This shouldn't change because you're the one who stands at the front of the squad."

We were silent for a moment. Up and down the river, frogs croaked and splashed into the black water. A white, crescent shaped moon was rising above the trees on the far side of the paddy. I thought about what I had to do the next day. I wondered what I would say to the older men when I had to tell them to do something. I thought about Trung and reporting to him every week. "I only want to put in my time," I said, "but now Trung will be watching me. If I fail, he'll punish me."

"You must not worry so far into the future," Cu said. "As long as you live in this country, you cannot control your future, so to worry about it is a waste of time." We were silent for a while longer, and then Cu stood up from his rock. "It's late," he said. "Tomorrow we'll organize the squad so your leadership will be easier."

The next day, Cu helped me make a list of chores that our squad had to accomplish. We made a sign-up sheet, and I explained to the squad how we would rotate each week to different assignments. Cu gave me many ideas when we were alone and told me to present them to the group as my own ideas. When I said I couldn't lie to the group, he laughed at me. "You're not lying," he said. "I gave you these ideas, so now they're yours. I wouldn't have them to offer unless I had learned them from someone else."

A few weeks passed, and I became comfortable with my new position. I continued to show respect to the older men, and they seemed to get used to my leadership. Phong returned from Saigon, but he was different from before. He was always tired and stayed away from the rest of the men. Sometimes we wouldn't see him for hours, then I would find him asleep on his bunk. I thought he must be depressed about his family, but I didn't ask him about it. Every time I got close to him, he would walk away.

One night while I was spreading out my blanket, I knocked the pillow off Phong's bed. When I put it back, I saw a hypodermic needle tucked halfway under his blanket. Cao was looking toward me, and I turned away so he couldn't see the surprise in my face. I didn't know what to do. I thought how Phong said drugs were his only escape, but I didn't understand. I thought about Loc and how sick the drugs had made him. I wanted to do something to help Phong, but I wasn't sure what to do.

That night I found Cu sitting alone by the river. I walked up to him and asked if we could talk. "Sit down, my son," he said, holding his arm toward the ground beside him. We both stared across the black water. It was the quiet, still time of the evening. Even the water moved with no sound.

"I need to ask you a question," I said.

Cu looked at me for a moment. "Then ask the question."

"I'm not sure what to ask. I don't know if I should be telling anyone about this, but I know I can trust you."

Cu did not have patience for too many words. "It may

not look like it to you, but I am busy here. Ask your question."

"I found a needle in the barracks. I don't know what I should do about it."

"Why must you do anything?"

"I know whose needle it is. It's Phong's."

"Why does this matter?"

"Phong is my friend; I don't want him to be sick."

"So what do you wish to do?"

"I think I should talk to him."

"Do you think you can change him?"

"I don't want to change him. I only want him to be happy."

"Isn't this the same as the communists telling you how to be happy?" Cu asked.

I had to think for a moment. "It's not the same. Phong is my friend, and if he uses drugs, he'll become sick."

"If you think you need to talk with him, then talk with him," Cu said, "but don't expect him to change for you. He has to find happiness within his own soul." I sat next to Cu for a while longer, but he stared straight ahead, ignoring me. I wanted to ask him what I should say to Phong, but he didn't seem interested, so I returned to the barracks.

After review that night, I told Phong I wanted to talk with him outside. He followed me to the washing docks, and I turned to face him. "I found your needle," I said.

He looked at me angrily, then took his glasses off with one hand and pushed my shoulder with the other. "Why were you snooping around in my bed?"

He wasn't very strong—his push didn't faze me, and I stood solidly in front of him. "I wasn't snooping. I was making my bunk, and my blanket knocked your pillow off. You're lucky that Dinh or Cao didn't find it."

"It doesn't matter. Nothing matters anymore."

"You told me you were happy to be off the drugs," I said, "and that it was the only good thing to happen to you in this camp."

He wouldn't look at me. He put his glasses back on and pushed them up on his nose. "It's my only escape," he said, his voice cracking as he forced the words past his emotions. "I'm a prisoner here, and I'm a prisoner at home with my family. I'm a prisoner anywhere I go in this country. Whether it's right or wrong, it's my life, and I have to live it." He looked up at me. "If you get out of this place, you have a family to go home to. You have hope for happiness and freedom. I have no hope. The only freedom I have is escaping the reality that surrounds me."

I didn't know what to say. He walked away and left me standing alone. I wanted to help him, but I felt there was nothing I could do. I went back to the barracks and crawled into my bunk. As I hung my mosquito net, I saw Cu looking up at me. I thought that Cu was right about Phong as I lay in my bunk, staring into the darkness. I considered turning him in so he would get off the heroin, but I couldn't do it. As he said, it was his life. If I judged him, I would be no better than the communist leaders I despised for judging me.

In the next few weeks, I watched Phong become more depressed until he finally told Trung he was sick and couldn't go to work. When we came home from the field that night, he was gone. Dinh was the first to notice that Phong's bag was missing. "Are you going to report this to Trung," he asked me, "or should I report it?"

I wasn't sure what to do. I didn't know if Phong had permission to leave or if he had escaped. "What's there to report?" I asked Dinh. "I'm sure Phong has permission to leave."

"Then I will report it," Dinh said.

I was standing in the doorway. Dinh tried to walk by me, but I held my arm out to stop him. "I'll report it," I said. I took my time walking to Trung's office. His door was open, so I knocked on the doorframe. He was sitting at his desk, staring into a book. He looked up and motioned for me to come inside.

"What is it, Viet?"

"Phong's bag is missing. Our squad is wondering if he has gone home."

Trung rose from his desk and rushed past me. I followed him out the door, around the barracks and into our room, where he jerked the covers from Phong's bed. "Where is Phong?" he demanded. Everyone smiled nervously but no one spoke. He raced out the door, and in seconds he was ringing the bell for us to assemble. We lined up, and he stood in front of us, waiting…and as he waited, anger filled his eyes. He made us count off, and when he was satisfied that only Phong had escaped, he dismissed us. He didn't say anything about the escape, but in a few days the word had spread through the company.

Our work became harder because Trung was always with us in the field. The days were long and hot. As I dug and chopped, I thought how Mr. Nguyen had told us we were being promoted to Xuyen Moc to focus more on self-motivation and less on labor, but the work was just as hard.

Sunday was our only break in the monotony of digging, eating and sleeping. There was nothing else to do, so I spent every Sunday in the library reading the communist books. As I read, I felt bad for the people who thought they were sacrificing their lives so our country could have equality. I thought how worthless they would feel if they knew how communism had divided the people even further, allowing some people to act like gods and making others slaves.

Toward the end of November, I found a book that wasn't just about Vietnamese heroes. It told of heroes all over the world who had dedicated their lives to helping people. I was in the library reading this book when Trung came in. I could feel him looking at me, but I kept staring at the book, pretending to be reading. After a few moments, he tapped my shoulder. I looked behind me, acting surprised to see him. "When you finish reading this book," he said, "I want to see you in my office."

I finished the book that evening to show how interested I was in it. It described how Stalin freed Russia and gave his people a chance for equality. It told how Gandhi used symbols to free the underprivileged people in his country, and how the socialist symbol of the hammer showed that we valued labor. When I was done reading, I went to Trung's office. He was sitting at his desk writing a letter when I walked in. I stood for a few minutes until he looked up. "Did you finish the book?" he asked.

"Yes, sir."

"Why did you pick that book to read?"

"I wanted to know more about the heroes in the book, and to learn how they helped their people."

"And what did you learn from this book?"

"I learned that these men taught by their example. The book said they lived meager lives and had little money, but they had so much influence because they wanted the best for their people."

He looked at me like a father looks at his son when he says his first words. "It is a shame you were born under the influence of the American fascist," he said, then he was silent for a moment. I was no longer frightened of him; I was confident that he trusted me. I realized that he saw me as an ignorant boy, and that he had no idea what went on in my mind. "What role do you see yourself filling in our new society?" he asked.

I actually dreamed that I would become a super powerful man and overthrow the communists, but what I replied to his question was that I didn't know because I had so much to learn. He stared at me for a moment, not satisfied with my answer. When the silence became intolerable, I continued. "I feel ashamed of my previous life. I want to spend the next few years learning as much as I can about our new society. I'll take whatever role is given to me."

He smiled at my response. "You have the motivation to learn, and you have the ability to know right and wrong. You will be rewarded."

For the next month, Trung gave me increasing responsibilities. When he went somewhere during the day, he left me in charge of the whole company. He had me lead the exercises in the morning and told me what had to be accomplished for the week, and then I would organize the company to get it done. During this time, I became friends with Tri and Quan. Our friendship started when I caught Tri behind some bushes with a woman from squad two. It was late in the evening, just as the sun was setting. I had gone to the river to wash and decided to walk downstream. I was looking for rocks to skip when I heard a noise. I thought it was an animal, so I picked up a round rock and crept through the bushes.

"Someone is coming," a woman's voice whispered. I froze, not knowing who was there. I heard a man's voice, but I couldn't tell what he said, then Tri and the woman walked out of the bushes. They stood in front of me with guilty faces.

"I'm sorry to have bothered you," I said. "I thought there was an animal in the bushes." I smiled at Tri, and he smiled back.

"Will you tell Trung?" he asked as I began to turn away.

"As far as Trung will know," I said, "I haven't seen you all evening." I walked back upstream, skipped rocks until the dinner bell rang, and returned to the barracks.

After that, Tri and Quan trusted me. Before that, Cu was the only other person I could talk openly to, but Cu was always serious. With Tri and Quan, I could be a boy again. On Sundays we went swimming in the afternoon, and in the evenings we pretended we were B-52s, bombing communist tanks, which were the thousands of insects that swarmed our barracks. We held rocks above them, made sounds like airplanes, and dropped the rocks. We kept score of direct hits per bombs dropped. It was a childish game, even for teenagers, but it occupied our time and made us laugh.

Tri made a corncob pipe, and we put our money together for a pouch of tobacco. In the evenings we sat by the fire, smoking the pipe. We limited ourselves to three puffs an evening, but it was enough to make our heads spin. When no one else was around, we openly criticized and made fun of Trung. Tri called him Boa, the giant snake. They made fun of me, and called me Boa's little boy, but they knew I was only playing the communists' game.

In December, Trung called me to his office and told me we were going to divide our company. Half would continue digging canals in the paddy, and the other half would begin working in the vegetable garden. "I need someone to be in charge of one of the groups," he said. "How do you feel about becoming my assistant?"

I had sensed that the promotion was coming, but I still wasn't prepared. Less than a year before, I had been hauled there in a cattle truck with no more value than an ox for labor. Now he wanted me to lead more than fifty people, all of them older than I. I stood speechless for a moment, then said I was honored that he had faith in me, but I wasn't sure if I was the right person for the job. He was disappointed with my answer.

"I understand your feelings because of the way you have been brought up," he said. "I agree that you have much to learn, the first thing being that in our new society, everyone is equal. You not only have to show respect to those older than you, but to every member of society. I chose you because I know you are the right person for the job. You owe it to your country to accept the challenge and to do the best you can." His words humbled me. I thanked him for the opportunity to prove myself, but my thoughts were different from my words. I knew that more responsibility meant less freedom, and I didn't have much freedom to give.

"When do I begin as your assistant?" I asked.

"You are not my assistant yet. I also have someone else in mind for the job. When we assemble tomorrow morning, the company will vote for their new leader."

The next morning when exercises were finished, Trung announced that we would be splitting into two groups and that he needed someone to be in charge of one of them. "I need a new assistant," he said. "Are there any nominations?" Tri stood up, smiling at me, and after a short speech about how I had shown self-motivation and appreciation of the value of labor, he nominated me. A few other people whom I didn't know well stood up and said they agreed with Tri.

I thought Trung must have told them what to say.

No one else was nominated, but Trung said there was another person who deserved a chance at leadership, and he nominated Tranh, the leader of squad 5. Tranh was one of the hardest workers and was nearly as big and strong as Trung, but he was always yelling at people who couldn't work as hard as he could, so he wasn't well liked. I thought Trung had picked Tranh because he knew the people wouldn't vote for him. A few people made speeches about how hard Tranh worked and then Trung started the voting. I kept my head down until he said, "Viet will be my new assistant," then everyone applauded and he motioned for me to come to the front of the company.

My stomach rolled with fear as I walked between the lines of people to stand next to Trung. He nodded for me to say something to the company. I cleared my throat and thanked them for picking me. "I will do my best to make our company better." I felt like I should say more, but I was tongue tied. I said thank you again and started back to where I was sitting, but Trung told me to come back.

"Are you going to dismiss the company, or will you leave them standing here all day?"

I turned to face the men and women. Tri and Quan were smiling at me. "The company is dismissed!" I shouted.

I walked back to the room as everyone patted me on the back and rubbed my head the way an uncle does to his nephew. Tri was laughing and mocking me: "The company is dismissed," he repeated over and over.

Camp Assistant

"Come in, Viet," Trung said. "We have much to do today."

I walked into his dark, damp office and stood in front of his desk. It was early morning, the second day of my assistantship. The day before, Trung and I had marked a line for a new canal in the vegetable field. I was to be in charge of squads six through ten, and we were to become the official canal diggers. "You will be working with Company D," he said. "You will report to Commandant Banh this morning, and he will give you special instructions."

I went outside and rang the bell twice, which was the signal for my squads to assemble, and then I led them to the field and found Commandant Banh. "Are you as young as you look?" he asked when I introduced myself. He was a small, plump man with big teeth.

"I'm sixteen," I said.

"You are even younger than you look," he said and held a cigarette out for me. I hadn't smoked a factory-rolled cigarette in more than a year. As I puffed on the smooth smoke,

Banh led me to the string that Trung and I had laid out the day before. "You should dig the canal from north to south," he said. "That way you don't have to fight the water as you dig."

We led the men to the north end of the string, and I told them to start digging a yard deep and two yards wide. Banh and I marked the string every twenty-five yards for flood gates, and then I helped with the digging. Being the leader was easier than I had thought it would be. The men had been digging canals for the past year, so everyone knew what to do. When we reached the first mark, I had Tri and Quan help me build the gate. By the end of the day, we had finished fifty yards of canal and put in two gates. After dinner that night, Trung called me to his office.

"Commandant Banh said you did a good job today. He was impressed with how hard you worked to set an example for the others." I lowered my head, embarrassed by the compliment. "I know you will continue with your efforts tomorrow. You are dismissed."

The next month went by without any major events. We finished the canal and began harvesting vegetables. I had to report to Trung every night, but we surpassed our goals every day, so all he said was to keep up the good work.

In February, we had an official visit and Mom came to see me again. There were many visitors this time, so we were allowed to sit outside the pavilion. She led me away from the other people, and when we sat down she said my escape was being planned again.

"Is Dad well?" I asked.

"He's fine now. He was happy to hear you're doing all right."

"I've become the assistant to our company leader," I

told her, and her mouth dropped, her eyes widened. "I've tricked him, and if I continue to trick him, he'll make me a cadre, and then I'll be able to come home whenever I like. I won't need to escape."

Mom seemed confused. "Why did he choose you?"

"Because I'm the youngest. I think he's using me to show that we're all equal, but it doesn't matter why he picked me. All that matters is that I'm the leader, and if I continue to do a good job, I think he'll let me come home."

"Will he let you come home for good?"

"I don't know, but I'm the leader now. If I meet the right people, maybe I can get the papers so all of us can leave the country."

Mom seemed stunned. She wasn't prepared for what I had told her. "What if they find out you're tricking them? What if they take you away? This could be your last chance to escape. Your father has arranged everything."

I felt guilty, but I told Mom I didn't want to spend the rest of my life hiding. I wanted to keep climbing the communists' ladder until I got out on my own. It was hard to explain to her what was happening, and I know she thought I had been brainwashed, but I was surviving. I was afraid to escape. If they caught me escaping, I would be worse off than before.

"Don't you see what the communists have done to you?" she asked. "It's not right for you to lead these people. The communists are only using you, and when they're through with you, they'll toss you away." I knew it wasn't right that I was put above the other people, but it was better than starving, or hiding, or going to a country I knew nothing about. "You have to escape soon," she said. "Your father has arranged it."

In normal circumstances, that would have been enough; I would not have gone against my father's wishes. But I hadn't seen my father in more than a year. "I'll be out of here soon," I said. "I've tricked the communists and I have an important position here. I have the best chance of getting us out of the country together."

"You mustn't try to do this," she pleaded. "You can't trust any of the communists—they'll trick you and they'll hurt you." The drivers began honking their horns for the visitors to assemble and go back to the coaches. "You must listen to me," she said urgently. "I'll bring money for you to escape; we've been saving it for you. You have to escape soon, or it might be too late." I was silent, but I nodded my head to say yes, and Mom turned away and walked to the coach.

Months passed, but she didn't return with the money. We harvested the rice, the monsoon season brought the rains, and the paddy flooded again. Once a month, Trung had to go to the communist party meetings, so he left me in charge for up to three days at a time. Everyone was more relaxed when he was away, but I had become the person that no one trusted. I wanted to tell people they could do as they pleased when Trung was away and they could trust me, but if I said anything, someone would tell him what I had said.

One evening after review, Trung called me to his office. "I found these hidden by the river," he said, pointing to some corncobs on his desk. "Someone stole them from the garden." I knew nothing about it, but the look on his face made me feel guilty. "What can you tell me about this?

"I don't know anything about it."

He stood up from his chair. "It is your responsibility to know," he snapped. "You have had time to take control of your men. Now who stole this corn?"

I had no answer. He marched by me and began pounding the bell. A few people were already lined up when I came out of the office. As I walked to my usual spot, a few of them asked me what was going on. I told them I didn't know, and they looked at me with disbelief. When we were all in line, the lecture began. "Some corn has been stolen!" Trung shouted. "Who will admit to this crime?" No one volunteered, and people were looking at me as though I were the one who had reported it. "The corn has been stolen from all of us," he said. "It is everyone's fault for letting this happen."

I was hoping he would say it was my fault for not noticing, so they would all know I didn't report it. Instead, he punished all of us. We spent the night running around the barracks and listening to his lecture. Afterwards, when we were walking back to the barracks, Tri asked me if I had reported the stolen corn to Trung. "Of course not," I said. "You should know me better than that."

"But we saw you walking out of Trung's office right before he rang the bell. Everyone must think you told him."

"I was in his office because he was lecturing me. Someone else found the corn, and Trung said I should know who stole it."

"Does he know who stole it?"

"If he knew, he would have pointed the person out. I think Dinh or Thanh found the corn. Or maybe they just told Trung they found it, so they could win his favor and make me look bad at the same time."

"I think you're right," Tri said. "Dinh probably made the whole story up."

When we got into the barracks, I could tell by the looks on the older men's faces that they thought I had reported it. But if I had told them the truth, Dinh would have reported me to Trung. All I could do was block it out of my mind and try to sleep.

The next day came too soon, and there were more angry glares from the men in my company. In the following weeks, there were more incidents that made people think I was spying on them and reporting wrongdoings to Trung. Few people would talk to me. Cu, Tri and Quan were the only ones who still trusted me.

When Trung went to the party meetings, I stayed in his office so I wouldn't have to see anyone. I could stay up and read as late as I wanted and go anywhere in the camp I wanted, but I still didn't feel that I was free. I thought he must have told the other company leaders to watch me, and I knew the men in my company were waiting for me to do something wrong so they could report me.

One night when Trung was away and I was reading in his office, I heard a noise by the fire. I crept outside and saw someone sitting by the fire. I thought it was someone who couldn't sleep and walked closer to see who it was. It was Quan, and I could see he had a few ears of corn, sitting on the edge of the coals. "What are you doing?" I asked.

Quan was startled. He stood up, trying to hide the corn that I had already seen. "I couldn't sleep," he said. "I came out to watch the fire."

I walked behind him and looked at the corn. "Where did you get this?"

His face became flushed with embarrassment. "We took it from the field."

"Who took it?"

"Tri and I took it last night."

"You know you can't help yourself to the corn," I said. "Trung already knows someone's stealing it. Why did you

318

do this?"

"Trung is away. No one will know."

Someone walked around the building. I tried to kick the rocks over the corn, but one ear was still in plain sight. I turned around to see who it was—it was Tri. "What are you doing?" he asked Quan. "Dinh sent me to find you." Tri glanced at the corn in the fire, then turned his eyes sharply away.

"Did you take the corn?" I asked him.

Tri looked to see if anyone were peeking around any corners, then kicked the corn into the flames. "I took it," he whispered, "but I didn't know Quan was going to cook it where everyone could see."

"Trung's gone," Quan said defiantly. "What does it matter?"

"Do you think no one will tell him?" Tri challenged, and Quan lowered his head.

"Both of you go to the barracks," I said, "and don't tell anyone about this."

I stayed in Trung's office that night. I was too worried to sleep and too tired to read. Trung returned from his meeting the next day, and after work, he called me to his office. I thought he wanted a report on how things went while he was gone, but when I walked into his office, I knew I was in trouble.

"Shut the door!" he shouted. I shut it and stood in front of his desk. "We know who is stealing from the garden," he said. "I have been told that you are directly involved." My heart sank, then my body tensed. "Who else is involved?" He stared at me with powerful, angry eyes.

"I don't know what you're talking about," I said.

"You lie to me!" Trung rose from his chair. "I trusted

you. I gave you my respect, and you give me lies. Tell me who the other traitor is!" My body was shaking; my mind was frozen. I couldn't have told him if I wanted to. "Go!" he shouted. "Bring me the traitor."

He pushed me out the office door so hard that I rolled across the dirt. When I looked up, I saw people from my company watching me. I crawled to my feet and ran around the end of the barracks. I thought about trying to escape, then I thought about Trung chasing me. I thought if I tried to escape, he would kill me. I went to my room and found Tri. Dinh was sitting on his bunk, and the way he was smiling made me think he was the one who had turned us in. I told Tri to follow me outside, where I told him what was going on.

"Quan and I will confess," he said. "It's our mistake."

"It's too late," I said. "Trung has already decided I'm guilty. He won't change his mind. But he only knows that one other person is involved. I think Dinh must have only reported Quan and me."

"But you shouldn't take the chance. If you lie, you'll be in more trouble."

"We're in serious trouble already. Trung knows I've been lying to him. He'll want revenge, and he'll send me away." Tri and I found Quan by the river and told him what was happening. As we walked to the barracks, Tri said again that he would confess.

"You can't confess," I said. "You're the only one who will help us. I don't know what Trung will do to us, but if he keeps me here, you have to help me escape."

I didn't have time to tell Tri my plan. I wasn't even sure what the plan was yet. Quan said we should make up a story, but all I could think about was Mom's visit. I worried that Mom would come to bring the money for my escape and I would be gone. She would think I had disobeyed my father and that I had become a communist.

"We'll tell Trung the truth," I said to Quan, "but we won't tell him Tri was involved. If he asks about Tri, tell him that Tri saw us, but he didn't steal the corn." We walked into Trung's office.

"So this is the traitor," Trung said. He walked from behind his desk and poked Quan in the chest. "What do you have to say for yourself?"

"I'm ashamed of my actions," Quan said.

Trung's neck swelled with anger and he turned toward me. "Why did you not report this man for stealing?" he asked. I didn't answer quickly enough, and his face grew fierce. He punched my chest. His blow knocked the wind out of me, and I fell to my knees. "Get up!" he commanded. "I'm not done with you yet." I stood up and caught my breath. "Tell me why!" he screamed. I managed to say I was wrong. "I know you're wrong," he said. "Tell me why you did not report this to me."

"I thought I could handle it myself. It was only some corn!"

"It doesn't matter what you stole! You lied to me twice! What else have you lied about?"

I was trying to think of how to answer when he punched me again. I fell to the ground and he kicked me in the stomach. I felt myself vomiting, then I felt him grab me by the back of my shirt and hold me up. "You did not plan to do anything. Quan is your friend, and you put friendship over the good of our company." He let go of my shirt and I fell to the floor. "You are unfit to be a leader. You've shamed the company. You've shamed me!" I saw his foot coming toward my face, and then everything went black.

When I regained consciousness, I was in a cage made of bamboo. Between the bars, I could see the company lined up in front of me. "These men have been caught stealing our food," Trung was saying. He was standing next to me, and Quan was in a cage on the other side of him. "They have acted like animals, so now they will be treated like animals!"

We spent the night in the cages, and the next morning, Trung led us to the field. "You will dig a canal along this string," he said, pointing to a string that stretched for a hundred yards. "When you finish this, we will decide what to do with you next."

Trung appointed Tranh as his new assistant, and they took turns watching us, driving us to work harder. They gave us a bowl of rice for breakfast and another for dinner, and when we finished work, they put us back in our cages. We had to sleep with our legs and arms folded because the cages weren't big enough to stretch out in. By the end of the second week, Quan's shoulder blade was rubbing through his skin.

Every day they marched us to the field, and we scooped at the thick, red mud. In the evenings, Trung called the company to the courtyard and lectured about stealing from society. He called us "the animals" and used us as an example for his lectures. "Without equality," he said, "men are no more than animals. Justice cannot exist in a world that is governed by animals. We must strive for equality! We must motivate ourselves to become equal!"

By the third week, with little food and the exhaustion of digging, I felt like my body was eating at itself. My muscles became weak, and pain shot through my legs when they pulled us out of our cages and marched us to the field. By the fourth week, I began to hallucinate. It was like I was dreaming, but my eyes were open. I would see the bars of my cage move apart, but when I tried to crawl between them, they would close again. I saw visions of my father and could hear his voice. I dreamed that he had killed us when the communists took over. I imagined myself floating through the air, passing images of people I knew and places I had been.

We finished the canal halfway through the fifth week, and that night some guards took Quan away. I was beyond the point of worrying for my life. I slept the night without waking, and when I woke the next morning people were walking by me. I could hear the rumble of their voices and when they had all passed, I leaned back and shut my eyes.

"Viet," I heard. Tri was kneeling beside my cage. "I will get you out of here," he said.

I barely had the energy to speak. "Have you had visitors yet?" I asked.

"I will get you out," Tri said again. He didn't seem to hear my question, and he began to walk away.

"Wait."

He turned around. I knew he was afraid someone would see him, so I pretended to be writing on my hand before he turned away again. I was trying to give him a signal to bring me something to write with, but I didn't know if he understood.

I spent the rest of the day in the cage. Trung came to me in the evening and stared at me for a moment, but didn't speak. It seemed as though he was deciding what to do with me next.

Later that night, Tri came to my cage again. He had understood my message and brought me a small piece of paper and a pen. I wrote my family's address and a note to Mom saying Tri was going to help me escape. "My mom is going to bring some money so I can escape," I told him.

"But I don't know when our visitors are coming," Tri said. "I should get you out of here now." There was a noise around the corner of the barracks, and he stood up to walk away. I shook my head and told him to wait, but he looked at me like he didn't understand what I was saying and kept walking.

For the rest of the week, I squatted in the cage. I lost hope that Mom would bring the money. I wasn't even sure if I would be able to walk if Tri broke me out of the cage. I stopped dreaming and didn't know if I was asleep or awake. I leaned against the side of the cage in a daze. Trung was getting his revenge: he was turning me into an animal.

Tri didn't stop at my cage again, but he and Cu threw food to me when they walked by. With the food they gave me, and the rice that Tranh gave me, I knew I could survive, but I didn't know how long Trung would leave me there. I prayed that he would send me to another camp, and then I prayed that I would die painlessly in the night and would never have to see him again. Then I would wake up the next morning and he would be staring into my cage. His eyes seemed to search inside me. He would stand for a while looking at me, then walk away without speaking. The uncertainty was worse than the labor. Each time I saw him, I hoped that this was the day. I hoped that he would send me away, or kill me, or do anything but leave me there.

I tried to keep track of time, but I would fall into a daze, and when I came out I wouldn't know what day it was. Sometimes I would think it was morning, then I would see the company returning from the field. Weeks must have passed by the time Tri came to my cage again. It was dark, but I had no idea what time it was.

"We're going to escape," he said. "I saw your mom. I

have the money."

I thought I had lost my will to live, but when I saw him, I felt an energy come into me. He pushed a saw blade between the bars, and I grabbed it. "Cut your way out," he said. "I will return in two hours." I didn't have time to asked questions. Tri disappeared around the side of the barracks, and I began cutting.

Escape from Communist Heaven

It was still dark when Tri returned. I had sawed through the bamboo bars, and he helped me out of the cage. My legs were stiff, but I was able to hobble along as he helped me to the river. We hid behind some bushes to catch our breath, and I stretched out my legs and arms. "Is Trung asleep?" I asked.

"I hope so," Tri said. "His light has been out for hours."

"Did you see my mother?"

"She came." His eyes were darting around in every direction, looking to see if we had been spotted.

"Did you get the money?"

"Yes, your mom gave me money and a map of the river. We have to steal a canoe."

Before I could ask what our plan was, he turned and moved cautiously along the river bank. "How will we get a canoe?" I asked from behind him.

He didn't answer until we got to the bridge. "I want you to hide here," he said. "I'll get the canoe, and I'll pick you up under the bridge." He turned and began to move away.

"Wait. This is the first place they'll look for me. I'll hide by the tree on the far side." I pointed toward a willow across the river, and Tri continued up the bank. I waded in and swam under the water for as long as I could. When I came up, I was across the river, but the current took me downstream from the tree. I turned back and saw the lights of the camp. Nothing was moving. The only sounds were the pigs, banging their feed troughs, snorting and squealing.

I swam toward the tree and then crawled with my hands along the bank. When I got under the tree, I pulled some branches over myself. I could see the camp between the branches, still no movements. I thought that even if they discovered I was missing, I would be safe there for an hour. I would have an hour of freedom before Trung captured me again.

I thought of Viet, and I thought about my father. I looked up the river—there was no sign of Tri. I wondered if he had been caught already and tried to decide how long I should wait for him. I imagined Trung looking under the tree and finding me. I would have to fight to the end. He would kill me anyway, or torture me so badly I would wish I was dead. I looked back up the river and saw a shadow moving through the water. I stopped breathing. The shadow moved closer and closer until I saw it was Tri. I took a deep breath and moved toward the river. Tri was sitting toward the back of the canoe. He maneuvered it close to the bank, and I climbed in without making him stop. The canoe tipped back and forth until I got my balance. He handed me a paddle, and I dug it into the water.

"I hope you know where this leads to," I said.

We paddled as fast and as hard as we could. The rice paddy stretched along one side of the river and the vegetable fields lined the other. We passed the paddy and I looked back. The lights of the camp faded behind us, and no one was chasing us. My heart seemed to be lifted. My spirit seemed to grow. I felt like I was free.

I looked around me. There was nothing but trees. Above me was an almost full moon; it was a bright night, but a cool gray mist was rising from the river. "What is the plan?" I asked.

"Your mother gave me a map," Tri said. "We are to follow the river to Ba Ria, and we are to meet a man in the market there. I think he's going to take us to Saigon."

"How long is this river?"

"I don't know exactly. The map doesn't have distances, only landmarks. We'll turn right at the first fork, then we'll go into a gorge. There's a waterfall somewhere in the gorge, but there's a path around it."

I wondered how we would know when the waterfall was coming. I couldn't believe Mom would send me to a waterfall. I worried that we wouldn't know when to get off the river. "How will we find the path?" I asked.

"It's by a calm spot in the river," he said. "There are rapids through the gorge, then a small lake before the waterfall. We're to paddle along the left side of the lake and there will be a break in the ledge overlooking it. We'll follow the break and it will lead us to the path."

I wondered if the plan would work. We were heading into thicker jungle where the trees began to hang over the river. The water became dark, and I couldn't see as far ahead. There were no rocks, but the current seemed to be moving faster. I had never been in fast water before and wondered if we would come to rapids soon. "How far will we go tonight?" I asked.

"I think we should camp this side of the gorge and take the rapids at first light in the morning."

"Are there rapids this side of the gorge?"

"There aren't any on the map."

The trees became bigger and thicker. Their tangled branches seemed to be moving in around us, and the current moved faster. I couldn't see the sides of the river, so I followed the thin line of stars between the trees. The air became thick with mist. The hiss of insects grew louder. I couldn't see three yards in front us, but above us I saw vines dropping down like snakes. I imagined horrible creatures who could see me through the darkness. A chill swept up my back, and I forced my eyes to see farther, and paddled faster.

We paddled for at least an hour before we came to an opening. The moon lit a field of grass to our right, and a light breeze swept across the water. My fear kept me from feeling any pain while we were in the dark, but as my body relaxed, soreness swept into my arms and legs. We slowed the rhythm of our paddling, then I pulled up my paddle and turned around. "Do you think Trung will chase us?" I asked.

"He'll try, but as long as we make it past the first fork, he won't know which way we went." Tri was still paddling lightly.

"How far do you think the turnoff is?"

"I don't know," he said. As soon as the words left his lips, I saw the river split. One channel went to the left into a tunnel of overhanging trees. The other channel went to the right and wound through the field. "Go to the right," Tri said.

We drifted right, and the current picked up speed. There

were still no rocks, but the river was becoming narrow, and the banks seemed to be sloping downhill. I put my paddle in to slow us down. "Pick up your paddle!" Tri yelled. Before I could pick it up, the canoe turned sideways. I felt it tip and I dug my paddle in and tried to push the front end forward. "Paddle harder!" he screamed.

He was paddling on the other side, trying to swing the back of the canoe around. I felt the cold water splashing on my arms. I paddled as hard as I could and the canoe straightened out. "Just go with the river," Tri said. We were going so fast that my eyes filled with mist. I wiped at the wetness and tried to see downstream. "If we turn to the left," Tri said, "paddle on the right side as hard as you can. If we turn to the right, paddle on the left side. Your job is to keep the front end of the canoe facing downstream."

"How do you know how to do this?"

"I just know."

We rode the current through the field and came to a pine forest. The trees weren't thick, but the moon was now low on the horizon and there was little light. The canoe seemed to move faster and farther with every stroke of my paddle. "When will we stop?" I asked.

"I want to make it to the gorge. We should be there soon."

Our speed increased until I could no longer see in front of me. The blackness was sweeping by. I thought at any moment we would hit a rock and tumble into the river. "We should stop," I said. "We're going to tip over!"

"Keep going!" I looked back and saw Tri paddling with all his strength. "Paddle!" he shouted. "Keep it straight." We rounded a curve to the right, and the current slowed. Then we rounded a curve to the left, and the current picked up again. The trees began to thin, and a rock wall on the left side of the river reached higher as we traveled. Then a wall on the right started and climbed until it was ten yards high on each side.

"This is it!" Tri cried. "We made it."

I was too busy paddling to think about where we made it to. We were stuck in the current and I didn't know how we would get out. The canoe was moving too fast. If we tried to go to shore, we would roll across the rocks. "Paddle left!" Tri yelled.

I paddled left and the canoe swung around. Before I knew what happened, we were drifting in calm water. We were only a few yards from the bank. I took another stroke, then climbed out and pulled the canoe onto the bank. Tri splashed through the water, carrying a basket. My adrenaline had been rushing so fast that I had forgotten how hungry I was, but when I saw the basket, I immediately thought of food. "What did you bring?"

He walked onto the bank and sat the basket by my feet. We both knelt beside it, and he handed me a piece of dry pork. "I brought as much as I could." We stared at the river. Just below us was a series of small waterfalls. We both saw them at the same time, then looked at each other and smiled. "We should hide the canoe," Tri said.

We looked around us for trees, but there were only a few pines growing through the rocks and some small bushes lining the water. There were bigger trees further up, but we couldn't carry the canoe up the steep bank. We dug rocks out behind the bushes, put the canoe into the hole we made, and camouflaged it with the rocks. "We should climb higher so we can see if anyone is coming down the river," Tri said.

He grabbed the basket and I followed him up the bank. My legs and arms were cramping. Tri found a flat spot behind a pine tree. The air in the gorge was cool, but I was sweating from the climb. When I sat down, my body began to shake. I thought I had become numb to pain, but this was a new pain—a deep throb within my bones. I couldn't control the shaking. "You should eat more," Tri said.

He handed me some fruit, then made a bed of dried leaves. When I finished the fruit, I lay in the leaves and he piled them around me. I continued to shake, but the pain was tolerable. In seconds, I was asleep.

"Wake up." Tri was shaking my shoulder. "We slept too long. We have to hurry."

I opened my eyes. The sun wasn't shining into the gorge, but the sky was already turning blue. "How long has it been light?" I asked.

"I'm not sure." Tri had the basket and was hurrying down the ledge. I stood up too quickly and the muscles in the backs of my legs seemed to rip. I fell back to the ground and my legs cramped, pulling my ankles behind me. My muscles burned as I rolled to my back and stretched my legs. "Hurry," Tri called from below.

By the time I crawled to the river, he had the canoe halfway into the water. "Sit in the front," he said. "I'll push us out." I climbed in and sat in the front. Tri tied the basket onto the canoe. "Remember what I told you. If I say left, you paddle on the left side as hard as you can. If I say right, you paddle on the right." He pushed us off and we floated to the middle of the river. As soon as we hit the current, the canoe went sideways. "Paddle left!" Tri shouted. I paddled left and the canoe straightened out. We floated over the first fall and crashed into a pool. "Paddle right!" We floated over the second fall. I could no longer feel pain, and my adrenaline had taken over. I paddled hard and we floated over the third fall, then crashed into another pool. The current caught the canoe and carried us downstream. "Stay in the white water," Tri said. "Paddle for the fastest current."

I wanted to stay away from the white water and in the slowest current, but Tri seemed to know what he was doing so I followed his command. We dodged rocks, slid sideways and recovered so many times that I became used to it. By the fifth recovery, Tri no longer had to tell me which way to paddle. Our canoe was tossed by the white water, then slid sideways and hit a rock. Tri pushed off with his paddle, I dug into the water with mine, and we rolled back into the current.

I couldn't see very far ahead of us. The river disappeared behind rocks or the gorge curved. I wondered if the map was right and whether we would be able to get out of the river before the big waterfall. We continued through the gorge. The walls were now at least twenty yards high, and scraggly pines grew through cracks in the white rock. We came over a small fall and splashed into a pool. The current slowed and the river widened. "Do you think this is the lake?" I asked.

"It looks bigger on the map," Tri answered.

We paddled down the left side of the river, looking for an opening in the bluffs. I could hear a faint rushing sound. As the river grew even wider, and the current almost stopped, I looked over my shoulder. "This must be the lake."

"Keep paddling." We stayed close to the bank. My heart began to beat faster and I tried to quiet my breathing so I could hear the rushing sound. It was getting louder. "Look!" I glanced over my shoulder and saw Tri pointing up the bluff. "The opening," he said.

There was an opening about twenty yards ahead. We

paddled to the bank and pulled the canoe onto the shore. A narrow ledge zigzagged from the water to the opening. It was just wide enough for us to walk up, but I didn't know if we could carry the canoe without falling. "Do you think this is it?" I asked.

"I don't know," Tri said. He pulled the map out of the basket and handed it to me. "What do you think?" I looked at the map. The waterfall seemed to be the same distance into the gorge as the gorge was from the turnoff. I wasn't sure if we had gone that far, but I didn't want to go farther without knowing what was around the bend.

"I think this is it," I said. "We should climb up and look down the river."

"If we're going to climb it, we should take the canoe," Tri said. We picked up the canoe and started up, holding it to the outside and leaning against the bluff. It was a light canoe, but it seemed to get heavier with every step. We made it to the first turn, then switched hands and walked up the next ledge. By the fifth turn, my legs began to shake.

"I need to rest," I told Tri.

He moved his hands toward the middle of the canoe so he would be carrying more weight. "We can't stop on this bluff," he urged. "Someone could see us." We continued upward, shuffling along the ledges. Each ledge took us a few yards higher. As we neared the opening, he called out, "I can see the path—one more turn and we'll be there." I stepped onto the next ledge and my foot slipped.

"Hold on!" Tri shouted. I held onto the canoe, and he pulled me onto the ledge. I looked down and saw the calm water ten yards below me. Less than a hundred yards downstream, the river met the sky. The rushing sound was louder now as we shuffled along the ledge to the opening. "This is it," he said. "We made it." I collapsed onto the ground.

"Did you bring water?" I asked. Tri pulled a leather flask from his basket and handed it to me.

"Don't drink too much. I don't know how long it will take us to get back to the river." I tipped the flask and filled my mouth, holding the water on my tongue until it became warm. Tri slid the canoe farther away from the ledge. "Eat some more fruit," he said. "We'll rest here for a while." I opened the basket to get some fruit. He had brought enough food for several days, as well as a machete. While I ate, he tied the basket onto the canoe.

"When did my mother come?" I asked.

"We had an official visit yesterday. I didn't have a visitor, so I gave the note to Cu. I don't know how he got it to your mother, but he did, and she gave him the money and the map. We're so lucky. I was going to leave before, but Cu told me to wait."

"What happened to Quan?"

"No one knows. I think they must have sent him to another labor camp."

"I'm lucky that Trung kept me as long as he did."

"And we're both lucky your mom came. I would never have thought of escaping down the river. I had no idea where it went."

"I don't think I could have walked. It's hard enough to paddle the canoe."

"You should rest for a while," Tri said. I lay back against a rock and shut my eyes. I waited for the pain to seep into my legs, but instead, they became numb. It seemed as though I had only rested a minute when Tri woke me. "We should go now," he said. "I don't know how long it will take us."

We lifted the canoe onto our shoulders and walked up

the path. It twisted through the rocks, then descended through some pine trees. The air was thick with heat, and mosquitoes and other insects swarmed around us. We couldn't see out of the forest, but we could still hear the pounding of the waterfall. We rested often, but by early afternoon, we made it to the bottom. The water fell from the top of the cliff about twenty yards above us and crashed into a small lake. We hid the canoe in a thick bed of flowers that lined the bank and walked into the water. "Are there crocodiles around here?" I asked.

"There are no crocodiles left in Vietnam," Tri said, and looked at me to see if I believed him.

"There could be some left, and if there are, this is probably where they would be."

Tri smiled and walked farther into the water. "The last thing I'm worried about is a crocodile. The snakes will get you before the crocodiles will." I walked in after him, and we soaked in the water. The walk had loosened my legs. I began to look for a shady spot on the bank to lie down, but before I found one, Tri said we should go. "I want to be sure we're close to Ba Ria," he said. "We're supposed to meet the man as the sun comes up tomorrow."

We pushed the canoe into the pool and paddled downstream. The current moved slowly, and we paddled with long, smooth strokes. "How long will it take us?" I asked.

"We should be there by nightfall. On the map, it looks like the waterfall is halfway between the camp and Ba Ria."

"I can't believe this is happening. I can't believe how easy it was."

"It hasn't been that easy. We aren't even halfway home. We've been lucky so far. I hope our luck holds out."

We had been paddling for an hour when we joined another river. The land around us was flat now, but the combination of the two rivers made the current swifter. "There should be a village around the next bend," Tri said. We paddled around the bend and I saw a small fishing village on the right side of the river. There were a few boats tied to the dock, and women sitting on porches that hung over the water. Below them, children were swimming and splashing. We paddled to the left side of the river and passed the village without anyone seeming to notice us. "I wonder why we saw no boats upstream," Tri said.

"The fishing is probably better toward the sea." We continued along the left bank, passing a few fishing boats, the men waving as we paddled by. "How will we know when we're close to the city?"

"There will be another river coming into this one. When we pass it, I think we'll be within an hour of the city."

We rounded another bend, and I could see the river getting wider in front of us. "There it is," I said. A small river twisted through a rice paddy to the north, and canals made squares across the green landscape. The sun was now low on the horizon behind us. "Where will we camp? There are no trees. Where will we hide the canoe?"

Tri was searching the river in front of us. "Keep paddling. There has to be some cover." We paddled until the sun set below the horizon. It would be dark in a half hour, and my body was begging for rest. We came around another bend and I could see houses on both sides of the river. Tri saw them at the same time. "Paddle to the shore," he said.

The sky was darkening, but there was a white glow ahead of us. "Is it Ba Ria?" I asked.

"It must be."

"Are we going to camp here?"

Tri looked around him before answering. The grass along the bank wasn't high enough to hide the canoe, and we couldn't see what was on the other side of the bank. As we paddled to the shore, the canoe slowed and mosquitoes circled around us. "We have no choice," Tri said.

The canoe glided onto shore. With one smooth motion, we both jumped out and carried it over the bank. There was a levee on the other side, and rice on the other side of that. It was all hidden from the river. "This will be perfect," Tri said.

The mosquitoes were still swarming, biting and leaving welts on my neck and arms. I didn't think it was perfect, but I thought it would be safe. We carried the canoe into the rice, lodged it in and covered it. The sky was dark by the time we had finished. The moon rose above the paddy, and the stars began to glow. We sat on the bank and ate the last of the pork.

"We're halfway home," Tri said. As I gazed at the stars, my mind was just beginning to focus on what was happening. I wondered if I would still be leaving the country. I hadn't thought to ask Tri what he would do when we made it to Saigon.

"Do you think we'll make it?" I asked.

"I think the hardest part is over. As long as we find the man in the market, and the officials don't search his truck, we're free."

"Where will you go?"

"My sister lives just south of Nha Be. I'll go there first. I don't know how long I can stay there." We were silent for a while. The mosquitoes buzzed around us, and we slapped at them. "What will you do when we get back?" Tri asked.

"I think my father has planned an escape for me."

"An escape to where?"

"Away from this country."

His eyes grew large. "How did he do this?"

"I'm not sure. He got a seat on a boat somehow."

"Your family must be very wealthy. I wish I could get out of this place."

"We're not wealthy, but my father's clever. I think he's helping other people escape, and that's how he got the seat on the boat."

"You're lucky. I've heard of people escaping. I heard they go to America."

I rested against the bank, trying to stay below the path of the mosquitoes. I couldn't decide if I was lucky or not. I wondered if they would have rice in America and if I would find my uncle. I had seen movies from America when I was young, and thought the whole country was filled with cowboys and Indians, fast cars and big houses. I wondered what the people would be like and if they would be nice to me. I closed my eyes and rested my head against the bank. When I woke, the stars were still out, but Tri was pulling the canoe out of the rice. "We need to hurry," he said. "It will be light soon."

We put the canoe into the river and paddled downstream, passing the houses and drifting between fields of thick grass. The lights of Ba Ria were in front of us. We came to another small village where fishermen were already on the docks, throwing nets and poles into their boats. As we drifted through the village and came into Ba Ria, the smell of the sea blew cold against my face and the water turned black, full of debris. Warehouses and fish markets crowded the bank. There seemed to be a thousand boats of all shapes and sizes tied to the docks and anchored in the water. Men stood on their bows, stretching and yawning.

"I think the market is behind these warehouses," Tri said. "Paddle to that dock. We'll leave the canoe there." He was pointing toward a dock on the far side of the last warehouse. We steered to it, I tied the canoe, and we climbed out. The morning air was cool and filled with the smell of fish. I took a deep breath and followed Tri around the warehouse. "We need to hurry," he said. "The sun will rise soon."

People hurried by us, carrying goods to sell. Pushcarts full of fish, squid and clams were arranged in rows that seemed to stretch on forever. I began to wonder if we would find the man. Tri asked a woman where Khang Le Street was. She pointed toward the west side of the market and hurried away without speaking. We walked along the warehouses but couldn't find any street signs. "How will we find him?" I asked. "Why did they tell us street names? They should have known there were no signs." Tri didn't answer. He asked another woman where the street was.

"You're standing on it," she replied.

As we walked through the carts, looking for a blue van, the sun was rising above the water. "There it is," Tri said. A blue van was parked on the corner of the street we were walking down and a path that crossed it. Beside the van were crates of vegetables and fruit. A small, gray-haired man was sitting on a melon beside the crates. "Ask him if his name is Ho," Tri said.

"Let's walk by him first and see if he watches us," I said. "I want to make sure it's him." We walked by the van, and the man's eyes followed us.

"It's him," Tri whispered. "I know it's him." He started to turn back, but I kept walking, and he followed me. "What are you doing?"

340

"Let's walk farther," I said. "I want to make sure."

We walked to the end of the row. There was another blue van, but it wasn't parked at a corner. A younger man sat on the bumper smoking a pipe, and the van was empty. "Let's go back before he leaves," Tri said.

My stomach fluttered as we approached the man. "Good morning, sir," I said.

"Good morning, son," he said. "Are you buying produce?"

"We have some fish to trade," I said. "We usually trade with a man named Ho, but he's not here today."

"I am Ho," the man said, smiling nervously. His eyes darted around to see if anyone was watching us. "You must be Viet." Tri and I smiled at each other, but my stomach was still fluttering.

"Get in the back of the van," Ho said to Tri. "Viet and I will hand you some crates." Tri climbed in, and we stacked the crates so there was a space in the middle. "Stay in the van," Ho said to Tri. He looked around to see if anyone were watching, but people were too busy making deals to notice us. "Climb in the van," he said to me. I got in, he stacked crates around us, and then he slammed the back doors shut.

We lay under the boxes, breathing the thick, dark air. In what seemed to be an hour, I heard the engine start, and the van jerked forward. It felt like a dream. I thought at any moment I would wake up in my cage with the morning bell ringing through my head. But I knew I wasn't dreaming when the van stopped and I heard a northern accent ask for Ho's papers. "How are you today, Mr. Ho?" the official asked. "Taking another load to Saigon?"

The two men talked for a minute, and we were on our way. We had to go through several more checkpoints, and every time we slowed down, my stomach turned and my head spun as I prayed that the back doors of the van would not be opened. But Ho seemed to know all the officials. At the last checkpoint, the official didn't even look at his papers. He just asked jokingly, "You don't have anything illegal in there, do you?"

Ho let us off at Hang Xanh market, which was close to Grandfather's house. He seemed almost as excited as we were that we had made it. When I gave him the money, he gave twenty piasters back. "Use this for a taxi," he said. "You should get to your grandfather's as fast as possible."

Tri and I thanked him. I felt like I couldn't thank him enough and wished I could do something for him. I wished that someday I would have the power, like him, to help people beat the communist system. Ho told us to hurry, then he got into his van and drove away. We were so close, but I knew that at any moment an official could grab my shoulder from behind and send me right back to prison. We flagged down a bike taxi, jumped in the front, and told him to take us to Phu Nhuan Road, where Grandfather lived. I told him we would give him ten piasters if he peddled as fast as he could, and we raced through the streets with our heads low.

Grandfather hugged both of us as we walked through the door. Then he pushed us further inside and looked down the street both ways. When he turned from shutting the door, I could see tears in his eyes. "You must be hungry!" He hid his face and went to fix us something to eat. I told him about our escape. My adrenaline was still pumping so hard, I felt like my body was moving even though I was sitting still. Grandfather said I would be staying with him for a while because the officials might be looking for me at my parents' house. After a few days, my parents would come and I would go with them to Mr. Vi's to stay on my father's new boat. It was docked there so Crippled Thanh wouldn't declare it the property of the people. Before we finished eating, Grandfather left to tell my parents I had made it back.

When our stomachs were full, I gave Tri the rest of the money so he could hire a taxi to the southern part of the city. It wouldn't be enough to get to his sister's house, but he would be able to walk the rest of the way by nightfall. "Thank you for helping me," I told him as he opened the door to leave.

Tri turned around and said, "You helped me first. Thank you." We told each other we would try to keep in touch, but neither of us knew where we would be in a week.

As soon as he left, I went straight for the shower. I stood soaking up the cool water until my loose skin wrinkled around my bones, then I searched the house for a kung fu book and found one between the mattresses of Grandfather's bed. I spent the next week feeling free. Even though I had to stay inside the house, at least I was out of Trung's cage.

Freedom

Mom and Dad came to Grandfather's house the next Thursday. I was waiting for them on the porch when they arrived. Dad didn't speak at first, but his face showed his joy and relief that I had made it. Mom rushed up the steps and hugged me. She rubbed my ribs and the thin stubble my hair had become. "What have they done to my son?" she asked.

I had lost most of my hair, and my body was marked with scabs. Grandfather had been feeding me at least five times a day, so I had gained energy, but I was still thin. "Thank you for getting me out," I said. "It feels good to be free."

"You're still not free," Dad said. "We must be careful, or you'll be caught and sent back to prison." His happiness seemed to fade, and his face became tight and serious.

"How did the escape go?" Mom asked. "Was the map right? Did Mr. Ho bring you here?"

"I couldn't believe how easy it was," I said. "Tri stole a

canoe. We made it to the market, and we found Mr. Ho."

"Who is Tri?" she asked.

"He's a friend who helped me escape."

"I was so worried about you," she said. "When I went to visit and you weren't there, I thought they had taken you away. I wouldn't have known what to do, but your friend Cu gave me the note."

"How did Cu get the note to you?" I asked.

"I was looking for you. I was beginning to worry, and I was walking toward your company leader when Cu asked if I was your mother. He asked me to sit with him and gave me the note. I was confused at first, but he explained what had happened to you. He convinced me that he knew you were going to escape, and he said you would have to leave soon, or it would be too late."

"I had to tell him about escaping," I said. "I couldn't have gotten out on my own."

"Cu seemed to be an honest man," she said. "I wouldn't have trusted him, but he seemed to be very concerned about you. He told me how they had been keeping you in a cage and said you would die if you didn't get out of the camp. I had no choice but to give him the map and the money."

"How did you know Mr. Ho would bring us to Saigon?"

"He's a friend of Vi's," Dad said. "Without Vi, none of this would have been possible."

"Am I going to leave the country?" I asked.

Dad didn't answer right away. Mom held her breath, and Dad seemed to reach deep inside himself before he spoke.

"The escape is planned," he said. "You will be leaving soon."

Grandfather brought us some rice and vegetables to eat, and no one spoke until we finished. I was stunned when I heard Dad say I was escaping the country. I knew the escape was still planned because I had asked Grandfather, but it was still hard to believe it was happening. The escape from Xuyen Moc was so easy that it made me think I was in control. It made me think that everything would go my way. I felt all powerful, and I had made myself believe that my country would change. I dreamed that I would go back to school, but the school would be different. They would teach us about the freedom to choose, and I could become an engineer or a doctor or have my own fishing business. I dreamed that my family would be able to live together. I would make new friends, and I wouldn't have to leave those friends and they wouldn't have to leave me. When I heard Dad say I was leaving the country, my thoughts became real again, and I realized my only chance for freedom was to escape.

After dinner, Mom asked why I was punished in the camp. "I was punished because I didn't report my friends to the company leader," I said. "Tri and another boy took some corn from the field. I caught them cooking it, but I didn't turn them in."

"What did they do to you?" she asked.

I told them about Trung beating me, and about the cage and digging the canal. Dad listened quietly, and Mom covered her face with her hands. When I finished the story, Dad rose from his chair. "The last bus will leave soon," he said. "I don't want to miss it."

"It's best that you're leaving this country," Grandfather said as we walked to the door. I hugged him and said I wished he was coming with me. "I'm too old to start a new life," he said, "but knowing you'll have freedom will give our lives meaning. You must use your freedom to learn, my son. You must use this opportunity to make a good life for yourself.

Be good to others. Tell your story to the people you meet. Your story will help others to learn the importance of freedom."

On the bus, heading back to our neighborhood, Dad told me we would go straight to our boat. "Can't I go home first?" I asked him.

"We can't risk letting your brothers and sisters see you," he said. "If they let the secret slip to one of their friends, we'd all go to prison."

Dad and I got off the bus by Vi's house, and Mom rode ahead to our neighborhood. Dad and I walked along the river, and when we came to Vi's dock, he pointed toward our new boat. It was much bigger than I had expected. The wooden planks were weathered and unpainted, but it looked solid. The boat must have been eight yards long, and the cabin ran half the length. "Get inside," Dad said. "I don't want anyone to see you."

I opened the door of the cabin and went inside. There were two beds, a cooker, a cabinet full of food, and an oil lamp so I could read at night. I sat on one of the beds, and Dad stood in the doorway. "You must not leave the cabin," he said. "And you must turn out the lantern early. If anyone comes here, you're to tell them you are Vinh." Dad handed me Vinh's ID card and his papers to travel on the river.

"What's the plan?" I asked. "When will I be leaving?"

"You're leaving Saturday morning," he said. "I'll explain the plan to you then."

He shut the door as he left, and the cabin seemed to shrink around me. I looked out the window and saw him walking over the hill. When he was out of sight, I left the cabin and sat on the dock. It was happening too fast. Even though I had no choice, I still wanted more time. I found myself not looking forward and not looking back. I was existing in the moment, and all I could do was feel lucky that I had made it that far.

The next morning, Mom came to the boat with a bag full of clothes and another full of food. She had a package wrapped in plastic and sealed tight, and her lips pressed together as she handed it to me. "These are some of our family pictures," she said. She buried her head in my shoulder; she was shaking. I felt a lump come up my throat, but I didn't cry.

"Can I see Tu and Vinh before I leave? Can I see my sisters?"

She pulled her head away from my shoulder. She was still shaking. "I know it's terrible, but we can't take the risk."

"What will you tell them?"

She clenched my forearm. "Your father will tell them we lost contact with you." Her fingers dug into my skin. "But you will see your brothers and sisters again. We'll escape soon. We will be together again."

I wanted to believe her, but if they didn't escape, my brothers and sisters would wonder if I was dead. It seemed like part of me was dying, and the other part was going to keep living somewhere far away. Mom pushed herself from me and looked at my face. She seemed to be imprinting it on her mind. Then she turned away and left the cabin.

Dad came later with two small boats hooked together. He tied one to the back of the boat I was in and the other one to the dock, then he came inside the cabin. "Are you well?" he asked.

"I feel fine."

He sat on the bunk beside me, but didn't look at me. "Sending you away is the hardest thing I've ever done. I'm doing this because I want you to live a free life. You must go to America if you can, and try to find Uncle Houng." He looked up, then closed his eyes and prayed. "Please God, take care of my son. Give him a safe journey. Take him to a place where he can be free."

He rose from the bunk and walked out. I could hear him talking with Vi on the dock. "Is everything ready to go?" Vi asked.

"The boats are loaded. We'll leave at first light."

"How is Viet?"

"He's better than we expected. When his grandfather came to our house last week, he said Viet was ill, but he seems to have plenty of energy now. His sores are healing well. I think he'll be fine."

I heard their footsteps coming toward the cabin, then the door opened, and Vi stepped in. "I heard about your escape," he said. "We were worried about you." I nodded, but didn't know what to say. "You'll be fine," Vi told me. "You're a lucky boy. I'm sure you'll make your father proud."

"Thank you for helping us," I said to Vi. "I know I'm lucky, and I'll do my best to get you all out of the country."

Vi smiled at me, then turned toward Dad. "You should reconsider my offer to help," he said. "Mr. Lanh's son has little experience with boats. I think it would be better if I went with you."

"It's best if you're not involved," Dad said. "If I get caught, I can trust you to take care of my family. If both of us get caught, we'll never escape the communists."

"Do you know where the big boat is waiting?" Vi asked.

"Mr. Lanh's son is the only one who knows," Dad said. "They wouldn't risk telling us."

"Why wouldn't they tell us?" I asked.

"They're afraid we'll take the boat for our own families," Dad answered.

"They've planned this escape for a year, son," Vi added. "There are many people who would steal Mr. Lanh's boat for themselves if they had the chance. We would never do this, but I can understand why they can't trust us."

"I should return home," Dad said. "I'll be back at dawn."

Before Dad left, Vi wished us both luck. "I'll pray for you," he told me. "May God deliver you to a land of freedom."

When they left, I climbed on top of the cabin and stretched out. I felt so alive. My blood seemed to be racing through my veins. I stayed outside for hours, thinking about my childhood, places Tam and I rode our bikes, all the people I had known. I wondered what would happen to the ones who had to stay in the country. I wondered if Phi was still in Vinh An and if Viet was still alive. And I wondered what America would be like and if the Vietnamese people there would help me learn how to speak English.

I woke the next morning when I felt a boat hit up against mine. I could hear my father talking to another man, so I pulled on my trousers and went outside. The man Dad was talking to was about my size, but he looked weak. His skin was pale, and I could tell he must have worked in the city all his life. Dad introduced me as his eldest son, and told me the man's name was Bao. "You'll take two boats," Dad said to me. "If we get stopped by anyone, tell them you're Vinh. Do you have his papers?"

I pulled the papers out of my pocket and showed them to him. "We can go fifteen miles south of Nha Be with these," he said. I put the papers back into my pocket, and he told me the plan. We were taking four small boats, including Dad's original small boat so the coast guard would be less likely to notice us. Three of the boats had engines. I would follow about fifty yards behind Dad, and Bao would follow fifty yards behind me. We would all stop under Rach Ong bridge, and then Bao would go up to the market and bring the people to the boats. Five people would be coming with me. When the people were settled in, I was to leave first and travel slowly down the river. Dad would pass me, and I would follow fifty yards behind him. Bao would then follow me.

We arrived at Rach Ong bridge, and in twenty minutes, Bao came back with eleven people. They looked working class from a distance, but when they got closer I could tell they had dirtied their clothes on purpose and had rubbed black grease on their pale skin so they would look darker. I told three of the boys to get into my net box and two men to get into the net box of the back boat. We floated silently down the river for twenty minutes before Dad passed us. The boys were poking their heads out of the box, and I kept pushing them down, telling them to lay there and wait. Bao caught up about a half hour later and stayed fifty yards behind me. Everything was going as planned.

I sat back, soaking up the sun and watching the scenery as we motored down the river. It was hard to relax, so I kept telling myself it was an ordinary day and I was just going out to fish. About every ten minutes, I looked back to make sure Bao was behind us, and the third time I looked he wasn't there. Dad was too far ahead to hear me, so I slowed down and hoped he would turn around. He saw me lag further behind him and came back. "Where is Bao?" he asked as we both drifted toward the bank. I told him I hadn't seen him for almost twenty minutes. I could see panic in Dad's face, but he told everyone to remain calm. "You stay here," he told me. "Keep those people's heads down! I'll go up the river and look for him."

We waited for an hour before Dad appeared around the

bend. He had Bao's boat hooked behind his, and they floated by without waving. I pushed my boats out, started the engine and followed them. We passed Nha Be and went left at the fork in the river. In a few minutes, Dad's boats drifted to a stop. When I caught up, I saw one of the men bent over the engine on Dad's boat. Bao was above the man, cursing down the back of his neck, and Dad was pulling Bao back, telling him to be quiet.

We were in the middle of the river, and their boat was rocking back and forth. I looked around to see if anyone was watching us, but there were no other boats in sight. The man who was trying to make the engine start was Dai, the boy whom Dad had said was the son of Mr. Lanh, the owner of the big boat we would escape on. I couldn't hear everything they were saying, but I figured out that he had been trying to make Dad's boat go faster and had overheated the engine, which was already straining from pulling Bao's boat as well. Now we had two dead engines and only the ten-horsepower engine on my boat to pull fourteen people through the river. We got all the boats to the bank and anchored two of them. We put the kids in the net boxes. Because Mr. Lanh didn't trust us enough to let us know the meeting location, Dai sat up in the front boat with Dad to direct him where to go. Bao and I sat in the back boat, and the rest of the adults stayed down and out of sight.

Dad didn't say a word, but Bao kept cursing at Dai. "I would throw you in the river if you weren't the only one who knows where we're going. How can you be so stupid?"

I knew we were supposed to be at the meeting point by late afternoon, and Dai didn't seem too worried, so I thought we must be getting close. We turned right at the fork in the river where Vi had taken us fishing the first time. The air began to smell like the sea. We crept along the bank in the shadows of the trees for a couple of hours until Dai told us to turn left into a smaller channel. We traveled for another hour up the channel. Dai began looking around like he was trying to figure out where we were, and Dad soon realized that Dai was lost.

"You must tell me where the boat is," Dad demanded. "You must trust me now. They will leave if we don't get there soon."

"It is at Ba Voi corner," Dai said. "I know it's close to here."

"Ba Voi corner!" Dad shouted. "We should have turned off the main channel an hour before you told us to! Dad began cursing to himself. Our boats had drifted close together and Bao jumped on top of Dai. They both tumbled into the water. Dai was bobbing up and down in the water, screaming that he couldn't swim, and Bao was grabbing for him. I couldn't tell if he was trying to save him or push him under. By the time I decided to help, Dad was already pulling Dai up over the side of the boat. Bao climbed back in with me. "Everyone needs to calm down," Dad said. "We can still make it, but we must work together. Help me row. It will take some strain off the engine."

Bao was still cursing at Dai who was curled up in the corner of the boat trying to get warm. "Both of you paddle now!"

We turned the boats around and headed back the way we came, but now we were going against the current. By the time we made it back to the main channel, my arms were aching like they had in prison. I wanted to quit, but I knew my father would keep rowing. His pride wouldn't let him give up. Dai had stopped paddling, so Dad made him lie on the floor of the boat and another man helped us. We made it back to the smaller channel that we should have turned onto before. The day was turning to night when the engine stopped. It was hours past the time we were supposed to meet the rest of the people. We were all silent until Bao began cursing at Dai again. "This is your fault," he said. "The boat will leave without us."

Bao splashed water onto Dai, but Dai didn't move. He stayed curled up in a ball, shivering. "At least you can help us row," Bao said. Dai didn't move.

"Save your energy," Dad said. "We have a long way to go." He pulled boards off the side of the boat and handed them to the other men. He put his paddle into the water and shouted "Row!" I looked around us to see if there were any lights. If the Coast Guard came within a few hundred yards of us, we would be caught for sure. I thought it was impossible. If we were having this much trouble getting to the sea, there was no way we would make it across the sea. The last thing I wanted to do was put my life in the hands of those people. I wanted to jump off the boat, swim to shore, and hide out where the communists couldn't find me. But I knew there was nowhere to hide, and that my only chance for freedom was to keep rowing.

It was the middle of the night when we came to Ba Voi corner. There was no boat. The women and children began to weep and the men were expressionless. My head was pounding with frustration. I knew we couldn't get everyone back to the city without the Coast Guard stopping us. It seemed my luck had run out.

Dad's face was still tight, and his eyes were fierce. I knew he wouldn't dump those people off and let them fend for themselves, but I felt I had done more than my part, so

I jumped in the water, swam to shore, and lay on the bank listening to them argue about what to do next. The ones who knew how to swim jumped in after me to wash off the soot and grease they had smeared on themselves. When they got the boats to the bank, Bao and Dad collapsed in the high grass next to me and rubbed their arms. I didn't want to listen to the people whining and crying any longer, so I went into the trees and found a place to lie down. My body was exhausted, and it fell asleep as soon as I got comfortable, but my mind stayed awake and wondered what would happen next. The sun was starting to climb over the trees when I heard people shouting, "The boat! The boat!"

I ran to the bank and could hear a boat engine, but it was around the corner, and we couldn't see it yet. Dad was trying to get the people to hide in the bushes in case it was the Coast Guard, but they wouldn't listen. They kept celebrating on the bank.

The sound of the engine grew louder and louder. I stood back in the bushes far enough to run, thinking it might be best if it was the Coast Guard and they hauled all those crazy people away. This way they wouldn't get the chance to drown me at sea. But when the boat came around the corner, the cheers grew louder. It was our boat. An old man was on top of the cabin yelling at my father and Bao.

Dad turned away from the boat and walked toward me as Bao explained to the man how his son broke the engine and then couldn't remember where the meeting point was. Dad hugged me so tight I could feel his heart beating. "This is the saddest day of my life," he said, "but it's also one of my happiest, because you have a chance for freedom. No matter what happens to us, you'll carry on our name and our memories. You must write us soon. Knowing you're free will give me the strength to keep on living, to keep working until all of us are together again."

I told him I would write, and that I would do whatever I could to get my family out of Vietnam. "I'll tell the whole world about the communists," I said. "Someday I'll come back and get you." I wanted to believe what I was saying and that I would make it, but at the same time, I was thinking those people would find a way to sink the boat. I felt small. I still had no control over what was happening to me.

The boat we were taking didn't look much bigger than the one I had been staying in, but it was sturdier. We transferred all the food and oil as fast as we could to avoid being seen. By the time it was loaded, the women and children were in the cabin. I didn't have time to meet the people who were already on the boat, but I thought they must have all been part of Mr. Lanh's family. I asked Dad how he would make it back home, and he told me Vi was meeting him not too far away. He could row there by early afternoon. As I climbed into the cabin, I heard Mr. Lanh thank Dad for bringing the rest of his family to the boat safely, and say that he was sorry for the trouble his son had caused. The last words I heard my father say were, "*Give my son freedom.*"

Almost twenty people were crammed into the cabin. The air smelled of motor oil and perspiration. I squeezed into the corner with my bag as Mr. Lanh crawled in and shut the door. The women said prayers in the darkness as the boat moved forward. The engine was strong and smooth for some time as we glided through the river. Then the boat rose and sunk lightly through swells, and I knew we were heading into the South China Sea. I fell asleep to the rhythm of the engine and the rocking of the swells.

When I woke, a child was lying on top of me. Bao was

reaching over bodies, poking at my side. It felt like we were flying for a few seconds, then I felt the boat crash back onto the water. Then I heard another crash of water on top of the cabin. My clothes were soaked and sticking to my skin. When I pulled at my shirt, I could feel chunks of something all over my chest. "The pump is clogged," Bao said, "and everyone is sick. I need you to help me."

I climbed over the people to the cabin door and stuck my head out for some air. Rain and salt water sprayed into my mouth. The two men who were steering the boat had ropes tied around them to keep from falling off as the swells tossed us. Bao and I spent the next ten hours bailing water out the cabin door. When the waves calmed, I climbed under the platform to clear the pump. Bao was asleep when I finished, but a few of the people were awake and whimpering from sea sickness. I stuck my head out the door and asked the two men if they wanted to get some sleep. "We can make it a few more hours," they said.

"You must know what you're doing to make it through that storm," I said. Both of them smiled, and one of them told me they had never been on a boat in the sea before. I smiled back, and they laughed nervously. I crawled over some people to an open spot and lay down to sleep. When I awoke, the boat was gliding smoothly across a calm sea. Bao wasn't in the cabin so I climbed out to the deck. One of the men was guiding the boat and the other man and Bao were sitting on top of the cabin. I started to climb up, but Bao jokingly said I should have a wash first. When I looked at myself, I saw regurgitated rice and chunks of vegetables hanging on my shirt. I lowered a bucket over the side for water and then dumped it over my head.

The man guiding the boat said his name was Khanh, and

he introduced the other man as Ty. They both smiled when I asked where we were going. "We're heading toward Singapore," Khanh said, "but we hope to be picked up by a ship in international waters. We may not have enough fuel to make it all the way."

Bao brought some food up from the cabin while Khanh showed me how to steer the boat. He told me to head straight into the swells to keep it from turning over. Khanh let me guide the boat by myself, and he checked our speed by dropping a line and timing how long it took to stretch out. He estimated that we should be close to international waters, but wanted to wait until morning to light the torches. "We've seen a few ships," Khanh said, "but we aren't sure if we're out of the Coast Guard's patrol area." He didn't say anything about pirates, but I knew they were on everyone's minds. There wasn't a person in Vietnam who hadn't heard the stories of pirates attacking refugee boats, stealing their money, raping the women, and throwing them all into the sea.

Ty and Khanh took turns sleeping for a couple of hours on top of the cabin. Neither of them wanted to go inside because of the foul smell. We talked about our lives in Vietnam and our dreams of America. Ty, Khanh and Bao had lived in the city all their lives. They were interested in my stories about prison and how I escaped. They said there was a man in the cabin named Hoa who had just escaped from Vinh An a few weeks before. I was anxious to talk to him about what had happened in Vinh An after I was transferred, and I was glad there was someone who would understand what it was like there.

The next morning a few people came out of the cabin. I could tell right away which one was Hoa. Khanh said our thin hair and skinny bodies made us look like twins. Hoa had been put into Vinh An right after I left. The way he described it, I could tell nothing had changed. I asked him about Phi, but he said he didn't know him.

Mr. Lanh lit smoke torches that morning, and we spent most of the day chasing ships. When we got close, they would take off and leave us behind. Every three or four hours we would see one, but we couldn't get close enough to see what countries they were from. I started to give up hope right away, but Khanh said we had fuel for three more days and food and water for six.

That night we saw a ship with so many lights it looked like a hotel, and we decided to try a different approach. We turned out all our lights and tried to sneak up on it. When we were about a quarter mile away, we could tell it was a cruise ship. We lit the torches and started screaming, "Help! Save us!" but all the lights on the ship went out like someone had thrown the main switch, and we heard the loud roar of the engines as the ship pulled away.

Bao and I stayed on top of the cabin for the whole night. I asked him why none of the ships would help us, and he said the people on them didn't want to take responsibility for us. If they picked us up, they would have to find a country that would let us in. He said the only place that would accept us was Singapore, and we would have to wait until a ship going there would take enough pity on us.

As the moon started to set and the sun was half risen above the swells, Bao started elbowing me and pointing over the water. I thought at first that he must have spotted a ship, but when I looked to where he was pointing, I saw dolphins racing beside our boat. They leaped in the air as they chased us through the water, and their backs glistened white in the moonlight. I couldn't remember ever seeing such a beautiful sight, but in minutes they faded away, and all that remained was the water and sky.

I fell asleep as the day was breaking but soon woke up to Dai shouting, "The water is gone!" Bao and I rushed over and saw that the valve on the tank was broken. The only water left was a few quarts below the valve. Mr. Lanh climbed out of the cabin and began screaming at Dai, but no one knew how the valve got broken.

"We'll ration the water," Mr. Lanh said. "No one will drink until we all drink." I began to feel thirsty right away. Dai measured the water and said we had enough to last for two more days if we conserved. I thought I could survive for a few more days after that, but everyone's eyes seemed a little crazy. The people in the family were all staying closer to one another. I thought I was one of the strongest men on the boat, but I was afraid the family members would team up against the rest of us so they could have the water for themselves.

We spent the morning chasing ships but didn't get close to any. There were no more in sight for the rest of the afternoon, but that evening we got another chance. This time, Mr. Lanh told the women and children to stretch out on top of the cabin so the people on the ship could see them. Khanh steered the boat at an angle, trying to cut the ship off. We were close enough to see people standing on the deck, and we knew they could see us, but the ship turned away and slipped into the blue swells. The women began to cry and the children followed them. Khanh turned our boat back on course, and I sat on top of the cabin, watching the ship fade into the distance.

I strained my eyes as I watched the black dot become smaller and smaller, until it disappeared. I thought again how I had no control over what happened to me. I looked down at the water tank and sucked hard on the dry sides of my mouth. When I looked up, the black dot had reappeared. I rubbed my eyes, and when I opened them again, the dot had grown bigger.

"The ship!" I shouted. "It's coming back."

It came closer and closer until it was only a few hundred yards away. I could see the name of the ship on the side of its bow. I couldn't read it, but Khanh shouted, "It's a British ship!" We heard the chains, and the anchor was lowered. I thought of the last thing I had heard my father say…*Give my son freedom. Give my son freedom.*

About the Author

Born and raised in the Midwest, Dennis Dunivan graduated with a Journalism degree from the University of Missouri. During an overseas work program, he met Viet Nguyen in London. After hearing Viet's story about escaping from a communist prison camp, he decided it was a story the world needed to hear. He moved to Viet's neighborhood, which was a Vietnamese community on London's East End. This is where the foundation of *Escape from Communist Heaven* was formed during months of interviews with Viet and some less extensive interviews with other refugees.

In 1994, before it was feasible for Dennis to conduct research in Vietnam, he was sponsored by U.S.A.I.D. on a mission to help Ukrainian farmers commercialize their businesses. This gave him firsthand experience in a country that was transitioning out of communism. Several years later, he finished the novel after traveling to Saigon and through the Mekong Delta of southern Vietnam. Although thousands of miles and the Atlantic Ocean have separated them for many years, Viet has always remained his best friend.

You can find out more about Dennis Dunivan and his work to advance the cause of human rights at www.communistheaven.com.

An Interview with Dennis W. Dunivan

What inspired you to write *Escape from Communist Heaven*?

I met Viet in London when we were both in our early twenties. He was the most interesting character I had ever met. We became friends and learned we both had strong tendencies to rebel against authority. He told me how he had escaped from a communist prison camp in Vietnam, and narrowly averted death at the age of fourteen. Compared to my up-bringing in rural America, this was an incredible story. The timing was great because I had just graduated from journalism school, and I was looking for something to write about. At first, I wasn't interested in the philosophical differences be-tween capitalism and communism, but as I learned how his captors used ideology to justify suppression and torture, it made me want to gain a better understanding of this practice. What I soon realized is this type of thing occurs all over the world at different levels. The interesting question is where our societies draw the line in terms of personal freedom.

Why should someone read this book?

Because it's entertaining. The book's number one goal is to entertain. If it fails at this, the reader will stop paying attention to the story. Viet is a strong character, and the situations he finds himself in are dangerous, uncertain and outside what most of us could ever imagine. If the reader is inspired to think more about personal freedom and human rights, if discussions happen around questions the story raises, and if these discussions turn into positive action, maybe we can move beyond the greed and desire for power that causes people to suffer.

What kind of research did you need to do?

I lived with Viet and several other Vietnamese refugees in a government housing project on London's East End. Most of the story comes from the events and descriptions of life in post-war Saigon that Viet told me about. I also interviewed other Vietnamese refugees and wove many of their stories into the novel. Because there was so little public information about what happened in Vietnam after the war, I relied mostly on Viet and his friends. Years were also spent in the library learning about socialism and communism and finding reports from human rights organizations that were doing work in Vietnam. After more than a decade of rejection letters from publishers, I traveled to Vietnam and did the best I could to retrace Viet's footsteps through Saigon. I also hired a fishing boat and floated through the Mekong Delta and into the South China Sea. This experience inspired me to revise the manuscript with more feel for the people and the landscape of the country.

How much of the story is historically accurate?

Many of the characters are fictional, and some are based on real people. For instance, Viet was and is a rebellious character who was arrested in the black market as a young teenager. The brainwashing, labor and torture in the reeducation camp were confirmed many times by the refugees I interviewed, and also by human rights organizations. I tried to confirm dates, street names, locations and events with historical documents and maps, but some details may not be completely accurate. Many of the stories Viet told me, such as the account of the abduction of his priest, were confirmed in the reports of human rights organizations.

Tell us about the writing process.

The bulk of the writing was done from 1989-1992. This is when I wove all the stories into a structure that was readable and made sense. Writing in the first person as a Vietnamese teenager was the greatest challenge and the greatest reward. Each chapter would start with a theme like The Wastelands or The Arrest, and there would be several stories within the themes. I would outline the story, and then I would have to become Viet to gain his perspective within the story. The best parts of the novel are when I became Viet in my dreams at night and would wake up abruptly to write it down.

What do you think about communism?

I am against anyone with power who intentionally suppresses other people. It should be our mission as humans to elevate the existence of all life. We should all be working to advance the goodness of our collective spirit.

I think Karl Marx, the most prominent author of communist ideology, wanted a positive outcome for people. But I believe much of his thinking was flawed, and his philosophy was incomplete. As has happened to many big thinkers and great leaders, his ideology was captured by criminals and used to create power for themselves. When this kind of ideological power is centralized and omnipotent leadership is created, the masses suffer: millions are persecuted, tortured and killed. I'm an optimist, and for the most part, I think people are good. Could it be that bad people try harder to control the good? Are the good ones too optimistic, or complacent, until it's too late? It has been fascinating to consider how this phenomenon played out with Stalin, Hitler, Mao, and several less well-known examples—including some current leaders, corporations and religions.

What are the major differences between capitalism and communism?

One of the promises of communism is to make everyone equal. This is where there is a clear differentiation between communism and capitalism. The competitive nature of people will not allow equality to exist, so all communism did was give the leaders omnipotent power. There was no freedom to challenge this power, and the South Vietnamese were suppressed, tortured and killed. The biggest difference between the ideologies does not lie in economics, which is where communism began. The biggest difference lies in human rights and freedom. If too much power is centralized in any society, the leadership will become corrupt. This is what happened in Vietnam, and it could also happen in more developed countries.

Was the spirit of the South Vietnamese people successfully suppressed?

Understanding the answer to this question was my favorite part of the conversations I had with refugees and the many stories that have surfaced mostly in the last decade. Vietnamese refugees are similar to people tortured by Stalin and Hitler and refugees from other parts of the world. This is my greatest learning from writing the novel. I am convinced that the goodness of the human spirit is stronger than any system of evil and suppression. The South Vietnamese refugees risked their lives for freedom. Most of them did not escape their country because of a fear of death. Viet definitely is not afraid of death. Most refugees would have survived in Vietnam, but they wanted a better life. They risked their lives for freedom. They would rather die escaping than to continue living under persecution. The spirit of these people was not and could not be suppressed. This is the essence of the story.

Many Vietnamese refugees do not want their story to be told. They don't want to relive the suffering and the shame. How do you respond to them?

Freud said, "Grandchildren want to remember what grandparents want to forget." I believe the grandchildren of refugees need to know their heritage. With this knowledge, they and others will more likely take action to help people who are going through similar persecution today. It is important for us to realize that there is no shame in being a victim of tyranny. The shame lies with the tyrants.

What advice do you have for young adults who would like to become authors?

Besides helping children, I think it's the most rewarding thing a person can do. But at least for me, it's hard, and you have to be committed. Never think about doing it for money. It has to be a passion to be worthwhile. The best advice I ever heard is, "Writers write."

An Interview with Viet Nguyen

How much of the novel would you say is about you?

Nearly all of it, but what happened to me happened to a lot of other people too, including people who weren't in prison. Part of who I am is my mum and dad, who both grew up in the North and escaped to the South when the country divided after the Second World War. My mum lost everything then. We lived in a society that was very open to other people— we all lived a lot of the time outside, everyone knew what was going on in everyone else's family, and you couldn't have secrets.

I grew up listening to my father tell the story of his life under communism in North Vietnam before he escaped to the South in 1954. If they wanted to cook chicken, which they could only get on the black market, they had to wait until night and could only boil it because if they fried or roasted it the neighbors would smell it and tell the authorities. That story stayed with me and I grew up with that view of communism. But the community where I grew up in the South didn't know what communism was like until 1975.

My mum and dad were a threat to communism, but the authorities couldn't do anything so they used me as an example, as a guarantor, so if my parents stepped out of line they would kill me. So the novel is also about my parents and about anyone who lives under a suppressive regime.

What happened after you were picked up in the South China Sea?

My understanding is that the tanker that picked us up was British and had a British captain, but was registered in Bermuda. They took us to Singapore, where we stayed for four months. The rule was that boat people went to the country where the boat was registered, but Bermuda did not want seven single men. So Bermuda made a deal with England that a family of seven that should have gone to England would go to Bermuda and the seven of us went to England instead. The rest of the people on the boat I escaped on all had relatives in other countries like Australia, US or Germany, so they went where their relatives lived.

I and three others who escaped with me still meet up with the captain and his wife from time to time. Not only did he rescue the four of us, but we all have children of our own now who wouldn't exist if he hadn't helped us.

Do you know what happened to your family?

All my family escaped too and came to live in England. My second brother escaped a year or two after me, and then my parents, two sisters and youngest brother escaped two years after that. My Uncle Houng and his family made it to California, where they are living now.

Is there anything you miss about Vietnam?

Yes and no. I've lived in England longer than I lived in Vietnam and have my children here so I don't miss it in the way my mum and dad do.

Would you like to go back to Vietnam?

Yes and no. I went back to visit in 2004, but for all the money in the world I wouldn't want to live there while it's still suppressive. When I visited, I only saw the surface, and even though I knew what to look for, I couldn't know what it is really like to live there. As I am now, with all the experiences I've had and what I know now, I don't think I'd survive two weeks if I went back to live there because I wouldn't be able to stop myself from saying what I think about what I see. But there is no perfect society or complete freedom of speech anywhere. True freedom is only in your head.

What would you say to other Vietnamese people who thought about escaping, but didn't?

I'd like to say, let's stand up and fight against the suppressive regime, and I'll help any way I can.

What would you like a reader of *Escape from Communist Heaven* to learn?

Any ideology, when it starts to impose itself on other people, becomes wrong; it doesn't matter how good the ideology is. You can only lead by example and hope that people join you, but if you impose your ideology on others it becomes wrong. This goes for any ideology—religion, politics, philosophy—that forces people to conform to it.

Viet, Vinh, Thanh Ha, Minh Ha, and Tu Nguyen

Viet Nguyen

Vinh Nguyen

Tu, Minh Ha, and Thanh Ha Nguyen

Viet Nguyen in London, 1987, when he and the author met

Viet Nguyen on his canal boat in London, 2006

Questions for Discussion

1. In the first chapter, Viet's father tells him they will try to give all the children to officials to put them on a plane to America. Discuss whether you think this was a right or wrong thing to do.

2. Describe the changing relationship between Viet and his father as the story unfolds.

3. If you were Viet's father, would you have done anything differently?

4. Is there anything Viet should have done differently?

5. Describe the differences in interests, temperament and behavior between Viet and his brother Vinh.

6. What are the similarities between growing up in America and growing up in Vietnam during the book's time period? Are the rules you are supposed to live by fair?

7. Describe the factors contributing to a strained relationship between Viet's mother and his grandmother from North Vietnam. (p. 126-143)

8. Describe Viet's father's experience with communism as a young boy in North Vietnam. (p. 21-23) Do you think it justified his fear of the communists and his plan to take his family's lives?

9. Do you think Ho Chi Minh was good or evil? Explain. (p. 287-288) Describe what you think his concept of Communist Heaven was.

10. Is it possible to achieve complete equality among people? Discuss why or why not.

11. Describe Phong's personal reality. (p. 309-310) Was there anything Viet could have done to help Phong escape from his reality? What do you think Viet should have done when he found the needle?

12. Do you think it's true that if power becomes too centralized in any society, the ones with power will suppress others for their own gain? How can we prevent this from happening?

13. Was it right or wrong for Viet to sell the stolen watch in the Black Market? What choice would you have made and why?

14. Are there any good things about communism? What parts of the ideology would you want to incorporate into your society?

15. What parts of communism would you definitely not accept?

16. *Escape from Communist Heaven* was written as a novel. Everything in the story likely happened to someone during this time period, but did not always happen to the real Viet. There is a tradeoff between factual accounts that may not provide much entertainment, and fictional accounts that are obviously not 100% factual. Discuss the potential value of each.

Glossary

ao dai: A traditional long gown with slits on each side, worn over silk pants.

black market: An illegal market in which goods or currencies are bought and sold in violation of government rationing and other controls. The black market activities happened in actual markets throughout Saigon and also included sales and bartering of private goods between neighbors and friends.

boat people: A term that usually refers to refugees, or asylum seekers, who emigrate in boats that are sometimes old and crudely made. The term came into common use during the late 1970s with the mass departure of Vietnamese refugees from communist-controlled Vietnam, following the Vietnam War.

cadre: In Vietnamese re-education camps, cadres were much like drill sergeants in an army. They had proven themselves to be supportive of communism, and they had learned about the ideology, so they could teach the prisoners how to think and act.

capitalism: A social and economic system where assets are mainly owned and controlled by private people, where labor is purchased for wages, capital gains belong to private owners, and a free market with competition helps to determine the price of goods, services and property.

Chairman Mao: Regarded as one of the most influential individuals in modern world history. Supporters praise him for modernizing China and building it into a world power. China's population almost doubled during the period of Mao's leadership, from around 550 to over 900 million. In contrast, critics have labeled him a dictator whose administration oversaw systematic human rights abuses, and whose rule is estimated to have caused the deaths of between 40–70 million people, mainly through starvation, forced labor and executions. It is likely that his rule caused the most people to be killed by genocide in human history.

communism: An economic and social system envisioned by the nineteenth-century German scholar Karl Marx. In theory, under communism, all means of production are owned in common, rather than by an individual. In practice, a single authoritarian party controls both the political and economic systems.

democracy: A form of government in which all eligible citizens have an equal say in the decisions that affect their lives. Democracy allows eligible citizens to participate equally— either directly or through elected representatives—in the proposal, development, and creation of laws. It encompasses social, economic and cultural conditions that enable the free and equal practice of political self-determinism.

fascist, fascism: A governmental system usually led by a dictator with complete power, which suppresses opposition and criticism, controls all industry, commerce, etc. In a fascist society, government control is more important than individual freedom.

Ho Chi Minh: He led the Viet Minh independence movement from 1941 onward, establishing the communist-ruled Democratic Republic of Vietnam in 1945, and defeated the French Union in 1954 at the battle of Dien Bien Phu. He officially stepped down from power in 1955 due to health problems, but remained a highly visible figurehead and inspiration for those Vietnamese fighting for his cause—a united, communist Vietnam—until his death. After the war, Saigon, capital of the Republic of Vietnam, was renamed Ho Chí Minh City.

Jean Baptiste Nho Dinh Diem: The First President of South Vietnam. His nationalism and drive to end communism made him a prominent figure. However, his favoritism of Catholicism and discontentment with Buddhists made him a target of generals from the Army of South Vietnam. The Army planned a coup d'état against him and his brother Nhu. America was humiliated by the corruption of Diem's administration, and they did not want to help Diem and his government. On November 2, 1963, Diem and his brother were assassinated.

Joseph Stalin: Rose to power within the Russian Communist Party from 1898 through the Russian Revolution in 1917 and beyond. Following Lenin's death, Stalin outmaneuvered rivals and by 1929 became the sole leader of the ruling Communist Party of the Soviet Union. A shrewd and ruthless political infighter, he built a tyrannical but powerful totalitarian state. Millions were "liquidated" in massive "purges." Stalin's outlook was shaped by his belief in a historically destined global victory for communism.

jute grass: Tall annual herb or sub-shrub of tropical Asia having velvety leaves and yellow flowers and yielding a strong fiber. The grass is used to make baskets, mats and hats.

Karl Marx: Marx's theories about society, economics and politics, collectively known as Marxism, state that human societies progress through a class struggle: a conflict between an ownership class that controls production and a proletariat that provides the labor for production. He called capitalism the "dictatorship of the bourgeoisie," believing it to be run by the wealthy classes purely for their own benefit, and he predicted that, like previous socioeconomic systems, capitalism would inevitably produce internal tensions that would lead to its self-destruction and replacement by a new system: socialism.

New Economic Zone: After the communist takeover, private enterprises were seized by the government and their owners were often sent to New Economic Zones to clear land. The farmers were coerced into state-controlled co-operatives. Transportation of food and goods between provinces was deemed illegal except by the government. Thousands of people who were sent to New Economic Zones died of starvation and malaria.

Nguyen Van Thieu: President of South Vietnam from 1965–75. He was a general in the Army of the Republic of Vietnam (ARVN), became head of a military junta, and then became president after winning a scheduled election.

He established rule over South Vietnam until he resigned and left the nation a few days before the fall of Saigon and the ultimate communist victory.

passive resistance: Resistance by nonviolent methods to a government, an occupying power, or specific laws, for example by refusing to comply, demonstrating in protest, or fasting.

pho soup: Delicate noodle soup, made from beef bones, ginger, onions and aromatic spices.

piaster: The standard monetary unit of Vietnam at the time the events of this book occurred. The piaster was replaced by the dong in May, 1978. The value of the dong was significantly changed many times by the communist government to help them control opposition. During the war, a piaster was worth only about a penny in American currency.

propaganda: Presenting facts selectively (possibly lying by omission) to encourage a particular synthesis, or using loaded messages to produce an emotional rather than rational response to the information presented. The desired result is a change of the attitude toward the subject in the target audience to further a political, religious or commercial agenda. Propaganda can be used as a form of ideological or commercial warfare.

Red Scarfs: A youth organization set up by the communist government to help influence the children, educate them on communist ideology and in many cases obtain information about their parents.

National Service: A program set up to control people with the potential to organize against the government. Although it was positioned as a volunteer program, people were required to leave their families and work in remote areas, draining swamps and clearing jungle to develop farmland.

socialism: An economic system characterized by social ownership of the means of production and co-operative management of the economy. "Social ownership" may refer to cooperative enterprises, common ownership, state ownership, or citizen ownership of equity. There are many varieties of socialism and there is no single definition encapsulating all of them. They differ in the type of social ownership they advocate, the degree to which they rely on markets or planning, how management is to be organized within productive institutions, and the role of the state in constructing socialism.

solidarity cell: A group of people in Vietnam that report to a communist leader. Usually the group is structured around a business such as the making of baskets and mattresses. All the production is given to the leader who sells it and theoretically divides the profits equally. The communists used solidarity cells to organize and control the population.

Tet: The Vietnamese New Year celebration, occurring during the first seven days of the first month of the lunar calendar.

Vladimir Lenin: As the leader of the Bolshevik faction of the Russian Social Democratic Labor Party, he took a senior role in orchestrating the October Revolution in

1917, which led to the overthrow of the Russian Provisional Government and the establishment of the world's first constitutionally socialist state. Immediately afterwards, Lenin implemented socialist reforms, including the transfer of estates to soviet workers. With Lenin as its leader, the Bolshevik faction later became the Communist Party of the Soviet Union, which presided over a single-party dictatorship of the proletariat.

Suggested Reading

These books are related to the subject matter of *Escape from Communist Heaven*. Some are specifically about Vietnam, and others address human rights issues in other parts of the world.

Between Shades of Gray, Ruta Sepetys, Philomel Books, 2011

Never Fall Down, Patricia McCormick, Balzer + Bray, 2012

The Kite Runner, Khaled Hosseini, Penguin Group, 2003

The Will of Heaven, Nguyen Ngoc Ngan and E.E. Richie, Dutton Adult, 1982

The Vietnamese Gulag, Doan Van Toai and David Chanoff, Simon and Schuster, 1986

Perfume Dreams, Andrew Lam, Heyday, 2005

Vietnam Under Communism, Nguyen Van Canh, Hoover Institution Press, 1985

Acknowledgments

Many thanks to the following people who helped make this book a reality:

My editor Connie Shaw and everyone at Sentient Publications who took a chance on this first novel. Your talent, wisdom and advice have been amazing.

The teachers who are bringing the book into their classrooms to share with their students. Viet and I hope the story will help them better understand the importance of freedom, and why we must do what we can for those who still struggle for basic human rights.

Captain Cy Beck, his wife, Anne, and the crew of the Port Hawkesbury for having the compassion to pick up Viet and the other passengers in the middle of the South China Sea.

Mom for always believing in me. Especially when the stakes are high.

Dad for always believing this book would be published. And thanks for the Mac Plus computer with a spell checker.

All my family and friends who helped and encouraged me to continue.

Everyone at Booth Media Group and Black Dog Design.

Cheryl, for your encouragement early on, not to mention your countless edits and suggestions that made such a difference.

Jack, Sam and Cole for understanding that much of our vacation time this year will be spent in bookstores and high school classrooms. It will be great to have you with Viet and me whenever possible.

And of course to Viet, for taking in the traveling writer with an expired work permit and trusting me to tell your story.

Dennis W. Dunivan
June 14, 2013

Sentient Publications, LLC publishes nonfiction books on cultural creativity, experimental education, transformative spirituality, holistic health, new science, ecology, and other topics, approached from an integral viewpoint. We also publish fiction that aims to intrigue, stimulate, and entertain. Our authors are intensely interested in exploring the nature of life from fresh perspectives, addressing life's great questions, and fostering the full expression of the human potential. Sentient Publications' books arise from the spirit of inquiry and the richness of the inherent dialogue between writer and reader.

Our Culture Tools series is designed to give social catalyzers and cultural entrepreneurs the essential information, technology, and inspiration to forge a sustainable, creative, and compassionate world.

We are very interested in hearing from our readers. To direct suggestions or comments to us, or to be added to our mailing list, please contact:

SENTIENT PUBLICATIONS, LLC

1113 Spruce Street
Boulder, CO 80302
303-443-2188
contact@sentientpublications.com
www.sentientpublications.com